THE CASE OF THE

Postponed Murder

by ERLE STANLEY GARDNER

Murder in Waiting

by MIGNON G. EBERHART

Published for the
DETECTIVE BOOK CLUB ®
by Walter J. Black, Inc.
ROSLYN, NEW YORK

THE DETECTIVE BOOK CLUB ®
Printed in the United States of America

The Case of The
Postponed Murder

Chapter One

~~~~~~

Perry Mason pushed himself slightly back from the desk and turned so that he was facing the young woman who had seated herself in the client's big, overstuffed, leather chair. Della Street, his secretary, handed him the confidential information card on which had been typed:

NAME	Sylvia Farr
AGE	Twenty-six
ADDRESS	North Mesa, Calif., 694 Chestnut St. Temporarily located at Palmcrest Rooms. Telephone number Hillview 6-9390.
NATURE OF BUSINESS	About sister
COMMENTS	When she opened her purse for compact, noticed a wad of folded bills and several pawn tickets.—D.S.

Mason turned the card face down on the desk and said, "You wanted to see me about your sister, Miss Farr?"

"Yes."

"Smoke?" Mason asked, raising the cover of his office humidor.

"Thanks. I have my own brand." She took a new package from her purse, tore open a corner, extracted a cigarette, and leaned forward for his match.

"All right," Mason said, settling back in his chair. "What about your sister?"

"She's disappeared."

"Ever do it before?"

"No."

"What's her name?"

"Mae."

"Married?"

"No."

"What about the disappearance?"

Sylvia Farr gave a quick, nervous laugh and said, "It's hard for me when you shoot questions at me. Could I tell you in my own way?"

"Certainly."

"Well, we live in North Mesa, and—"

"Just where is North Mesa?" Mason interrupted. "I don't recall the place."

"You wouldn't," she said. "It's in the northern part of the state, off the main highways. It's awfully rural. There hasn't been any building activity for years. We did manage a new post office, but that doesn't mean anything in particular."

"So much for North Mesa," Mason said with a smile. "Now how about Mae?"

"Mae," she said, "left North Mesa over a year ago. It was the opposite of the conventional, short-story situation. She was the household drudge. I was the— Well, I was considered prettier, not," she added quickly, with a deprecating smile, "that that means much in North Mesa.

"But you know the conventional setup. I should have been the one to get impatient at the small-town stuffiness and head for the big city, try to crash the movies, wind up making a living waiting on tables in a cheap restaurant, then marry a prince charming—or go broke and return home, disillusioned, bitter, and cynical, to find that my homely sister had married the local undertaker, had three children, and was known all over the countryside for her wonderful disposition and fine apple pies."

Mason's eyes twinkled. "Mae," he asked, "didn't run true to form?"

"I'll say she didn't. She got fed up with North Mesa and decided she was going to see the world."

"Where is she now?"

The laughter faded from Sylvia Farr's eyes. "I don't know," she said.

"Where was she when you heard from her last?"

"Here."

"Was she working?"

"She'd had several jobs," Sylvia Farr said guardedly. "I think she tried to make up for some of the things she had lost in North Mesa

She formed a few friendships and enjoyed them immensely. She became quite a playgirl."

"Older than you or younger?" Mason asked.

"A year and a half older. Don't misunderstand me, Mr. Mason. She knew what she was doing. . . . But what I mean is that her attitude changed. In North Mesa, there was no animation about her. She seldom laughed. She felt she was just marking time there while life was slipping through her fingers, and her actions showed it. After she came to the city, she apparently had an entirely different outlook. Her letters really sparkled. They were quite clever, and . . . Well, I didn't dare show all of them to Moms. I remember that Mae said that in the city a girl had to play with fire and that the art of keeping fingers from getting burnt was not to try to control the fire but to control the fingers."

"When did you hear from her last?"

"A little over two months ago."

"What was she doing then?"

"She was working as secretary to a man in the stationery business, but she didn't give me the address of the firm. She was staying at the Pixley Court Apartments, and she seemed to be having a wonderful time."

"You have a letter?" Mason asked.

"No. I destroyed all of her letters—that is, nearly all of them. She used to write me things in confidence. Occasionally, she'd write a letter for Moms to read, but they were mostly little notes."

"Did she ever come back to North Mesa after she left?" Mason asked.

"Yes, she was back about six months ago, and I was never so flabbergasted in my life. I've never seen such a complete change in any human being. Her complexion was never good, and her hair was inclined to be coarse and dry. Her features aren't what you'd call beautiful, but, my heavens, to see what she'd done to herself! Her clothes were smart. Her complexion was a lot better. Her eyes danced. She'd been taking care of her hair and her hands, and she was full of wisecracks and all the latest slang. She made us North Mesa girls feel hopelessly out of things.

"You know, Mr. Mason, I'm not the moody type. I take things as they come and live life as I find it, but I never felt as blue as when Mae had left and we settled back into the old rut. Things weren't so bad while she was there. Just being around her made all of the girls feel sort of urban and sophisticated, but after Mae left, the steam was all out of the boiler, and we couldn't carry on. . . ."

"I think I understand," Mason said. "I think we've covered the preliminaries fairly well, Miss Farr."

"Well," Sylvia Farr went on hastily, "a month or so ago I wrote Sis, and she didn't answer. Then I sent her another letter about two weeks ago, and the letter was returned with a note from the apartment house saying that she'd moved and had left no forwarding address."

"She sounds as though she'd developed an ability to take care of herself," Mason said. "I would hardly think there was any cause for worry."

"In her last letter," Sylvia Farr explained, "she mentioned a Mr. Wentworth who had a yacht. I understand he's a gambler and rather wealthy. She'd been out on the yacht with him and wound up the letter by saying something like this: 'Good Heavens, Sis, if you come to the city, lay off of people like Penn Wentworth. What I've told you about playing with fire doesn't fit him. He goes through life taking what he wants, not asking for it. You can't control either the fingers or the fire with men like that.' "

Mason said, somewhat impatiently, "Your sister isn't the first girl in the world to find that you can't make hard and fast rules about playing with fire, as she called it. You don't need a lawyer, Miss Farr. You need a private detective if you need anyone. If you'll take my advice, you'll return to North Mesa and forget all about it. Your sister is able to take care of herself, and the reason she has failed to communicate with you is undoubtedly because she doesn't want you to know where she is. The police can tell you that this frequently happens. If you want a good detective, the Drake Detective Agency in this same building has several very skillful operatives, and you can absolutely trust the discretion and honesty of Mr. Paul Drake, the head of the agency. He does my work."

And Mason swung about in his chair as an indication that the interview was terminated.

Sylvia Farr crossed over to the desk and stood looking down at him. "Please, Mr. Mason," she said, with desperation in her voice, "I know it sounds silly. I just couldn't tell it the way it was. I can't make you see Sis the way I know her. I tell you I *know* this is something different. I think—think—that she's dead, been murdered."

"What makes you think that?" Mason asked.

"Oh, just several things, knowing her and—because of things she said in that last letter."

"You didn't keep that letter?"

"No."

Mason said, "If you're absolutely convinced in your own mind that there's something seriously wrong, go to the police. They'll investigate. You may not be pleased with what you find out."

"But I want you to investigate this, Mr. Mason. I want you to. . . ."

"All I could do," Mason said, "would be to hire a detective agency. You could do that just as well yourself and save yourself money. I presume money means something to you, doesn't it, Miss Farr?"

"Yes, it does," she said. "But Sis means more to me than money, and I just know there's something wrong."

Mason said, "Go see Paul Drake. In all probability, one of his operatives can locate your sister within twenty-four hours. If it turns out your sister is in any difficulty and she needs legal help, I'll still be available."

Della Street said, "This way, Miss Farr. I'll take you to Mr. Drake's office."

Chapter Two

Paul Drake, long and loose-jointed, entered Mason's private office with the familiarity born of years of intimate association, and said, "Hi, Perry. Hi, Della. How's tricks?"

He crossed over to the client's chair, swung around so he was seated crosswise in the seat, and let his legs hang over one of the arms. "Thanks for the case, Perry," he said.

"What case?"

"The girl you sent me yesterday."

"Oh, you mean Miss Farr?"

"Uh huh."

"Any money in it?" Mason asked.

"Oh, so-so. Enough to cover a preliminary investigation and report. I figured it shouldn't take over three or four hours to locate the girl."

"Find her?" Mason asked.

"No, but I found out a lot about her."

Mason grinned and reached for the cigarette humidor. "Smoke, Paul?" he asked.

"No, thanks," Drake said. "I'm chewing gum today."

Mason turned to Della Street. "He has something on his mind, Della. When things are coasting along, he smokes cigarettes and sits in the chair like a civilized human being. When you see him tie himself up in knots like a snake with a stomachache, you know he has something on his mind. And chewing gum is another infallible sign."

Drake tore the cellophane end off a package of gum and fed three sticks into his mouth, one after another, rolled the wrappers into a tight ball, and tossed them into Mason's wastebasket. "Perry," he said, "I want to ask you a question."

Mason flashed Della Street an obvious wink. "Here it comes, Della," he said.

Drake said, "No kidding, Perry, you did call the turn on me."

"I know I did," Mason said. "What is it, Paul?"

"Why the devil did you interest yourself in that girl's case?"

"I didn't."

"You didn't *take* it," Drake said, "but from what she told me, you must have given her quite a bit of time."

"Did she think so?" Mason asked.

"No," Drake said. "She was sore. She thought you'd thrown her out on her ear. I explained to her that you were one of the highest-priced trial lawyers in the city and that darn few people ever got as far as your private office. That smoothed her down some."

Mason said, "I darn near took her case at that, Paul."

"That's the way I figured it. Why?"

Mason grinned and said, "You found the sister was in a fair-sized mess of trouble, didn't you, Paul?"

The detective nodded, watching Mason warily.

"A fugitive from justice?" Mason asked.

"Nope," Drake said. "Forgery."

"I thought so," Mason said.

Della Street looked at the lawyer curiously. Drake said, "Come on, Perry. Give me a break. How did you figure it?"

The lawyer's eyes narrowed somewhat as they looked past the detective. "Darn it, Paul," he said. "I wish I didn't take such a keen interest in people and in mysteries. If there'd been just a little more mystery about that case, I'd have taken it and found myself donating five thousand dollars' worth of work for a fifty-dollar fee."

"What was the mystery?" Drake asked.

"Did you locate Mae Farr?" Mason countered.

"No, we can't find her."

Mason made a gesture with his hand as though tossing something onto the big desk in front of him. "There," he said, "is your answer."

"What do you mean, Perry?"

Mason said, "Look at the setup. This girl comes to see us about her sister. Her sister has disappeared. She thinks her sister is in some sort of trouble, doesn't know anything at all about what it might be, but is filled with vague forebodings.

"Notice the way she's dressed—shoes that are the best on the market, a skirt and jacket smart in design but not new, a coat that apparently *is* new, of the cheapest sort of material cut along flashy lines with a fur collar and trim which looks as though it came direct from an alley cat."

"Well," Drake asked as Mason hesitated, "what's the answer?"

Mason waved back the question with a quick gesture. "Her nails," he said, "were manicured carefully. Her hair was slicked back. Her face had very little makeup on it. There was virtually no lipstick on her mouth, and then to clinch matters, her purse was full of money—and pawn tickets."

Drake, nervously chewing away at his gum, looked across at Della Street, then back to Mason, and said, "I don't get you, Perry. You're leading up to something, but hanged if I know what."

Mason said, "It's a column of figures that doesn't add up, that's all. What does a country girl do when she goes to the city? Puts on her best clothes, tries to look her best. The country girls—the good-looking ones—are the ones who try to look sophisticated. They're the ones who go heavy on makeup when they're calling on a lawyer. They're particularly careful to have their hair done as soon as they get to the city."

"She was worried," Drake said."She didn't have time to go to a hairdresser."

"She had had time to get her nails manicured," Mason said, "and she'd been to a hairdresser. Her hair was pulled back to make her look as plain and unsophisticated as possible. A country girl would have economized on shoes, and put what she saved into getting a better coat, unless she was the type who liked that kind of a coat. In that event, she wouldn't have ever had the shoes Miss Farr was wearing. The coat didn't go with the clothes. The coat didn't go with the shoes. The hair didn't go with the nails. The face didn't go with the story."

Drake chewed away at the gum with nervous rapidity, then suddenly straightened in the chair. "Cripes, Perry, you don't mean that she . . . that she was . . ."

"Sure, she was," Mason said. "She was a fugitive from justice. She wanted a lawyer to pull some chestnuts out of the fire. She didn't dare use her right name, so she posed as sister Sylvia."

"I," Drake announced slowly and impressively, "will be damned. I believe you're right, Perry."

"Of course I'm right," Mason said, as though disposing of a matter which was entirely elementary. "That's why I almost took her case. I wondered what kind of character she possessed, what sort of a scrape she was in, what mental quirk had given her the resourcefulness and ingenuity to think up that approach. Most girls would either have sought refuge in tears or hysterics or would have been hard-boiled enough to brazen the whole thing out. She wasn't particularly hard-boiled. She looked as though she knew her way around. She was frightened, but she wasn't giving way to tears. She was self-reliant and, all in all, pretty resourceful. She'd hocked all her valuables, bought herself a flashy coat, had her hair done so that it made her look as plain as possible, but entirely overlooked her shoes and the fact that her nails were freshly manicured."

Drake resumed his gum chewing. He slowly nodded. "Well," he said, "she's in a jam."

"How much of a jam?" Mason asked.

"A forged check for eight hundred and fifty smackers for one thing," Drake said.

"Who cashed the check, Paul?"

"Stylefirst Department Store."

"Some cash and some credit?" Mason asked.

"Credit on a nine-hundred-and-fifty-dollar balance," Drake said. "The department store received the check in the mail, put it through without paying very much attention to it, had it returned marked as a forgery, and got peeved about it. In the meantime, Mae Farr had evidently got wind of what had happened and skipped out."

Mason pushed his chair away from the desk, got to his feet, and started walking the floor, his eyes staring in frowning concentration at the carpet as he walked. "Paul," he flung over his shoulder, "I'm going to ask you a question. I hope the answer to the question is 'no.' I'm afraid it's going to be 'yes.' Was that forged check signed by a man named Wentworth?"

"That's right," Drake said. "Penn Wentworth, and it was a lousy forgery."

Mason whirled to stare steadily at the detective. "It was what?" he asked.

"A lousy forgery," Drake repeated.

Mason once more made that characteristic tossing gesture with his right hand. "There you are, Paul," he said. "Another figure in the column which throws the account out of balance. That girl wouldn't have committed a poor forgery. Notice her hands and fingers—long, slender, tapering, artistic, swift and sure about everything they did.

"When she was in here, she was nervous as the devil, but she opened her purse, took out a fresh pack of cigarettes, tore off a corner of the package, took out a cigarette and put it in her mouth, all with smooth, swift grace. That girl can play a piano, can probably paint, and would never, never be guilty of committing a crude forgery."

"Well, she's done it this time," Drake said. "I saw the check. It was payable to Mae Farr in an amount of eight hundred and fifty dollars and was endorsed on the back, 'Pay to the order of Stylefirst Department Store, Mae Farr.' "

"How about her signature on the endorsement?" Mason asked.

"What about it?"

"Did it look all right?"

Drake raised his eyebrows in surprise. "Why the devil wouldn't it look all right?" he asked. "Cripes, Perry, no one is going to forge an eight-hundred-and-fifty-dollar check just to show a department store a good time."

"What," Mason asked, "does Wentworth say?"

"Apparently, Wentworth is very much concerned," Drake said. "Now, here's a funny thing. When that charge account was originally opened, Wentworth guaranteed it."

"So he'd be stuck on the account anyway?" Mason asked.

"Yep."

"Then the forgery wouldn't have actually injured him," Mason said. "He was obligated to pay anyway."

"No," Drake said, "if the girl had paid, he wouldn't have had to. His okay was as a guarantor."

"And he's burnt up about the forgery?"

"I'll say. Says that the girl is a base ingrate and that he's going to put her behind bars regardless of what comes of it."

Perry Mason heaved a deep sigh. "Paul," he said, "the whole business is screwy."

Drake glanced across at Della Street. "How's he doing, Della?" he asked. "He's got me interested now. But what about Perry?"

Della smiled. "He's been interested all along," she said, "only he hasn't admitted it to himself until just now."

Mason said, "By gosh, Della, I think you're right." He turned to Drake and said, "Okay, Paul, tell her I'll handle her case. When she comes in, tell her this forgery is a serious business and we should do something to protect her sister. Don't let on that you know the sister business is a stall. I want to spring that on her after she figures she's got away with something—when it'll come out of a clear sky."

"Okay, Perry," Drake said.

"And one more thing," Mason went on. "How about a photostatic copy of that forged check? Do you think you could get me one?"

"Nothing to it," Drake said. "The bank had it photographed. Whenever they turn down payment of a check on the ground that it's forged, they protect themselves by having photostatic copies made. I managed to get one."

"Okay, Paul. Wire the Motor Vehicle Department for a photostatic copy of Mae Farr's driving license. That'll have her signature, among other things. When you get her signature, I'm going to send the photostatic copy of the check and her signature over to a handwriting expert."

"But, my gosh, Perry," Drake protested, "you don't need a handwriting expert to tell that check is a forgery. It's a tracing, and you can see it's a tracing. All the little tremors of the hand which are characteristic of that type of forgery show up plain as day."

Mason said, "I don't want to get an opinion on Wentworth's signature. I want an opinion on the signature of Mae Farr on the endorsement."

The detective's forehead knitted into a perplexed frown.

"Get the picture?" Mason asked. "A department store has a bill of nine hundred-odd dollars against a Mae Farr with a Penn Wentworth as guarantor. They get a check, apparently drawn by Wentworth, payable to Mae Farr, and endorsed over to the department store. They shoot it through in the ordinary course of business. The check is a forgery. It comes back to the department store on the first bounce. They notify Wentworth, and Wentworth goes straight up in the air. Naturally, everyone supposes Mae Farr forged the check because apparently she's the one who stands to profit by the forgery."

"Well?" Drake asked. "You can't get away from that reasoning."

Mason grinned. "Suppose," he observed, "that Mae Farr's signature is also a forgery."

"I don't get you," Drake said.

Mason's grin broadened. "Think it over for a while, Paul. The situation has possibilities."

Mason nodded to Della Street. "Take a letter, Della," he said.

She whipped a shorthand book from the desk drawer and held a fountain pen poised in readiness.

Mason dictated, "To Mr. Penn Wentworth. Drake will give you his address. 'Dear Sir: Miss Sylvia Farr of North Mesa, California, has retained me to locate her sister, Mae Farr, who formerly lived at the Pixley Court Apartments in this city, and to act as her legal representative in any difficulties in which she may be involved.' Paragraph. 'From information contained in some of Mae Farr's letters to her sister, it occurs to me that you may be in a position to give me some information as to the present whereabouts of the party in question. In the event you should, by any chance, be in direct communication with her, please assure her that her sister has made all necessary arrangements for this office to represent her to the extent of its ability.' Paragraph. 'Thanking you in advance for any information you may be able to give, I am very truly yours.' "

As Mason finished dictating, he glanced across at Paul Drake. "Unless I miss my guess," he said, "that letter will get us plenty of action."

Chapter Three

Della Street, entering Perry Mason's office with the morning mail, said, "Your bread on the waters seems to have returned in the form of cake."

"What bread?" Mason asked.

"The letter you sent yesterday to Penn Wentworth."

"Oh, that," Mason said, and grinned. "I'm afraid I'll have to send you to cooking school, Della."

"Why?"

"That bread on the waters," Mason remarked, "isn't going to return in the form of cake. It's going to return in the form of dough."

"Dough?" she asked.

"Exactly," he said. "Mazuma, coin of the realm. How long's he been waiting, Della?"

"About half an hour. He's fit to be tied."

"Bring him in," Mason said.

Penn Wentworth was in his early fifties. He had apparently tried to hide the evidence of those years by devoting a great deal of careful attention to grooming. His clothes were faultlessly pressed. His grith, compared with his chest, the fit of his clothes, and his carriage, indicated that the natural sag of his stomach was held in check by an elastic belt.

His hands were well cared for, the nails carefully manicured. The face, pink and velvety from the ministrations of a barber, was in sharp contrast with the grayish green of his pale eyes. He wore a small, neatly trimmed mustache carefully waxed at the ends.

"Good morning, Mr. Mason," he said.

"Hello," Mason observed casually. "Sit down."

Wentworth accepted the indicated chair. His eyes appraised Mason as the eyes of a skillful bridge player sweep over the cards when he first picks up his hand. "Nice weather," he said.

Mason's face became granite-hard. "Think it'll rain?" he asked.

"No," Wentworth said. "Just a high fog. I received your letter, Mr. Mason."

Mason said, "Personally, I think it's going to rain. What about the letter?"

"I feel that an explanation is due you."

Mason said gravely, "That's fine. I always like to get everything that's due me."

"Don't misunderstand me, Mr. Mason."

"I won't," the lawyer said.

"What I meant was that you have undoubtedly been tricked. A man of your standing, reputation, and ability certainly wouldn't have agreed to represent Mae Farr if he had known all the facts."

"Smoke?" Mason asked.

"Yes. Thank you."

Wentworth's hand came across to the humidor which Mason extended. His fingers picked out a cigarette. He seemed glad of the interruption.

Mason scraped a match into flame, lit the cigarette, tossed the match carelessly into the wastebasket, and said, "Go on."

"It will perhaps come as a surprise to you to learn that Miss Farr is a fugitive from justice," Wentworth said.

"Indeed," Mason observed tonelessly.

"The police hold a warrant for her arrest."

"What's the charge?" Mason asked.

"Forgery."

"Of what?"

"Of a check," Wentworth said indignantly, "a check which constituted a base betrayal of a friendship. The girl is a gold digger, an ingrate, a selfish, scheming—"

"Just a moment," Mason said, pressing a button.

"As I was saying," Wentworth observed, "she—"

Mason held up his hand, palm outward. "Wait just a moment," he said. "I've rung for my secretary."

"Your secretary?"

"Yes. I want her to take down your comments about the moral integrity of my client."

"Look here," Wentworth said in sudden alarm, "you're not going to try to use any of this."

Della Street opened the door from the outer office. Mason said,

"Della, I want you to take down Mr. Wentworth's comments about Mae Farr."

Della flashed a glance of calm appraisal at the uncomfortable visitor, then came across to the desk and slipped Mason a note.

The lawyer, unfolding the interoffice memo, read, "Harold Anders waiting in outer office. Wants to see Penn Wentworth about a personal matter which he refuses to disclose. His address is North Mesa, Calif. Said he was told Wentworth was here and said he will wait for Wentworth to come out."

Mason slowly tore up the sheet of folded paper, dropped the pieces into the wastebasket.

Wentworth said, "What I was saying was just between us."

"Surely," Mason said, "you wouldn't make such serious charges against a young woman unless you could prove them."

Wentworth said, "Don't try to trap me, Mason. I came here in good faith to warn you about the type of person with whom you're dealing. I don't intend to expose myself to a suit for defamation of character."

"Rather late to think of that now, isn't it?" Mason asked.

"What do you mean?"

Mason turned abruptly to Della. "Send Mr. Anders in," he said. "Tell him Mr. Wentworth will talk with him right here."

Wentworth half rose from his chair. He looked at Mason with eyes that held some measure of suspicion and alarm. "Who," he asked, "is Anders?"

As Della Street slipped quietly through the door to the outer office, Mason said soothingly, "Just a chap who wanted to see you on a personal matter. He's been trying to locate you, heard that you were here, and followed you."

"But I don't know any Anders," Wentworth said, "and I don't think I want to see him. Can't I leave through this exit door, and . . ."

"But you don't understand," Mason said. "He comes from North Mesa. I think he wants to see you about Miss Farr."

Wentworth got to his feet. He had taken two steps when Della opened the door from the outer office and a tall, rawboned man in his early thirties came striding into the room.

"Which one of you is Wentworth?" he asked.

Mason waved his hand in an affable gesture. "The gentleman heading toward the exit door," he said.

Anders strode across the room, moving with a deceptive swiftness which cut off Wentworth's retreat. "Wentworth," he said, "you're going to talk with me."

Wentworth tried to brush past him. Anders grabbed him by the shoulder of his coat. "You know who I am," he said.

"I've never seen you in my life."

"Well, you know of me."

Wentworth said nothing.

Anders said, "Of all the slimy, contemptible tricks I ever heard of, this business of having Mae arrested takes the cake. A lousy eight hundred and fifty bucks. Here, here's your eight hundred and fifty. I'm making the check good."

He pulled a roll of bills from his pocket and started peeling off twenties. "Come over to the desk where we can count this money. I want a witness, and I want a receipt."

"You can't pay off that check," Wentworth said.

"Why not?"

"Because the entire matter is in the hands of the district attorney. I would be compounding a felony if I accepted this money. Mr. Mason is a lawyer. He can tell you that's right. That's true, isn't it, Mr. Mason?"

"Consulting me professionally?" Mason inquired.

"Oh bosh! I'm merely commenting on what is general information."

"Put your money away, Anders," Mason said. "Sit down. You too, Wentworth. While you're both here, I have something to say to you."

"I have nothing further to say," Wentworth said. "I came here in the utmost good faith, thinking that I could spare you an embarrassing experience, Mason. I didn't come here to be trapped, tricked, or insulted. I suppose that you carefully arranged this meeting with Anders."

Anders' face showed surprise. "What are you talking about?" he asked. "I never heard of the man in my life."

Wentworth looked longingly at the door.

"No, you don't," Anders said. "I've been chasing you all over town. We're going to have a showdown right here and now. Try to get out that door, and you'll wish you hadn't."

"You can't restrain me," Wentworth said.

"Probably not," Anders observed grimly, "but I can beat the living hell out of you."

Mason grinned at Della Street, leaned back in his chair, and crossed his ankles on the corner of his desk. "Don't mind me, gentlemen," he said. "Go right ahead."

"What kind of a trap is this?" Wentworth demanded.

"There's no trap at all," Anders said, quivering with indignation. "You've pulled a dirty, stinking trick. I'm here to tell you you can't get away with it. Here's your eight hundred and fifty dollars."

"I refuse to touch it," Wentworth said. "It isn't the money, it's the principle of the thing."

Abruptly, he jumped to his feet. "You try to stop me," he said, "and I'll call the police. I'll sue you for conspiracy, for . . ."

Mason said to Anders, "Let him go, Anders," and then to Wentworth, "I just wanted you to know that I am representing Mae Farr. It may also interest you to know that I've submitted a photostatic copy of that check to a handwriting expert."

Wentworth, with his hand on the doorknob, stopped to stare at Perry Mason.

Mason said, "My guess is that if *your* signature is forged, *so is that of Mae Farr*."

Wentworth said, "It serves me right for trying to do you a good turn. I should have had my lawyer with me."

"Bring him, by all means," Mason invited, "and when you bring him, you might explain the matter of that check to him and ask him for his advice."

"What do you mean?"

"You," Mason said, "have accused Mae Farr of forging that check, acting purely on the assumption that because the check was sent to the Stylefirst Department Store to be credited to her account, she must have been guilty of the forgery. I submit that you haven't any evidence to back that claim, that you can't prove she mailed the check, that you can't prove she wrote it because the evidence of the handwriting expert will be that she didn't, and that, therefore, the check was forged by some third party."

Wentworth hesitated for a moment, then he said cautiously, "Well, of course, if that is true . . ."

"If that's true," Mason said casually, "you have been guilty of defaming the character of Mae Farr. You have made slanderous assertions to the effect that she is a forger and a fugitive from justice. You have made these to the police and to other persons. You have apparently sworn to a complaint charging Miss Farr with a criminal act. . . .

Do get your lawyer, Wentworth. I am sure he will advise you to instruct the bank to pay that check. Come in to see me any time. Ring up my secretary for an appointment. Good day."

Wentworth stared at him with consternation showing in his eyes. Then abruptly he jerked the door open and stepped out into the corridor, leaving Harold Anders staring in perplexity at the lawyer.

"Sit down, Anders," Mason invited.

Anders walked over to the big leather chair which Wentworth had just vacated and sat down.

"The trouble with me," Mason observed conversationally, "is that I am a natural-born grandstander. My friends call it a flair for the dramatic. My enemies call it four-flushing. That, coupled with a curiosity about people and an interest in anything that looks like a mystery, is always getting me into trouble. What are your bad habits?"

Anders laughed and said, "I lose my temper too easily. I can't take 'no' for an answer. I'm too much in love with the soil, and I have a hick outlook."

Mason studied him with twinkling eyes. "It sounds somewhat as though the list had been compiled by a young woman who left North Mesa to come to the city," he said.

"It was," Anders admitted.

Mason said, "I've been retained to represent Mae Farr. As nearly as I can find out, her entire trouble is over this forged check with which you seem to be familiar. I don't think we're going to have any further trouble with that."

"But look here," Anders said, "it's a cinch she didn't forge that check. Mae wouldn't do a thing like that, but what I can't understand is, who did it."

"Wentworth did it," Mason said.

"Wentworth?"

"That's right. We probably won't be able to prove it on him, but he's the one who did it or had someone do it for him."

"Good Lord, why?"

Mason said dryly, "It is quite probable that Wentworth is another individual who can't take 'no' for an answer."

Slow comprehension dawned on Anders' face. Abruptly, he placed his hands on the arms of the big chair, pushed himself to his feet, and had taken two quick strides toward the door when Mason's voice arrested him. "Wait a minute, Anders," the lawyer said, his voice kindly yet packed with authority. "I'm running this show. Come back here. I want to talk with you."

Anders hesitated a moment, his face flushed, jaw pushed forward.

"Come on back and sit down," Mason said. "Remember, I'm acting as Miss Farr's lawyer. I don't want anything done which wouldn't be in her best interests."

Slowly Anders came back and sat down. Mason studied the rugged features, the bronzed skin, the deep tan at the back of the neck. "Rancher?" he asked.

"Uh huh," Anders said.

"What kind of a ranch?"

"Mostly cattle, one patch of alfalfa, some hay."

"Much of a place?" Mason asked.

"Fifteen hundred acres," Anders said proudly.

"All cleared?"

"No, some if it's in brush. A lot of it's hill land. It's all under fence."

"Good," Mason observed.

For several seconds the men sat in silence, Mason calmly regarding the man who sat across from him. Anders, his angry flush subsiding, studied the lawyer with growing approval.

"Known Mae for some little time?" Mason asked.

"Nearly fifteen years."

"Know the family?"

"Yes."

"Mother living?"

"Yes."

"Brothers or sisters?"

"One sister, Sylvia."

"Where is she?" Mason asked.

"She's there in North Mesa, working in a candy store."

"How did you find out Mae was in trouble?"

"Sylvia got worried about her. She hadn't heard from her for some time, and then one of her letters was returned saying that Mae had moved and left no forwarding address."

"You don't hear from her regularly?" Mason asked.

Anders hesitated a minute, then said shortly, "No."

"You keep in touch with her through Sylvia?"

"That's right," Anders said, in a tone that implied he considered the question none of the lawyer's business. "But this time she called me to say she was in trouble over a forged check for eight hundred and fifty dollars."

"Have you located Miss Farr?"

"No, I haven't. I wanted you— Well, I'm her friend. I want her address."

"I'm sorry," Mason said. "I don't have it."

"But I thought she employed you."

"The young woman who employed me," Mason said, "explained that she was doing it on behalf of Mae Farr. She said that she didn't know where Mae could be reached."

Anders' face showed disappointment.

"However," Mason said, "if you keep on searching, I feel quite certain you'll be able to locate her. When did you leave North Mesa?"

"Two days ago."

"Where is the sister—Sylvia? Is she still in North Mesa, or did she come with you?"

"No, she's still there, holding down a job. The girls support their mother. Mae has contributed most of the money."

"She stopped sending checks a few months ago?" Mason asked.

"No, she didn't. That's why I was trying to find Wentworth. Sylvia received three checks from Wentworth. He said that Mae was working for him and had asked him to send part of her salary direct to Sylvia."

"I see," Mason observed thoughtfully.

"Look here, Mr. Mason. I don't think we should let this thing rest. I think we should—well, do something about Wentworth."

"So do I," Mason agreed.

"Well?" Anders asked.

"I don't like to jump to conclusions when I haven't sufficient evidence to point the way, but it looks very much as though this is about what happened. Wentworth, as I understand it, is something of a gambler. I don't know the exact nature of his business. Apparently, he's rather wealthy. Miss Farr went to work for him. She didn't care particularly about having her friends know where she was working."

Anders said uneasily, striving to keep doubt from his voice, "That bill in the department store, that . . ."

"That undoubtedly means," Mason assured him, "that she was acting as a hostess in some place which Wentworth controlled, or was doing some work for him which necessitated her coming in contact with the public. He insisted that she should be well dressed and probably sent her to the department store with a letter of guarantee. You'll notice that he didn't agree to pay for the merchandise outright, and, in view of the fact that he sent the checks to Sylvia, it's reasonable to suppose that he kept the bulk of Mae's salary, the understanding being that he was to apply part of it toward paying off the bills at the department store and make the remittances to the sister."

"But she said in her letters that she was working for him and . . ."

"Exactly," Mason amended, "but she didn't say just what she was doing. If she was hostess in a nightclub or something of that sort, it's quite possible that Mae didn't want to tell Sylvia about it."

"I see," Anders said, and then, after a moment's thought, his face brightened. "By George," he said, "that would explain the whole thing. Mae was afraid her mother would find out what she was doing. Her mother's rather old-fashioned and straitlaced. She's not well, and Mae was afraid she might worry."

"Exactly," Mason said.

Anders got to his feet. "Well, Mr. Mason, I won't make a nuisance of myself. I know you're a busy man. I'll— Look here, Mr. Mason, I'm at the Fairview Hotel, three-nineteen. If you see Mae, would you tell her that I'm here and want very much to see her?"

"I'll tell her," Mason said. He stood up as Anders came across to shake hands. The two men were much the same build, tall, muscular, and rugged of feature. Anders' bronzed hand gripped Mason's. "I can't begin to tell you how much I appreciate this," he said. "Look here, Mr. Mason, how about your fees? Can I—"

"No," Mason interrupted, "I think Miss Farr would prefer to make all arrangements herself. Don't you?"

"Yes," Anders said, "she would. Please don't tell her I suggested it."

Mason nodded.

"And you'll let me know if you hear anything?"

"I'll tell her where you are."

Anders said, "Gosh, Mr. Mason, I'm certainly glad I met Wentworth here. Otherwise I'd probably have made a fool of myself. Goodbye."

"Good-bye," Mason said.

Anders hesitated a moment uncertainly, then bowed to Della Street, who had sat silently throughout the conversation. "And thank you very much, Miss . . . ?"

"Street," Mason said. "Della Street, my secretary."

"Thank you very much, Miss Street."

Anders walked to the exit door with the long, free stride of a man accustomed to the outdoors.

When the door had closed behind him, Della glanced up at Perry Mason. "Do you believe that story?" she asked.

"What story?"

"The one you told Anders, the explanation for Mae Farr's conduct."

Mason grinned. "Gosh, Della, I don't know. It was the best I could do offhand. Dammit, I wish I didn't get so interested in people and so sympathetic with their problems."

Della Street's eyes were a trifle wistful. She said thoughtfully, "It was a peach of a story."

Chapter Four

∿∿∿∿∿∿∿∿∿∿∿∿∿∿∿∿∿∿∿∿∿∿

Mason, relaxed from a hot shower, clad in thin, silk pajamas and sprawled out in a reclining chair, was immersed in a mystery story. Ominous thunderheads, which had been gathering all afternoon over the high mountains to the north and east, had begun to drift toward the city, and the rumble of distant thunder became increasingly audible as Mason turned the pages of the book.

Abruptly the telephone rang.

Mason, without taking his eyes from the book, stretched out his arm and completed a groping search by closing his fingers around the instrument. He lifted it and said, "Mason speaking. What is it?"

Della Street's voice said, "I think you'd better come down here, Chief."

"Where?"

"My apartment."

"What's wrong?"

"I have a couple of rather excited clients here."

"You've talked with them?"

"Yes."

"And think I'd better come?"

"If you can."

"Okay, Della. Be there in fifteen minutes. Remember, apartment walls are thin. Excited voices always attract attention. Put a muzzle on them until I get there."

She said, "The place is under gag rule right now. I figured you'd want to hear the details firsthand."

"Good girl," Mason said. "I'll be right over."

He telephoned the night man at the garage to have his car waiting, dashed into his clothes, and beat his promised schedule by a minute and five seconds.

In Della Street's apartment he found his secretary clothed for the street, a raincoat over her arm, her hat on, a shorthand notebook and a purse under her arm.

Seated side by side on the davenport across from her, looking very white-faced and big-eyed, were Harold Anders and Mae Farr.

Mason nodded his approval at Della Street's preparedness and said to Anders, "Well, I see you've found her."

Mae Farr said, "You mean that you really did know all along?"

"About you being Mae and not Sylvia?" Mason asked.

She nodded.

Mason said casually, "Of course. That was all that interested me in the case in the first place. What's the trouble?"

Anders started to say something. She placed her hand on his forearm and said, "Let me tell him, Hal. Penn Wentworth is dead."

"What happened?" Mason said.

"Someone shot him."

"Where?"

"On his yacht, the *Pennwent*."

"How do you know?" Mason asked.

"I was there."

"Who killed him?"

Her eyes faltered.

"I didn't," Anders said.

"No," she said hastily, "Hal didn't."

"Who did?"

"I don't know."

"How did it happen?"

She said, "I was struggling with him, and someone leaned down through the open skylight in the cabin and shot him."

Mason's eyes narrowed. "You looked up?" he asked.

"Yes."

"See anyone?"

"No. The flash and the shot made me a little goofy, I guess. I didn't see— Well, I could see a shadowy figure. That was all."

Mason, frowning, stared steadily at her.

"You see," she explained hastily, "it was light there in the cabin. This figure was standing against the darkness up above. The skylight was open because it was so airless and—well, I had my hands full. Penn was trying to—trying to—"

"Okay," Mason said. "You don't need to draw me a diagram. What happened?"

"I'm not certain whether it was Penn who said something, but I heard someone say something. I couldn't tell just what the words were, and Penn looked up."

"What was your position?" Mason asked.

"I was twisted around. My hips were on the cushion in one of the seats in the cabin. His knee was in my stomach. His right hand was trying to choke me. I had twisted my shoulders around so I could bite at his wrist and keep him from getting a good hold on my throat. Both of my hands were clawing at his bare arm."

"Bare?" Mason asked.

"Yes."

"Did he have any clothes on?"

"Someone called something, and I think Wentworth must have

"Just his underwear."

"What happened?"

looked up at the skylight, and then—then *bang*, it happened."

"Kill him instantly?"

"He rolled off the cushioned seat, doubled up with his hands over his face, and ran aft out of the cabin."

"Then what?" Mason asked.

"I looked up and could see someone moving. I heard steps on the deck. I ran back to the door that goes to the after cabin. I called out to Penn to ask if he was hurt. He didn't answer. I tried to open the door. He must have been lying against it. I couldn't push it open."

"It opened *into* the after cabin?"

"That's right."

"Then what?" Mason asked.

"Then I ran up on deck."

"Where did you meet Anders?"

"On the deck," she said, shifting her eyes quickly.

Mason scowled and glanced at Anders.

Anders said, "Here, let me tell this, Mae."

"By all means," Mason said.

"I distrusted this man, Wentworth. I thought he might know where Mae was or that Mae might try to get in touch with him. I went down to the Yacht Club where he keeps his boat."

"So you found her?"

"Yes. About nine-thirty she drove up to the Yacht Club."

"What happened?" Mason asked.

"She left the car and went aboard, and I . . . well, I . . ."

"Go ahead," Mason said impatiently. "What did you do?"

"I lost my nerve," Anders admitted. "I thought she'd gone aboard voluntarily and—and that perhaps she'd thank me to keep out of her business."

"A wise assumption," Mason said. "Let's have the rest of it."

"Well, I sat there, feeling like a heel, lower than a snake's belly, and—"

"For the love of Mike," Mason interrupted. "I know how you felt. I know the thoughts that were going through your mind. I want facts! We may have to move fast. What happened? Give it to me straight from the shoulder and fast."

"I heard Mae scream," Anders said. "I jumped out of the car and started toward the yacht. She screamed again. The yacht was tied to a float. There's a walk running the length of the float, and then a lot of U-shaped stalls. . . ."

"I know all about that," Mason said. "You don't need to go into those details."

"No, but it's important," Anders insisted. "You see, Mr. Mason, my eyes were blinded by watching the lights on the yacht, and I was running fast—"

"—and he fell in," Mae Farr interposed.

"I fell in," Anders said.

Mason looked from one to the other and said grimly, "The hell you did."

"That's right. I fell in, and it must have been just at that moment when the shot was fired. You see, I didn't know anything about it. It happened while I was in the water."

"You swim?" Mason asked.

"Oh yes. I'm a good swimmer."

"A champion swimmer," Mae Farr amended.

"Well, I've won a few events, no big competition, just interscholastic stuff."

Mason looked at his dry clothes and said, "What happened to your clothes?"

"I changed them," Anders said, "while Mae was telephoning your secretary."

"Where?"

"In the car."

"Carried an extra suit with you in the car?" Mason inquired skeptically.

Anders said, "I was—wearing overalls."

"Don't you see?" Mae Farr explained. "He was trying to shadow Penn, and he thought he needed a disguise. Penn had already seen him, you know. So Hal put on some overalls and one of those round caps that workmen wear, and—"

"And your other clothes were in the car?" Mason interrupted.

Anders nodded.

"Did you have a gun in that car?" Mason asked.

"Yes."

"Where is it now?"

"I— We threw it away."

"Where?"

"Driving back from the Yacht Club."

"When?"

"About thirty or forty minutes ago."

Mason shifted his eyes to Mae Farr. "You called the police?" he asked.

She shook her head.

"Why not?"

"Because no one except Hal knew I was aboard the yacht, and—

well, finding Hal there with his clothes all wet, it would have been impossible."

"Why did you go aboard the yacht?" Mason asked.

"I wanted to try and make Penn listen to reason."

"You'd tried before, hadn't you?"

"Yes."

"Get anywhere?"

"No—but you don't understand."

Mason said, "All right then. Go ahead and make me understand."

"Penn," she said, "wanted to— Well, he wanted me."

"I gathered as much," Mason said.

"But he was willing to do anything. You know, he wanted to marry me."

"And you said 'no'?"

She nodded.

"Ever say 'yes'?" Mason asked.

"No," she said, with an indignant shake of her head.

Mason said, "Well, you've made a sweet mess of it now."

"I know," she said, blinking her eyes rapidly.

"Cut it," Mason ordered sternly. "Don't start bawling."

"I'm not going to," she said. "I don't cry. Tears are a confession of weakness, and I *hate* weakness. I *hate* it."

"That vehemently?" Mason asked.

"A lot more than that."

Mason noticed that Anders seemed distinctly uncomfortable.

"Who knew you were going down to the yacht to see Wentworth?" Mason asked.

"No one."

"No one at all?"

"No."

"Where's your car?"

Sudden dismay showed in Mae's eyes. "My God," she said, "we left mine down there. Hal rushed me over to his car and—"

"Your car or one you'd rented?" Mason asked.

"One I'd rented from a drive-yourself agency," Anders said.

Mason's eyes narrowed. "All right," he said, "let's get going. We drive back to that Yacht Club. You go aboard the yacht. Disarray your clothes the way they were during your struggle. . . . How was this struggle? Any bruises?"

"Good Lord, there should be. We fought enough."

"Let's take a look," Mason said.

She hesitated for a moment, glanced at Anders.

Mason said, "Forget it. This is no time to be coy. Go in the bathroom if you have to, but *I* want to see those bruises."

Mae took hold of her skirt on the left side and pulled it up midway on her thigh. "There's one," she said.

Mason nodded. "Any more?"

"I don't know."

"Go in the bathroom with her," Mason said to Della Street. "Take a good look. I want to be damn certain she has bruises."

As the girls went into the bathroom, Mason stared at Harold Anders and said, "Your story stinks."

"It's the truth."

"It stinks just the same," Mason said. "What are you holding back?"

Anders said, "Mae thinks I'm weak. She hates me for it."

"Are you?" Mason asked.

"I don't know. I don't think so."

"What makes her think you're weak?"

"Because I hung around there carrying a gun. She said a real man would have stepped out of the car and grabbed her before she'd gone aboard the yacht, or followed her aboard the yacht, or gone aboard and given Wentworth a damn good beating."

Mason said moodily, "She may be right at that."

The bathroom door opened. Mason had a glimpse of Mae Farr in flesh-colored underwear struggling back into her dress. Through the crack in the door, she saw Mason's eyes on her and said, "Do you want to look, Mr. Mason?"

Mason glanced at Della Street. "Any luck?" he asked.

"Lots," she said. "She's been mauled all right."

"No," Mason said to Mae Farr. "Get your dress on."

Della Street closed the bathroom door. Mason started pacing the floor. When Mae Farr emerged from the bathroom, Mason said, in a low voice, "All right, you two. Anders, you go to your hotel, have a chat with the night clerk, get him to notice the time. Tell him you can't sleep. Stick around the lobby. Mae, you're going back down to that Yacht Club with me. You're going aboard the yacht. After looking the situation over to make damn certain there's nothing that's going to prove you a liar, you start screaming for help. You'll run up on deck with your clothes disarrayed. Scream and keep on screaming until someone notices you. Then you tell your story."

"You mean about coming here and . . ."

"Certainly not," Mason said. "You were struggling with Wentworth. Someone shot him. He ran into the after cabin. You tried to follow. You were half unconscious from the struggle. You tried the door. His body was jammed against it so you couldn't open it. You tried and tried. You don't know how long—it seemed forever. Finally, you succumbed to hysteria and began screaming for help. Think you can do that?"

"Yes, I guess so."

"Well," Mason said, "it's the only way you can get yourself out of the mess. Your car's down there. Your fingerprints are all over the cabin. I don't suppose you thought to wipe your fingerprints off, did you?"

She shook her head.

"Wentworth in his underwear. There are probably fingernail marks on his arm. Your clothes are torn and your body is bruised. The police won't take more than two guesses to figure out what he was doing."

"But why shouldn't I try and get out of it?" she asked. "Why shouldn't I wipe my fingerprints off the knobs, get my car, and . . ."

"Because they'll start looking for the woman in the case, and then start looking for her boyfriend," Mason said. "They'll trace Anders and pin a first-degree murder rap on him. As it is now, they'll only ask for second-degree or manslaughter, and if worst comes to worst, and you can make the story of that struggle sound realistic enough, we can get a justifiable homicide out of it. But you two try to cover the thing up, and here's what'll happen: The D.A. will claim you'd forged a check, that Wentworth was holding it over you, that you went down prepared to offer him almost anything to square the rap."

"They can see," she said, "that I was fighting for my honor."

Mason stared steadily at her. "They can see it," he said ominously, "unless they can prove that you'd already been his mistress, and if they can prove that, God help you."

She stared steadily at the lawyer, her face utterly devoid of expression.

"All right," Mason said, "let's get started. We've wasted too much time already."

"How about me?" Anders asked. "Do I stay at the hotel until— the police come?"

"No," Mason said, "but stay there until I call. I want to look the thing over. I'll telephone you before the police can possibly nab you. Then, probably, the thing for you to do will be to go to another hotel, register under an assumed name, and lie low, pretending that you were planning on taking other steps to get in touch with Mae, and didn't want anyone to know what they were. I'll give you a ring. Come on, Mae. Let's go. Della, I'm playing with dynamite. You can keep out of it if you want to."

"I don't want to," Della Street said, "not if I can possibly help."

"Okay," Mason said. "Come along."

Chapter Five

A few scattering drops of rain spattered against the windshield when the car was halfway to the Yacht Club. Behind them, the stars were blotted out by great banks of clouds from which came the flash of lightning, the crash of thunder. By the time they reached the harbor, they had left the thunderstorm behind.

"Which way?" Mason asked the girl at his side.

"Turn right at this next intersection. Now go slow. You have to make another turn within a few hundred feet. It's right along in here. It's just by that fence. There it is. Turn here. There's a place to park cars over on the left."

"Where is your car parked?"

"Right over there."

Mason said, "Wait a minute. Tell me your license number and describe the car."

"It's a Ford convertible," she said. "The license number is WVM five-seven-four."

Mason said, "Sit here for a few minutes."

He switched out the lights, said, "Keep an eye on her, Della," slid out of the car, and walked around the parked automobiles until he spotted the car Mae Farr had described. After a few minutes he came back and said, "Everything's quiet along here. Let's get aboard that yacht and look things over. Della, you'd better stay here."

Della said, "Let me go. You may want to take some notes."

"All right," Mason said. "If you feel that way about it, come along. You show us the way, Mae."

Mae Farr hung back, a trembling hand on Mason's arm. "Gee," she said, "I don't know if I can . . . can face it."

Mason said, in a low voice, "If you haven't nerve enough to make the play, let's not take a crack at it. I have no great desire to stick my neck out. As far as you're concerned, it's the only way you can save your boyfriend. Do you love him that much?"

She said very emphatically, "I don't love him at all. He thinks he loves me. Perhaps he does. I don't know. I put him out of my life when I left North Mesa. I was never cut out to be the wife of a rancher."

Mason looked at her curiously.

She went on to say calmly, "I'm doing this for him because I think I owe him that much. I'd much prefer that he stayed home and minded his own business, but he did what he could to help me."

Mason said quietly, "Do you think he shot Wentworth, Mae?"

Mae Farr tightened her grip on Mason's arm. "I don't know," she said. "Sometimes I think— No, he wouldn't lie about it."

"All right," Mason said. "I can't hold your hand through the mess that's going to come next. How about it? Do you want to go through with the thing the way I suggested or telephone the police and give them the whole story?"

"The way you suggested," she said quietly, "but give me a minute to get my breath. I hate to go back in that cabin."

Mason cupped his hand under her elbow. "If you're going to do it, get started. If you're not going to do it, say so."

"I'm going to do it," she said.

Mason nodded to Della Street. The three of them walked from the parking lot down to the long float where a miscellaneous assortment of boats were crowded into U-shaped stalls, a tangle of masts stretching up to where the edges of advancing clouds obscured the starlight.

"That thundershower's catching up with us," Mason said.

No one answered. Their feet sounded on the cross boards of the float. A vagrant breeze, springing up, sent little ripples of water slapping against the sides of the boats.

Mason asked, "Where is this yacht?"

"Down toward the far end," she said.

They walked on. At intervals they passed yachts in which there were lights. From some of them came the sounds of merriment, from one, the twang of a guitar. From another, a girl's voice, sharp with indignation, asked someone where he thought he got off, told him he was no gentleman but a four-flusher, a cad, and a cheapskate.

Mason said, "Well, where the deuce is this yacht?"

"It shouldn't be much farther."

"Do you know it when you see it?"

"Of course. I've . . . I've cruised on it quite frequently."

"A big one?"

"Uh huh. Pretty big, about fifty feet."

"Motor and sail or just motor?"

"A motor sailer. It's an old-timer, what Penn called a 'character' boat, but the whole thing is the last word. Lots of electronic equipment and even what they call an Iron-Mike."

"What's an Iron-Mike?" Della asked.

"An automatic steering thing," Mae Farr said. "You switch the thing on, and it's connected in some way with the compass and the steering wheel. You set the course you want the yacht to travel, and it never gets off that course. As soon as it starts to veer, the compass sets an automatic mechanism into action. I don't know the details, but it works perfectly."

Mason said, "Well, there are three boats between here and the end of the landing. Is it one of those three?"

Mae Farr stood stock-still, staring incredulously. "No," she said, "it isn't."

"You mean we've passed it?" Mason asked.

"We couldn't have—but I think we've come too far."

"Okay," Mason said, "let's go back. Keep your mind on what you're doing. Watch for the yacht carefully."

They walked slowly back along the landing until they could once more see the parking lot. Mae Farr said, in a half whisper, "It isn't here."

"All right," Mason said. "Let's find out where it was. Can you remember what boats were next to it?"

"No," she said, "I don't think I can. When I came down, I just walked along here until I saw it."

"Then it wasn't near any of the large yachts?" Mason asked.

"No. I remember it was between two rather small yachts. Oh, wait a minute. I think one of them was the *Atina*."

Mason said, "Okay, let's look for the *Atina*."

They walked slowly back toward the end of the float, and Mason said, "There's the *Atina* just ahead. There's a vacant space next to it."

Mae Farr stood staring, then turned to Mason. "I remember now," she said, "that it was here. I remember that water barrel near the end of the slip there. She's gone."

Mason's eyes narrowed. "Is there a watchman here?" he asked.

"Yes, he lives in that houseboat. I don't know what they have him for except to answer the telephone and take out messages. I think they lock the place up around midnight. You know, that gate that we drove through. The club members have keys."

Heavy raindrops began to spatter down on the landing and in the water.

Mason said, "All right. That thundershower is going to catch up with us. Get back to your car. I'll drive into town. You drive right behind me. Now, how about this place where Anders tossed the gun? Do you think you can find that place?"

"Yes, I think so. I know about where it was."

"All right," Mason said. "When we come to that place, blink your headlights on and off. We'll stop. I have a flashlight. We'll get out and pick up that gun."

"But what could have happened to the *Pennwent*?" she asked.

"Only one thing," Mason said. "It was moved and probably under its own power."

"Then that means—that someone—would have had to be aboard."

"Exactly," Mason said.

"Who could it have been?"

Mason stared at her with narrowed eyes. "How about this boyfriend of yours?" he asked. "Does he know anything about engines or yachts?"

"He . . . Yes, I think he does."

"What makes you think so?"

"When he was going through college, he worked one summer up in Alaska on some fishing boats, and I think he's been on at least one cruise from San Francisco to Turtle Bay."

Mason said, "All right. Let's get out of here. We'll talk that over later."

He piloted Mae Farr over to her car, said, "You'd better drive out first and keep the lead until we hit the main boulevard back to town. If anyone stops you, I'll do the talking. After we hit the main boulevard, I'll take the lead. If anything's going to break, it will happen before then. Remember to blink your lights when we come to the place where Anders threw the gun."

"I will," she promised.

"Feel all right? Think you can drive the car?"

"Yes, of course."

"All right. Get going."

The rain was falling more rapidly now, the flashes of lightning were more brilliant, and, at intervals, thunder crashed.

Mason and Della Street climbed back into Mason's car. The lawyer started the motor, switched on the lights, and followed Mae Farr out of the parking place, the windshield wiper swishing back and forth monotonously.

"Think she's lying?" Della asked quietly.

"I don't know," Mason said. "She's a woman. You should know more about it than I do. What do *you* think?"

"I don't know," Della admitted, "but it seems that she's keeping something back."

Mason nodded absently, watching the red glow of the taillight on the machine ahead. "The more I think of it," he said slowly, "the more I'm relieved that I didn't get aboard that yacht."

Della said, "I suppose there's no use pointing out to you that you were taking an awful chance."

"No use whatever," Mason said with a grin. "I have to take chances. When I take on a case, my duty and loyalty are one hundred percent to my client. I do everything in my power to get at the facts, and sometimes I have to cut corners."

"I know," Della said quietly.

Mason glanced at her. "That's no sign that you have to stick *your* neck out," he said.

Apparently Della considered the statement called for no comment.

They drove along in silence for five or six minutes until they reached the boulevard. Then Mason swept on past Mae Farr's car. Della Street asked, "Want me to keep an eye on her headlights?"

"No, I can watch them in the rear-view mirror," Mason said.

The rain was lashing down in torrents. Bolts of lightning zigzagging across the sky illuminated the landscape with weird greenish flashes followed almost instantly by deafening crashes of thunder.

After some fifteen minutes the lights behind Mason blinked on and off. The lawyer pulled his car over to the side of the road and stopped. Mason turned up the collar of his coat against the rain and sloshed back to where Mae Farr's car was standing with idling motor, the windshield wiper clacking back and forth. The headlights showed the falling raindrops, turned them into golden globules.

Mae Farr rolled down the window as Mason came abreast of the car. "I think it was right along in here," she said.

"How positive are you?"

"Pretty positive. I remember that hot-dog stand across the road behind us. I think we'd passed it just about fifty yards."

Mason looked back at the white building. "It's dark now," he said. "Was there a light in it then?"

"Yes."

"What did he do?" Mason asked. "Stand here and toss the gun, or did he throw it, or did he just open the door of the car and drop it out?"

"No. He got out, stood by the car, held the muzzle of the gun in his hand, and threw it as far as he could throw it."

"Over that fence?"

"Yes."

Mason stared for a moment at the ditch which had already commenced to collect drainage water, and said, "All right. Wait here," walked back to his car, took a flashlight from the glove compartment, climbed over the barbed-wire fence, and started searching through the wet grass, playing the beam of his flashlight around in circles. Whenever other cars approached, he switched out the flashlight and remained motionless until they had passed.

At the end of fifteen minutes, with the batteries in his flashlight running down, Mason climbed back over the fence, fought his way up the slippery embankment at the side of the road, and said to Mae Farr, "It's no use. I can't find it. I'm afraid to hunt any longer."

"I'm quite certain it was right near here."

"Well, we'll know more in the morning."

"What do you want me to do?"

"Where have you been staying?"

"At the address I gave you, the Palmcrest Rooms."

"And we have your telephone number?"

"Yes. I'm awfully sorry, Mr. Mason, that I tried to deceive you. You know, about telling you that I was Sylvia and . . ."

"You'll have a lot of time to make those apologies," Mason said, "when I'm not standing out in the rain listening to them. I feel a lot more forgiving when cold rainwater isn't dribbling down the back of my neck and when my feet are dry."

"What do you want me to do?"

Mason said, "You have Della Street's telephone number."

"No. We called the office and . . ."

"It's all the same," Mason said. "There's a day number and a night number. The night number is Della Street's apartment. I have an unlisted telephone. She's the only one who has my number. You drive on back to town. Go to the Palmcrest Rooms and go to bed just as though nothing had happened. If anyone drags you out of bed and starts asking questions, don't answer. Don't say a word. Don't admit, don't deny, and don't explain. Insist that you be allowed to call me. I'll do the talking."

"And if—well, suppose no one does say anything?"

Mason said, "Get up, have breakfast, and get in touch with me in the morning. And for God's sake, keep out of trouble between now and then."

"What do you mean?"

Mason said, "Lay off of Harold Anders. Keep your eyes open and your mouth shut."

She placed her hand on his. "Thank you so much, Mr. Mason," she said. "You don't know how much I appreciate this."

"That can also keep," Mason said. "Good night."

"Good night, Mr. Mason."

The lawyer turned and his wet feet pumped water with every step back to his automobile.

Della opened the car door for him. "Find it?" she asked.

Mason shook his head.

Mae Farr started her car, pulled around them, sounded her horn in two quick blasts by way of farewell, and accelerated down the black ribbon of road.

Della Street opened her purse and took out a small flask of whiskey. "Where did this come from?" Mason asked.

"Out of my private cellar," Della said. "I figured you might need it. Gosh, Chief, you're soaking wet."

Mason offered her the flask. She shook her head and said, "You need it more than I do, Chief. Drink it down."

Mason tilted the flask to his lips, then handed it back.

"Better take some, Della."

"No, thanks. I'm fine. You certainly were out there long enough."

"I wanted to find that gun," Mason said.

"Think she remembered just where it was?"

"She should have. That hot-dog stand was her landmark."

"It's hard to find anything like that in the dark."

"I know," Mason said, "but I made a pretty thorough search, covered an area seventy-five paces wide by seventy-five long, and what I mean is, I covered it, darn near every inch of it."

"Gosh, you certainly are sopping."

Mason started the car and threw it into gear. "Well," he said, "that's that."

"Make anything of it?" she asked.

"No," he said, "not yet. That whiskey certainly was a lifesaver, Della."

"Where do we go now?"

"To a telephone," Mason said, "and call Hal Anders at the Fairview Hotel."

They drove for miles in silence. The rain became a drizzle, then finally stopped. They found a telephone in an all-night restaurant on the outskirts of the city, and Mason called the Fairview Hotel. "I know it's rather late," he said, "but I'd like to have you ring Mr. Anders. I believe he's in room three-nineteen."

"Was he expecting a call?" the clerk asked.

"It will be quite all right if you ring him," Mason said. "It's a matter of business."

There was an interval of silence, and then the clerk said, "I'm very sorry, but Mr. Anders doesn't answer."

"Perhaps he's in the lobby," Mason said. "You might have him paged."

"No, he isn't here. There's no one in the lobby. I haven't seen Mr. Anders since early this evening."

"You know him?"

"Yes. I didn't think he was in, but I rang his room to make sure."

"Is his key there?"

"No."

"Ring the room again, will you, please? Push down hard on the bell button. He may be asleep."

Again there was an interval of silence. Then the clerk said, "No, sir, he doesn't answer. I've called repeatedly."

Mason said,"Thanks.

He hung up as the clerk started to say, "Any message?"

Mason beckoned Della Street from the automobile. They had a cup of hot coffee at the lunch counter. "Any luck?" she asked.

"None whatever," Mason said. "He wasn't in."

"Wasn't in?"

"No."

"But you told him particularly . . ."

"I know," Mason said grimly. "He wasn't in. I think I'll have some ham and eggs, Della. How about it?"

"Sold," she said.

Mason ordered the ham and eggs. While they were waiting for their order, they sat side by side in silence, sipping coffee. Della Street's eyes were frankly troubled. Mason's profile showed patience, grim determination, and thoughtful concentration.

Chapter Six

~~~~~~~~~~~~~~~~~~~~~~~~~~~~~~~~~~

Mason entered his office to find Paul Drake and Della Street in conference.

"Hello, gang," he said, scaling his hat onto the bust of Blackstone by the door. "Why the gloom?"

Drake, looking at the lawyer with eyes that were expressionless, said, "Wentworth is dead."

"The deuce he is," Mason observed cheerfully. "Well, that would seem to simplify matters as far as Mae Farr is concerned."

"Or complicate them," the detective said.

Mason walked over to his desk, sat down on the swivel chair, flashed a swift glance at Della, and received by way of reply a cautious wink.

"Well," Mason said, "let's take a look through the mail. Anything important, Della?"

"Nothing that can't wait."

Mason riffled through the stack of letters and shoved them to one side of his desk. "Well, Paul," he said, "what's the dope? How did Wentworth die?"

"Brain hemorrhage," Drake said.

Mason raised his eyebrows.

"Caused," Drake continued, "by a bullet that went into the right side of the head, struck some of the blood vessels so that there was profuse bleeding, and apparently caused a slow hemorrhage into the substance of the brain, which was the cause of death."

"Death instantaneous?" Mason asked.

"Apparently not."

"Who did it?"

"No one knows."

"When?"

"Sometime last night. They haven't established the exact time."

Mason turned to Della Street so that his face was partially concealed from the detective. "Did you notify our client?" he asked.

"I gave her a ring," Della said. "She wasn't available."

"Where is she?"

"No one knows. She doesn't answer the telephone at her apartment."

"Now that," Mason said slowly, "is *something*."

"You don't know the half of it yet," Della said significantly, with a slight gesture of her head toward Paul Drake.

"Okay, Paul," Mason said, "let's have the other half. You do all the talking for a while, and after I have all the facts I'll do a little thinking."

Drake coiled himself up in the big leather chair and fed three sticks of chewing gum into his mouth. His eyes remained veiled and expressionless. The rapid motion of his jaws as he chewed the gum into a wad furnished the only indication of any nervousness.

"Wentworth," he said, "has a yacht, the *Pennwent*. It's around fifty feet, rather an elaborate affair, with lots of gadgets, including an Iron-Mike. In case you don't know about an Iron-Mike, Perry, it's a device by which the skipper of a boat can link the steering mechanism up with the compass. It enables the ship to be placed on a certain compass course and kept on that course with a very small margin of deviation. The manufacturers claim that a boat is steered by that mechanism a lot more accurately than is possible when there's a man at the wheel."

"Uh huh," Mason said. "I know something about them. Go ahead, Paul."

"About daylight," Drake said, "somewhere off San Diego, the Coast Guard picked this yacht up."

"Why the Coast Guard?" Mason asked.

"Well, it's quite a story," Drake said. "A tanker, headed up the coast, had to change course to avert a collision. This yacht ignored signals, seemed to have no lookout aboard, and was running full speed. The skipper of the tanker was considerably peeved. He radioed in a report. A Coast Guard cutter that happened to be cruising in the vicinity picked it up. An hour or so later it saw the yacht plowing along through the water. The cutter signaled it without getting any response, and finally, by a clever piece of navigation, managed to get a man aboard. He found Wentworth's body in the main cabin. Apparently, Wentworth had tried to stop the flow of blood without success. He'd been able to get to the after cabin and returned to the main cabin. He finally keeled over, became unconscious, and died."

"Police find the bullet that did the job?" Mason asked, his voice showing only a casual interest.

"I don't know," Drake said. "I haven't a whole lot of details."

Mason whistled a few bars of a tune, drummed with his fingertips on the edge of his desk. "No one else aboard the yacht, Paul?"

"No."

"Any evidence that anyone had been aboard the yacht?"

"Apparently not. They will, of course, take fingerprints and then they'll know a lot more about it—perhaps."

"Any estimates on how long he'd lived after the shot was fired?" Mason asked.

"Not yet. Anyway, long enough to wander around a little."

"Find the gun?"

"No."

"Where did he keep the yacht?" Mason asked. "Do you know?"

"Yes. He had a berth at the Yacht Club. It would have taken him about twenty minutes to have cleared the harbor from that berth."

Mason continued to drum with the tips of his fingers on the edge of the desk. Della Street avoided his eyes. Paul Drake, chewing gum rapidly, kept his eyes fastened on the lawyer.

At length Drake asked, "What do I do, Perry? Call the whole thing off or stay on the job?"

"Stay on the job," Mason said.

"Doing what?"

"Getting all the dope you can about that death. Any chance it was suicide?"

"Apparently not," Drake said. "The police don't think so."

"Of course, if he lived long enough to move from cabin to cabin," Mason pointed out, "he could also have tossed the gun overboard."

"There were no powder burns," Drake said, "and the angle of the shot pretty well rules out suicide."

Mason said, "I want to know a lot about this man, Wentworth, Paul. It may be important. I want to know about his friends and associates, his life, his liberties, and his pursuit of what he probably thought was happiness."

"I'm getting quite a bit of that stuff lined up," Drake said. "Part of it was routine that I handled in connection with the job I was on. Some of it is stuff I can get pretty easily, and I figured you'd want it."

"How much of it do you have available now?" Mason asked.

"Not a great deal. He'd been married, and was having some domestic difficulties."

"No divorce?" Mason asked.

"No, that was the rub. His wife is part Mexican—beautiful, olive complexion, streamlined figure, snappy black eyes."

"And a hell of a temper," Mason said.

"And a hell of a temper," Drake agreed. "They separated over a year ago. They couldn't come to terms on a property settlement."

"Why didn't she go to court and let the court give her a slice?" Mason asked.

"Wentworth," Drake interrupted, "was too smart for that racket."

"Lots smarter men than Wentworth have got hooked," Mason said.

"But not such fast workers," Drake said. "Wentworth knew his way around. Apparently, Juanita wanted to marry a man by the name of Eversel, Sidney Eversel. He cuts quite a wide swath. He hangs around with the yachting crowd, has a boat of his own, and takes in all the Catalina cruises and all that jazz. Juanita met him on a club cruise to Catalina. Evidently, it was something of a binge. Juanita became impulsive, and Wentworth objected. After that, Juanita and Wentworth didn't jibe so well. Two months later they separated."

"Had she been seeing Eversel in the meantime?" Mason asked.

Drake shrugged his shoulders and said, "Wentworth employed detectives. Juanita didn't sue for a divorce. You can draw your own conclusions."

"Where was Juanita when Wentworth was shot?" Mason asked.

"I don't know," Drake said. "That's one of the things I'm working on."

"What are the other angles?" Mason asked.

Drake said, "Wentworth got around quite a bit. You know, Perry, a man's home is his castle, but his yacht is his own damn business. Down at the Yacht Club, the party has to get awfully rough before anyone says anything. The only people around are those who have their own boats or their guests. Watchmen of yacht clubs usually go to bed early and don't have good hearing. They have poor eyesight and poorer memories, if you know what I mean."

"You mean Wentworth entertained women aboard his yacht?"

"Scads of them," Drake said. "I have a hunch that there was a party aboard the yacht before it pulled out. Of course, you can't figure that Wentworth was shot and then started putting out to sea. On the other hand, if someone murdered him at sea, did the murderer just step off the yacht into the drink? It's goofy no matter how you look at it. Just on general principles, I'm checking pretty carefully to find out who was aboard the yacht last night. I'm already working on a good lead. A young woman who had been aboard the *Pennwent* several times and was known by sight to some members of the club was down at the Yacht Club last night. One of the members saw her getting out of her car."

"Know who she was?" Mason asked.

"He either doesn't or says he doesn't," Drake said, "but the D.A.'s outfit hasn't really started to work on him yet. When they do, they'll probably get results. I also have some men working on it from another angle."

Mason said, "I'm not so certain that angle is important, Paul."

"I thought you wanted all the dope."

"I do."

"Well, this is part of it."

Mason said, "It might get some innocent girl in an awful jam, Paul."

"Why innocent?" Drake asked.

"Because I don't believe that Wentworth would have taken the yacht out to sea after he'd been shot."

"All right," Drake said, "figure out how someone could have shot him on the high seas and then called a taxicab. Anyway, this girl is in it now right up to her neck. The D.A.'s office will identify her before they get done."

Mason sighed. "Okay, Paul. You can't find out anything sitting in here and gassing."

"I've got five men on the job," Drake said. "Do you want any more?"

"Use your judgment, Paul. I want the facts. I would like to get them in advance of the police if I could."

"You can't," Drake said. "I can pick up crumbs here and there, but the big dish is being served to Homicide. They're working on the case. They have the facilities. And they have the authority."

"Just a minute," Mason said. "How was he dressed when he was found?"

"You mean the color of clothes, or . . ."

"No. Was he fully clothed?"

"Why, yes, I guess so."

Mason said, "Find out, will you, Paul?"

"Okay. I just took it for granted he was dressed because no one said anything to the contrary."

"All right," Mason said. "Get busy and keep me posted."

Drake made no move to get up out of the chair. "You seem to be in a hell of a hurry this morning, Perry."

Mason motioned toward the stack of mail and said, "I have to work for a living. Look at that mail."

"I'm looking at it," Drake said. "I'm also looking at you. This is the first time I ever saw you in such a stew to tackle a pile of correspondence. Let's talk a little sense, Perry. Suppose it was Mae Farr who went aboard that yacht last night?"

Mason raised his eyebrows. "Why pick on her?" he asked.

"Why not?"

"For one reason," Mason said, "she and Wentworth weren't particularly cordial. Wentworth had her arrested on a forgery charge."

"I know," Drake said. "Miss Farr might have figured she could square that forgery rap if she had a few minutes alone with him."

"There was nothing to square," Mason said. "It was a frame-up."

"I know," Drake said, "but the question is did Mae know?"

"Of course she knew," Mason said. "Her boyfriend was in here when we ripped Wentworth to pieces."

Drake said, "She may have gone down there, Perry."

"What makes you think she did?"

"The description fits."

"Whose description?"

"The man who saw the girl getting out of the car. He knew she was Wentworth's property."

"Wentworth have a brand on her?" Mason asked.

"No, but you know how those yachtsmen are. The stick together. A good-looking, unescorted girl, rubber-necking around at yachts, wouldn't have much difficulty finding some yachtsman who was willing to show her around, but when she belongs to one of the crowd, that's different."

"I don't like that assumption of ownership," Mason said.

"You know what I mean, Perry. A girl who's coming down to call on some particular yachtsman."

Mason said, "Mae Farr is our client."

"I know," Drake rejoined. "The ostrich sticks his head in the sand. You wouldn't want to have any sand in my eyes, would you, Perry?"

Mason said impatiently, "Oh, get the hell out of here, and let me figure this thing, Paul. I'm worried because we can't get in touch with Mae Farr."

Drake said to Della, "Have you tried her boyfriend?"

Della shook her head.

"It might be a good thing to try him," Drake said to Perry Mason.

"It might," Mason agreed.

Drake sighed and began to uncoil himself. He got to his feet, stretched, yawned, and said, "Have it your own way, Perry. You know what you're doing. I'll keep you posted."

He walked slowly across the office, opened the exit door, and then turned as though about to say something, but he thought better of it and moved silently out into the corridor.

As the door clicked shut, Mason and Della Street exchanged glances.

Mason said, "All right, Della. You're elected. Take your shorthand book."

She picked up her shorthand book from the desk. "Long?" she asked.

"Very short," Mason said.

"All right, I'm ready."

Mason said, "Write 'demand' in caps at the head of the page and then put on a dateline and the words, 'Demand is hereby made that you produce for the inspection of my attorney the original check purported to be signed by Penn Wentworth on which you have refused payment, claiming the same is a forgery. This is a check payable to the undersigned, Mae Farr, and purported to have been endorsed on the back thereof "Pay to the order of Stylefirst Department Store, (signed) Mae Farr".' "

Della Street's pen flew rapidly over the shorthand notebook.

"Put a blank for a signature on that," Mason said. "Type it out, then put on your hat, and go hunt up Mae Farr."

"You mean go to her apartment?" Della Street asked.

"Go anyplace," Mason said. "Find out all you can. Remember this Demand is your protection, in case anyone asks questions. You're simply looking for her as a part of your duties as my secretary. I want this Demand signed by her so we can serve it on the bank."

"You mean it's just a stall?" she asked.

"Just a stall," he said, "to protect you in case anyone starts checking up."

"How long do I stay on the job?" Della asked.

"Until you find her," Mason said, "or until I give you different instructions. Telephone in every hour or so and let me know what you're doing. Try and get a line on her. Find out if anyone saw her come in or saw her leave. Find out where she keeps her car. Check up on it. In other words, I want everything you can dig up. Feed the facts to me as fast as you get them. If anyone tries to get rough, be wide-eyed and innocent. I dictated this Demand to you and told you to get Miss Farr's signature. You're trying to get it."

Della Street nodded. "On my way," she said, and went out.

At eleven-thirty, Della Street telephoned her first report. "I've located her automobile," she said.

"Where is it?"

"In the garage where she ordinarily keeps it."

"Can you find out what time it came in?"

"Yes, about three o'clock this morning."

"Who drove it in?"

"She did."

"Find anything about her?"

"Not yet."

Mason said, "Do everything you can on that angle, Della. Remember that's one place where we're ahead of the police. I want to get the information before they do."

"I think," she said, "I could work faster if I had one of Paul Drake's men to help me."

"No, that's exactly what I don't want," Mason said. "We can trust Paul, but we can't trust his men. As my secretary, you can be on the job getting a paper signed, and that's all there is to it. If police ask one of Drake's men why he happened to be looking for her, it wouldn't be so good."

"I get you," Della Street said. "What time are you going to lunch?"

"Not until after you telephone again," Mason told her. "Snoop around a little bit and see what you can find."

"Okay, I'll call you back."

Her next call came in less than thirty minutes later. "Someone," she said cautiously, "has taken the lid off the bean pot, and the beans are spilled all over everything."

"What did you find out, Della?"

"Two men," she said, "drove up about nine o'clock this morning and pounded on the door of Mae Farr's apartment until she answered. The men walked right on in and didn't take their hats off. The woman who has the apartment across the court saw that much."

"That," Mason said, "is all she needed to see. Come on back to the office, Della, and we'll go to lunch."

Chapter Seven

Paul Drake was waiting for Mason when the lawyer and Della Street returned from lunch. "Well, Perry," the detective said, "the best I can do is to give you this information about an hour in advance of publication. The newspapers will have it on the street in the early afternoon editions."

"Shoot," Mason said.

"It doesn't look so good for Mae Farr or her boyfriend. I don't know just what lead the police followed, but they followed it right to Mae Farr. I understand the man who saw her leave her car has identified her absolutely."

"Anything else?" Mason asked.

"Yes. They have a lead on the boyfriend."

"Did they find him?"

"I think they had the devil of a time finding him," Drake said. "They picked him up out of town somewhere. The story I get is that they found him up at North Mesa."

"Then what?" Mason asked.

"I understand the girl's sitting tight, but telegraphic advices from the north are that when representatives of the district attorney's office flew up to San Francisco to meet local authorities who had brought Anders down that far, Anders made a fairly complete confession."

"Confession?" Mason asked.

Drake nodded and then said, after a moment, "You're not looking well, Perry."

"What's wrong with me?"

"You don't look right around the eyes. You've been on pretty much of a strain lately. Why don't you take a vacation?"

"Why?" Mason asked, "would I want a vacation?"

"I thought it might be a good idea," Drake said. "If I were you, I'd start right away."

"What," Mason asked, "did Anders say?"

"I don't know," Drake admitted, "but it was something pretty hot, I think. The tip that came to the newspapers was that a prominent attorney was going to be implicated."

Mason said, "Bunk. Anders can't implicate anybody."

"It might be well if you were out of the picture for a day or two until I can get all the dope," Drake said. "I can turn the whole thing inside out if I have forty-eight hours."

"To hell with that stuff," Mason said. "Can't you see the field day the police would have if I suddenly took a powder? They'd smear it all over the newspapers that I'd left hurriedly on being advised of Anders' statement."

"Do they," Drake asked, "have anything on you?"

Mason shrugged his shoulders and said, "How do I know what they have? How did they get Anders to talk?"

"Same old scheme," Drake said. "They told him Mae Farr had confessed to the whole business and was going to take the blame, and he got chivalrous and said it wasn't her fault, and spilled his guts."

Mason said, "Well—" and broke off as the telephone buzzed. Della picked it up, said, "Hello," hesitated a moment, then covered the mouthpiece. She looked up at Perry Mason and said, with no expression whatever in her voice, "Sergeant Holcomb of the Homicide Squad and Carl Runcifer, a deputy district attorney, want to see you at once."

Drake said, "Oh *oh*, those birds get around fast."

Mason jerked his head toward the exit door. "Slip through there, Paul," he said. "Okay, Della, go out and bring them in."

Drake covered the distance across the office with long, easy strides and opened the exit door. A man's voice said, "Hold it. Stay where you are."

Drake stood motionless.

Before Della Street had reached the door to the outer office, it was shoved open by Sergeant Holcomb, who came pushing his way into the office behind a cloud of cigar smoke, his hat tilted back on his head, his eyes hard with hostility.

The man in the corridor called out, "Here he is, Sergeant."

Holcomb strode over to the corridor door, took a look at Drake, and said, "He's just a stooge. Let him go. Come on in, Runcifer."

He held the door open while Carl Runcifer, a tall man in his late thirties with heavy features and gray eyes, walked somewhat sheepishly into the office.

"I thought it was Mason from the description I had," he said.

Mason, behind the desk, said affably, "No apology's necessary, Runcifer. You're one of the deputies I haven't met. Come on in and sit down."

Runcifer, seeming ill at ease, moved over to the client's chair and sat down.

Mason glanced at Sergeant Holcomb and said, "And how are you, Sergeant? I haven't seen you for a while."

Sergeant Holcomb did not sit down. He stood with his legs spread apart, his hand shoved down into the side pockets of his coat. "Looks as though you've made quite a slip, Mason," he said.

Mason said to Runcifer, "You haven't been in the office long, have you?"

"About three months."

Sergeant Holcomb took the cigar out of his mouth. "Don't try to pull that casual line with me, Mason, because it won't work."

Mason countered, "Don't try to pull that get-you-on-the-defensive line with me, Sergeant, because *it* won't work. If you want to know anything, come out and say so."

"Where's the gun?" Sergeant Holcomb asked.

"What gun?"

"The gun that killed Wentworth."

Mason shrugged his shoulders and said, "You can search me."

"You're damn right I can," Holcomb said grimly.

"Got a warrant?" Mason asked.

"I don't need one."

"It depends somewhat on the viewpoint," Mason observed.

Holcomb came over and sat down on a corner of the desk. "It's one thing," he said, "to act as a lawyer and hide behind this professional-confidence business and this privileged-communication gag. It's another thing to stick your neck out so far that you become an accessory after the fact."

Mason said irritably, "Go ahead. Say it. Get it out of your system."

Runcifer interrupted. "Perhaps, Sergeant, I might ask Mr. Mason a few courteous questions before we make any serious accusations. After all, you know, Mr. Mason is an attorney and . . ."

"Oh hell!" Sergeant Holcomb exclaimed disgustedly, and then, after a moment, said, "Go ahead," and walked across the office to stand in front of the window, deliberately turning his back on Runcifer and Mason.

"I believe you're aware that Penn Wentworth was found dead on his yacht at an early hour this morning?" Runcifer asked.

Mason nodded.

"He had been shot. Circumstances pointed the finger of suspicion at a girl named Mae Farr and a man by the name of Harold Anders. The girl was undoubtedly around last night at the scene of the shooting. Anders admits it, admits that he was in the vicinity of the yacht when the shooting took place. From his story, it probably isn't first-degree murder, but it's undoubtedly a homicide which will have to be cleared up by a jury.

"According to Anders' story, you sent him to his hotel and told him to stay there after Mae Farr had told you all about the shooting. Anders began to think things over and decided that he wanted to consult his own attorney, a friend of long standing who has an office in the county seat where Anders lives. He went down to the airport, chartered a plane, and flew north. He stated all of the facts to this attorney, who advised him to get in touch with the police without delay and make a clean breast of everything. The attorney seemed to—"

"Oh hell!" Sergeant Holcomb interrupted, spinning around from the window. "Why mince words? The attorney said that Mason had given Anders the worst possible advice that a lawyer could give a man."

Mason said, "That's nice."

Sergeant Holcomb went on, "I always told you, Mason, that someday you were going to come a cropper. This is it."

Mason said, "All right, let's quit the schoolboy grandstand stuff and get down to brass tacks. I know you're a smart detective. You should be promoted to a captaincy. You've predicted my downfall for a long time. Anders' lawyer says I gave Anders bum advice. All right, what if he did? I don't care. Anders goes ahead and has kittens. Just because this lawyer gave him the kind of advice you want, you think he's right and I'm wrong. What do *you* want?"

Sergeant Holcomb said, "We want that gun."

"What gun?"

"The gun that killed Penn Wentworth."

"I haven't got it."

"That's what you say."

Mason's face darkened. His eyes narrowed slightly. "That," he announced with cold finality, "is what I say."

"Okay," Sergeant Holcomb said. "We wanted to give you an out. If we have to do it the hard way, we can do it the hard way."

"Go ahead," Mason said, "do it the hard way."

Sergeant Holcomb said, "Just a minute. You stay here with him, Runcifer," and strode across the floor, jerked open the door to the outer office, walked out to the reception room, picked up a small handbag, and returned.

Mason watched him calmly while he opened the handbag, reached inside, then stood for a moment as though setting the stage for a dramatic act.

"Go ahead," Mason said, "pull out the rabbit."

Sergeant Holcomb jerked out a pair of shoes. "Look at these," he said. "Tell me if they're yours, and remember that anything you say will be used against you."

Mason looked at the muddy shoes, reached out, took one, examined it, and asked, "Where did you get these shoes?"

Holcomb said, "Don't think you're going to pull that kind of an act, Mason. I got them with a search warrant."

"Who the hell gave you a warrant to search my apartment?"

"A judge," Sergeant Holcomb said, "and that's not answering the question, Mason. Are those your shoes?"

"Of course they're my shoes. You got them in my apartment, didn't you?"

"Were you wearing them last night?"

"I don't remember."

"The hell you don't."

Mason said, "You're asking the questions. I'm answering them. Never mind the comments. You might get into trouble."

Sergeant Holcomb said, "Don't try bluffing me because it won't work. If I drag you down to headquarters and book you on the charge of being an accessory after the fact, you'll sing a different tune."

"Not to any music you can play," Mason said.

Runcifer said placatingly, "Now, let's not lose our tempers, Mr. Mason. You must appreciate that the evidence is incriminating, to say the least. You must also realize that the minute we take any action, the newspapers will give you publicity which will be highly disadvantageous. Now we are here for the purpose of eliciting information in a courteous manner."

"Why don't you follow your charted course then?" Mason asked.

Runcifer said meaningly to Sergeant Holcomb, "I think we will. Sergeant, if you'll pardon me, I'll do the questioning."

Sergeant Holcomb shrugged his shoulders and turned away contemptuously.

Runcifer said, "Mr. Mason, I am going to be frank with you. Anders has made a complete statement. He said that Miss Farr boarded the *Pennwent*, that he heard her scream and heard sounds of a struggle. He rushed to her rescue. In running across the float, he missed his footing and fell into the water. As nearly as he can judge, the shooting took place while he was in the water because he insists that he did not hear the sound of the revolver shot although he had heard Miss Farr's cries for help quite plainly. Upon boarding the yacht, he ran to the open skylight and looked down into the main cabin. Miss Farr was arranging her clothes, which apparently had been badly disarrayed. She ran up on deck. Upon seeing him aboard the yacht, she became greatly confused and embarrassed, asked him what he was doing there, and when he told her that he came in response to her cries, asked him if he had a weapon with him. Upon being assured that he had, she rushed him off the yacht in the greatest haste.

"Later on, and as they were traveling toward the city in his car, she told him that Wentworth had been shot and that she wanted to rush him off the yacht because she was afraid that persons from neighboring boats would be attracted by the shot and that Anders would be accused of the shooting. Anders thereupon, fearing that such might be the case, decided to get rid of his gun. He stopped the car near a hot-dog stand which he describes perfectly and threw the gun off to the side of the road across the fence which borders the highway. Then they drove to town.

"Thereafter, Anders tells a story which I find it difficult to believe. He claims that—"

Sergeant Holcomb interrupted. "Are you going to tell him every single fact we have in our possession?"

"Absolutely," Runcifer said, his tone reflecting the obstinacy of a man who lives in a world of books, who has acquired his knowledge from abstract study and looks upon the events taking place about him from an academic viewpoint.

"Show 'im all the trump cards you hold before he plays his," Sergeant Holcomb said, "and he'll know which ace to trump."

"I think this is the only ethical way to handle the matter, Sergeant," Runcifer said with cold finality. "Your methods resulted only in an argument which brought us no additional information and was personally distasteful to me."

Sergeant Holcomb said, "Nuts."

Mason said to Runcifer, "You were saying?"

"Let's see," Runcifer said, frowning. "Exactly what *was* I saying? Oh yes, about what Anders told us took place when he returned to the city. He said that he consulted the telephone directory to see if you had a resident telephone. He found there were two numbers for the office, one a day number, the other a night number. He called the night number, and your secretary, Miss Street, answered. He tried to tell her what had happened over the telephone, and she instructed him to come with Miss Farr to her apartment at once."

Runcifer placed the tips of his fingers together and concentrated his gaze upon them, apparently more concerned lest his summing up of the case should miss some significant detail than in the reactions of Perry Mason.

Sergeant Holcomb stood glowering at the deputy district attorney, apparently of half a mind to step in and assume charge but hesitating because of orders to act under Runcifer's direction.

"Now then," Runcifer went on, in calm, academic tones, "comes the part of the story which seems utterly incredible to me. I cannot understand your actions in the matter, Mr. Mason. However, I will first outline what Anders said. He claimed that Miss Street called you, that you came to her apartment, that you advised both of them to refrain from notifying the authorities, and that you yourself accompanied Miss Farr to the yacht harbor for the purpose of finding some way of keeping her name from being brought into the case.

Anders swears that the *Pennwent* was moored at the float when he left. As you know, the yacht was subsequently found cruising off San Diego, steering a course which would have taken it into the Mexican coast in the vicinity of Ensenada. The body of Penn Wentworth was found fully clothed. Nevertheless, Anders states that Miss Farr insisted that during the struggle with her, he was clad only in his underwear.

"Now then, Mr. Mason—oh yes, one thing more. The police officers naturally wished to check Anders' story. They went to the place where he said he had thrown the gun. He was in the car and indicated the exact spot. You'll remember that there was a thundershower last night, Mr. Mason, and the officers were surprised to discover that someone had made a very thorough search of the ground where Anders had thrown the gun. The footsteps were quite plainly evident in the soft mud which covered much of the field.

"The officers made plaster casts of those footprints, and your shoes make identical marks. Now then, Mr. Mason, there is no other conclusion which seems logical other than that you went to the Yacht Club, that you and Miss Farr, and perhaps your secretary, Miss Street, boarded the *Pennwent*, that you found Penn Wentworth dead, that you desired to keep Miss Farr's name out of the case and to protect her good name in the event she should be dragged into it. Therefore, you placed clothes on Wentworth's body, started the yacht, took it out to the headland, set the automatic steering mechanism on a course to Ensenada, and then left the yacht."

"That's interesting," Mason said. "How did we leave?"

"Probably by having some other boat come alongside."

"Then what?" Mason asked.

"Then you returned to search for the gun, found it, and removed it."

"All this," Mason asked, "is predicated on Anders' story?"

"His confession."

"What did he confess to?"

trouble."

"Being aboard the yacht, armed and, as he admitted, looking for trouble."

"That's not much of a crime," Mason said. "What did he do?"

"According to his story, he didn't do anything."

"And all that you have against me," Mason said, "is that he told you I left for the Yacht Club with Miss Farr, and he surmised that I had done this and that. Is that right?"

"His surmises are quite reasonable."

Mason said, "Well, I'm sorry I can't help you. I didn't go aboard the *Pennwent*. I didn't dress the corpse. I didn't have anything to do with it. I don't know who did."

"You knew that the dead body of Penn Wentworth was aboard that yacht, Mr. Mason?"

"No."

"You didn't? Why, Anders insists that Miss Farr told you."

"As far as the conversation which occurred between my client and myself is concerned," Mason said, "it's confidential. I have no right to repeat any statements which she made to me or any advice which I gave to her. Therefore, it's out. You can't inquire into it here. You can't inquire into it before a grand jury, and you can't inquire into it in court."

"Subject to certain specific qualifications, that," Runcifer admitted, "would seem to be correct. However, the law of privileged communications is subject to certain well-defined exceptions."

"All right," Mason said. "I'll advance the law. You advance the exceptions. I'm telling you you can't question me concerning the advice I gave a client.

"Now then, we come to the rest of it—a claim by Anders that I went to the Yacht Club and he thinks I must have done certain things while there."

"His deductions are most logical," Runcifer insisted.

Mason said, "You'll pardon me if I fail to agree with you."

"What is your explanation?" Runcifer asked.

"I have none."

"Well, I'll put it this way, Mr. Mason. Wherein do you find any departure from logic in Anders' statement?"

Mason said, "That's something I'll argue in front of a jury."

"But look here, Mr. Mason, you were in that field walking around looking for a gun."

"What if I was?"

"You had no right to do that. You should have reported the crime to the officers."

"How did I know there was a crime?"

"You had been advised of the shooting."

Mason said, "Let me ask you a question. Why did you go and look for the gun?"

"We wanted to check up on Anders' story."

"In other words, you thought that it was open to some doubt?"

"Well, it was rather unusual. We thought perhaps he was keeping something back."

"All right," Mason said. "Suppose I say I also felt his story was open to some doubt and decided to confirm it?"

"The gun constituted a complete confirmation."

"What gun?" Mason asked.

"The gun that was there."

"What," Mason asked, "makes you feel that a gun was there?"

Runcifer said somewhat irritably, "Mr. Mason, I didn't come here to bandy words with you. You know perfectly well that the gun was there."

"You looked for a gun this morning?" Mason asked.

"Yes."

"Why?"

"We wanted to check on Anders' story, I tell you."

"In other words," Mason said, "you went out to look because you weren't certain that a gun was there. I should certainly have the same privilege."

Runcifer said, "I don't think that's a fair answer, Mr. Mason. It was the duty of the officers to search for that gun in order to find it and preserve it as a part of the evidence."

Mason said, "So far you've talked about Anders. Why don't you give me the benefit of the story that Miss Farr told?"

"Unfortunately," Runcifer said, "Miss Farr refuses to make any statement whatever. That, I consider, is very much opposed to her best interests."

"You told her about Anders' statement?"

"Naturally," Runcifer said. "We—"

"For God's sake," Sergeant Holcomb interrupted, "we came up here to get information, not to hand this bird everything we know on a silver platter."

Runcifer said, "That will do, Sergeant."

Sergeant Holcomb took two indignant strides toward the exit door of the office, then checked himself and stood with flushed countenance and angry eyes.

Runcifer said, "I don't think your attitude shows a desire to co-operate, Mr. Mason. I have been perfectly fair and frank with you. Because you are an attorney, I don't want to have you placed under arrest without giving you an opportunity to explain."

Mason said, "I appreciate your sincerity and your motives, Runcifer. However, you have nothing to say about it. You're acting under orders. You don't determine the policy of your office. You came here with certain specific instructions. Those instructions were given to you for a purpose. Your office isn't as considerate as you are. If there'd been any grounds on which they could have arrested me, they'd have done so. However, they can't do it. All Anders knows is that I suggested to Miss Farr that we should go to the yacht harbor. I had a right to do that in order to verify her story. That much you will certainly grant.

"As for all this cock-and-bull yarn about dressing the corpse and putting the yacht out to sea, your office has one thing and one thing alone on which to act—the cockeyed guess of a man who tells a rather remarkable story, namely, that he had been watching Wentworth's yacht, lying in wait with a gun in his pocket; that the girl he loved boarded Wentworth's yacht; that he claims he heard sounds of a struggle taking place, started to run aboard the yacht, and fell into the drink; that at the exact moment when his ears were submerged under water, and his sight of the yacht had been blotted out by a cross section of the Pacific Ocean, some obliging individual stepped aboard the yacht, shot Wentworth, and then withdrew; that Anders, climbing from the water to the float, completed his journey to Wentworth's yacht only to find that the woman he loved was straightening her disarrayed clothing.

"That story, gentlemen, is worse than lousy. It stinks. If you think any jury is going to believe that story, you're crazy as hell. And because that story is so cockeyed, the district attorney's office and the police aren't quite ready to crack down on me as an accessory after the fact, but they did have enough information to send you and Holcomb up here to ask me for a statement, the idea being that I might be unwise enough to say something which would furnish something by way of corroboration."

"We have those shoes for corroboration," Holcomb said. "That's all the evidence we need."

"The most you can claim for the shoes," Mason said, "is that they prove I was walking around in a field."

"You found the gun," Runcifer charged, "and concealed it."

"Where did I conceal it?"

"We don't know."

"In that event," Mason said, "you'd better get some more evidence before you make any statement of accusation."

Runcifer stared thoughtfully at Mason for several seconds, then he once more regarded his spread-out fingertips. At length he looked up at Sergeant Holcomb. "Any questions, Sergeant?" he asked.

"Questions?" Sergeant Holcomb said in disgust. "You've told him everything you know now, and he's told you nothing he knows. Questions, hell!"

Runcifer said, "I find your attitude insubordinate rather than helpful, Sergeant."

Sergeant Holcomb made some half-strangled, half-articulate reply. "Let's go," he said.

Runcifer got to his feet.

Sergeant Holcomb angrily threw the shoes into the bag, locked it, and strode toward the exit door.

Runcifer followed him, turned at the door, bowed, and said, very precisely, "Good afternoon, Mr. Mason."

Mason, his eyes twinkling, said, "So long, Runcifer."

Chapter Eight

Mason rang for Della Street and when she entered the office said to her, "Della, use our regular office forms. Prepare a writ of *habeas corpus* for Mae Farr. I'm going to make them either file a charge against her or turn her loose."

She studied the granite-hard lines of his countenance with solicitous eyes. "How was it?" she asked.

He shrugged his shoulders.

"What did they do?"

"Not much," Mason said. "It could have been a lot worse. Evidently, Holcomb was under orders to let the D.A.'s office run the show."

"And how did they run it?"

"Their timing was bad," Mason said, "but Runcifer was a gentleman. I don't think he has had much experience as a trial lawyer. He wanted to be certain he'd covered every single detail about which they wanted to question me."

"What did Sergeant Holcomb do?"

"Tried to get rough," Mason said, "found he couldn't get away with it, and turned sullen."

She said, "Paul Drake telephoned that he had some important information and wanted to come in as soon as the coast was clear."

"Okay. Tell him the coast is clear. Get out that application for a writ of *habeas corpus* and ride herd on that outer office. I don't want to see any routine clients, don't want to think about any routine business."

She nodded. "Follow the same procedure as in that Smith case?" she asked.

"Yes. Use the files in that case for form. You can check them over and get the typists started doing the work. I want it right away."

With self-effacing efficiency, Della glided through the door to the outer office. A few minutes later Paul Drake knocked on the corridor door and the lawyer let him in.

"How was it, Perry?" Drake asked.

"Not so bad," Mason said.

"What did they want?"

"The man from the district attorney's office wanted facts," Mason said. "Sergeant Holcomb wanted me."

"Didn't get you, did he?"

"Not yet. What's new?"

Drake said, "A lot of things. Here's the latest paper."

"What's in it?"

"The usual hooey and statements that by throwing out a dragnet, police were able to apprehend Anders in a northern city where he had fled, that he's made a partial confession, that as a result of that confession, police are investigating the activities of one of the best-known criminal attorneys in the city, that police are searching for the gun with which they feel the murder may have been committed, that Anders admits having a gun which he threw away. Police were rushed to the scene where they found that virtually every inch of the territory had been covered by a man who made a search sometime after the rain started last night."

"What's the photograph?"

"Sergeant Holcomb holding up a pair of shoes and showing how they fit the plaster-of-paris casts made of the footprints that were found in the soft soil."

"Say where he got the shoes?" Mason asked.

"No, that's one of the things on which the paper reports the officers are working, but are not as yet ready to divulge any information because of the sensational conclusions which may be drawn when the evidence is finally put together. . . . Are those your shoes, Perry?"

"Yes."

Drake said, "That looks rather bad, doesn't it?"

Mason brushed the question aside with a quick gesture of his hand. "Never mind the postmortems," he said. "Give me the facts. What's that other picture?"

"Photograph of the field where police think you found the gun."

"Let me see it," Mason said.

He took the newspaper, folded it over, and studied the newspaper reproduction of a photograph showing a field alongside the highway.

"Line of high tension poles running along the right of way," Mason said musingly, "barbed-wire fence, concrete pipe lines for irrigation—not much opportunity to conceal a gun there, Paul, just clumps of grass and weeds. Why don't they cultivate that ground if it's under irrigation?"

"It's tied up in litigation," Drake said.

"What else, Paul?"

"Quite a bit of stuff—a whole mess of dope on the tastes and habits of Wentworth."

"Yachting his hobby?" Mason asked.

"Yachting, women, and coin collecting," Drake said.

"Why the coins?"

"You can search me. Coins, boats and horses, wine and women, that represented Wentworth's life."

"What did he do for a living?" Mason asked.

Drake grinned and said, "I think that's going to be a sore subject with the police. Evidently he was a bookmaker. He had a partner by the name of Marley—Frank Marley."

Mason said, "I've heard of him. Wasn't he arrested a while back?"

"Two or three times," Drake said.

"What happened to the charges?"

"Postponed, transferred, continued, and dismissed."

"A payoff?"

Drake said, "I'm not saying anything. Perhaps you can read my mind."

"I'm reading it," Mason said, and grinned. "How about Marley? Can we drag him in?"

"I have an idea we can," Drake said. "Incidentally, Marley also has a boat. He went in for fast stuff, an express cruiser with powerful motors, twin screws, mahogany finish—nothing you'd want to be out in a heavy sea in, but something that would scoot over to Catalina and back in nothing flat."

"Where was he last night?"

"Apparently in a hospital. He was scheduled to have an operation this morning—nothing serious. He'd had a couple of attacks of appendicitis, and the doctor told him to have it out when he could spare a few days from his business. He reported to the doctor yesterday and went to the hospital yesterday afternoon."

"Did he have the operation?" Mason asked.

"No. There was nothing particularly urgent about it. When he heard of Wentworth's death, he called off the operation, claims he can't afford to be laid up right now. There's too much business to be handled."

Mason said, "Not that it means anything, but just for the purpose of keeping the records straight, that hospital business doesn't mean a damn thing."

"I know," Drake said. "I've checked on it, however. He had a private room. A special nurse was to come today after the operation, but he was on general last night. Directions called for him to have a capsule of sodium amytal."

"Did he get it?"

"Yes. The nurse gave it to him."

"Would that make him stay put?" Mason asked.

"Yes, I think it would," Drake said. "And the floor nurse looked in on him three or four times during the night."

"Does it show on his chart when she looked in on him?"

"No, but the nurse says it was at least once before midnight, a couple of times after midnight, and once this morning. The special came on duty at eight o'clock. He was to have been operated on at ten."

"Did they tell him about Wentworth?"

"They weren't going to, but he insisted on talking with Wentworth over the telephone before he went under the anesthetic, said he had some last-minute instructions to give and wanted to verify certain matters. They tried to keep it from him but couldn't."

"How about Wentworth's wife?" Mason asked.

"She was down in San Diego. It looks as though Wentworth had an appointment with her for this morning."

"Where?"

"At San Diego."

"And the wife's boyfriend?"

"I don't know, yet. But he has a yacht."

"Where is it moored?"

"Outer yacht harbor, just inside the breakwater."

Mason and the detective exchanged glances.

"Better check him pretty carefully," Mason said.

"I'm doing that. He's quite a sportsman, polo, yachting, and airplanes."

"Airplanes?"

"Yes. He has an amphibian he plays around with."

"Where does he keep it?"

"In a hangar on his estate."

"And that's where?"

"On a rugged promontory overlooking the ocean about ten miles from his yacht mooring."

"Can you find out if the plane has been doing any traveling lately?"

Drake said, "I'm going to try to get a look at the log of the plane."

"How about traveling? That wouldn't be in the log."

Drake shook his head and said, "Barring accident, we can't find out about that."

Mason drummed with the tips of his fingers. "Can you get in the estate, Paul?" he asked.

"It's difficult," Drake said, "but I think I have an operative who could do the job."

Mason said, "There was rain last night, Paul. It came down pretty heavy for a while. If an airplane taxied off a dirt field, it would leave tracks, particularly if it was a little slow on the takeoff."

Drake said, "I get you, Perry."

"How about servants? Can you find out if they might have heard the sound of the motor?"

Drake said, "I could tell you the answer to that in advance, Perry. It's 'no.' "

"How come?"

"There wasn't a servant on the place last night. Eversel gave them all a night off and had the chauffeur put a car at their disposal."

Mason raised his eyebrows.

"That's what I thought, too," Drake said, "but it turns out it's not particularly unusual. Eversel has a hard time keeping servants. The estate is isolated. There are no picture shows, beauty shops, or any sort of amusement facilities available. Naturally, you can't expect servants to stay on a job like that seven days a week, fifty-two weeks a year. When they have time off, Eversel has to provide them with transportation if they're going to leave the estate. So he frequently sends them out on a skylarking expedition, especially when he doesn't expect to be home."

"I see," Mason said, his voice casual enough, but his eyes narrowed into thoughtful slits.

"The bullet," Drake went on, "was fired downward, apparently through the skylight or when Wentworth was leaning forward. Probably the shot was fired through the skylight. The windows of that skylight roll back. They're controlled from the inside. In warm weather, while the ship was moored or cruising through calm waters, Wentworth would roll the windows back and get ventilation through the opening."

"It was warm last night," Mason said.

"There's no question but what the glass was rolled back when Anders went aboard," Drake said. "Anders admits that in his statement to the police. He claims that's the reason he could hear Miss Farr pleading with Wentworth and struggling."

"Anyone else hear any screams?" Mason asked.

"No. Apparently, the screams weren't particularly loud. People on yachts don't listen for those things anyway. Some pretty wild parties go on at times. Most of the time the screams that come from a yacht are referred to as 'the squeals of synthetic virtue.' I'm getting a file of photographs taken by one of the newspapermen, showing the interior of the cabin just after the yacht was brought into the harbor. Incidentally, Perry, Wentworth was probably dead before the rain started."

"How come?"

"He hadn't closed the skylight. He would have . . ."

Della Street slipped quietly through the door from the outer office and came over to Mason's desk. She slid a folded paper across to him. He unfolded the paper and read, "Frank Marley, partner of Wentworth, in the office. Wants to see you at once on an urgent matter."

Mason thought for a moment, then slid the memo across to Drake. The detective read it and said, "Oh, oh."

"Send him in, Della," Mason said.

The men waited in silence until Della Street escorted Marley into the office and quietly withdrew, closing the door behind her.

Marley, a small-boned, dark, thin man in his late thirties, kept his face without expression as he stood still, glancing from Mason to Paul Drake.

"Come over and have a chair," Mason invited. "I'm Mason. This is Paul Drake, who handles my investigations."

Marley's large, dark eyes, the sheen and color of ripe olives, moved from one man to the other. He smiled, then came forward and extended a hand to Mason. "Very pleased to meet you, Counselor," he said.

Mason's big hand closed over the small, tapering fingers, received in return a grip of surprising strength. Then the huge diamond in Marley's tie flashed as he turned to shake hands with the detective.

His hand dropped to his pocket and took out a cigarette case. A diamond on his ring finger made a glittering streak of light as he conveyed the cigarette to his lips. "I only have a few minutes, Mr. Mason," he said significantly.

"Go right ahead."

Marley smiled. His eyes were without expression. In a low, well-modulated voice, he said, "My information is very confidential."

Drake glanced at Mason, raising his eyebrows. The lawyer nodded, and Drake said, "Okay, Perry. See you later." He studied Marley for a long moment, then he said, "Glad I met you, Marley. Probably see you again."

Marley said nothing.

When he had gone, Mason said, "Well?"

Marley said, "Too bad about Penn."

Mason nodded.

"However," Marley went on, "I'm a man of the world, and I take it, Mr. Mason, that you're a businessman."

Again Mason nodded. "Better sit down."

Marley eased one hip over on the arm of the chair which Drake had just vacated. "You're representing Mae Farr?" he asked.

Mason nodded.

"A nice girl, Mae."

"Know her?"

"Yes. Penn carried a torch for her. I was close to Penn. Sometimes we'd cruise on his yacht, sometimes on mine. It depended on the weather. My boat performs best on a smooth sea. Penn had an all-weather yacht."

Mason nodded.

"Mae's an independent kid," Marley said, almost musingly.

"Any idea who killed him?" Mason asked abruptly.

Frank Marley's dark eyes bored steadily through the light blue haze of cigarette smoke which framed his features. "Yes," he said.

"Who?" Mason asked.

"Suppose I tell you a story first."

"It's your show," Mason said. "Go ahead and run it."

Marley said, "I want something."

"You don't look exactly like a philanthropist," Mason observed.

"What I want means a lot to me and not much to you."

"Go ahead," Mason urged.

"I always figured you were the best mouthpiece in the business. I made up my mind that if I ever got in a jam, I'd come to you."

Mason's acknowledgment was less than a bow, almost a nod.

"I'm apt to be in a jam on this thing."

"How come?"

"Penn was never divorced. He and his wife could never agree on a property settlement. She tried to wear him down. He wouldn't give her a divorce, and she wouldn't give him one. Neither one of them could have had a divorce without the other's consent. It would have resulted in a lot of mudslinging, and a judge would have kicked them both out of court."

"They didn't get along?" Mason asked.

"At first they did. Afterwards, it was just like two cats tied by the tails and thrown over a clothesline."

Mason said, "I suppose that was after you started playing around with her."

Marley's face didn't exactly change expression. It merely stiffened as though he had frozen his facial muscles into immobility at the impact of Mason's remark. After a long moment, he puffed calmly on his cigarette and said, with equal calmness, "What gave you that idea, Mason?"

"Just a shot in the dark," Mason said.

"Don't make them," Marley warned. "I don't like them."

Mason ostentatiously pulled a sheet of paper toward himself, and scribbled a rapid note on it.

"What's that?" Marley asked suspiciously.

"Just making a note to have my detective look up that angle of the case."

"You," Marley announced, "are hard to get along with."

"Not for those who shoot square with me," Mason said. "When a man sits on the other side of the desk and starts trading horses, I trade horses."

"Better wait until you hear the horse trade I have lined up," Marley said, "before you start getting rough."

"I've been waiting ever since you came in," Mason reminded him.

"As I was saying," Marley said, "I think you're a swell mouthpiece. I'd rather have you in my corner than in the other guy's corner. Juanita is still Wentworth's wife. I don't think Penn left a will. She'll have the job of winding up the estate. As the surviving partner, I'll have to account to her for partnership business."

"Well?" Mason asked.

"It's going to put me in a spot," Marley said.

"Why?"

"There were things that Penn knew all about," Marley said, "which wouldn't look so well in black and white. I did certain things. I asked Penn about them before I did them. He gave me his okay. It was all word of mouth, nothing in writing. Naturally, I didn't think he was going to get bumped off."

"So?" Mason asked.

"So I want you to be in my corner."

"For what?" Mason asked. "The preliminary fight or the main event?"

"Just a preliminary," Marley made haste to assure him. "There isn't any main event as far as I'm concerned. I want you to represent me in straightening out the affairs of the partnership."

"That all?"

"That's all."

"How much," Mason asked, "were you prepared to pay?"

Marley said hastily, "Before we start talking about that, I'll tell you some more about the horse I have to trade."

"What about it?"

Marley said, "I don't have too much use for the cops. I've been in business too long. I'm sorry Penn got croaked. Being sorry can't help him any. He's gone. I'm left. I have to look out for myself. All right, here's the proposition: Mae Farr killed him. I have a witness who can prove it. You play ball with me, and I play ball with you."

"I don't like that sort of a ball game," Mason said. "You call all the strikes and let me pitch all the balls."

"No, it isn't like that, Mason, honest. Look here, I'll put my cards on the table. Mae Farr bumped him. I think she was entitled to do it. I think a jury would think so, but it would be a lot better for her if she didn't have to go in front of a jury and tell all that stuff.

"You know, Penn was always on the make for her. I don't think she was any virgin, but she just didn't care for Penn. Perhaps she got a kick out of holding him at arm's length and watching him pant. Some women are like that."

"Go ahead," Mason said.

"Hell, do I have to draw you a diagram?"

"Yes."

Marley sighed and said, "Oh well, here it is. A certain party who shall be nameless was at the Yacht Club late last night and early this morning, sitting in an automobile waiting."

"For what?" Mason asked.

"What do you think?"

"I don't know."

"Well, we'll let it go at that then. She was waiting. She knew Penn. She knew me. She knew our boats. She didn't know Mae. While she was sitting in her car waiting and getting sore because she thought her boyfriend had stood her up, she saw the lights of a boat coming into the float. She thought at first it was the one she was waiting for, then she saw it was my cruiser, the *Atina*."

Mason shifted his eyes to watch the smoke which drifted upward from the tip of Marley's cigarette.

"The party handling the *Atina* didn't make such a good landing, scraped and bumped around a little bit, finally got the motors shut off, and jumped out with the mooring lines. She saw it was a girl. She didn't know the girl, but she got a good look at her face. Later on, she heard about the murder. She put two and two together. She told me about it. She described the girl. The description checks with Mae."

"Well," Mason said, "she—"

"Just a moment," Marley pleaded, holding up his hand. "I want you to have it absolutely straight. I had photographs taken on cruises, showing Mae Farr. I showed this girl the photographs. She's positive that Mae was the one who had my cruiser out."

"Well?" Mason asked.

"You can figure what that testimony will do to you," Marley said.

"It won't do a damn thing to me," Mason told him.

"Well, it will to your client."

"Testimony," Mason said, "is one thing. Conversation is another. Don't forget I have a right to cross-examine witnesses. There are a lot of questions I can think of right now that I'd like to ask this witness of yours. There'll probably be a lot more by the time I know more about the case."

"Sure there will," Marley said, his enunciation becoming more rapid. "That's what I'm getting at. You're dangerous, Mason. I know it. I'm not kidding myself a damn bit. You can probably beat the rap on Mae Farr. She's a good-looking baby, and jurors fall for that stuff. She can put on a great story about fighting for her honor. It's a cinch. Good-looking women have lived with men for months and then killed them to defend their honor, and weeping juries have brought in verdicts exonerating the dames and asking for their telephone numbers afterwards. It's a cinch you can beat it."

"If I can beat the rap," Mason asked, "what have you got to trade?"

"Simply this," Marley told him. "If you play ball with me, there won't be any rap. They'll concentrate on Anders and try to pin the kill on him. They can't do it. They can get so far, and then it sticks. Anders didn't do it. Mae did."

"What makes you so positive?"

"After I heard what had happened to my boat, I went down and looked her over."

"When was that?"

"About two or three hours ago."

"What did you find?"

Marley said, "You know, Mason, I wasn't born yesterday."

"What did you find?" Mason repeated.

Marley said, "I found that a lock had been smashed, that someone had had the boat out. I always leave the boat with a full tank of gas. As nearly as I can tell from the gas guage, she'd gone maybe ten miles. I know a little something about fingerprints—I learned it in the hard school of experience. I sprinkled some powder around where it would do the most good on the steering wheel, on the handle of the throttle, on the lighting switches."

"What did you find?" Mason asked.

"Fingerprints."

"Whose fingerprints?"

Marley shrugged and said, "I wouldn't know. It would be up to the police to tell whose fingerprints they were."

"What's your proposition?" Mason asked.

Marley said, "I'll give you five grand in cash right now. I'll take an oiled cloth, go down and scrub off every fingerprint on the boat. I'll buy this witness a ticket to Australia, and let her stay there until the case is over. You advise me about how to wind up the partnership business."

"Why can't any attorney do that?"

"I tell you, it's a mess. I've been careless. I've relied too much on conversation and not enough on records. I did virtually all of the business recently. Penn got so he left things more and more to me."

"Why do you think I could handle the widow better than any other lawyer?" Mason asked.

"You have the reputation. What's more, you have the knowledge, and if she gets too tough, you could bring a little pressure to bear on her. You know, let her feel that you were going to rip her wide open when she came into court to testify. Penn had some stuff on Juanita. She's nobody's fool. She knows that."

Mason said, "That's all of your proposition?"

Marley nodded.

"Pardon me a minute," Mason said as he rang the buzzer for Della Street.

When she opened the door, he said, with a nod to Frank Marley, "Mr. Marley will be leaving shortly. Tell Drake that he can come back. And tell him to make adequate preparations to report progress on everything that happens from now on. Emphasize *everything*. Do you understand?"

She nodded. "I'll tell him, Mr. Mason. Is there anything else?"

Mason shook his head and she closed the door.

"Sorry for the interruption," Mason said, turning back to face Marley. "I don't like your proposition."

"I could up the cash a little—not very much because I'm short right now, and Penn's death is going to . . ."

"No," Mason said, "it isn't the cash."

"What is it?"

"It's the idea."

"What idea?"

"Of suppressing evidence, for one thing."

Marley looked at him in surprise. "You mean to say that you're going chicken on a little thing that's done every day of the week?"

"You can call it that if you want to."

Marley said, "Well, look. We don't have to do anything. We can simply . . ."

Mason shook his head.

"Listen," Marley said, "this is on the square. There's just the two of us here. It isn't any trap. It's a straight-out business proposition."

Again Mason shook his head.

"For God's sake," Marley said, "don't tell me you're going to pull that line. If you're going to act like that, it's your duty to see that this witness tells her story to the police."

"It may be at that."

Marley said, "Look here, Mason, don't be a fool. You're in business. You know which side of the bread has the butter."

Mason said, "From where I sit, it doesn't seem to be your side."

Marley said indignantly, "You mean I'm apt to sell you out? You mean you think you can't trust me?"

Mason said, "I'm not interested."

"Think it over for an hour or two," Marley said. "I think you'll figure it's the only thing to do. Anders has spilled his guts. You're in a spot. I'm in a spot. Mae Farr is in a spot. If we play this thing right, we can all get off the spot."

Mason said coldly, "I like to lead my own aces, Marley."

Marley said, "I know. You think I'm bluffing. You think there isn't any witness. You think that I'd simply go down and clean the inside of the yacht, tell you I'd sent the witness to Australia, and be sitting pretty."

"You could do just that," Mason pointed out.

"Don't be a damn fool," Marley said.

"I'll try not to," Mason assured him.

Marley sighed, said, "Cripes, if you haven't any better sense than that, I don't want you for an attorney. I think you're vastly overrated."

"Sometimes I think so myself," Mason said.

Marley started for the door, paused with his hand on the knob to look back at Mason. "No," he said thoughtfully, "you aren't dumb. You're smart. You figure you can make *me* the fall guy. Well, think again, Mason."

Frank Marley jerked open the door, then slammed it shut behind him.

Mason picked up the desk telephone and said to the operator in the outer office, "Get Della Street for me right away."

Almost immediately he heard Della's voice on the line. "Okay, Chief, what is it?"

"Did you get my message straight for Paul Drake?"

"I think so. You meant that you wanted Marley shadowed?"

"Yes. I was wondering if you'd get it."

"Two operatives will be in the lobby," she said. "Another operative is being planted at the elevator. She'll put the finger on Marley for the two detectives downstairs. Drake had to work fast, but he did it."

"Good girl," Mason said.

Chapter Nine

~~~~~~~~~~~~~~~~~~~~~~~~~~~~~~~~~~~

It lacked ten minutes until five o'clock when Paul Drake entered Mason's office with news. "Marley," he said, "left here and went directly to the Balkan Apartments on Windstrom Avenue. He kept buzzing the apartment of Hazel Tooms until he decided he was drawing a blank. Then he started out toward the harbor on Figueroa Street. My operatives are tailing him. Does this Tooms girl mean anything to you?"

"Not so far," Mason said. "Look her up. See who she is. See if she's a nurse."

"Okay. Here's something else. The police have found the murder gun."

"They're certain?"

"Yes. The bullets tally exactly."

"Where did they find it?"

"That's the funny thing," Drake said. "They found it right where Anders says he threw the gun."

"What do you mean?"

"Get this," Drake said. "The highway is banked way up at that particular place, probably eight or ten feet above the level of the surrounding country. There's a deep drainage ditch on each side of the highway."

"I know," Mason said. "Just how did they find the gun and just where did they find it?"

"Anders stood on that highway and threw it as hard as he could throw it," Drake said. "The gun evidently hit the high tension post on the side of the road and dropped back into the ditch. It started to rain a short time later, and quite a bit of water gathered in the drainage ditch. During wet weather, water stands in there two or three feet deep. The water went down this afternoon, and some smart photographer who had been sent out to photograph your footprints happened to notice it lying there in the water.

"It's a thirty-eight-caliber Colt, police-positive. Police rushed a test bullet through it, and compared it with the fatal bullet. They were both fired by the same gun."

Mason said, "What does Anders have to say to that?"

"I don't know," Drake said. "It doesn't make very much difference what he does have to say to it. It puts him in an awful spot."

"Numbers on the gun?" Mason asked.

"I guess so. Remember, Perry, this is last-minute news, hot off the wire. My friend on the newspaper handed it to me as a flash."

"Well," Mason said, "I guess they'll turn Mae Farr loose now. I filed *habeas corpus* on her."

"They'll want to hold her as a witness," Drake said.

"They will and they won't. She cuts both ways. Once they can pin the kill on Anders, it's up to him to show the circumstances which would justify or extenuate his actions. That means it's up to him to keep Mae Farr where he can put his finger on her. She's more important to the defense than to the prosecution."

"Listen, Paul, get busy on that Tooms girl, find out all you can about her. Keep men on Marley and see if you can scare up anything more on Eversel. How about Mrs. Wentworth? I presume the police have been checking on her?"

"I guess so. She went up to the D.A.'s office shortly after noon, was in there for about an hour. As I get it, she took it right on the chin, said that it was a shame that it had to happen, that naturally she regretted it, that she and Wentworth were estranged, that she wasn't going to pretend they were good friends any longer, that differences over property affairs had become very bitter, that naturally his death came as a shock to her.

"My newspaper friend slipped me a bunch of photographs. Among them is a swell one of Juanita Wentworth just leaving her automobile in front of the courthouse."

"Why leaving the automobile?" Mason asked.

Drake said, "These newspaper photographers are instructed to get lots of leg in the pictures. You can't very well pose a widow that way. It's in poor taste. So they got a 'candid camera' shot just as she was getting out of the automobile."

"I see," Mason said, and then added, after a moment, "How about her story, Paul? Did the D.A.'s office ask her for more particulars, or did they just hit the high spots?"

"I don't know just what"—Della Street slipped through the door from the outer office. Drake broke off to glance up at her for a moment, then finished quickly—"what they talked about, Perry."

Della said, "Mae Farr's in the office."

Mason jerked his head toward the door. "Beat it, Paul," he said. "I want to get the lowdown on some stuff. Anything she tells me is privileged unless a third party like yourself overhears it. Then it is no longer privileged communication and we might all be in a spot later on. Keep working on things and dig up all the information you can."

"I will," Drake said, "and you'd better work fast with Mae Farr, Perry."

"Meaning what?"

"Meaning that she's outside now, but I have a hunch she won't stay out long."

"Why, Paul?"

"Just the way things are looking," Drake said. "I'm on my way, Perry."

"So long," Mason said, and nodded to Della Street.

Della went out and brought Mae Farr into the office. She crossed over to Perry Mason, her head held high, a defiant smile on her lips. "Hello," she said. "Are we speaking or aren't we?"

"Why not?" Mason asked. "Sit down and have a cigarette."

"Do you want me?" Della asked.

Mason shook his head. "And see that we're not disturbed, Della."

"I'm closing up the office now," she said, and walked swiftly through the door to the outer offices.

"Why," Mason asked Mae Farr, "shouldn't we be speaking?"

"I'm afraid I got you in something of a spot."

"That's nothing. I'm accustomed to spots. What did you tell the police?"

"Not a thing."

"What do you mean by that?"

"Exactly what I said. I told them nothing."

"Did they read Anders' statement to you?"

"They told me about what he'd said first—with a lot of variations of their own, and then they let me see their signed statement, which differed quite a bit from what they'd said it was."

"And you told them absolutely nothing?"

"Not a thing. I said that I was a working girl with my reputation to think of, and I didn't care to make any statement whatever."

"What did they say to that?"

"They said that I'd get in more deeply than ever by adopting that sort of an attitude. I told them that was fine. They've given me a subpoena to appear before a grand jury. They say I'll have to talk then. Will I?"

"Probably," Mason said. "If you didn't kill him, you'd better talk."

"I didn't kill him."

"Did Anders kill him?"

"I can't believe he did, but if he didn't, who did?"

Mason said, "Let's go back to last night. You started back to town with me. Then you went on ahead. Now then, what did you do after that?"

"Kept right on going to town," she said.

"To your apartment?"

"Yes."

"Then what?"

"Then this morning detectives from the Homicide Squad came and got me out of bed, and held me for questioning."

Mason said, "You didn't, by any chance, turn around after you left me and double back to the Yacht Club, did you?"

"Good heavens, no! Why?"

"Someone tried to tell me you did."

"Who?"

"A man by the name of Marley. Do you know him?"

"Oh, Frank," she said scornfully, and then, after a moment, "What does he know about me?"

"Don't you know him?"

"Yes. I mean, what does he know about me being down at the Yacht Club?"

"He says you were. He says you were the one who took his cruiser out."

"Nonsense," she said. "He was out himself, and he's trying to cover up."

"What makes you say he was out in the boat?"

"Because he has one of those devious minds that never approaches anything directly. He works around in a circle. If you want to know where he's going, you never look in the direction in which he's headed."

"I see," Mason said with a smile.

"He's clever," she added hastily. "Don't overlook that."

"You know him fairly well?"

"Yes."

"Seen a good deal of him?"

"Too much," she said.

"You don't like him?"

"I hate the ground he walks on."

Mason said, "Let's get things straight, Mae. How well did you know Penn Wentworth?"

"Too damn well."

"His wife?"

"I've never met her."

"Was Frank Marley playing around with Wentworth's wife?"

"I wouldn't know," she said.

"Would you have any ideas on the subject?"

"If Juanita Wentworth left the door open, Frank Marley would walk in," she said.

"Why," Mason asked, "do you hate him? Did he ever make a pass at you?"

"Lord, yes—and never got even halfway to first base."

"Is that why you dislike him?"

"No." She met his eyes steadily and said, "I may as well be frank with you. I don't object to men making passes at me. I like it if they go about it in the right way. I don't like it if they whine about it or try to appeal to my sympathies. I don't like Frank Marley because of his dishonesty—no, not his dishonesty either. I don't object to a man cutting corners if he is clever about it. I've known men who weren't exactly honest. Some of them have fascinated me. What I don't like about Frank is his sneaky, underhanded intrigue. You just can't tell about him. He'll be suave and friendly and reach around you as though to put a friendly arm around your waist, and there'll be a knife in his hand. He'll stick it in to the hilt, and never change expression. He never raises his voice, never bats an eyelash, never gets flustered. And he's dangerous."

Mason said, "Let's talk about you for a while."

"What about me?"

"Quite a lot of things," Mason said, "for instance, about what happened on the *Pennwent*."

"Well, what about it?"

Mason said, "When you told me about that, your boyfriend was with you."

"Well?" she asked.

"Did you," Mason asked, "sort of expurgate the account because he was there?"

She stared steadily at him and said, "No. It would take more than Hal Anders to make me lie. Look here, Mr. Mason, I'm going to tell you something about myself. I pay my own way as I go through the world, and I want the privilege of living my own life. I left North Mesa because I couldn't do just that. I have my own code, my own creed, and my own ideas. I try to be true to them, all of them. I hate hypocrisy. I like fair play. I want to live my own life in my own way, and I'm willing to let other people live their lives in their way."

"How about Anders?"

"Anders wanted me to marry him. I thought for a while I was going to. I changed my mind. I hate weak men."

"What's wrong with Anders?"

"What isn't wrong with him," she said bitterly, and then added, after a moment, "Oh, he's all right, but he needs a lot of fixing. He can't get along without having someone pat him on the back and tell him he's doing all right, that he's a wonderful young man, and all that stuff.

"Look at what happened in this case. You told him what to do. You told him particularly to go to his hotel and stay there until he heard from you. Did he do it? He did not. He never even got as far as the hotel. He had to have someone else give him advice. That's the trouble with him. He's never learned to stand on his own two feet and take things as they come."

Mason said, "I'm not certain but what you judge him too harshly."

"Maybe I do," she admitted.

"Don't you think perhaps he's tried to advise you, tried to interfere with your life, and you resented that, but that you really care a lot for him and are trying all the harder to fan your resentment into flame because the fuel doesn't want to burn?"

She smiled and said, "You may be right at that. I've always resented him because he was so darn *good*. Everyone pointed him out as a model young man. He didn't drink, didn't smoke, didn't gamble, worked hard, was nice to old ladies, kept his lodge dues paid, his hair cut and his nails clean. He read all the best books, listened to the best music, raised the best stock, and got the best prices.

"Everything he ever does is carefully worked out and programmed —and it's always on the advice of someone else. The horticultural commissioner tells him about how to handle his land. His lawyer tells him about his contracts. His banker tells him about how to handle his finances. That's what makes me so darn *tired* of him. He's always attentive, always learning, always right, but he's always right because he's taken the advice of someone who knew. He has good judgment. He usually knows which is the best advice and he acts on it."

"Don't we all live our lives that way?" Mason asked. "At any rate, to a greater or lesser extent?"

"I don't," she said simply, and then added, with feeling, "and I don't want to."

"You resented his coming to the city to look you up?"

"Yes, I did. It was very decent of him to offer to pay the amount of that check, but I'm perfectly capable of living my own life. If I get into something, I want to get out of it through my own efforts. If I can't, I want to stay there. I don't want to have Hal Anders rushing into the city to lift me up out of the gutter, brush the mud off my clothes, smile sweetly down at me, and say, 'Won't you come home now, Mae, marry me, settle down, and live happily ever after?' "

"He still wants you to marry him?"

"Of course. He's rather single-minded when he gets an idea in his head."

"You don't intend to?"

"I do not. I suppose I'm an ingrate. I know I'm in a jam. I suppose he'll come to my rescue with money and moral support, and I should be grateful and fall in his arms when it's all over. Well, just for your personal, private information, Mr. Perry Mason, I'm not going to do anything of the sort."

"All right," Mason said. "Let's talk about what happened on the yacht."

"I've told you what happened."

"You said Wentworth was wearing his underclothes."

"He was."

"When the body was found, it was fully clothed."

"I can't help that," she said. "When he was shot, he was wearing his underwear, and that's all."

"How did it start?"

"Oh, he said he had to take a cruise that night and asked me if I'd excuse him while he changed his clothes and put on his overalls. He said he had some work to do on the motors. He went to the after cabin to change. He'd left the door open. I didn't know it. I strolled back towards the engine room. I could look right in the cabin where he was changing. I guess that gave him ideas. He started working on me instead of the engines."

"How loudly did you scream?"

"I didn't know I screamed," she said. "Hal says I did. I think he's cockeyed. I think I did a little cussing, some kicking, and a little scratching and biting. If I screamed, I was screaming at Penn and not for help. I got myself aboard that yacht, and I could get myself off of it. I never was one to yell much for help."

"Were you nervous, hysterical?"

"Me?" she asked in surprise.

"Yes."

"Good Lord, no! I was being crowded into a corner," she said, "and I was getting pretty tired. I didn't know how much longer I was going to hold out. Look, Mr. Mason, I've fought men off before, and I'll probably do it again."

"Do you," Mason asked, "inspire men to violence?"

"I don't think so," she said. "A lot of men try caveman tactics because a lot of girls fall for them. I don't. The minute a man starts pushing me around, I want to hit him with anything I can get my hands on. I think I have more trouble that way than most girls because I'm inclined to be independent, and men resent that. A lot of girls make a habit of saying 'no' in such a way they make the man like it. When I say 'no,' I say 'NO.' I don't give a hang whether he likes it or doesn't like it."

"When did you see Frank Marley last?"

"Sunday, a week ago."

"Where?"

"We went on a cruise—a bunch of us."

"Was Wentworth along?"

"Yes."

"On the *Pennwent*?"

"No," she said, "on Marley's cruiser, the *Atina*. We took a quick run over to Catalina."

"Can you run that boat?"

"Yes. I brought it back all the way. I wish I could like Marley as well as I do his boat. It's a honey."

"What about you and Wentworth?"

She said, "We met some time ago. I did some work for him. I saw he was taking quite an interest in me. He asked me to go on a cruise. You know what those cruises are apt to be. I told him straight from the shoulder. He said it was okay by him. All he wanted was my company. I went. Okay, he was going to open up a bookmaking office. It was against the law, but he claimed he had it squared with the officers. He wanted me to be in the place to class it up and sort of check on Marley. He knew that Marley's line didn't go across with me, and he was a little suspicious of Frank. Frank was handling most of the money end of the business. Pen thought it would be a good idea to have someone around who could check up on him.

"To tell you the truth, I don't think Frank liked the idea. If you started prodding around in Frank's accounts, I think you'd find something rotten. I told Penn that."

"What did Penn say?" Mason asked.

"Not very much. He told me I was wrong, but I could see he was turning what I'd said over in his mind."

"And the clothes?" Mason asked.

She said, "I get mad every time I think about that. It was a straight business proposition from first to last. Wentworth wasn't to pay for those clothes unless something happened and I didn't go to work. I was to go to work and pay the bill out of my salary in installments. The whole thing was explained to the credit manager at the time the account was opened. I tell you it was a business proposition."

"But you didn't pay for the clothes?"

"No, of course not. I never went to work. There was a shake-up in city politics. The men they thought they could control were transferred around to other districts. They didn't give up the idea entirely but marked time trying to establish new contacts.

"Well, that was the understanding we had when he put the proposition up to me. I was out of work. I wasn't to draw any regular salary until the place opened. I was to spend a good deal of time with Penn, meeting his friends and getting to know who they were. Penn was to send my sister a small check every three weeks and to pay my living expenses. I was to have enough clothes to make a good impression. In a way, I was to be the official hostess on his yachting parties.

"I didn't need anyone to tell me what it looked like. It looked like the devil. I didn't need anyone to tell me that in the back of Penn's mind was the idea that I'd become dependent on him, get under his control, and become his mistress. I didn't care what was in his mind. I knew what was in my mind. I didn't sail under any false colors. I told him so right at the start. He knew the way I felt. He thought he could make me change. All right, it was a fair deal and no favors."

"But your family?" Mason asked.

"There the shoe pinched. I was out of work and couldn't get any satisfactory job. I figured this would open up into something that would pay. I also knew darn well that there was a chance the place might be raided and I'd find myself dragged into court. I didn't think they'd do anything to me, but I didn't know. I knew it would hurt Mother terribly if she thought I was mixed up in a business like that.

I didn't want to lie to them, so I just quit writing. But I also knew Sylvia needed some help with finances, so I arranged to have Penn send her some money until my regular salary began. By that time, I expected to have money to send her. Now then, that's the story."

Mason said, "It's a good story if it's true."

Her eyes darkened.

"Don't get excited," Mason said. "I'm talking particularly about what happened after you left me. A witness will claim that you took Frank Marley's cruiser out for a spin."

"That *I* did?"

"Yes."

"When?"

"Sometime after we made our trip to the Yacht Club."

"I did not."

"The witness says you did."

"The witness lies. What in the name of reason would I want with Frank Marley's boat?"

Mason said, "If Hal Anders had gone back to the *Pennwent*, instead of going to his hotel, and had taken it out to sea and started it heading down the coast in the direction of Ensenada, you *could* have taken Marley's cruiser and gone out to pick him up. The *Atina* was at least twice as fast as the *Pennwent*."

"That's absurd. Hal went directly to North Mesa so he could consult his old family lawyer."

"He went to North Mesa all right," Mason said. "I'm not so certain about the direct part of it."

"Well, I've told you the truth."

Mason got up, reached for his hat, and said, "Okay, we'll let it go at that."

"What do you want me to do?" she asked.

Mason said, "Go back to your apartment, act just as though nothing had happened. Newspaper reporters will call on you. People will ask questions. Photographers will want pictures. Give them all the pictures they want. Remember, newspapermen are working for a living. They're sent out to get stories, pictures, and interviews. If they come back with something good, the boss pats them on the back. If they come back without anything, the boss snarls at them. So give them something to come back with. Let them pose you any way they want to, give them all the pictures they want, and tell them that you're not discussing the case."

"I get you," she said.

"As far as the newspaper reporters are concerned," Mason said, "tell them all about your romance with Hal Anders."

"It wasn't any romance."

"That's what I want you to tell them. Tell them just about the way you've told it to me."

"About his being weak and always asking for advice—"

"No, not that," Mason interrupted. "The part about how he's such a model young man who never makes any mistakes and how you got tired of it all. You wanted to come to the city and see life for yourself. And tell them all about Wentworth's proposition that you should go to work for him, only don't let on that you knew it was a bookmaking business. Simply say that it was a downtown office he intended to open up, and he wouldn't tell you very much about what it was only that it was to handle some of his investments. But about the things that happened last night, keep mum. You'd like to talk, but your attorney has told you to say absolutely nothing."

"In other word," she said, "I'm to give them something they can turn into copy, is that it?"

"That's right."

"Okay, I'll do that little thing."

"How about it?" Mason asked. "Are you nervous and upset?"

She shook her head and smiled. "It's all part of the game," she said. "Sometimes you're on top and things are easy. Sometimes you're on the bottom. There's no need to let it worry you."

Abruptly, she thrust out her hand, smiled up into his face, and said, "Good night, Mr. Mason."

Mason stood for a moment holding her hand, looking down into her eyes. "Did they," he asked, "try to browbeat you, try to make you nervous?"

"Did they?" She laughed. "All of them yelled questions at me and asked me to reenact what happened at the time of the shooting, and then when that failed, accused me of having been his mistress and lying to Hal about it because I wanted to marry Hal in order to be on financial easy street. I guess they tried everything, Mr. Mason."

Mason grinned and said, "I guess they did. Okay, on your way. Think you can remember all I've told you?"

"Sure," she said.

She flashed him a quick smile from the door, then Mason could hear her heels click . . . clack . . . click . . . clacking down the corridor toward the elevator.

Mason put on his hat, went out to the other office, and said, "All right, Della. I'm going out into the highways and byways. Get yourself some dinner and stick around the telephone."

She reached up to take possession of his right hand, caressing it with hers. "You'll be careful, Chief?" she asked.

Smiling down at her, he once more shook his head.

She laughed and said, "I could have saved my breath, but keep your eyes peeled, and if there's anything I can do, let me know."

"Okay, Della, but I want you to keep out of circulation for a little while. I don't want to have them drag you into the case. They've subpoenaed Mae Farr to appear before the grand jury. They'll probably subpoena me."

"And me?" she asked.

Mason nodded.

"What'll we tell them?"

Mason said, "We won't commit any perjury. We won't play into their hands. And we won't betray the interests of our clients. We'll generally adopt the position that just about everything that happened was a privileged communication, confidential, and not the subject of a grand jury investigation. That'll raise a lot of technical points. Oh, we'll come out all right, Della."

"I suppose you want me to say nothing."

"Be like the clam," Mason said.

"At high tide?"

"What's the difference?" he asked.

"You gather clams at *low* tide."

"Right," Mason said. "Be like a clam at high tide."

As the door closed behind him, the telephone rang. Della picked up the receiver and answered.

"Hello, beautiful," said Paul Drake. "Let me speak to the boss."

"He's just stepped out," said Della, "and I think he is looking for action."

"Oh, oh," said Paul. "I was waiting for him to give me a ring after Mae Farr left. The D.A. has sent the story out. The papers aren't mentioning names right now because they're afraid, but the D.A.'s office is mentioning names. They state that they're prepared to prove Mason was out last night looking for that gun, that he's going to be subpoenaed to appear before the grand jury, and that in the meantime he's being kept under the closest surveillance. He—"

Della said, "Gosh! Let me try to catch him at the elevator, Paul."

She slammed down the receiver, dashed out of the door, raced down the corridor to the elevators, and frantically jabbed at the button. When one of the elevators stopped, she said breathlessly to the operator, "Listen, Sam, rush me down to the ground floor, will you, please? I have to get there right away."

The elevator operator grinned, nodded, and, disregarding the curious stares of the other passengers as well as various stop signals along the way, dropped the cage swiftly to the lower corridor.

Della pushed people to one side, running toward the street exit. She was just in time to see Mason enter a taxicab fifty feet down the street. She called to him, but he couldn't hear her. The taxicab swung out into traffic. Two men in plainclothes, sitting in an automobile parked in front of a fireplug, eased their car into motion and in behind the taxicab.

Della looked quickly up and down the street, could find no cab in sight. A red traffic signal held up traffic coming her way while the cab containing Mason and the car with the two officers turned to the right at the next intersection and were swallowed up in traffic.

Della Street turned and went slowly back to the office.

Chapter Ten

Mason discharged the taxicab a block from the Balkan Apartments and reconnoitered carefully. The two plainclothesmen who had followed the taxicab drove on past without so much as a look in Mason's direction. Mason walked the block to the apartment house and looked at the directory for the name of Hazel Tooms.

As he pressed the button opposite her name, a man came walking briskly down the street from the opposite direction, turned into the apartment house, and fished in his pocket for a latchkey.

The electric door release buzzed, and the man who had been looking for his latchkey pushed against the door and went on in. Mason followed him, passed him in the corridor, walked to the elevator, and went to the fifth floor. He found 521 near the end of the corridor and tapped gently on the panels of the door.

The young woman who opened the door was taller than average and was dressed in lounging pajamas. She carried herself firmly erect. Her brownish hair had highlights. Her eyes, blue and cautious, surveyed Perry Mason in frank appraisal. There was neither nervousness nor fear in her manner. She seemed quite capable of taking care of herself in any emergency.

"I don't know you," she said.

"A situation which I wish to remedy at once," Mason replied, lifting his hat and bowing.

She looked him over from head to foot, then stood to one side. "Come in," she said.

When Mason had entered the apartment, she closed the door, indicated a chair, and then, instead of seating herself, stood with her back to the door, her hands on the knob.

"All right," she said. "What is it?"

Mason said, "My name is Mason. Does that mean anything to you?"

"Not a thing. If this is a mash, save your breath. I don't go out with strangers."

Mason said, "I'm doing a little investigating."

"Oh," she said.

"I have reason to believe," Mason went on, "that you have some information in which I'd be interested."

"What about?"

"About the *Pennwent*."

"What about it?"

"When you saw it last and about Frank Marley's *Atina* and when you saw it last."

"A detective?" she asked.

"Not exactly," Mason said.

"What's your angle?"

"I'm representing someone who wants the facts."

"What's in it for me?"

"Nothing."

She left the door then and sat down across from Perry Mason. She crossed her legs and hugged one knee with the interlaced fingers of large, capable hands. "Pardon me for being cautious," she said, "but you read so much stuff these days of men getting into women's apartments, slugging them over the head, choking them, and playful little practices of that sort, and I was taking no chances."

"Did I," Mason asked, "look like one of those?"

"I don't know," she said. "I don't know what they look like."

Mason laughed. Hazel Tooms smiled slightly.

"Well," Mason said, "let's get back to my question."

"About the boats?"

"Yes."

"What about them?"

"When did you see Frank Marley's cruiser last?"

She smiled and said, "Really, Mr. Mason, I'd prefer to get back to *my* original question."

"What's that?"

"What's in it for me?"

"Exactly what I told you the first time," Mason said. "Nothing."

"Then why should I answer?" she asked.

"Let's look at it another way," Mason suggested, with a slight twinkle in his eye. "Why *shouldn't* you answer?"

She said, "Charity may begin at home, but it ends up in the poor-house."

Mason said, "All right. I'll put my cards on the table."

"Aces first, please," she said.

"I'm a lawyer. I'm representing a Miss Mae Farr in connection with—"

"Oh, you're *Perry* Mason."

He nodded.

"Why didn't you say so in the first place?"

"I didn't think it would do any good."

She looked at him, her brows puckered together, her head tilted slightly to one side. "Well," she said at length, "so *you're* Perry Mason."

Mason said nothing.

"And interested in information you think I have. Is that information going to get me in trouble?"

"I don't know," Mason said.

"Listen," she told him, "I don't want to go on the witness stand."

"You're not on the witness stand now."

"No, but you might put me there."

"Again, I might not."

"Would you promise not to?"

"No."

She caressed her knee with the tips of her fingers, her eyes distant and preoccupied with a survey of the possibilities of the situation. Abruptly, she brought her eyes into hard, sharp focus on the lawyer's face, then said, "All right, I'm going to take a chance. I'm strong on taking chances."

Mason settled back in the chair and shifted his eyes slightly so that she could talk without being conscious of his gaze.

She said, "I can't go on the witness stand because a smart lawyer would make me out a sorry figure. I've always loved the outdoors— tennis, riding, skiing, all sports. Especially, I like yachting. You don't get invited on boat trips by cultivating the company of impecunious young men of regular habits and virtuous intentons.

"You've heard of gold diggers? Well, I guess I'm a yacht digger. Whenever there was a cruise over to Catalina, I met all the yachtsmen I could. Whenever they wanted my telephone number, I gave it to them. That's all I give them, my telephone number, my company, and a lot of laughs.

"Lots of times yachtsmen want girls along who are good sports, know something about handling a boat, are willing to do a good share of the work, and can keep the gang laughing.

"I suppose I could have used the same amount of mental effort in some commercial activity and made money. I work like the devil thinking up wisecracks, games, stunts, and how to drink a lot without getting too awfully drunk. If you've never tried it, eating a lot of butter before the drinking starts is a swell stunt."

"I have a recipe which beats that," Mason said.

"You have?"

"Yes."

"Be a good sport and give it to me. That butter stunt is the best I've ever found."

Mason said, "Mine is more simple. I don't drink much after the drinking starts."

"Oh," she said, her voice showing disappointment. "I thought you were really going to say something."

Mason said, "Don't let me interrupt you."

"I won't—not again. Well, Mr. Mason, here's the lowdown. Penn Wentworth took a shine to me. He was on the make. When you say 'no' to Penn, he starts wrestling, and when he wrestles, he gets out of control. Personally, I don't like to be manhandled. My eyes, my judgment of distance, and my timing are all pretty good. I just won a tennis championship the other day.

"Well, when the party got just so rough, I warned him. Warning didn't do any good. He was past that point. So I slipped my shoe off, doubled up my leg, waited my chance, and shot my heel straight to the chin."

"Connect?" Mason asked.

"Of course I connected."

"What happened to Wentworth?"

She said, "I thought I'd killed him. I poured water on his face, rubbed his chest and ribs, and fed him brandy with a teaspoon. It seemed like an hour before he came around, and he was still punch-drunk for another thirty minutes."

"Then what?" Mason asked. "Did he come up for round two, or did he toss in the towel when the bell rang?"

She grinned and said, "He tossed in the towel, and it made the start of a swell friendship. I got so I cared a lot for him after that, and he respected me. We had one of those friendships that are so rare between a man and a woman, just perfect pals. He found out that I liked boats, and he liked to have me with him. Occasionally, he'd go off on a trip just by himself when he didn't want anyone around to bother him and talk to him. He never cared about yachting as yachting but used the yacht simply for incidental pleasure—attending the cruises, staging parties, and things of that sort. That's why he had all those gadgets on the *Pennwent*.

"This is the part you're not going to believe. However, it happens to be the truth. When Wentworth would have a fit of the blues, he liked to go on a cruise. He'd leave the handling of the boat pretty much up to me. He'd let me do the cooking. Sometimes we'd take an entire cruise wtihout saying a word except a few comments about what he wanted to eat and about handling the boat. That suited me right down to the ground. I love to head out into the ocean with my hands on the wheel. It gives me a thrill, a sense of power. I know the ocean is cruel and merciless. I know that you can't make any mistakes with the ocean. I like to play that kind of a game."

She hesitated a moment, studying Mason's face, apparently waiting for some comment. He made none. She said, "Naturally, I got to know Frank Marley. He's different from Penn. Frank never made a pass at me. If he ever does, he'll have all the dice loaded against me. He waits and watches and thinks and schemes, and you never know what he's thinking about from what he says.

"Penn was a good egg. A girl couldn't trust herself around Penn Wentworth for five minutes. He'd try a line, and if that didn't work, he'd try massage, and if that didn't work, he'd get rough. But there was one thing about Penn. You always knew where he stood, and he was never a hypocrite. Any girl who went out with Penn Wentworth knew that Penn was—well, sticky. Once you got past that first round with him, he made a swell friend. Penn had a lot to him. He was shrewd and fair. He had a sense of humor, and he could be a very good companion when he didn't have the blues. When he had the blues, he wanted you to leave him alone, and he'd leave you alone.

"Frank Marley was the exact opposite. I've been out with Frank a lot of times. I've handled his boat a lot. He'd be sitting or standing somewhere nearby all the time, smoking cigarettes and watching me with half-closed eyes through the cigarette smoke. He was always a perfect gentleman, always quiet, always well behaved—and always waiting."

She stopped to study Mason's face curiously, then said, "Oh, go ahead and look at me. I'll keep on talking just the same."

"No," Mason said. "I'm listening. I listen with my ears and look with my eyes. I can't do two things at once and really concentrate on them. Right now, I'm listening to your voice."

"Don't you think you can tell more about a woman by watching her when she talks than by listening to what she says?"

"Not always," Mason said. "A lawyer trains himself to listen. Witnesses have usually rehearsed their story pretty well—at least to the extent of making the mannerisms and gestures more or less mechanical, but they rehearse silently. People really should cultivate the art of talking to themselves. They'd learn a lot about voices if they did."

She laughed and said, "You make me feel frightfully naked—sitting there with your head turned and your ears taking in every word."

"I didn't intend to. You have a very observing mind."

"Think so?"

"Yes."

"Thanks."

"Well," Mason said, "that's that. We were talking about Frank Marley's boat."

"I was talking about the yachts and the men," she said. "Late in the afternoon, Wentworth called and said he'd like to see me. I drove down and went aboard. He said that he had to be in San Diego the next day for an appointment with his wife. He told me that he had finally decided to give her an ultimatum: either she would give him a divorce on reasonable terms or he would sue Sid Eversel for alienation of affections. Then he suggested that I go with him and that we take the *Pennwent* to Ensenada. He'd drive to San Diego to meet his wife. Of course, I'd stay aboard; he didn't want his wife to know I was with him.

"Well," she said, "that suited me right down to the ground. I told Penn I'd have to go get some clothes and that there were some provisions we needed. He gave me some money and told me to stop on the way back and pick up the supplies at one of the all-night markets. As soon as I returned, we'd sail.

"I drove back. The *Pennwent* was gone. I thought perhaps he'd taken it out for a trial spin. He'd never stood me up. Ours wasn't that sort of a friendship. I knew he wanted me to sail the boat for him. I stuck around. I thought for a while I'd go over and see if anyone was aboard Frank Marley's boat, then I saw that it, too, was gone.

"Ordinarily, I wouldn't have waited very long, but I did want that trip to Ensenada, and I felt certain that anything that had taken Penn away would be a real emergency. I knew that he'd have left word if he'd had to pull out wthout me.

"There's a message board up by the clubhouse, a place with a lot of little mailboxes where people can leave messages for the various yachts. I looked in Penn's box. There wasn't any message. I went back to the car and waited some more."

"Just a minute," Mason interrupted. "What time was all this?"

"I don't know what time it was," she said. "I remember it started to rain when I was buying the groceries. Does that mean anything?"

Mason nodded.

She said, "I don't think it rained down at the Club for half or three-quarters of an hour after that. The showers were drifting in from the mountains.

"Well, I dropped off to sleep, sitting there in the car and dozing. I'd been playing tennis all afternoon—a small tournament—amateur stuff. I'd won the medal for second place in the women's division, and the girl who'd beat me had done every dirty trick in the cards. God, how I hated to lose to that woman.

"I guess I had the blues myself. Anyhow, the thought of that boat trip down to Ensenada soothed my mind. I kept waiting and dozing. Then I heard a boat coming in. I thought it was the *Pennwent*. I opened the door and started to get out of the car. Then I saw it was Frank Marley's *Atina*. I figured he'd know where Penn was, but I wasn't certain Marley was alone. You know yachting etiquette is a little different from other stuff. You wait to make certain the man's alone or else you give him a chance to make the play.

"Well, first rattle out of the box, this girl showed on deck, running ashore with the lines. I could tell from the way the boat was handled that she was alone on it. Boy oh boy, I sure looked her over."

"Jealous?" Mason asked.

She said, "It might add up to that. I figured if Frank Marley was generous enough in his softer moments to let a girl take his cruiser and just sail out on parties of her own—well, it was an interesting idea."

"Did you recognize this girl?"

"Not then," she said. "I've found out since that it was Mae Farr."

"How do you know?"

"I've seen photographs of her."

"Who showed them to you?"

"That," she said, "is something we won't discuss right now. I haven't that party's permission."

"Was it Frank Marley?" Mason asked.

"We won't discuss it."

"Then what?" Mason asked.

"I waited about half an hour after the girl had left," Hazel Tooms said, "and then gave it up as a bad job. I figured something had happened and Penn had been called away without even having time to leave a message for me. I came home, climbed into a hot tub, and then went to bed."

Mason said, "You jumped at this trip to Ensenada?"

"Yes."

"You were going alone with Wentworth?"

"That's what I said."

"That," Mason observed, "would be rather bad for the sake of appearances."

"Well, what of it?" she asked defiantly.

"Exactly what I was getting at," Mason said. "You don't seem to care much for appearances."

"I don't give a damn for them."

"You have your own car?"

"Such as it is, yes."

"And you're able to leave on a moment's notice to go on trips?"

"What are you getting at?" she asked.

Mason smiled and said, "Perhaps it's my habit of leading up to something through cross-examination. What I'm really trying to find out is what are your means of support?"

"Oh," she said, "that. I guess a lawyer could put me in a funny position before a jury with a line of questions like that, couldn't he?"

Mason nodded.

"Well," she said, and hesitated.

"Go ahead,"Mason prompted.

"Do they inquire into that on the witness stand, Mr. Mason?"

"They could be asking questions in just about the way that I ask them."

"I see. Then they'd force me to go into it in front of the jury, wouldn't they?"

"Well," Mason said, "it would be up to you."

"I don't want to be a witness," she said.

"You still haven't given me the answer to the question."

She said, with flashing eyes, "I don't think it's any of your damn business," and then after a moment added, with a twinkle, "incompetent, irrelevant, and immaterial to you, Mr. Perry Mason."

He bowed and said, "The objection is well taken, Miss Tooms."

She laughed at that. "You and I," she announced, "could be friends.

Listen, you said I had an observing mind. I've had to develop it. I'm crazy about tennis. I like all sports. A girl can't work in an office and get very much time for outdoor recreation."

"That," Mason observed dryly, "is axiomatic."

She said, "I might have an ex-husband somewhere in the background who is paying a small amount of alimony."

"Have you?" Mason asked.

"I thought you said the objection was well taken."

"It was."

"Then I don't need to answer the question."

He shook his head.

She said, "Things don't look so good for Mae Farr, do they?"

"I would say that Hal Anders was in the toughest spot," Mason observed.

"You know, she *could* have been working with him. He could have killed Wentworth right there in the harbor, and he could have taken Wentworth's boat out and set it on the course for Ensenada. She could have tagged along in the cruiser, picked him up, put him ashore at some other dock, and then returned Marley's boat."

"What," Mason asked, "gave you that idea?"

She laughed and said, "Just reading the papers and thinking things over. Naturally, as soon as I read the papers, I appreciated the significance of what I'd seen."

"Did you tell anyone about it?"

She shook her head.

"Why not report to the police?" Mason asked.

"The police?" she said, and shrugged her shoulders.

"Well, why not?"

"Several reasons."

"Such as?"

She said, "I don't want to have to go on the witness stand."

"And, therefore, decided that you'd say absolutely nothing to anyone about what you'd seen?"

She pinched the fold in the leg of her lounging pajamas between her thumb and forefinger and slid her hand down the crease, then sighted along it with a critical eye as though to see if it was absolutely straight.

"Well?" Mason asked.

"Look here," she said abruptly, "I've long ago come to the conclusion that a person can get what he wants out of life, if he wants it badly enough."

"I have heard others advance the same idea," Mason commented.

"Well, I've lived my life according to that theory. I get what I want, but it's not particularly easy. You have to want what you want with every ounce of energy and vitality you possess."

"And so?"

"And so I've learned to be absolutely cold-blooded and selfish," she said, meeting his eyes defiantly.

"Most successful people are selfish," Mason said. "Most strong people are selfish. Here and there, you find the exception which proves the rule. I'm discussing generalities. If you're selfish, don't apologize for it."

"I'm not apologizing."

"Then," Mason said, "I take it you're leading up to something."

"I am."

"Then lead up to it."

"All right. Look here. If I go to the police, I'll have my name in the paper. I'll have to go on the witness stand. They'll have photographs of me. I think I'd photograph rather well—for newspaper purposes. That proposed trip to Ensenada would be magnified and distorted."

"I thought you didn't care for appearances," Mason said.

"I don't, but I do care for reputation."

"So what?"

"So, Mr. Mason, if I go on the witness stand, I'm going to hurt your client. Your client shouldn't want me to go on the witness stand. This man Anders shouldn't want me to go on the witness stand. *You* shouldn't want me to go on the witness stand. *I* don't want to go on the witness stand.

"I would like to take a trip. I know someone who has a yacht. I won't mention any names. That someone and I could start on a cruise to the South Seas. We'd have all kinds of bad luck. The engine would break down. We'd be blown off course, would make a landing at some isolated tropical island, would be out of fuel, would have to repair the mast and sails, and it would be weeks or months before we'd be heard of again."

"Rather a dangerous way to avoid going on the witness stand, isn't it?" Mason asked.

"I don't think so. I'd love it."

"What seems to be holding you back?" Mason inquired.

She said suddenly, "Oh, I see what you mean. You think it's Frank Marley. No, it isn't. Frank has to stay here. This person has a small auxiliary. Marley's boat could never make a long ocean voyage. It would be foolishness to even try."

"Well, I'll put it another way," Mason said. "What's holding this other person back?"

"Money," she said.

"Money?"

"Yes—or the lack of it, if you want to put it that way."

"I see."

"Mr. Mason," she said eagerly, "it wouldn't take very much money to do the trick, and—in case you have a conscience—you wouldn't be paying me to stay off the witness stand. It would be simply a proposition of financing me on a little trip I've always wanted to take. A thousand dollars would cover the whole cost."

Mason shook his head.

"Seven-fifty?" she said.

Again Mason shook his head.

"Look, Mr. Mason. I'll do it for five. It would be quite a job because we'll have to be gone for a long time, and this other party has certain obligations, but we could do it for five."

Mason said, "No. It isn't a matter of price."

"What is it?"

"It's a six-letter word," Mason said. "I'm not certain you'd understand."

"Oh, *please,* Mr. Mason. You don't know how much it means to me."

Mason shook his head, got up from the chair, pushed his hands down deep into his trouser pockets and stood for a moment lost in thought. Then he started pacing the room, not the aimless pacing of mental preoccupation, but a slow, studied tour of inspection along the baseboard of the four walls of the room.

"What is it?" she asked, watching him with apprehensive eyes.

"Just thinking," Mason said.

"You're looking along the floor."

"Am I?"

"Yes."

Mason continued his slow progress around the room.

She walked over to stand at his side. "What is it, Mr. Mason?" she asked. Then, as he didn't answer, she placed a pleading hand on his shoulder. "Look, Mr. Mason. It wouldn't cost you a thing. Harold Anders is rich. He has lots of money and lots of land. I'm a poor girl. Gosh, what he'd have to pay me wouldn't be a drop in the bucket compared to what he'd pay you for defending him."

"I'm not his lawyer," Mason said.

She paused suddenly, thinking that over, then after a moment said, "Oh."

Mason finished his tour of inspection.

"Who is Mr. Anders' lawyer?" she asked.

"I don't know. He's consulted someone up north, someone around North Mesa."

"In North Mesa?"

"Probably in the county seat."

"You don't know his name?"

"No."

She said, "Listen, Mr. Mason, will you do me a favor? As soon as you find out just who is representing him, will you give me a ring and let me know? You could do that much and—and it might amount to the same thing."

Mason said, "Under the circumstances, you'd better read the newspapers and get your information from them."

"All right, I will. Look here, Mr. Mason. I put my cards on the table with you because I had that proposition to make you. You won't take advantage of me, will you?"

"How do you mean?"

"This trip to Ensenada and what I've told you about what I do—how I get my yachting trips?"

Mason said, "When you put your cards on the table, you can't very well expect the other man not to know what you're going to play."

"You wouldn't do that to me, would you?"

"I don't know," Mason said. "It would depend on what you did to me."

"But I'm giving you a fair deal."

Mason raised his voice. "All right, let's hope so. In any event, I won't pay five cents to suppress your testimony. I won't let my client pay five cents."

"You aren't going to tell the police about what I saw?"

Mason said, "Don't worry. I'm not working up a case against the district attorney." He picked up his hat and moved toward the door. "Good-bye, Miss Tooms."

She made a little grimace. "Oh, Mr. Mason, I had hoped you'd be reasonable."

"And do what?"

"You know."

Mason said, "People have different ideas about what's reasonable. It depends somewhat on the viewpoint. Good night."

She raised her eyes to his. "Don't forget, Mr. Mason."

"I won't."

It was as he started down the hall toward the elevator that she called to him. "And don't forget I have an observing mind."

The door closed gently but firmly.

Chapter Eleven

Mason found a little hotel two blocks from Hazel Tooms' apartment. He called Paul Drake from the telephone booth. "Hi, Paul," he said. "What's new?"

Drake's voice showed excitement. "Lots of stuff, Perry. Listen. You were tailed when you left the office. Della tried to get you but was too late. A couple of plainclothesmen followed that taxicab. Where did you go—any place important?"

"I figured as much," Mason said. "I went to see a witness. She kept making me offers, saying that she would skip out if my clients would give her some money."

"Well?" Drake asked.

Mason said, "About the third time she made the proposition, it sounded awfully fishy to me. I walked around the apartment to see if I could find any evidence of its being bugged."

"Find any?"

"No. They were too smart. A bug is hard to locate, but usually when one is installed on a hurry-up job, a little fine plaster dust will adhere to the baseboard."

"Then you think this witness was planted?"

"No," Mason said slowly, "I don't think she was a plant. I think she's a witness, but she may be trying to buy her way out of something with the police. You know, if they could catch me in a scheme to spirit a witness out of the country, they'd let her get off to a running start, then drag her back with a big fanfare of trumpets, and the fact that I'd tried to get rid of her would raise the devil with my client and with me. Her testimony would automatically become the most important evidence in the case."

"You didn't fall for it?"

"Hell, no!"

Drake said, "I've got those pictures here."

"Have you got an extra gun around there anywhere, Paul?"

"Why, yes."

"One you don't think much of?"

"I have a couple of cheap revolvers that some of my operatives took away from ambitious lads who played with grown-up toys. Why?"

"How far," Mason asked, "could you throw one?"

"Shucks, I don't know, a hundred feet perhaps."

"Ever tried it?"

"No, of course not."

Mason said, "Better get Della Street, Paul, and meet me at that restaurant where I sometimes eat lunch. Della knows the place. Had anything to eat?"

"Yes, I grabbed a bite."

"Well, I'll take a taxi there, eat something, and be ready to go. I think Della will have had dinner."

"I doubt it," Drake said. "She was all worked up about getting word to you about those shadows. Where are they now, Perry? Did you ditch them?"

"Damned if I know," Mason said. "Probably not. I looked around but didn't spot anyone. However, a man came through the door of the apartment house when I was ringing the bell for this girl's apartment. He may have been one of them."

"What'll that mean, Perry?" Drake asked. "Anything serious?"

"Hell, I don't know," Mason said. "I can't afford to waste time figuring what the other man is going to do. I have to work fast."

Drake said, "I have some hot dope on Eversel."

"What is it?"

"His plane went out and returned twice—once before and once after the rain."

"You're sure?" Mason asked.

"Yes. One of my operatives got the chief gardener of the estate to give him a job as an assistant. It's a steady job. He's on the place, so he can get anything we want."

"Can you call him?" Mason asked.

"No, I can't call him, but he calls me for instructions."

"Okay," Mason said. "I have an idea or two. Get your stuff together, pick up Della, and meet me at the restaurant. See you there. Good-bye."

He went out to stand in the doorway of the hotel. He saw no one who seemed to be taking any undue interest in his motions.

Mason summoned a taxi and went to the restaurant where he had time for a sandwich, coffee, and piece of pie before Paul Drake joined him.

"Della with you?" Mason asked.

"Yes, sitting outside in the car."

"Has she had anything to eat?"

"She grabbed a sandwich and says she's not hungry now."

"Did you bring that gun?"

"Yes."

Mason said, "Let's get a couple of five-cell flashlights. I want to see how far I can throw that gun."

"Where are you going to do the pitching?" Paul Drake asked.

"Down where Anders did."

Drake surveyed Mason with alarm. "That," he said, "may be dangerous."

"Why?"

"It might not sound good in court."

Mason said, "Love letters don't sound good in court, but people go on writing them just the same."

"Go to it," Drake said. "It's your party. Were you followed here, Perry?"

"I don't think so, but I'm not sure," Mason said. "I went through the usual maneuvers without turning up anybody."

On the way out to the car, Drake said, "My operative out at Eversel's estate certainly had a lucky break. The gardener's a Scot. He's sort of a privileged character, has a little cottage of his own and isn't really classed as one of the servants."

"Where does your operative stay?" Mason asked.

"In a room in the basement."

"Find out anything?"

"Lots. The gardener didn't go on the whoopee party with the servants, although he was supposed to. He's just about as taciturn as a granite rock—unless, like my man, MacGregor, you happen to come from a certain section of Scotland."

They stepped out to the curb. Mason saw Della Street sitting in Drake's automobile, grinned, and said, "Hi, Della."

She said, "Gosh, I was worried about you. I was afraid you were going to walk right into a trap."

Mason said, "I may have at that. What did your man find out, Paul?"

Drake slid in behind the wheel. Mason eased in beside him. Della made herself comfortable in the back seat.

"Where to?" Drake asked.

"Down to the place where Anders says he threw the gun," Mason said. "You might see if anyone's on our tail, Paul."

"Okay," Drake said. "Do I get violent about it and let them know we're wise to them?"

Mason thought for a minute, then shook his head and said, "No. Do it casually, Paul. Pretend that we're looking for an address. That'll give you a chance to do a little turning and twisting."

"Okay," Drake said, "but my hunch is they won't try to follow us if they haven't quit already. A wise shadow usually checks out when the man he's after steers a zigzag course, no matter what the pretext —that is, unless he's told that it doesn't make any difference whether the suspect spots him or not."

"Well," Mason said, "you do whatever you can get away with and make it look innocent. What about the gardener at Eversel's?"

Gliding out into traffic, Drake said, "The gardener opened up. It seems that after the servants had left, Eversel came in with his car. After a while he took his plane, went somewhere, and came back.

When he came back, a woman was with him. My operative thinks the gardener knows who it was, but the gardener wouldn't say. Understand, my man had to beat around the bush getting this out of him."

"I understand," Mason said. "Give me what you have, and we'll fill in the blanks."

"Well, Eversel came home with this woman and went directly to a room that Eversel keeps fitted up as a darkroom. It seems he's quite a camera fiend."

"Mrs. Wentworth still with him?" Mason asked.

"The woman, whoever she was."

"Then what happened?"

"Then it started to rain. Eversel went down and warmed up the motor on the plane. About fifteen minutes later, they took off. He was gone nearly all night, came back along toward morning. He came back alone."

Mason said, "Mrs. Wentworth was supposed to have been in San Diego."

"Uh huh," Drake said. "The plane could have taken her down rather easily. I have my San Diego correspondents checking to find out if the plane was seen there."

"Where was Eversel's yacht?"

"Apparently moored in the outer yacht harbor."

"What speed does she turn up?"

"About two knots an hour faster than Wentworth's boat at cruising speed, and she can go about five knots faster."

"Where was Mrs. Wentworth staying in San Diego, Paul?"

"On a yacht with some friends. She also had a room at one of the hotels. You know how it is on a yacht, Perry. You have lots of conveniences, but it's hard to take baths, get beauty appointments, and things like that. Many of the women get a room and spend part of the time there when their yachts are in a city. Sometimes they'll all pitch in and get a room together."

Mason said, "Did you find out anything about where Juanita Wentworth was that night?"

"The people on the yacht said she went to a room at the hotel. As far as the people at the hotel are concerned, they know nothing. If they do know, they aren't making any comments."

"If it came to a pinch, think she could prove that she was in the hotel?"

"She might," Drake said. "I doubt if anyone could prove that she *wasn't.* . . . Well, this looks like a good place, Perry. We'll swing around the block and stop down on one of the side streets, turn the spotlight on a house number or two, then drive on for another block and stop."

"Okay," Mason said, "go to it."

Drake turned the corner, ran two blocks, then turned another corner.

"Oh, oh," Della Street said. "Headlights behind us."

"Don't look around," Mason said. "Paul can watch them in his rear-view mirror."

Drake turned the corner, stopped the car, played the beam of his flashlight over the house numbers, and then moved into slow motion.

The car behind them also turned to the right, came straight toward them, the occupants showing no sign of interest in the car that was parked at the curb.

"Keep your head turned away from it," Mason instructed in a low voice. "Roll your eyes for a quick glance."

He had just finished talking when the other car, which had slowed its speed appreciably, speeded up and swept on past.

Drake looked at the taillight going straight on down the street and said, "I think that's the last we'll see of them, Perry."

"Think they know we're wise?"

"I wouldn't doubt it. Anyhow, they gave me the idea they were signing off."

"Same here," Mason said. "When's that operative down at Eversel's place going to report again?"

"In an hour."

Mason said, "Let's go. I want to perform an experiment with guns, and then I want to be within reaching distance of Eversel's place when your man telephones. He'll telephone directly to the office, Paul?"

"Yes."

Mason said, "Better telephone your office, Paul, and tell them to hold this man on the line when he comes on. We'll want to talk with him."

"Okay, Perry."

Drake started the car once more. They ran down the side street for some fifteen blocks, turned and crossed the main boulevard intersection, then kept on going until they reached another parallel boulevard.

"Try this one," Mason said.

They made the boulevard stop, swung left, and shot into quick speed. Della Street, looking behind through the rear window, said, "No one turned into the boulevard from our street, Paul."

Drake said, "I tell you they've quit. Their instructions were to shadow you as long as you didn't get suspicious. The minute you got suspicious, they were to quit."

Mason said, "Okay, Paul. Show a little speed. Stop at the first store you see that will be selling flashlights. I want to get a couple of five-cell lights."

"I have one pretty good flashlight," Drake said. "It's only three cells, but . . ."

"We'll use that," Mason said, "and also get a couple of bigger ones."

Five minutes later, Drake found a drugstore where he was able to get the flashlights and phone his office. Another fifteen minutes found them driving past the hot-dog stand which Mae Farr had pointed out to Mason.

Mason said, "Take a run down the road half a mile, Paul, turn around and come back. Drive slowly as you go past the place. Let's see if anyone's on guard."

Drake drove down the road, turned the car in a U-turn, swung back, slowed down, and said, "Looks deserted, Perry."

"All right, stop," Mason said. "Pull well over to the side of the road. Shut off your motor. We'll listen and see if we can see or hear anyone over there."

Drake shut off the motor, pushed the lights down to dim, and the trio sat listening for several minutes.

At length Mason said, "Okay, Paul. Nothing ventured, nothing gained. You get out and you, too, Della. We'll wait for a moment when there are no cars passing. I'll throw the gun with my right hand. I'll try and keep the beam of this flashlight on it with my left hand. You folks can each hold a flashlight and try and follow the course taken by the gun."

"What's the idea?" Drake asked. "Trying to show that it would only have hit the high tension pole once out of a thousand times?"

Mason said, "No, that line isn't worth a damn in front of a jury. There's always someone among the twelve who likes to believe that the hand of an all-wise providence betrayed the criminal to his own undoing. Let him get an idea like that through his head, and he becomes a fanatic, feels that if he brings in a not-guilty verdict, he's defying providence. No, Paul, I just want to see how far I can throw the gun."

"Well," Drake said, "here's a good time as soon as that car passes."

"Okay," Mason said, looking up and down the road. "Let's get ready."

He took the gun which Drake gave him, hefted it by the barrel, flexed his arm like a baseball pitcher.

A car tore past them at high speed, vanished down the road, the sound of its tires on the pavement a high-pitched snarl.

Mason said, "Okay. Here we go. One . . . two . . . three."

The gun sailed up in the air. Mason's flashlight caught it, followed it, lost it, caught it again. Della Street's flashlight caught it and held it. Drake's light groped uncertainly for a moment, then focused on the moving object.

Together they watched it sail out across the fence over the pasture and down to the ground.

Drake said, "That was a darn good throw, Perry. I might be able to sign you up with the Coast champions—if you could keep away from murders long enough."

Mason said, "Let's go see just where it lit. Take a bearing for direction, Paul. Let's go."

Della said, "How does a lady climb over a barbed-wire fence in the presence of two gentlemen?"

"She doesn't,"Mason said. "Ladies are always lifted over."

Della laughed, put her hand on Mason's arm for support when her shoes slipped as they made their way down the steep side of the road, and they crossed the muddy ditch to the barbed-wire fence on the other side. Mason and Drake lifted her clear, swung her over the fence. They held down the top wire, stepped over, and walked across the soft, moist earth.

Mason said, "Don't use your flashlights any more than necessary. When you do, shield them the best you can."

They trudged silently for several seconds, then Drake said, "There it is, Perry, right ahead."

Mason stopped and looked the ground over. "That," he said, "is farther than I'd figured."

"It was a darn good throw," Drake said. "I couldn't do it."

Mason said, "No, but you're not an outdoor man. You don't live on a cattle ranch, ride horses, and rope cattle. This must be a good ten feet beyond that concrete pipeline."

"It is," Drake said. "What's the idea, Perry?"

Mason said, "Do you know, Paul, it's occurred to me that there are just two places that haven't been searched."

"Where?"

"One of them," Mason said, "was the drainage ditch. That ditch had some water in it. The police neglected to search it right at the start. The newspaperman found the gun there later. The other place the police didn't search is the overflow pipes on this concrete pipeline. There's water in the bottom of those big pipes."

Drake said, "It would have been expecting a lot to throw a gun and have it light ker-*plunk* right in the middle of a pipe. What's more, the police have found the gun with which the murder was committed. So why look for any more guns?"

Mason said, "Because I figure there are some."

"Well, I guess you're the only one who feels that way about it. You want to take a look down those concrete standpipes?"

"Yes."

"Just how?"

Mason said, "I don't know. I think our flashlights will penetrate enough to show whether there's anything like a gun lying at the bottom."

Drake said, "Well, there are only about three pipes that he could possibly have hit. The road makes a swing fifty yards above here. The pipeline continues to run straight."

Mason said, "Let's take a look."

The detective bent over one of the pipes. Mason walked on to the next one. Della Street turned back down the pipeline.

Mason found the big concrete pipe protruding some four feet above the ground. He leaned over, pushed his flashlight well down into the interior, and switched it on.

The beam of the light, striking the rough, white sides of the pipe, diffused into light-spray which made it hard for Mason to focus his eyes on the place where the main pencil of light entered a body of murky water.

After playing the flashlight around for a minute, he suddenly stepped back and called, in a low voice which however penetrated, "Oh, Paul, take a look at this, will you? Bring Della with you."

Mason stood by the side of the concrete pipe, his lips twisted into a faintly sardonic smile. He could hear the steps of Della Street and the detective approaching through the darkness.

"Here," he said. "Take a look at this."

Della had to raise herself on her tiptoes and prop her elbows against the edge of the pipe. Mason and the detective leaned over. Mason switched on his flashlight.

After a moment Paul Drake said, "I see it down there under the water. By George, it *is* a gun."

Della Street said nothing. Mason looked up to encounter her eyes, troubled and apprehensive.

Mason said, "Well, it looks as though I'm due to get my feet wet."

He removed shoes and socks, rolled up his pants, and said, "I can't get out, Paul, unless you lean over and give me your hand. Let's make sure you can make it."

Drake leaned over and down the side of the concrete.

Della said, "I can hold his legs."

"You may have to at that," Drake said.

Mason said, "I don't want to scratch my bare feet. Ease me down as much as you can, Paul."

He clasped the detective's right forearm, holding it around the wrist with both of his hands. Drake, with his left arm and leg clinging to the edge of the pipe, lowered Mason down into the murky water.

"Brr-r-r-r," Mason exclaimed. "This water feels almost freezing."

A moment later he let go his hold, dropped a few inches, then, assuming almost a sitting posture, groped with his hand down in the water.

"Here it is," he said.

He brought up a gun, his bent, right index finger sticking through the trigger guard. Gently, he sloshed it back and forth in the water, getting the mud removed from the metal.

Taking his flashlight from his coat pocket and flashing the beam on the gun, he said, "This is a Colt thirty-eight special on a forty-four frame. Okay, Paul, give me a hand up."

Drake said, "Unless you planted that gun sometime this afternoon, this is the damnedest coincidence I ever heard of."

"No coincidence to it," Mason said, as he put the gun into one pocket of his coat and the flashlight in the other. "These pipes are arranged at just about the distance a good strong man would heave a gun. They're not very far apart. At least three of them are within a throwing radius. The pipes are about four and a half or five feet in diameter. Reduce that into square feet, and you'll see that it's not at all unreasonable to suppose the gun would hit one of these pipes—oh, say, once out of five."

Drake stretched down his right arm, braced himself with his left. Mason seized the hanging wrist, and, by the joint efforts of Della Street and the detective, was pulled up to a point where he could climb over the edge of the concrete pipe.

"Gosh," he said, "a guy jumping down there without friends to help him would be up against it."

Gathered around the outside of the pipe, they inspected the gun.

"What are you going to do with it?" asked Drake.

Mason said, "That's the problem." He swung out the cylinder and said, "Six shells, none of them fired."

"Can't you notify the police?" Della asked.

"And have them say I'd planted the gun?"

"You think this is Anders' gun, Perry?" Drake inquired.

"Sure, it's the sort of gun he'd carry. It's the one he threw away."

"Then how did the murder gun get there?"

Mason shrugged his shoulders.

Della started to say something, then checked herself.

Drake said, "Gosh, Perry, there's nothing you *can* do. If you turn this gun in, they'll claim you planted it. If you drop it back in the pipe, you can't get the police to do any more searching. They've found the gun they want, and even if someone did find this gun, they'd claim it had been taken out and planted long after the murder."

Mason took a handkerchief from his pocket and carefully folded it around the gun to dry it off.

Out on the highway a car swerved violently with the sound of screaming tires. Mason, looking musingly at the highway, said, "Now what the devil do you suppose scared *that* driver?"

Della said quietly, "I think there's a car parked without lights, Chief. I had just a glimpse of it when the headlights of that automobile picked it up."

"Right on the highway?" Mason asked.

"No, off to the side, but the driver evidently didn't see it until he was right on top of it, and then got frightened."

Drake said, "Let's get out of here, Perry."

"Just a minute," Mason said. "I want to get the numbers on this gun."

Holding the gun in his handkerchief, he held the flashlight on the numbers and read them off to Della Street, who jotted them down.

Drake said, "We could all of us testify to the finding of the gun."

Mason shook his head. "It wouldn't do a damn bit of good," he said. "Holcomb would still think I'd planted it. Anyway, I'm satisfied in my own mind."

"What are you going to do with the thing, Perry?"

"Drop it back into the pipe," Mason said.

He extended his hand over the opening of the concrete pipe, holding the gun by the trigger guard.

Suddenly a blinding light bathed them with white brilliance, etching their figures against the black background of the night shadows. A voice from the darkness said, "Hold it. Stay just as you are."

Mason remained motionless.

The authoritative voice said, "Get that gun, Jim, before he drops it."

Dim shadowy figures, moving behind the shaft of bright light, converged on the group gathered around the pipe. The beams of individual flashlights crisscrossed to converge upon the motionless figure of Perry Mason. A man ran into the cone-shaped shaft of the light, the glare illuminating his set profile, reflecting from the gold shield which was pinned to his coat. "Don't make a move," he warned.

He grabbed the gun from Mason's hand.

Drake said, "What's the idea?"

Della turned so that her eyes were shielded from the glare. Sergeant Holcomb ran into the area of illumination. "You're under arrest," he said.

Mason said, "What's the charge, Sergeant?"

"Lower that searchlight," Sergeant Holcomb ordered.

The beam of the searchlight dropped so that its glare was not in their eyes.

"Compounding a felony," Sergeant Holcomb said.

"Doing what?" Mason asked.

"Planting evidence."

"We weren't planting anything," Mason said. "We found this gun in the pipe."

"Yeah. I know," Holcomb said.

Mason said, "I'm telling you. Suit yourself, Sergeant. Don't say I haven't warned you."

"You're in a hell of a position to give anyone a warning," Sergeant Holcomb said.

Mason shrugged his shoulders.

"What's that other gun?" Sergeant Holcomb asked Paul Drake.

"A gun we used for an experiment," Drake said. "Mason wanted to see how far he could throw it."

"Give it here," Sergeant Holcomb ordered.

Drake passed over the gun.

"Thought you were pretty smart, didn't you, Mason?" Holcomb said.

Mason glanced across to Sergeant Holcomb's triumphant face. "If the term is relative," he said, "the answer is 'yes.' "

Holcomb said, "None of your wisecracks, Mason. Save those for the judge."

"I will," Mason assured him.

Holcomb said, "Here, boys, put a string around this gun for identification. And keep it separate from the other one until we all get back to headquarters and label them for exhibit."

Mason, propping himself against the water pipe, casually dried his feet with his pocket handkerchief, put on his socks and shoes.

Sergeant Holcomb said, "We figured you'd be down here just as soon as you thought you'd ditched the shadows. We didn't miss it far, did we, Mason?"

Mason said nothing.

Drake said, "Look here. All three of us can testify that that gun was in that pipe lying under the water."

"Sure it was," Holcomb said. "Who put it there? Perry Mason."

Mason finished tying his shoelace, stretched and yawned, then said to Drake, "Well, there's no use sticking around here, Paul."

Sergeant Holcomb said, "I guess you didn't hear me say you were under arrest."

"I heard you," Mason said, "but the words don't mean anything. If you've been watching this place, you saw what happened. You saw me go down inside that pipe and pull out the gun."

"A gun you'd planted," Sergeant Holcomb said.

"Any evidence of that?" Mason asked.

"I don't need any. You were getting ready to drop the gun back down the pipe when we stopped you."

"Too bad you stopped me then," Mason said casually, "if you wanted to make out any sort of a case."

He turned away from Sergeant Holcomb and started toward the road. "Come on, folks, let's go."

For a moment Sergeant Holcomb stood undecided, then he said, "I'll let you go this time, Mason, but you won't get far."

Mason flung back over his shoulder, "I haven't far to go, Sergeant."

Della Street and Paul Drake exchanged glances, then followed the lawyer. A group of officers around the concrete pipe stood still while Mason, Drake, and Della, lighting their way with flashlights, crossed the slippery field in silence.

"Over the fence she goes," Mason said to Drake.

They lifted Della over the fence. Mason and Drake climbed over.

Drake said to Mason, "I don't like this, Perry. I think we should have stuck around. You can't tell what they'll do."

Mason said, "I don't give a damn what they do. When is your man due to telephone in from Eversel's place, Paul?"

"About twenty minutes from now."

"Let's get to a telephone," Mason said.

"You want to go toward Eversel's?" Drake asked.

"Yes," Mason said, "and when your man telephones, tell him that we want to talk with him. We'll drive out to the grounds, and he can arrange to meet us."

They drove silently for several minutes, then Drake said, "Look here, Perry. How much of a spot are we in?"

Mason grinned and said, "We'll get some newspaper notoriety. You can trust Sergeant Holcomb for that."

"And then what?"

"That'll be all," Mason said.

"You mean they won't do anything about planting evidence?"

"We didn't plant any, did we?"

"No, but that isn't going to keep them from trying to do something about it."

Mason said, "Forget it."

Della said to Paul Drake, "Don't you get the sketch, Paul? He knew that those officers were going to be there."

Drake took his eyes from the road to stare at the lawyer. "Did you, Perry?"

"Well," Mason admitted, "when we started out toward the harbor and ditched the follow car, I had an idea Sergeant Holcomb might think we were headed toward that field. I didn't know just what sort of reception he'd plan for us."

"But why stick your head into a lion's mouth?" Drake asked.

"How else would you have gotten the police to consider the possibility that there was more than one gun?"

"Did you know that gun was there, Perry?"

"I didn't *know* it was there. I thought it *might* be there."

Drake said, "Well, that's a load off my mind. I thought they'd caught you off first base."

"They did," Mason said with a chuckle, "and so we're going to run to second."

"And what'll happen if they throw the ball to second?"

"Then we'll steal third," Mason said.

Drake sighed. "An optimist like you has no business playing baseball," he said, and devoted his attention to driving the car.

Mason consulted his wristwatch from time to time. At length he said, "How about this little roadhouse café, Paul? It looks as though they'd have a telephone."

Drake slowed the car and swung it from the highway to the graveled driveway beneath the red glare of the neon sign. "Yes," he said, "they have a public phone. There's a sign."

Mason turned to Della in the back seat. "How about a bowl of hot soup, Della?" he asked.

"It would go fine," she admitted.

Mason said, "Let's eat. If you get your man on the phone, Paul, hold him on the line, find out who's home down at the estate."

"Okay," Drake said.

They entered the restaurant, seated themselves at a table for four, and ordered hot soup and coffee. Paul Drake had a hamburger in addition.

Mason grinned and said, "Eating our dinner on the progressive installment plan."

"I'm loading up with grub," Drake admitted, "on the theory that jail fodder won't agree with me."

"They say you get accustomed to it after a while," Mason observed cheerfully.

"Yes, I know. The first eight or ten years are the hardest."

When Drake was halfway through his hamburger, Mason, consulting his wristwatch, said, "Well, Paul, just to be safe, you'd better get on the telephone and hold the line to your office."

Drake nodded, scraped back his chair, entered the telephone booth, and remained closeted for some three minutes, then opened the door and beckoned to Mason.

The lawyer crossed over to him.

"My man's on the line," Drake said. "The servants are out again. The gardener's gone to bed. My man says we can drive out and he'll meet us at the gates."

"You know the way?" Mason asked.

"Yes."

Mason said, "Okay, let's go."

"It'll take us about twenty minutes to get out there," Drake said into the telephone. "You'd better be there waiting."

He hung up the telephone and turned to Mason. "Of course, Perry," he said, "if anything happens and our man gets caught, it spoils the perfectly swell connection. There's not one chance in a thousand I could get another operative planted in time to do us any good."

"I know," Mason said, "but it's a chance I have to take. Fortunately I like to take chances."

Drake said lugubriously, "I'll say you do."

Mason paid the check. When they were once more on the road, Drake asked, "Exactly what are your plans, Perry? Not that I want to interfere, but in case you expect police officers to be there, I'd like to know about it in advance. My heart won't stand many more of those little surprises."

"Oh, this is all right," Mason said cheerfully. "I don't think the officers will follow us any more tonight. The worst we can expect now is to be arrested for burglary."

"Perry!" Drake exclaimed. "You're not going to try to get in that house?"

"I am if I can make it," Mason said.

"Good Lord, why?"

Mason said, "We've overlooked one of the most significant things in the entire case."

"What do you mean, Perry?"

"No one heard the shot."

"Well, what if they didn't? The man was shot. His body shows that, and Mae Farr's statement shows it."

Mason said, "Did it ever occur to you, Paul, that if the shot was fired just at the moment when Hal Anders was dunking in the waters of the bay, it was timed to a split second?"

"Well, it was, wasn't it?"

Mason said, "I don't think so. I don't think there was any shot."

Drake slapped on the brakes so that he could turn to stare incredulously at the lawyer without wrecking the car. "You don't what?" he exclaimed.

"Don't think there was any shot," Mason said.

"Then Mae Farr is lying."

"Not necessarily."

"What do you think happened?"

Mason said, "I'll tell you more about that when I've indulged in a little high-class housebreaking."

Drake groaned and said, "Gosh, Perry, I should have known better."

"*You* don't need to go any farther than the gate," Mason said.

"That's far enough," Drake said, and then, after a moment, added, "it's too damn far."

Mason settled back against the cushions, his eyes staring steadily through the windshield at the lighted ribbon of highway which flowed smoothly toward them. Della Street, in the back seat, kept her own counsel, glancing from time to time at the back of Mason's head, studying the set of his shoulders, studying what she could see of the angle of his jaw. Drake, driving the automobile carefully, was given to periods of contemplation during which he would slow the car appreciably, then, catching himself, would push the speedometer needle up another ten or fifteen miles an hour.

Mason gave no sign that he noticed the irregularities of the driving, and Della surrounded herself with an observant, self-effacing silence.

Drake turned to the right from the main highway, drove several miles, then turned left, following a road which snaked its way up the side of a sharp headland. To the left could be seen the glittering lights of a city and roads studded with automobile headlights. To the right, occasional glimpses of moonlit water finally resolved themselves into a magnificent view of the ocean as the road straightened out on the relatively level ground at the top of the headland.

Drake slowed the car until it was running at a scant twenty-five miles an hour. He said, "There's a turnoff right around here some-place. It—." He interrupted himself to swing the wheel sharply to the left, and the car climbed a short pitch to disclose the gables of a house silhouetted against the sky, a long sweep of hedge, and, after a few moments, in front of the headlights the forbidding barrier of locked iron gates crossing a driveway.

Drake switched off the headlights, turned on the dome light, and said, "Well, here we are."

"Your man's supposed to be here?" Mason asked.

"Yes," Drake said. "Here he is now."

A lighted cigarette glowed as a red coal in the darkness. A moment later a man in rough clothes and with a trace of a Scottish accent said, "You're a bit late."

"The coast all clear?" Drake asked.

"Yes."

Mason took a good look at the man's face, then switched out the dome light as Drake introduced Della Street and the lawyer.

"Exactly what was it you wanted to know?" the man asked.

Mason said quietly, "I want to get in the house, MacGregor."

There was a moment's stiff, uncomfortable silence, then the operative said, "I'm afraid that's going to be a pretty tough order."

"How tough?" Mason asked.

"Plenty tough. Old Angus goes to bed early, but he always reads for an hour or two before he turns out the light. He's a light sleeper."

"Where does he sleep?"

"In a cottage down near the hangar."

"You have a key to the gate?" Mason asked.

"Gosh, no. I'm just an assistant to the gardener. I sleep in a cubby-hole in the basement."

"The door from the basement to the other part of the house un-locked?" Mason asked.

"I could get in. Of course, I'd be fired if I were caught. Then I could either produce my credentials and show I was a private detective on a job, or be sent to jail as a burglar."

"Do you know how long they're going to be gone?"

"The servants won't be back until one or two o'clock. The chauffeur took them to see a picture show in town. God knows when Eversel will show up."

"Doesn't he usually send the servants away when he plans on spending the night elsewhere?"

"He didn't the other night," MacGregor said. "He sent them away to get rid of them."

Mason grinned and said, "Well, let's take a chance."

"You can't leave the car there," MacGregor said, "and I can't get it through the gates. You'll have to drive it back down to the main road and park it."

"I'll take it down," Drake said.

"And stay in it?" Mason asked.

Drake took a deep breath. "Hell, no, Perry," he said. "I'll stay with you. I don't want to, but you may need my moral support."

Mason glanced inquiringly at Della Street. By way of answer, she opened the door and slipped out of the car to stand by the driveway. "We'll wait for you here, Paul," she said.

Mason said, "Look here, Della. I don't know just what I'm getting into. This may be embarrassing, and it may be dangerous."

"I know," she said quietly, in a tone which completely disposed of the discussion.

Drake slipped the car into reverse. Mason joined Della Street at the driveway, quietly closed the door. "Don't make any more noise than necessary, Paul," he said.

"It's all right," MacGregor told him. "Lots of cars come up here on moonlit nights—not an awful lot, but enough so Angus gets accustomed to hearing them turn back when they come to the locked gates."

Abruptly Mason signaled Paul Drake, walked over to stand near the front left-hand window of the car. "On second thought, Paul," he said, "I think you'd better stay with the car, and you'd better take Della with you."

Della Street quietly shook her head.

"Why not?" Mason asked.

"You may need a witness," she said. "I'm going to stay with you."

Mason said to Drake, "Go back to the main highway, drive about three hundred yards up the road, stop the car, turn out the lights, and wait until you hear from me. If things go all right, I'll join you inside of half an hour. If, at the end of half an hour, you haven't heard from me, beat it back to town."

"If I can help, Perry," the detective said, "I want to. . . ."

"No," Mason told him. "Go on. Beat it. I don't know just what we're getting into. MacGregor's here. He can stand by if it comes to a showdown. You'd better keep on the sidelines, Paul, and get started. Time's precious."

"Okay," Drake said, "thirty minutes," and drove away.

Mason turned to MacGregor. "Let's go," he said.

"We'll work through an opening in the hedge down here about twenty yards," he said. "I'll lead the way."

Casting black, grotesque shadows in the moonlight, the three moved quietly along the hedge. MacGregor led the way through the opening. Inside the grounds, he paused to listen, then whispered, "Just where do you want to go?"

"The room that Eversel went to when he returned to the house," Mason said. "Paul Drake told me it was a darkroom."

"It is. It wasn't built as a darkroom, but it's been fixed over. He has a lot of equipment there, does quite a bit of amateur photography."

"Let's go," Mason said.

"Do you want me to take you all the way up?"

"Yes."

MacGregor said, "Be as quiet as possible. If we use flashlights, cover them with your hand and let as much light as you need work out through your spread fingers. Angus might see lights shining on the windows."

"All right," Mason said. "Let's go."

They crossed the moonlit yard, entered a basement door. Mac-Gregor led the way across the cement floor to a flight of stairs. The door at the head of the stairs was unlocked. They entered a back hallway, passed through a kitchen, and reached a flight of stairs near the back of the house. MacGregor piloted them to an upper corridor and down the corridor to a door. "That," he said, "is the room. Don't turn on any lights."

"We won't," Mason promised.

"Where," MacGregor asked, "do you want me?"

"Someplace on the lower floor," Mason said, "where you can keep watch but can manage to get back to your room in case anything happens. If anyone drives through the gate, slam the nearest door, and slam it hard, then go back to your room. Keep your ears open. If you hear any commotion, come running. Keep in the character of a servant who has been asleep, was wakened by the commotion, and is loyal to his employer, unless I give you a signal. In that case, come out in the open and take orders from me."

"Okay," MacGregor said quietly. "I'll slam that kitchen door. You can hear that from here if you are listening."

"We'll listen," Mason said.

MacGregor retraced his steps down the hallway. Mason turned the knob of the door and entered the room.

It had evidently been a small bedroom at one time. Now it had been completely done over. The windows were darkened. A battery of light switches led to safelights, enlarging cameras, wired printing boxes, and electrical washers. Shelves were well filled with photographic supplies. A long sink ran the entire length of the room, divided into various tanks for developing, printing, and washing. A long shelf held graduates and photographic chemicals.

Mason said quietly, "I think we can turn on a light here, Della. The room is lightproof."

He experimented with the switches, finally located one which controlled a shielded white light.

"What," she asked, "are you looking for, Chief?"

Mason said, "I think they came here to develop a photograph. After that photograph was developed, it was probably printed in an enlarging camera. We'll look around and see what we can find."

Della Street said, "Here is a file of negatives, Chief."

"How are they listed?" Mason asked. "By dates or subjects?"

"Subjects," she said, "alphabetical order."

Mason said, "This room is too darned orderly to be a good darkroom. Look around for a wastebasket, Della. Hang it, it doesn't look as though the place had been used for a month, and yet they must have developed a picture here."

Della said, "You don't think Eversel killed him, do you?"

"I don't know," Mason said.

"I've been wondering about that Farr woman," she said. "Do you believe her story, Chief?"

Mason said, "There's no particular reason why I should. She first came to the office with a lie which she had ingeniously worked out—but she's our client, Della. You can't keep clients from lying, but that doesn't relieve you of your responsibility to see they get a square deal."

"Do you think she . . ."

"That she what?" Mason asked as her voice trailed away into silence.

"Oh, I don't know," Della said. "Forget it. We'll see what we can find here. I can talk about Mae Farr later."

Mason said, "We're licked before we start. Hang it, I never saw such an orderly darkroom."

"We might try running through those negative files," she said.

"Yes, we could," Mason agreed dubiously. "I don't think we'd get anywhere."

"What's that big thing that looks like a toy frieght car?" Della Street asked.

"Horizontal enlarging camera," Mason said, "nine-inch condensers, takes up to a five-by-seven negative. That screen over there on the track holds the enlarging paper. Let's find the switch for that enlarger, Della. I want to see about how much of a blowup there was on the last negative in there."

Mason clicked switches near the work shelf, turning on first a red light in a printing box, then a white light, then, on his third attempt, clicking the huge bulb of the enlarger into light.

Della Street gave a quick, involuntary gasp.

On the white surface of the easel which held the enlarging paper was thrown the image of an enlarged negative, held in the big enlarging camera. Save for the fact that blacks and whites were reversed, it was as though they stood looking down through the skylight of a yacht into a cabin beneath.

A man, with his face half turned as though he had twisted it suddenly to look upward, was struggling with a woman whose face was concealed from the camera. Much of her body was shielded by the man's body. Her arms and legs showed in arrested motion as though the figures had suddenly been frozen into immobility.

Mason said, "That's it, Della."

"I don't understand, Chief."

Mason said, "Wentworth wasn't shot when he was struggling with Mae Farr. What she saw wasn't the flash of a shot, but the flash of a bulb that was synchronized with the shutter of a camera. Those flash bulbs are instantaneous, just a quick burst of light synchronized to the fraction of a second with a camera shutter."

"Then you mean . . ."

"That Eversel took that photograph," Mason said. "You can figure for whom he took it and what he wanted with it."

"And that's why no one heard the shot?"

"Yes."

"Did you know that in advance, Chief?"

"I suspected it," Mason said. "Gosh, I'd like to mix up some developer, put in a sheet of bromide paper, and pull a print of that negative. We could—"

His words were interrupted by the reverberating boom of a slamming door on the lower floor.

Mason looked at Della Street. "In case you don't know it," he said quietly, "this is a felony."

"Of course I know it," she said. "What do you think I've been working in a law office for?"

Mason grinned, pulled up the slide in the enlarging camera, took out the negative holder, removed the negative, and slipped it in his pocket. He switched out the lights and said, "Come on. Let's go."

They ran on tiptoe down the corridor to the back stairs, down the back stairs and through the kitchen to the basement.

MacGregor was waiting for them at the foot of the stairs. "Eversel just drove into the garage," he said quietly.

"Can you get Miss Street out of the grounds?" Mason asked.

"I don't know," MacGregor said. "I can if something occupies his attention. If he happens to be looking out of the window, we're sunk— it's moonlight, you know."

Mason slipped the negative from his pocket. "Let me have your purse, Della."

She gave him her purse. Mason slipped the negative between the leaves of the small notebook which she carried in the purse. "Think you know what to do with this?" he asked.

"The thing you said you'd like to do up there?"

"Yes. You and Paul Drake beat it. Get that done on the largest scale possible. I'll join you in town."

"What are you going to do?" she asked.

"Pay a social call," he said. "I'll get back."

Mason nodded to MacGregor.

MacGregor led them out of the basement door. Mason walked quietly around the house. MacGregor waited for his signal to cross the yard.

Lights blazed on in the front of the house. Mason, walking around the corner, signaled MacGregor, climbed the front steps, and rang the bell.

For a moment there was no response, then Mason heard the sound of quick steps in the hallway. He stepped back a few paces to look out across the moonlit yard. He glimpsed two fleeting shadows as Mac-Gregor and Della Street made a dash for the break in the hedge. He glanced back toward the ocean. In a low, white building at the far end of the garage he saw lights come on, then go off. A moment later he heard the sound of a door rolling back on a steel track.

Abruptly the porch light flooded him with brilliance. A wicket in the front door swung back. Mason was conscious of a pair of intense eyes staring steadily at him. A voice, ominously calm, said, "Who are you and what do you want?"

"My name's Mason," the lawyer said. "I want to talk with you."

"Are you Perry Mason, the lawyer?"

"Yes."

"What do you want to talk with me about?"

"About Penn Wentworth."

"I don't care to discuss him with you."

Mason said, "I think you do."

"Well, I don't," the voice said. "This is private property. I don't allow trespassers. I'll give you thirty seconds to get started for the gate. At the end of that time, I'll telephone the police."

The lights on the porch switched out. After a moment the lights in the front of the house went out. Mason was left standing on the front porch in the moonlight.

"Very well," Mason said. He turned, walked down the front steps, but instead of turning to the right toward the gate, turned to the left and strode rapidly toward the hangar.

He was almost at the door of the hangar when he heard the slam of a door in the house behind him and running steps on the graveled walk.

Mason entered the hangar. His flashlight explored the interior, showed a trim, white amphibian plane. Seated in the cabin was a beautiful, olive-skinned woman with dark eyes.

Mason climbed up on the step of the plane and opened the cabin door.

The woman's voice said reproachfully, "You blinded me with that flashlight, dear."

Mason entered the cabin. "I'm sorry, Mrs. Wentworth," he said.

At the sound of his voice, she stiffened to attention. Mason saw her lips twitch with emotion. The cabin door jerked open, and the voice of Eversel behind him said, "Get the hell out of here."

Mason calmly sat down in one of the seats.

Eversel said, "Get the hell out."

Juanita Wentworth switched on the lights in the plane, illuminating the cabin, showing Eversel, a bronzed, young giant with reddish-brown, excitable eyes, holding a gun in his right hand.

Mason said, "Better put away the gun, Eversel. Don't you think we've had enough gun play?"

Eversel said, "This is my property. I'm ordering you out and off. If you don't go, I'll treat you as I would any other trespasser."

"I wouldn't advise you to," Mason said. "You're in deep enough already. A witness has identified you as the man who climbed aboard Wentworth's yacht just before the shooting."

He settled back in the seat.

"That's a lie," Eversel said.

Mason shrugged his shoulders.

Juanita Wentworth said, "Please, Sidney—no trouble."

After a moment Eversel asked, "What do you want?"

"A complete statement," Mason said, "admitting that you were the one who boarded the *Pennwent* while Mae Farr was struggling with Wentworth in the cabin."

"I wasn't there," Eversel said.

Mason arched his eyebrows. "After that, you took this airplane and flew to San Diego."

"What if I did? This is a private plane. I go where I damn please."

"An amphibian, I notice," Mason said casually. "While you were flying to San Diego, did you, perhaps, happen to fly over the *Pennwent* and look down into the lighted interior of the cabin?"

"What the devil are you talking about?"

"Just asking questions," Mason said.

"Don't do it. It isn't healthy."

Mason said conversationally, "Do you know, Eversel, I have a peculiar idea about what happened aboard that yacht. You're quite an amateur photographer. It's a funny thing about that shot. No one heard it."

"Well, what's strange about that?" Eversel asked belligerently. "People in the other boats were making whoopee. If they heard a noise, they'd take it as the backfire of a truck or a boat engine."

Mason said, "Do you know, Eversel, I was wondering if it couldn't have been a flashlight bulb that Mae Farr thought was a shot. Wentworth knew he was trapped as soon as the picture was taken. He ran back to the after cabin and held the door tightly shut while he was getting into his clothes. He thought perhaps it was a raid."

Eversel said, "I suppose you'd like to cook up some cock-and-bull story like that in order to get your client, Mae Farr, acquitted of murder."

"She's a little adventuress," Mrs. Wentworth said.

"It was just an idea I had," Mason observed almost apologetically.

"Well, it's an idea that didn't pan out," Eversel said sharply, "and if you make any insinuations like that in court, I'll sue you for slander."

"Of course," Mason went on conversationally, "you hoped that as soon as Wentworth realized the full import of what had happened, he would decide to get in touch with his estranged wife and meet her terms on a property settlement. He knew that photograph would put him in rather a bad light."

"You're crazy," Eversel said.

"You and Mrs. Wentworth wanted to get married," Mason said. "You'd been just a little too eager. Wentworth wouldn't let his wife have an uncontested divorce. You were pretty desperate. You couldn't afford to have your name dragged into a scandal."

"I tell you you're crazy."

Mason went on calmly, "I don't think it was only a question of money. It was probably also a question of jealousy on Wentworth's part. He was fascinated by the woman he had married and who had grown to despise him." The lawyer turned to Mrs. Wentworth and made a little bow. "Seeing Mrs. Wentworth, one can well appreciate how he felt."

Eversel said, "You're not only crazy, but you're insulting. By God, I won't stand for it."

Mason said, "The preliminary hearing is tomorrow morning. Through an understanding with the justice of the peace, witnesses whom I think important are subpoenaed."

"Juanita is going to be there," Eversel said.

"So I understand," Mason observed, taking a folded subpoena from his pocket and extending it to Eversel, "and so are you, Eversel."

Eversel dashed the subpoena from the lawyer's hand to the floor. "Not by a damn sight," he said.

Mason shrugged his shoulders and said, "Suit yourself. You can figure whether it's better for you to be there and answer routine questions, or to make yourself conspicuous by your absence and force the Justice to take proceedings to enforce your attendance."

"This is outrageous," Eversel stormed. "It's the work of a shyster criminal lawyer."

Mrs. Wentworth said, "Let me talk with him, Sidney. Please," and then to Perry Mason, "What is it you want, Mr. Mason?"

"I want a square deal for my client," Mason said. "I want you to attend that preliminary hearing and tell the truth."

"What do you mean by the truth?"

"That it wasn't a shot which was fired when Mae Farr was aboard the yacht, it was the taking of a flashlight photograph."

"By whom?" Mrs. Wentworth asked.

Eversel said, "Juanita, don't—"

"Please, Sidney," she interrupted.

Mason said, "By Eversel."

She said, "Mr. Eversel holds several important positions. He's on the board of directors of a bank, a trust company, and other important corporations. He simply can't afford to have any scandal connected with his name."

"Taking a picture doesn't necessarily mean a scandal," Mason said.

"It would in this instance."

"Was fear of scandal," Mason asked, "the hold that Wentworth had over you?"

She met his eyes steadily and said, "Yes."

"And what were you holding out for?"

She said calmly, "Money for my parents. Sidney offered . . . I could have secured it elsewhere, but I was just as obstinate as Penn was.

My parents lived on a large hacienda in Mexico. The government took their land and gave it to the peons. They were impoverished. It was only fair that Penn should make some financial settlement. He took an unfair advantage by threatening to drag Sidney's name into the case. I knew Sidney couldn't afford to have the publicity, and Penn knew it too. Penn threatened to sue Sidney for alienation of affections. I knew how to handle Penn. There was only one way. I had to fight him and master him. Otherwise, there would never have been any peace for us."

"How about Eversel?" Mason asked Mrs. Wentworth. "How did he feel about it?"

"He was impulsive," she said. "He was . . ."

"Juanita, please don't drag me into this," Eversel said. "He's a shrewd lawyer, and he's just trapping you."

"The truth can't hurt us," she said, and then added, after a significant moment, "now."

"Were you," Mason asked, "glad that your husband was killed?"

"I am not glad to have anyone killed."

"You were relieved?"

She met his eyes and said, "Naturally. It was a shock to me of course. There was much about Penn that was good, and a lot more that was all bad. He desired to dominate people. He wanted to get them in his clutches and in his power. He was a brute—particularly as far as women are concerned."

Mason said, "Well, there's your subpoena, Eversel. You can't say I didn't give you a chance to play fair. If you're going anywhere, you can drop me at an airport where I can pick up a car, and," Mason added with a smile, "when I say drop me, I use the term figuratively."

Eversel said, "To hell with you. You can go back the way you came."

Mason said, "My friends have left. I thought I might have to wait all night to serve the subpoena."

Eversel eyed him suspiciously.

Mrs. Wentworth said, "Please, Sidney. We could leave him in Los Angeles. You don't want to go away and leave him here, do you?"

That idea appeared suddenly disquieting to Eversel.

"Please," Juanita Wentworth asked, flashing him a glance from her limpid, dark eyes. "This is once, Sidney, when I think I know best."

Eversel hesitated a moment, then shoved his gun into a hip pocket, moved over to the pilot's seat in the plane, fastened the seat belt in sulky silence, and operated the starting mechanism which sent the motor roaring into life. He taxied out to the level field and sat grimly silent while he warmed up the motor of the plane.

Mrs. Wentworth, raising her voice so it could be heard above the sound of the motor, said, "Don't you think, Mr. Mason, it would be better for your client to tell the truth and face the consequences instead of trying to drag us into it?"

Mason, pushing his hands down deep in his trouser pockets, sunk his chin on his chest and stared moodily at the floor of the plane. "That," he said musingly, "is something that's been running through my own mind."

Chapter Twelve

Daylight found Mason sitting in the narrow confines of Paul Drake's private office, studying huge, glossy paper enlargements with a magnifying glass.

Drake, seated across the desk, chewed gum nervously. His eyes surveyed the lawyer speculatively. "That," he said, "was the biggest enlargement we could make and still keep any detail in the print. As it is, you'll notice it shows considerable grain. The negative was wire-sharp and fine-grained, but we've blown it up to a point where it commences to get fuzzy. Each one of those prints represents only a quarter of the negative."

"I understand," Mason said, not looking up, but continuing his patient search with the magnifying glass.

"And this other one, the one my pals slipped me," Drake said, "is an eleven-by-fourteen enlargement, from the negative taken after the *Pennwent* was brought into port. I was lucky to get that print. I can get bigger enlargements, but it will take time and a little manipulation."

"Time," Mason said, "is the one thing we haven't got. That preliminary hearing is called for ten o'clock this morning."

"Exactly what," Drake asked, "are you looking for, Perry?"

Mason said, "I'm looking for a lucky break."

"What do you mean?"

"I'm hoping to find something in one photograph which isn't in the other."

"You mean the figures, a person . . ."

"No," Mason said, "some significant difference in the furniture. For instance, look at this cigarette tray. In the picture Eversel took, it has half a dozen cigarette stubs in it. In this picture taken after the body was discovered, there are only two."

"Well?" Drake asked. "What's wrong with that?"

Mason shook his head. "A person committing a murder," he said, "doesn't bother to tidy up the place and empty the ashtrays. If he should do that for any reason, he doesn't stick around to smoke two cigarettes."

Drake frowned. "Exactly what are you getting at, Perry?" he asked.

Mason said. "I'm darned if I know exactly, Paul, but I'm working on the theory of elimination. I'd like to find something to substantiate my idea. If I could—. Hello, what's this?"

His magnifying glass remained stationary over a section of one of the enlargements.

Outside, the first rays of sunlight tinted the tops of the office buildings, made the electric light in Drake's office seem artificial and unreal. The morning light, pouring through the window, showed Mason's skin oily with fatigue, brought into prominence the tips of stubble which had grown out on his chin during the last twenty-four hours.

"What is it?" Drake asked.

Mason passed the photograph across to him, indicated a section with his finger, and said, "Take a look, Paul."

Drake studied it through the magnifying glass and said, "Gosh, Perry, it doesn't look like anything to me. It's something round in a case, some kind of a rare coin, I suppose. Wentworth, you know, was quite a collector."

"Uh huh," Mason said. "Let's assume that it is a coin. It isn't so much what the object is as where it went. You'll notice that it doesn't appear in this other photograph, yet it was up on the shelf, and there's something else across the top of that case."

"It looks like a cartridge," Drake said, studying it carefully.

"It does," Mason said, "but I don't think it is a cartridge. Remember, Paul, this picture was taken by a flashlight which makes the lighting rather harsh, and we've enlarged it from rather a small negative. Even so, that could hardly be a revolver cartridge. It would have to be a rifle cartridge, judging from its length."

"Well, why not?" Drake asked.

"The modern rifle," Mason said, "uses a bottleneck cartridge. This is straight across like a revolver shell."

"Couldn't a revolver cartridge be that long?" Drake asked.

"Yes," Mason said, "I guess it could, but—that's rather a big coin, Paul. I wish we could make out some of the details on it."

"You can only get a line here and there," Drake said, "not enough to tell what kind of a coin it is."

Mason narrowed his eyes. "That coin," he said, "must mean something. One thing's certain, Paul. Wentworth wasn't killed at the time it's been generally assumed the shot was fired. He had an opportunity to dress, empty the ashtray, cast loose the lines, start the motor, and put out to sea."

Drake shook his head. "Someone else did that for him, Perry. You can't figure a man being killed on the high seas on a yacht without anyone else being around—not without some evidences of a struggle. A man certainly isn't going to let someone else board his yacht, and . . ."

"Not strangers," Mason said. "A friend might be different."

"Well," Drake said, "even supposing you're right, I don't see what this coin has to do with it particularly."

Mason said, "I'd like to have the *Pennwent* searched from stem to stern to see if we can find that coin."

"It's been gone over with a fine-tooth comb for fingerprints and everything else," Drake said. "The Homicide Bureau of the Police Department has inventories of everything that was found. I can find out if that coin was located."

"It should be a cinch," Mason said, "because it's evidently in a case with a hinged cover. That would mean it's a valuable coin. You can get just a hint of the design, Paul. There's something running across it, a band of crisscross lines."

"Uh huh," Drake said, "probably some sort of a coat of arms."

"It might give us a clue," Mason said thoughtfully, "if we could—"

There was a knock at the door of the offitce. Drake called, "Come in."

One of his operatives opened the door. "Want to see the papers?" he asked. "There's a lot in there about—about Mr. Mason."

Mason straightened from a contemplation of the photograph. "It'll be a change for my eyes," he said. "What do they say about me?"

"Darn near everything," the operative said with a grin. "It seems you're guilty of just about everything except murder, including bribing a witness to leave the country."

"Bribing a witness?" Mason asked.

"Yes, a girl named Hazel Tooms. It's the theory of the police that someone who wanted her out of the way gave her five hundred dollars to make a trip out of the country. She admitted that much to officers when they served her with a subpoena."

"Mention my name?" Mason asked.

"Not in so many words," the operative said.

Mason spread the paper out on the desk and read in headlines: "OFFICERS CLAIM LAWYER CAUGHT RED-HANDED—POLICE CLAIM PROMINENT ATTORNEY APPREHENDED PLANTING GUN."

Mason turned to Paul Drake with a grin. "Well, Paul," he said, "looks like we're in the news."

Drake placed his extended forefinger on a paragraph midway down the article. "Notice this," he said. " 'Grand jury subpoenas have been issued and will be served sometime today. Police have insisted that the grand jury make a sweeping investigation into the activities of a lawyer whose methods have been noted for dramatic originality rather than a strict adherence to conventional routine. It is rumored that a detective agency which subsists largely on work furnished by the attorney in question will be the subject of a sweeping investigation. If criminal charges are not brought, police intimate that they will at least take steps to prevent a renewal of the agency's license.' "

Mason grinned again at Paul Drake. "How about a little breakfast, Paul?"

Drake said, "Five minutes ago, it would have sounded swell. Right now, I'd have to choke the food down. Gosh, Perry, I hope you know the answer to *this* one."

Mason said, "I think we have enough facts to go on, Paul. What we need right now is a chance to do a little thinking. I'm going to a

Turkish bath, get a shave, some breakfast, and I'll meet you at the preliminary hearing."

"What'll happen there?" Drake asked.

Mason said, "One thing about the justice of the peace, Paul. Emil Scanlon is fair. He doesn't like to have cases tried in the newspapers. In view of these accusations, he'll give me every chance to examine witnesses."

"What'll he do with the district attorney?" Drake asked.

"Give him the same chance," Mason said.

Drake ran his fingers through his hair. "And I," he announced mournfully, "am a witness. I'll have you both on my neck."

Emil Scanlon was a unique justice of the peace with an appreciation of the dramatic, a keen sense of humor, and a desire to see justice done at all costs. His basic philosophy of life made him as bigheartedly sympathetic with the living as he was scientifically detached with the dead. Taking his role of office conscientiously, he felt himself the representative of both the living and the dead.

Scanlon's first career was that of a professional baseball player of no mean ability who retired to Southern California after an injury shortened his playing days in the early twenties. Elected justice of the peace the first time he ran, he was "grandfathered" into office when California substituted municipal judges for justices of the peace in the larger cities; and even though he had no formal legal background or even a high school education, the new law permitted him to be re-elected to the office of justice of the peace year after year to the consternation of a succession of district attorneys and impatient young law school graduates whetting their teeth as defense attorneys.

Scanlon watched Mae Farr as she sat in whispered consultation with Perry Mason and decided that she was far from the cold-blooded killer the district attorney's office claimed. His knowledge of Perry Mason was founded upon various personal contacts, dramatic preliminary hearings when Mason, using a quick wit, keen logic, and unconventional methods, had sprinted first across the tape as a spectacular winner from a position hopelessly behind the field.

There was nothing in Emil Scanlon's voice or face to reflect the determination which crystallized in his mind that, even if the hearing took all night, he was going to see that the various parties had a square shake.

Mae Farr whispered her confession to Perry Mason. "I gave you a raw deal," she said. "I lied to you when I first came to your office and I've been lying to you ever since. When you didn't find Hal's gun there where he'd thrown it over the fence, I became convinced that he'd doubled back, picked up the gun, and gone down to take the *Pennwent* out to sea and sink it, taking the chance of rowing back in the little skiff Wentworth kept aboard.

"I doubled back and took Marley's cruiser and went out to pick him up."

"Find him?" Mason asked.

"No," she said. "I didn't search very long because I became convinced the Coast Guard had been notified of the killing and was looking for me."

"What made you think that?"

"A Coast Guard airplane flew over me, circled three of four times, and then went on out to sea."

"How do you know it was a Coast Guard plane?"

She thought for a moment, and said, "I don't know. I presumed it was. What other flyer would have taken such an unusual interest in a yacht? And that Tooms woman saw me when I came back with Marley's boat, and I understand Marley had a fingerprint expert go over the steering wheel and throttle and develop my fingerprints. I suppose I'm in for it now."

Hal Anders, tall, sunburned, and ill at ease, came over to Mae Farr. "I'm sorry, Mae," he said simply.

She looked at him with troubled eyes.

"The D.A. has dismissed the case against me," Anders went on. "I don't know what that means."

"It means they're going to concentrate on me," she said.

"It was my gun they found there in the pipe," Anders said. "They thought Mason had planted it, but by checking up on the numbers, they found where the sale had been made directly to me, and they uncovered some other evidence. I don't know exactly what it is, but they've dropped the charge against me."

"That," she said, "is very nice. Congratulations. You seem to have saved yourself a disagreeable experience. Thanks to the advice of your very competent and very ethical family lawyer."

"Please, Mae, don't be like that."

She turned her face away from him.

Anders, conscious that the eyes of spectators were on him, knowing that reporters with high-speed lenses were surreptitiously clicking candid-camera shots, leaned forward until his lips were close to the ears of Mae Farr and Perry Mason. "Please don't, Mae," he said, "and listen, Mae. I did one thing for you. I did this on my own without *anyone's* advice. I managed to get in touch with Hazel Tooms this morning. She won't be here. She's on a plane to Mexico where a friend has a yacht. They're going to leave at once on a cruise for—and I quote—destination unknown."

Mae Farr's expression showed utter incredulity. "You did *that*?" she asked.

Mason's eyes hardened. They surveyed Anders with cold hostility. "I presume you realize," he said, "that I'll get the blame for that."

"No, you won't," Anders said quietly. "If it comes to a showdown, *I'll* take the blame."

Scanlon said, "I've already viewed the body of the deceased. The autopsy surgeon has pointed out the course of the bullet and the cause of death. It was a gunshot wound in the head. That much of the case is so clear that we don't have to waste the doctor's time in having him come down here."

He cleared his throat, glanced from Perry Mason to Oscar Overmeyer, a deputy district attorney, and Carl Runcifer, who represented the district attorney's office. He said, "Proceedings are going to be short and informal. We're going to get at the facts. I don't want any delaying, technical objections from anyone to any of the testimony. I don't want any fancy legal arguments raised. If I think it will speed things along and help us get at the truth, I'll ask some of the questions myself. There isn't going to be any rambling cross-examination of witnesses just so the lawyers can make a showing of doing something; but if the attorneys for any of the interested parties want to ask questions purely for the purpose of clearing matters up, explaining or bringing out facts which the witnesses have neglected to state, I'm going to permit those questions."

Carl Runcifer started to make some objection to Scanlon's unorthodox procedures, but Overmeyer, who was familiar with Scanlon's temperament, pulled him back into his seat.

Judge Scanlon's clerk walked up to his informal podium and handed him a note. This gave Sidney Eversel time to march militantly over to Perry Mason. "I suppose," he said ominously, "you think you've been very, very clever."

"Now what?" Mason asked.

"I discovered the real object of your trip to my house early this morning," Eversel said. "I suppose you thought I'd keep my mouth shut and that you could blackmail me into doing almost anything you wanted in order to keep my connection with it a secret. For your information, I went at once to the police and notified the district attorney's office. I am advised then that you were guilty of burglary in taking that negative. The only thing we lack is absolute proof. Produce that negative, Mr. Perry Mason, and you'll go to jail. *That* is where I stand." He turned on his heel and walked off.

Mason said to Mae Farr, "Well, you always claimed that Anders was too conservative and wouldn't do anything without taking advice. He seems to have cut the apron strings with a very sharp pair of scissors. I'll leave you two for a few moments to fight it out."

He arose from his chair and walked back along the aisle of curious, staring spectators to engage in a whispered conference with Paul Drake and Della Street. "Called your office, Paul?"

"Yes, just a minute ago," Drake said. "I have a last-minute report, but it doesn't mean anything. I simply can't get anything on Hazel Tooms. She's apparently a playgirl who goes in for outdoor sports."

Mason said, "She told me all that herself. Where is she now, Paul?"

"She's under subpoena," Drake said, "and should be here. Good Lord, Perry, you haven't spirited her away, have you?"

Mason said, "No. Personally, I wish she were here."

"How are things looking?" Della asked in an anxious whisper.

Mason's eyes glinted with a frosty twinkle. "They look like hell, Della," he admitted. "Eversel got a burst of courage and went to the police, claimed the negative had been stolen, evidently told them all about taking the picture. That put Mae Farr right in the middle of a very hot spot. The police will now claim that she had a gun of her own, that she went back to the Yacht Club, took out Frank Marley's boat, overtook the *Pennwent,* killed Wentworth, returned to the Yacht Club, drove to the place where she'd seen Anders ditch the gun, and dropped the murder gun where it would be found as soon as the drainage waters evaporated."

"Isn't that going to make a strong case against her, Perry?" the detective asked.

"Very strong indeed," Mason said dryly. "I hadn't counted on Eversel overcoming his fear of publicity. Apparently, he's determined to get me. He reported the theft of the negative to the district attorney's office. Of course, the evidence about the taking of the picture gives them an entirely new slant on the case. They have left Anders out of it. They're concentrating on Mae Farr—and on me."

"Go to it, Chief," Della Street said. "Tear into them."

Mason grinned and said, "I don't know just how much tearing I can do. However, I have one ace up my sleeve. If I can play it at just the right time and in just the right manner, I can probably take the trick I want. If I can't, I'm hooked."

"What's the ace?" Drake asked.

"Just a hunch," Mason said. "I'm going to put a witness on the stand without knowing in advance what he's going to say. If he says the right thing, his very evident surprise will register with the J.P. Otherwise, it will look like a desperate attempt to drag a red herring across the trail."

Drake said, "Gosh, Perry, you did lay yourself wide open, going after that negative. Why the devil do you violate laws in order to get justice for your clients?"

Mason grinned and said, "I'll be damned if I know, Paul. I guess I'm just made that way. When I start unraveling a mystery, I can't seem to find a brake. Every time I put my foot down, it hits the throttle."

"I'll say it does," Drake agreed.

Della Street said calmly, "As a matter of fact, Chief, I was the one who took that negative out of the house. They can't get you for that."

Mason grinned and said, "You did it under my instructions, Della. You keep out of this."

"I will not," she retorted. "I'll take my share of the responsibility."

Emil Scanlon finished reading his note, whispered instructions to his secretary, and said, "Very well, we'll proceed with the preliminary hearing on the case of People against Mae Farr."

Oscar Overmeyer got to his feet. "May it please the Court," he said. "We understand your desire for an informal, expeditious hearing. However, within the last few hours, I may say within the last few minutes, the district attorney's office has come into possession of evidence which materially changes the entire complexion of the case.

"We are now prepared to show by witnesses that the murder did not take place as was originally supposed. In fact, we might refer to it as the case of the postponed murder. What Harold Anders really believed to have been a shot and what Mae Farr said she believed was a shot was in reality not a shot, but the explosion of a flash bulb.

"We understand, of course, that the Justice wishes to move this hearing along as fast as possible. For that reason, we call our first witness, Sidney Eversel, and call the Justice's attention to the fact that the testimony of this witness will be so pertinent, in fact I may say so spectacular, as to cause a complete change in our order of calling other witnesses."

Scanlon frowned a moment in thought, glanced surreptitiously at Perry Mason, saw no evidence of an objection, and said, "Very well, for the purpose of getting to the bottom of this case in the shortest possible time, I'll let you call Sidney Eversel."

Sidney Eversel marched forward and was sworn.

"Do you," Scanlon asked, "know anything about this murder?"

"I know this much about it," Eversel said. "I know when it was *not* committed."

"Exactly what do you know?" the Justice asked.

Sidney Eversel said, "I'm going to make a clean breast of things. I have long been in love with Juanita Wentworth. I met her and fell in love with her while she was still married to Penn Wentworth, while she was living with him as his wife. The intensity of my emotion made me indiscreet."

Eversel paused and swallowed. Evidently he had memorized this much of his testimony but found the recital of it more difficult than he had anticipated. After a moment, he went on, "Wentworth was diabolically clever. He found out all about our affair. I believe he was insanely jealous of me. He wanted Juanita—Mrs. Wentworth—to return to him. She had left him shortly after meeting me. He threatened that unless she did return, he would sue me for alienation of affections. He refused to give her a divorce. His entire actions were those of a man who is utterly selfish and acting without consideration."

"Never mind that," Scanlon interrupted. "Just what do you know?"

Eversel said, "I rankled at the injustice of it because I knew that Wentworth was entertaining numerous women aboard his yacht. I determined to get evidence which would put Wentworth on the defensive—in a position where he would be forced to listen to reason and give his wife a divorce without dragging my name into it."

"What did you do?" Scanlon asked.

"On the night of the twelfth," Eversel said, "I lay in wait at the Yacht Club watching his boat. I knew that Miss Farr had been a frequent visitor aboard that yacht. The night was hot and stuffy. Wentworth had the skylight in his cabin open. I crept closer and closer to the yacht, listening. When I thought the time was ripe, I boarded the yacht and looked down through the skylight. I saw Wentworth in a very compromising position. His face was away from the camera. I put my finger on the shutter release and called his name softly. He didn't hear me the first time. I called a second time, and he looked up in alarm. At that moment, I pressed the trigger and a flash bulb, synchronized with the shutter of the camera, exploded, giving me a sharp, clear picture."

"What did you do?"

Carl Runcifer whispered to Oscar Overmeyer, "This is the most incredible substitute for a legal proceeding imaginable. Are you going to let Scanlon get by with this type of hearing? Aren't you going to object to his examining the witnesses?"

"Won't do a bit of good," Overmeyer whispered back. "This is the way Emil Scanlon always runs his show; and surprisingly enough, it always comes out okay."

"I turned and ran from the yacht," Eversel continued. "I drove home and developed the picture. It was a perfect negative. I could hardly wait. I knew that Mrs. Wentworth was in San Diego. I jumped in my plane and flew to San Diego, explained the circumstances to her, and brought her back with me. By the time we returned, the negative was dry. I put it in the enlarging camera and made a print. Naturally I felt very jubilant. Then I flew Mrs. Wentworth back to San Diego.

"Subsequently, that negative was stolen from my house. At the time of its disappearance, Perry Mason, the attorney representing Miss Farr, was prowling around the grounds. I demand that that negative be produced. When it is produced, I intend to prosecute him for burglary."

Emil Scanlon pursed his lips thoughtfully and assiduously avoided glancing at Perry Mason. "Well," he said after a moment, "if anything like that happened, it's something that's entirely apart from this case. As I see it, your testimony may show that the murder wasn't commited at the time we had supposed. That's all that relates to the present investigation."

Oscar Overmeyer said, "May I ask a question if the Justice please?"

"Yes."

"When you were flying to San Diego the first time," Overmeyer asked, "did you take a direct course a part of the way over the water?"

"Yes," Eversel answered. "My plane is an amphibian. The night was calm. The rainstorm hadn't begun then, and the safety factor in night flying induced me to keep over the ocean."

"While you were near the outer entrance of the harbor, did you notice by any chance a yacht?"

"I did."

"What yacht was it?"

"It was the express cruiser *Atina* belonging to Frank Marley."

"And who is Frank Marley?"

"A partner of Wentworth's."

"You know him?"

"I know of him, and I know him personally. I am quite familiar with his boat."

"You were flying low?"

"Yes."

"What did you do, if anything?"

"I circled the cruiser several times, thinking that it was rather significant that it was heading out to sea."

"Did you have any means of illumination by which you could . . ."

"Yes, I have a pair of searchlights in the wings. I turned them on the cruiser."

"What did you see?"

"I identified the *Atina* absolutely. I saw that someone was at the wheel. I could see that someone was a woman, and that she was wearing clothes of the identical color that had been worn by Mae Farr when she went aboard the *Pennwent* earlier in the evening."

Overmeyer bowed and smiled. "If the Justice please," he said, "that is all."

Mason raised his eyebrows at the J.P. and Emil Scanlon nodded.

"Did you fly over any other yachts while you were en route to San Diego?" Mason asked casually.

Overmeyer said, "If the Justice please, that has nothing to do with this case. It is an attempt to confuse the issues and—"

"I would have asked the question myself if Mr. Mason hadn't," the
J.P. interrupted. "I said I didn't want any purely technical objections.
Let's hear the answer to that question."

Eversel squirmed uneasily in the witness chair. He glanced appeal-
ingly at Overmeyer, then averted his eyes.

"Answer the question," Emil Scanlon said, his voice taking on the
edge of authority, like a ballplayer telling the umpire that he missed
the last call.

"Well," Eversel said, "naturally in taking a course for San Diego,
I was flying on just about the course a ship would have taken in going
to Ensenada."

"Never mind the explanations," Scanlon said. "You can make those
later. The question was whether you flew over any other yachts."

"Yes, I did."

"Did you," Scanlon asked, "recognize any of those yachts?"

"I recognized one of them."

"Was it the *Pennwent*?" Scanlon asked sternly.

Eversel kept his eyes straight ahead. "Yes, it was," he said in a
strained voice.

"And did you circle over her?"

"Just once."

"What did you see?"

"I saw her plugging along with the skylight in the cabin open."

"Was there anyone at the wheel?" Scanlon asked.

"I don't think this witness could see that distinctly," Overmeyer
objected. "It's asking rather much . . ."

"No, it isn't," Scanlon said. "A witness who could look at one
yacht and testify to the color of the *clothes* worn by the person at the
wheel could certainly see if anyone was at the steering wheel of another yacht. Answer that question, Mr. Eversel."

Eversel said, "No one was at the wheel."

"You only circled the yacht once?"

"Yes."

"Are you certain no one was at the wheel?"

"Yes."

"Where was the yacht then?"

"About a mile off shore and about ten miles below the breakwater."

"And how far from Frank Marley's boat?" Mason asked.

"About three miles, I should judge."

Mason said, in a very conversational tone of voice, "You knew that Wentworth had a violent temper, didn't you, Mr. Eversel?"

"I did."

"And you knew that if he caught you aboard the *Pennwent*, he might resort to violence?"

"Yes."

"You knew he was a powerful man?"

"Yes."

"I suppose," Mason said, "that's why you went armed."

"Well, I carried a weapon. I didn't propose—" The witness suddenly broke off as the full significance of Mason's question dawned upon him.

"And saw no reason for removing that weapon before you stepped into your airplane?"

"To tell you the truth, I forgot all about it."

"So that at the time you were circling over Wentworth's yacht, you were armed. Is that right?"

"I don't like the way you put that question."

"Never mind whether you like it or not," Scanlon said. "Answer it."

"Yes, I was," Eversel snapped.

"What kind of a revolver?"

"A thirty-eight—a Colt."

Mason smiled affably. "That," he said, "is all."

Scanlon frowned. "I am not certain that I care to have the examination concluded at just this point," he said. "Well, perhaps we'll let the matter rest temporarily. You'll remain in attendance, Mr. Eversel."

"Just one more question," Mason asked. "You stated that you made an enlargement of that negative, Mr. Eversel?"

"I did."

"Where is it?"

"I gave it to the deputy district attorney."

"Mr. Overmeyer?"

"No, Mr. Runcifer."

Mason smiled. "Would you mind producing that print, Mr. Runcifer?"

Runcifer said, "I certainly would. That's a part of the confidential files of the district attorney's office. I object to any such a demand. If you want that photograph in evidence, produce it yourself, and when you do so, account for the fact that you have that negative in your possession."

Emil Scanlon, in a voice that was suavely courteous, said, "If there are no more questions of Mr. Eversel, he will be excused. But remain in attendance."

Eversel left the witness stand.

Runcifer exchanged a triumphant glance with his associate.

"And now," Overmeyer said, "we will call Hazel Tooms as our next witness."

"Thank you very much," Scanlon said, "but the Justice has his own ideas about who should be the next witness. Mr. Runcifer, will you please come forward and be sworn?"

"Me?" Runcifer exclaimed. "I most strenuously object on the ground—"

Scanlon nodded affably and cut Runcifer in midsentence. " . . . Just step right up to the witness stand, Mr. Runcifer."

Oscar Overmeyer said in a loud half-whisper: "You'd better go if you don't want a contempt citation. This guy means business."

Runcifer moved slowly forward, held up his hand, and was sworn.

Emil Scanlon said, "Do you have in your possession a photograph which purports to be a print of the flashlight photograph taken by the witness who last testified?"

"Your Honor, I object to that," Oscar Overmeyer said. "That is a part of the—"

"I don't want any objections," Scanlon said. "I want that photograph if you have it."

There was a moment of tense, dramatic silence. Then Runcifer said, "Very much against my wishes and over my protests, I produce the photograph the justice of the peace has requested." Runcifer could not keep a condescending tone out of his voice when he said "justice of the peace."

He opened his briefcase and took out an enlargement on glossy paper which he handed to the Justice. At the same time he favored Perry Mason with a glance of savage hostility.

"While we're about it," Scanlon said casually, "you seem to have a lot of other photographs there. What are they, pictures showing the interior of the *Pennwent*?"

"Yes."

"Let's have them," Scanlon said.

Runcifer took out a series of pictures, explaining that they showed the posture of the body when it was discovered, the interior of the cabin when the yacht had been brought in, the exterior of the yacht, the yacht in its berth at the Yacht Club, and an airplane view of the club showing the floats to which boats were moored. Scanlon marked them all in numerical order and announced them as exhibits. "That's all, Mr. Runcifer," he said. "Thank you."

Runcifer stalked stiffly back to his seat.

"Well," Scanlon said, "let's hear from Hazel Tooms. Will you come forward and be sworn, please?"

There was a craning of necks, but no rustle of motion usual when a witness moves toward the witness box.

Scanlon frowned and said, "Wasn't she under subpoena?"

Runcifer said acidly, "She was under subpoena. She stated that at least one attempt had been made to get her to leave the country. When she was subpoenaed, we believe she was about to put herself beyond the jurisdiction of the court."

"I'm not concerned with that," Emil Scanlon said. "We're holding only one postmortem, and that's on the death of Wentworth and the probable involvement of the accused, Mae Farr. The question is, where is this witness now?"

"I don't know," Runcifer said.

Scanlon's eyes turned to Perry Mason and became suddenly stern. "Mr. Mason," he said, "I think I'll now ask you to take the stand."

Mason obediently took the witness stand, realizing that any protest would be quickly overruled.

"Do you know this witness, Hazel Tooms?" Emil Scanlon asked.

"I do."

"Did you talk with her about the case?"

"I did."

"Do you know where she is now?"

"I do not."

"Do you know how she happened to leave?"

"Not of my own knowledge, no."

"Were you directly or indirectly responsible for her departure?"

"No."

"That's all," the Justice said.

Runcifer said eagerly, "I'd like to ask this witness one or two questions."

Scanlon hesitated a moment, then said, "I didn't give him an opportunity to ask you any questions."

"This is different," Runcifer said.

"I'll hear the question and see if I permit it," Scanlon said.

"When you talked with Miss Tooms, wasn't the subject discussed that she might leave the country for a financial consideration, and didn't you discuss with her the amount of money necessary?"

"You might put it that way," Mason said calmly. "She made the proposition. I turned it down."

"Oh," Runcifer said, his voice filled with sarcasm. "You went to her apartment. She told you that she had testimony which would be very damaging to your client, and offered to leave the country, and you were too ethical to even entertain such a proposition. Is that the idea you wish to convey?"

Scanlon said, "You don't have to answer that question, Mr. Mason. Now then, Mr. Runcifer, we're not going to have any more such bursts of sarcasm from Counsel. We're here to try and find out whether there's enough evidence to hold this accused for trial in Superior Court for the murder of Penn Wentworth. That's all. You can air your grievances some other place than in my courtroom."

Mason said, "Begging Your Honor's pardon, I'd like to answer the question."

"Go ahead," the Justice said.

Mason crossed his long legs in front of him, smiled down at Runcifer, and said, "Your question assumes an erroneous fact, Mr. Runcifer. The testimony which Hazel Tooms was to have given, in place of being detrimental to my client, was really most advantageous. I regret that she isn't here."

"All right," Runcifer said triumphantly. "Since you've opened the door as to the nature of her testimony, I'll ask you this question. I assume the Justice will admit it. He's let in everything else. Isn't it a fact that she said she had gone to the Yacht Club to call on Wentworth, that Wentworth had advised her he was going to Ensenada that night and asked her to go along, that she went back to get some groceries and some clothes, and when she returned, the yacht was gone, that she waited for some time, and while she was waiting, she saw Frank Marley's boat come in to its landing, that she watched to see who had been piloting that boat, and that the only person who left it was Mae Farr, your client."

"That," Mason said calmly, "is substantially what she said."

"And you consider that that is to the advantage of your client?" Runcifer asked.

Mason nodded gravely. "I do."

There was a moment's astonished silence, followed by a whispered conference on the part of the deputy district attorneys.

Scanlon said, "I guess that's all, Mr. Mason. I think that's all the examination I'll permit anyway. You may leave the stand."

Mason returned to his chair.

Runcifer got to his feet and said, almost pleadingly, "Won't the Justice permit me to ask Mr. Mason one more question?"

"I don't think so," Scanlon said. "You seem to have covered the situation pretty well. What was the question you wanted to ask?"

"I wanted to ask Mr. Mason just how he could possibly claim that that testimony was of any advantage to his client?"

Scanlon shook his head. "That would mean just a lot of argument," he said.

Mason, from his chair, said, "I think perhaps if Your Honor permitted that question and I answered it, it might clear up a lot of misunderstandings right now."

"Go ahead and answer it," Scanlon said. "To be perfectly frank, I'm interested in the answer although I consider the question somewhat improper and an attempt to take advantage of a witness who apparently has been very fair and frank. Go ahead and answer it, Mr. Mason."

Mason walked up to Scanlon's bench where the photographs were spread out and said, "In answering that question, it's going to be necessary to correlate certain facts at some length."

"Go ahead and correlate them," Scanlon invited. "That's what we're here for. Just make it terse and logical and keep within the facts, and we'll listen. We don't want to hear any impassioned argument."

"I'm not going to make any," Mason said with a smile.

"Go ahead," Scanlon invited, "and answer the question."

Mason said, "I think the tag which was given to this case by learned counsel for the prosecution is perhaps the best description of the case. Your Honor will remember that he referred to it as 'The Case of the Postponed Murder.'

"Quite obviously, Penn Wentworth was shot from a distance. There are no powder marks on his clothing or on his body. He was evidently shot from above, as Your Honor knows from talking to the autopsy surgeon. It is quite natural to suppose that he was shot through the skylight of his yacht by someone who was well above him, a distance, let us say, that was not less than six or eight feet and which stretches indefinitely into space as far as anyone could have accurately aimed a gun and fired a bullet. For instance, I believe that Mr. Eversel is an expert revolver shot and has acquired some reputation as an authority on firearms. I believe that's correct, Mr. Eversel?"

Eversel hesitated and nodded curtly.

"Your Honor, if we're still taking testimony, I suggest that witness Eversel be asked to return to the witness box," Runcifer exploded.

"You let me worry about that, won't you?" Scanlon said evenly.

Mason continued: "And you would back the statement I have just made from your knowledge of the case and your experience with firearms?"

Eversel made no move to answer. Mason went on affably, "Well, it's of no moment. I merely mentioned it so that we can keep in mind the position of the person who fired the shot and the position of the man who was the target.

"Now let's examine the possibilities. Let's first consider Anders. He could hardly have committed the murder. The evidence shows that Wentworth's yacht was only a couple of miles ahead of Marley's cruiser when Eversel saw them. Wentworth had much the slower boat. However, making all due allowances for speed, it would seem quite apparent that Wentworth must have pulled out with his yacht very shortly after Mae Farr and Anders drove away, perhaps within half an hour. Anders says that he threw his gun away. Mae Farr also testifies to that. The evidence shows that the murder gun was found. It certainly wasn't the gun Anders had or was carrying. Moreover, Anders went to the city and almost immediately started for North Mesa, and I understand that the police have been able to trace his movements so that they are convinced he didn't return to the Yacht Club after his conversation with me.

"Miss Farr and I drove to the Yacht Club. We found the *Pennwent* gone. We returned and Miss Farr stayed with me until after I had passed the place where Anders threw the gun. She then doubled back and took Marley's cruiser."

"You're admitting that?" Runcifer asked incredulously.

"Of course I'm admitting it," Mason said. "Now let's look at it from her viewpoint. Suppose she had gone out and overtaken Wentworth's yacht, as could well have happened. She couldn't have put the *Atina* alongside the *Pennwent* without Wentworth's knowing it was there. It's a physical impossibility to do that without bumping and jarring. Moreover, she couldn't have kept her boat at cruising speed, laid her alongside the *Pennwent,* left the wheel, and made fast to Wentworth's yacht without help. She would have required either that Wentworth slow down or that someone help her, or both.

"However, suppose that Wentworth did slow down, suppose that Mae Farr boarded the *Pennwent.* Wentworth would have had to help her. They could have gone down to the cabin together. Wentworth had an automatic pilot on his yacht. There was no necessity for him to be at the wheel. But there is no likely combination of circumstances by which he could have been in the cabin and Miss Farr could have stood on the deck and shot him through the open skylight.

"Let's take the case of Eversel. He is an aviator. He flew low over the yacht. He was armed. He's an expert shot. But before I go into that, I want to call your attention to a significant item in these photographs. Notice the photograph which was taken by Eversel. I want to call Your Honor's attention to this little shelf. You will notice a circular object in a case with a cylindrical object near it."

Runcifer got to his feet and walked quickly to the Justice's bench to examine what Mason was pointing out. "That," Runcifer said, "is a rare coin. Wentworth was a prominent collector of rare coins."

"Quite possibly," Mason said. "And with a magnifying glass you can notice certain distinctive marks on this coin. There are two parallel lines with interlacing, diagonal lines in between them."

The Justice studied it through the magnifying glass. "Just how is that significant, Mr. Mason?" he asked.

"One moment, Your Honor," Mason said. "Examine this picture of the cabin taken through the skylight by the police after the *Pennwent* was returned. There is the same shelf. But the objects are missing."

Scanlon nodded.

"Now then," Mason said, "we are confronted with this situation. Whatever those objects were, they were on the *Pennwent* when Eversel took that flashlight photograph. As soon as that photograph was taken, Eversel left the yacht. Wentworth ran back to the after cabin.

Miss Farr ran out on deck and joined Anders. The two of them left the yacht together. There's no evidence showing that Eversel, Anders, or Mae Farr ever returned to that yacht.

"But here are two objects clearly shown in one photograph and clearly absent from a subsequent photograph. Why? Where did they go? Who took them?"

Scanlon said, "You have some theory about that, Mr. Mason?"

"I have," Mason said. "I'd like to call one witness."

"Well, I don't know that the State has rested," Overmeyer said hesitantly in hopeless confusion.

"Oh, what does that matter when we're trying to clear up this case?" Scanlon said. "Go ahead, Mason. Call whoever you want to."

"Mr. Robert Grastin," Mason announced.

A tall skinny man with sunken eyes, thin lips, and high cheekbones came forward. He was in his early fifties, a man with long arms and legs, quiet and unhurried in his manner. He said, "I hate to disappoint people, but I don't know one single thing about this case. I don't know any of the parties."

Mason said, "That's quite all right. Just take the stand, and we'll see what you know, Mr. Grastin."

Grastin slipped into the witness chair.

Mason said, "I believe the subpoena that was served on you called for you to bring certain records with you."

"Yes."

"Now just so the Justice can get the picture," Mason said, "kindly explain to him who you are and what your occupation is."

Grastin said, "I am the secretary and treasurer of the Interurban Amateur Athletic League. That is an association of amateur atheltes sponsored by an interurban busline for the purpose of promoting civic relations and—"

"And traffic?" Mason interrupted with a smile.

"And traffic," Grastin admitted. "The theory being that interurban matches are arranged at places which are most advantageously reached by the interurban service. Prizes are awarded. Competition is encouraged, and the line receives a certain amount of advertising."

"Now then, on the twelfth," Mason said, "you sponsored certain athletic activities?"

"Yes, sir. On the twelfth, the open tennis tournament reached the stage of finals."

"And on that day," Mason asked, "do your records show who won second place in the women's division?"

"*Second* place?" Grastin asked.

Mason nodded.

"Just a moment," Grastin said, and took from his pocket a leather-backed notebook filled with typewritten sheets of paper. He ran down the page to which he had opened the book, and said, "Our records show that second place was won by Miss Hazel Tooms who resides in the Balkan Apartments."

"Exactly," Mason said. "Now, I am interested in going back over the records of other athletic activities. Do you have an alphabetical index showing the names of winners?"

"We do."

"That is with you?"

"It's in my briefcase."

"Get it, please."

Grastin walked to his seat in the front of the room, picked up a briefcase, returned with it to the witness stand, and took out a large looseleaf notebook.

"Look under the name of Tooms," Mason said, "and see what else you find."

Grastin ran through the pages. Suddenly he said, "Wait a minute. I remember that name now. She's won quite a few championships; she's quite an all-round athlete."

"All right," Mason said. "Just look through your records. Now, what do you find in connection with swimming?"

"In each of the past two years," Grastin said, "she has won the women's long-distance swimming championship. Last year, she also won the four-hundred-meter free-style swimming event for women. In—"

"I think that's enough," Mason said. "It's enough to prove my point in any event. Now, I'm going to show you this photograph, Mr. Grastin, and call your attention to a coinlike object contained in a case and shown on this shelf." Mason handed him the photograph and pointed. "Please look at it with this magnifying glass. Can you tell what it is?"

Grastin held the magnifying glass in position, then said slowly, "Why, yes. That's the medal we had struck off for second place in the women's tennis tournament. That series of lines across it represents a tennis net."

Mason smiled affably at Justice of the Peace Scanlon and said, "I think, Your Honor, by the time the district attorney's office puts two and two together, it will have an answer to its question of who killed Penn Wentworth; and it wasn't Mae Farr."

Chapter Thirteen

Mason, Della Street, Mae Farr, and Paul Drake sat in Mason's office. Mae Farr seemed dazed at the swift turn of events. "I don't see how you figured it out," she said. "I thought I was up against a certain conviction."

Mason said, "It was mighty thin ice. Almost as soon as I talked with Hazel Tooms, I sensed she was altogether too eager to get out of the country. My first reaction was that her eagerness was due to the fact that her apartment had been bugged and the police were trying to trap me. When she saw I wasn't walking into the trap, she tried too hard to get me in.

"Later events caused me to change that opinion. If, then, her anxiety to escape hadn't been a scheme to trap me, what *was* the cause? That opened up an interesting field of speculation. I knew that she was an all-round athlete. I could tell by looking at her, and she had told me of winning second place in that tennis tournament. I also sensed that she had really cared a great deal for Penn Wentworth, and I believe, though I can't prove it, that theirs was more than a platonic friendship.

"It was quite obvious to me that Wentworth either must have been shot from an airplane or by someone who had been aboard the *Pennwent* with him and had been able to swim ashore after the shooting.

"I knew that Marley's alibi wasn't cast-iron, but he didn't impress me as being a man who could have swum ashore, landed virtually naked, and made his way back to the hospital without showing some evidence of his experience. Mrs. Wentworth might have done it, but it was quite evident that she was in San Diego. Unless Eversel had shot Wentworth from the airplane, I couldn't connect him with it. You were out in Marley's boat. You brought it back. For the reasons I mentioned, I didn't think you could have done the actual killing.

"As soon as I realized that what you had taken for the flash of a pistol was probably the release of a flashlight bulb, I knew that the murder had been postponed from that moment until a later one.

"Once I had that theory, it was easy to reconstruct what must have happened. Hazel Tooms won the second-place medal in the tennis finals. She went down to Wentworth's yacht to be congratulated. Knowing what we do of Wentworth, we can be sure that his idea of congratulations would require the use of lipstick by Hazel Tooms after those congratulations were received. When she had repaired the damage, she put the medal and the lipstick on the shelf in the cabin.

"Wentworth then told her of his plan to sail to Ensenada that night and asked her if she'd like to go with him. She was delighted but pointed out that she'd have to get some clothes and that they needed some provisions. So she left the *Pennwent,* drove home to pack, and on the way back stopped to pick up the provisions.

"During the time she was gone, you, Mae, boarded the *Pennwent* and had your struggle with Wentworth. Eversel boarded the boat and took the photograph of Wentworth in a compromising position, then left. Anders boarded the boat to rescue you. Then you two left.

"Some time after that, probably not long after, Hazel Tooms returned with the provisions, boarded the *Pennwent,* and she and Wentworth set sail for Ensenada.

"Wentworth was undoubtedly angry and upset. He knew he had been photographed. He reacted instinctively by doubling up and covering his face. He could guess that that photograph might make it very much more difficult for him to arrange a divorce on reasonable terms when he met his wife the next morning. He probably told Hazel Tooms all about it.

"Whether or not Wentworth had promised to marry Hazel if and when he got his freedom, I think Hazel assumed that was his intention and he made it plain that was a ridiculous assumption. For whatever reason, she was filled with murderous rage. He was probably sitting there laughing at her when she pulled the gun and shot him.

"She thought she'd killed him outright. The impact of the bullet must have knocked him out before he came to and wandered around. And she had to get off the boat. I believe she carried one of those canvas bags people take aboard instead of suitcases—just as I believe she always carried a gun in case one of the yachtsmen she picked up got too rough. I think she took off her clothes, stuffed them in the bag along with the swimming medal, the lipstick, and the gun, set the automatic pilot on the course for Ensenada if that hadn't already been done, dove overboard with the bag, and swam ashore.

"At first, I couldn't understand why she would have taken along the murder weapon instead of dumping it overboard. Then I put myself in her place and realized what she was up against. She'd arrive on shore naked at some strange place. She'd have to put on her wet clothes and find some motorist who would pick her up as a hitchhiker and take her to within walking distance of the Yacht Club where she had left her car. As a matter of protection, she decided to keep her revolver with her.

"She got back to the Yacht Club in time to see Mae Farr coming in aboard the *Atina*. Then she went home. The next morning, in the news coverage of the murder, she learned where Anders had thrown his gun. She drove down and 'planted' the murder weapon. Sometime that morning she also told Frank Marley about seeing Mae Farr bringing in the *Atina*."

"That's quite a reconstruction, Perry," Paul Drake said, "but I still don't see how you can figure that a normal, well-balanced, athletic girl like Hazel Tooms would commit murder."

"She might have fooled me if it hadn't been for one thing, Paul."

"What's that?"

"No matter what other facts we may get by surmise, one fact stands out as absolutely true. The person who killed Wentworth took the murder weapon down to the place where Anders had thrown his gun and planted it in hopes that it would clinch the case against Anders. In other words, the murderer was quite willing to send Anders up for a life sentence or a death penalty for a crime he hadn't committed. That showed that the person who had done the killing knew that there was some possibility a subsequent investigation might be made, that that person might be suspected, and strove to forestall both the investigation and the suspicion by deliberately trying to build up an iron-clad case against Anders."

"That," Drake said, "is right."

"What'll they do with her?" Mae Farr asked.

Mason said, "Well, that depends. First, they'll have to catch her, which I don't think will be easy. Then, they'll have to convict her, and that's going to be quite a job. That photograph Eversel took will come pretty close to getting her an acquittal if she testifies that Wentworth made the same sort of attack on her that he made on you."

"Planting that gun will look like the devil as far as her case is concerned," Drake said.

Mason grinned and said, "In one way, yes, but—oh come on, Paul, you can't convict a woman with a figure like hers of anything worse than manslaughter."

"How about Eversel?" Drake asked.

"He shook hands and made up," Mason said. "He was so darned afraid I was going to accuse him of the murder and make it stick that the real solution came as a great relief to him. He'd been scared stiff. Moreover, when he realized that because of my activities, an innocent woman had been liberated, he began to think I wasn't such a bad egg after all. In fact, Della, he's invited us down for dinner next week."

"Are we going?" she asked.

"Why not?" Mason asked. "In the meantime, let's climb in the car and go places."

"Where?" she asked.

"Oh, take a trip," Mason said. "Why not drive up toward North Mesa and look that country over?"

"Would you risk it?" Mae Farr asked.

"Risk what?"

"You'll probably come to blows with Hal's family lawyer."

"Fiddlesticks," Mason said. "I have no feelings like that. Actually the man was right."

"Well," she said, "I'm going that way myself this afternoon."

"You *are*?" Della asked in surprise.

She nodded.

Mason said, "Well, well, well! How did that happen?"

She flushed and said spiritedly, "It's a woman's prerogative to change her mind, isn't it? Maybe I've changed mine about Hal."

Mason said, "He does seem to have developed a lot of independence lately."

Mae Farr laughed nervously. "Yes. He's picked up quite a few ideas of his own. I think this murder case may have been a good thing—for him. I wish you would come and have dinner with us tomorrow night, Mr. Mason. It's going to be a special occasion."

Mason looked at Mae Farr with a twinkle in his eyes. "A sort of celebration?" he asked.

She nodded. "I'm going to tell Hal I'll marry him."

"Good girl!" Mason said, then he turned to Della Street. "How about it, Della?"

"Leaving it up to me, Chief?"

He nodded.

"Let's go to North Mesa," she said, "if you *really* want us, Miss Farr."

"Oh, but I really do," Mae Farr said eagerly.

Paul Drake got to his feet, fed a stick of gum into his mouth, and said, "Well, nice to have known you."

"Aren't you coming, too, Mr. Drake?" Mae Farr asked.

"Not me," Drake said. "When wedding bells ring the enthusiasm is apt to be contagious. What would a detective do with a wife?"

"Wrong again," Mason said cheerfully. "What would a wife do with a detective?"

Drake paused in the outer doorway for a parting shot. "Particularly a detective who works for a lawyer who keeps him up all night, running around committing felonies," he said, and punctuated his remark by banging the door shut behind him.

THE END

Murder in Waiting

The judge lay in the shadow, but the eerie red light from the burglar alarm flashed from its box under the eaves of the house at swift intervals and momentarily lighted lawns, shrubbery and the inert figure.

Bea bent over him. "Uncle Judge—Uncle Judge."

One arm clad in a white shirt threshed a little; the judge moaned. Then he said clearly, "Doctor . . . Will . . . Seth . . ." and died.

The flashes of light from the house sent out tremors of rosy reflections which touched the tall pines, the glossy laurels, the stone wall beyond the shrubbery. The alarm kept squawking raucously.

But he can't be dead, Bea thought, and knew that he was. His hand had relaxed and dropped. She tried to remember whatever she had vaguely heard about resuscitation: move his arms, move his chest so his heart will keep beating, breathe air into his lungs. It was no use. Without being aware of her own action, she had found his wrist and hunted for a pulse, but there was not even the slightest flicker in that suddenly flaccid arm.

The burglar alarm kept on: wow-wow-wow. The whole countryside must hear it. Surely the doctor would hear it; the Thorne house lay across and only a couple of hundred feet down the road. Rufe Thorne, too, would hear the alarm and come.

Instead there was the nearby sound of a car racing behind the stone wall, and then it shot into the Salcott drive. It had a red light too, whirling and flashing on top of it: police car. The alarm connected with the Valley Ridge police station, and somebody there must have radioed a patrol car. Before Bea could more than stumble to her feet, two men were getting out; she could see their black silhouettes against the car lights. She ran, calling to them, "Here! He's here—"

They heard her, turned and came plunging toward her. She seemed to be shouting, yet her voice sounded thin and faraway in her own ears. "The judge! He's dead! Down there—"

Each man had an enormous flashlight. The lights turned upon her,

dazzling her, showing every fold of the blue dressing gown she had yanked
on when the burglar alarm went off.

She cried to them to hurry. She could be mistaken; the judge, so full
of energy and determination, could not have died so quickly.

One of the men said, "All right, Miss Bartry. Take it easy—"

They jogged on, their flashlights dancing everywhere, down toward the
wall and the crowding thickets of the laurels and pines—and the judge.

She had to tell Clara. She saw then that the study door at the end of
the terrace was open as she had left it. Clara stood there, her little figure
clear against the light behind her. "Bea," she called. "Bea! Is it the
judge?"

Bea made her way toward the terrace and Clara. The alarm was now
very near, shrieking to all the world that the judge was dead.

Clara didn't need to be told. "That man Meeth! He was let out yesterday. He said he'd kill the judge when he was released. He killed him."

"I don't know. Come back into the house, Aunt Clara."

"He killed him! I knew he would. He swore he'd kill him—"

"Aunt Clara—" She drew her back into the study. "Dear, I think he
fainted or . . . or something." Her attempt at a lie sounded unconvincing.

Clara knew. "No. No, he's dead. He was murdered."

"I'll call the doctor, he said to call the doctor. He said to call Seth—"

"Neither Seth nor the doctor can help now. How did he kill him? I
didn't hear a gunshot."

"I don't know. He might have had a stroke and lost consciousness. You
know the doctor warned us—"

Clara pointed at Bea's dressing gown. "He didn't have a stroke. That's
blood."

Bea looked down. There were vividly red, wet blotches along the front
of her dressing gown and on one sleeve. She remembered that she had
tried to lift the judge. Suddenly the unusually warm spring night seemed
cold. She felt it in her bones. "I'll call the doctor. The judge said to—"

"He talked to you? Didn't he say what happened?"

Bea reached for the telephone on the judge's big desk. She dialed the
doctor, a number she had always known well, especially since Rufe came
back from Vietnam.

Clara stood like a statue in her prim dressing gown, belted at her plump
little waist; her gray hair was neatly netted, her pretty round face stony.
As Bea waited for the ring of the telephone she saw the judge's jacket
lying on the desk. It was old and shabby but the judge loved it; it was

almost a part of him. The burglar alarm was still going. Somebody ought to turn it off; it will run down the battery, Bea thought. The judge couldn't have been murdered. Yet that man Meeth *had* been released from prison; he *had* sworn to kill the judge. A feminine voice said thinly in her ear, "Dr. Thorne's answering service—"

"I want the doctor. I must have the doctor—"

Footsteps came running across the terrace and Rufe Thorne plunged into the study. "Bea—Aunt Clara—Bea—"

"I'm calling your father," Bea said.

He came to her, took the telephone and put it down. "He's coming. He heard the alarm. He's down there with the police. Can't you turn off that thing?"

Bea said something, but Rufe ran out of the study and up the stairs to the panel controlling the alarm in the linen closet.

A sudden silence fell upon the night. Bea took a long breath. But then she heard clearly the metallic sound of voices coming from the drive, calling the police station. Soon there would be more police. Rufe came back into the study. "They're calling Obrian—" Obrian was the Valley Ridge chief of police.

Dr. Thorne came slowly in from the terrace. Accustomed to night calls, he had got into a dark turtleneck sweater; he carried his small medicine bag as if it were a part of him. "I'm sorry, Clara."

Clara gave him a stony look. "I know that man—that Meeth killed him, didn't he?"

Dr. Thorne's face was set too; he looked older and very tired. He was the family physician and their friend. "I don't know."

"But it was murder," Clara said. "I know it was murder. We heard the alarm and Bea found him."

Dr. Thorne came to Clara and put his hand on her wrist. "Yes. He was murdered. He was shot—"

"I knew it! That man Meeth—"

"Now, Clara—" The doctor took her arm, his silvery head towering above her. She went with him as if she didn't know what else to do.

Rufe came to Bea and put his arm around her. It couldn't be very late, for he was still dressed. "I'm sorry about the judge." He looked at her dressing gown. "Bea!"

"Yes. I leaned over him. I tried . . . I couldn't believe . . . but then he died. He just died."

"Bea!" He held her close to him, his face down upon her own. "Dear, don't tremble like that."

She clung to him, thankful for the warmth of his arms and the solid rock of his body. "Oh, Rufe, he died. And he didn't forgive me. He only said something about your father. Get the doctor I think he meant. Oh, Rufe, I wish he had forgiven me. We quarreled tonight—after dinner."

"About me." It was a statement.

"Yes. He said . . . well, you know the judge. Lately he's been so difficult."

"A kind word for it. But then the poor old guy couldn't help it. My father explained it to me."

"Your father told me too, and Aunt Clara. He said we mustn't let him be upset or excited. He said— Oh, Rufe, I feel as if I had killed him myself. That quarrel!"

Rufe's arms held her tight. "You couldn't have killed him."

"I lost my temper and said that as soon as you had your appointment we were going to be married and that he couldn't stop us. He turned so red—"

"Yes, he was like that with me."

Bea's head jerked up. "With you! You weren't here!"

"Yes, I was. I knew he'd get himself worked up when you told him we were going to be married, so I came across the road after dinner and tried to talk to him. It was no use."

"I didn't know you were here!"

"You and Aunt Clara were upstairs. I could hear her television going. I came here to the study door and saw his light. He was still moody."

Bea waited a moment. "I suppose he said the same things to you that he said to me."

"I imagine stronger."

"He told me that he wouldn't let me marry you. I reminded him that I'm of age. And I— Oh, Rufe!"

"There, there, Bea. Things will be all right."

"Rufe, if it's murder . . ."

"If this man Meeth did it, it shouldn't be hard to run him down."

"What else did Uncle Judge say?"

"He said that I had only passed the examinations, and that the Foreign Service is a long and demanding career. He said you'd been accustomed to every luxury, that he had given you every care and an expensive education. He said that he'd been like a father to you—"

"He always was. Until lately."

"He couldn't help his recent condition. But then—"

"I know. He said it to me too. He said—" Bea swallowed hard. "He said that I probably expected all Aunt Clara's money and his too—what there was—to come to me eventually. He said that it was a great help to a young Foreign Service officer to have a wife with money, or even expectations of money."

"He said all that to me and more. I reminded him that he had helped me all along the line—character reference, study of international law, everything. He was really worked up. He said that he wouldn't have helped me if he'd known that my intention was to marry you and eventually get his money and Clara's. He said—" Rufe checked himself for a moment and then went on. "Well, never mind all that. I lost my temper too, so I thought I'd better leave. He was so furious, I was afraid he'd blow up then and there. Bea, how did you know he was out there?"

"I didn't know. I was half asleep. The burglar alarm went off. Aunt Clara and I both ran into the hall. I knew she had set it, thinking that the judge had come upstairs. She's done that a time or two and it made him very angry. Its still new to us—the alarm, I mean. Aunt Clara had it installed when she learned that Meeth was to be paroled. We were supposed to phone the police if it was a false alarm. It's connected with the station. The men who installed the alarm said that all the doors and windows downstairs, and both front and back stairs too, were—he called it bugged."

"Go on."

"Then the judge didn't come upstairs. I ran down. The lights were still on in the study and the terrace door was open. I thought he'd gone out for a stroll around the place; he did that sometimes. I thought the door must have blown open, or something. I expected him to have heard the alarm and come back to the house, and when he didn't I was afraid he'd fainted or had a stroke or—I didn't know what. So I ran down to the hedge along the stone wall. All the time the alarm kept going. I ran along the laurels, and then I stumbled over his feet, I think, and fell and . . . he said something about the doctor and . . . and died. I felt his pulse and he was dead. Like that."

"He must have had only a moment of consciousness."

"Not more than that. He just said 'Doctor . . . Will . . . Seth . . .' He must have meant for me to call Seth too. I only thought of your father. Rufe, who is Will?"

"I don't know. We'd better call Seth."

"We don't need a lawyer!"

Rufe's face changed slightly; it seemed guarded. "Well, he'll know what to do. The police will question everybody."

"But surely it was that man he sent to prison. Who else could have killed him?"

"I'll call Seth."

"Is he in town?"

"I saw him on the street yesterday. Do you know his number?"

She couldn't think of it. When Rufe let her go, she felt she couldn't stand without his supporting arms. He hunted through the telephone book, and then, as he dialed, said, "But I don't know any Will!"

"Oh, of course! He didn't mean Will Somebody. I know what he was thinking of. He told me that if I married you, he and Aunt Clara would change their wills. He accused you of being a fortune hunter. He must have meant that Seth was to draw up new wills. He didn't realize that he was dying."

Rufe spoke into the phone. "Seth? Rufe Thorne. Something awful has happened. The judge was murdered."

Bea could hear the rumble of Seth's powerful voice. Rufe replied, "Shot. A few minutes ago. Seth, can you come? The police are here. A patrol car came and by now they've sent for help, and Aunt Clara and Bea are alone except for me and my father." Seth's voice came again; no words were clear, but Rufe replied, "I think Aunt Clara is all right. My father took her upstairs. He's seeing to her." There was another pause, a short one, and then Rufe said, "Tony was in the patrol car."

Tony? Bea thought, and remembered: of course, Tony Calinas. He and Rufe had known each other since they were boys; they had been inducted into the service at the same time. Rufe had written: "We were in the same outfit at first. I really miss him now."

Rufe replied to something Seth said. "I don't know, I'll ask . . . All right." He put down the telephone. "He'll be here, right away. He's only a mile away. He said not to talk to anybody, police or anybody."

"What did you say you would ask?"

"If either you or Aunt Clara had heard a gunshot."

"No, only the alarm. Aunt Clara was watching a Western on her bedroom television. She's a little deaf, so she turns it very loud. It was full of gunshots; I could hear them from my room. She must have turned it off only a little before we heard the alarm."

Rufe went to the door and looked out. Over his shoulder she could see headlights and hear the racing roar as still another car came hurtling into the drive.

"Obrian must be here by now. I'll go down and see what they're doing." Rufe gave a swift glance to the smears on her dressing gown. Again his face seemed to alter a little. "Bea, go upstairs and take that off. Put on a dress."

She started numbly for the living room and the hall but he caught her by the shoulder and turned her back. "Bea, the police will have to question you and Aunt Clara. Don't talk to them till Seth gets here. Take as long as you can about dressing. It will give you time to pull yourself together." He leaned over, kissed her swiftly and then ran out the terrace door.

She went slowly through the living room, as if she were drugged, and pulled herself up the stairs which she had come down so short a time ago to find the judge, to placate his wrath at Clara for setting the alarm too early—so short a time, yet so long a time.

Bea couldn't remember when the judge had not been an important figure in her life. It was true, he had told her—accused her in a way—that he had stood between her and the world; he had taken her in when her own parents had died; her only claim was that she was the daughter of his nephew. He hadn't been particularly fond of her mother, but he and Aunt Clara had made her their child. Nothing was too good for her.

At the top of the stairs she met Dr. Thorne coming from Clara's room. "She's all right," he said quickly. "I gave her as strong a sedative as I dared. Her heart is really better than she thinks, you know, but still, she's not young." He gave her a faint smile. "She's a bit of a hypochondriac, as we all know, but I won't let the police talk to her tonght. How about you?" His eyes and Rufe's eyes had the same piercing concentration. "I think I'd better give you something to make things easier for you, just for a while. Come on. You'd better lie down until the police—" He broke off and, as Rufe had done, stared down at the smears of red on her dressing gown. "How did you get those?"

"I leaned over him. I thought I could do something—"

"Take it off." He spoke as tersely as Rufe.

From off in the distance there rose an ululating wail. Dr. Thorne's head lifted.

"Is that—" she began.

He nodded. "The ambulance. Don't worry, child. Here—" He went into her room with her, gently took off her dressing gown, disappeared into the bathroom and returned. "I hung the thing over the shower rail. They'll find the stains, of course, but don't worry. Perfectly clear how you got them. Don't look like that, child."

"Doctor, was there anything I could have done for the judge?"

He considered it. "No. He must have been unconscious—"

"He spoke to me. Just a few words."

"He couldn't have lived, Bea. Here, get back into bed."

Her bed was tumbled as she had left it. The doctor opened his medicine bag, got a capsule from a small bottle and gave it to her. "Take that. It won't put you to sleep but it'll calm you down a little." Again he lifted his head sharply and listened. "H'mm, they got here in a hurry."

"You mean the Valley Ridge police—Obrian and—"

"Oh, they were on their way when I came. I expect they've called in the state police."

"State . . ."

"We don't have many murders in Valley Ridge. Fact is, I can't remember one. The state police have facilities we don't. Besides, the judge was an important man. Now take it easy, Bea." He went out. The door closed behind him. Though he and Rufe, father and son, naturally resembled each other, Dr. Thorne was thin where Rufe was strong and sturdy, and now the doctor's frosty hair retained only a tinge of red, while Rufe's was still a stubborn auburn.

For a long time she sat on the bed. She was aware of a tumult and activity around the house—cars dashing into the drive, doors opening and closing, voices—but the capsule the doctor had given her began to dull the sounds for her. After a long time she began slowly to dress. She'd wait until they sent for her. The state police!

A voice from below her window shouted, "We looked in the barn right away. Nobody there!"

Another voice shouted back, "Search the house."

TWO

They searched the house, room by room, swiftly. Two troopers in state uniform knocked politely at Bea's door, then went through the room, the closet, the bathroom, even the wastebasket, like two terriers clad in smart gray uniforms. When they thanked her and departed, one of them was carrying her blue dressing gown with its sickening red patches.

She knew that the nearest state police barracks was in Welbury, not far from Valley Ridge. Dr. Thorne had said the state police had "facilities" —he must mean for the detection of criminals. She thought vaguely of fingerprints and guns. Guns! The judge had had one in the drawer of his big desk. But he would never have killed himself. She sat on the bed again, huddled against the pillows. She wouldn't budge; she wouldn't speak to anybody until Seth came. Suppose . . . suppose the police found out that not only had she quarreled with the judge, but that Rufe had actually been in the house not long before the judge was killed and that he too had quarreled violently with him about their marriage. Yet the judge had had nothing against Rufe; he had done everything possible to help him during his training to enter the Foreign Service.

Rufe was a part of her being. There had been few things in her life that Bea loved. One was Clara's library; another, her dog Shadders. But the most important, for as long as she could remember, was Rufe. She loved Clara and the judge and was grateful to both. But Rufe she loved with all her deepest instincts. She had adored him when she was a gawky girl in her early teens and Rufe, older, would come home for vacations and skate with her or take her for a ride in a sled with Shadders bounding happily beside them. She had adored Rufe even when he was in love with Lorraine, Clara's niece, and couldn't stay away from the house because she was there. She had prayed when he went to Vietnam; she had hated Lorraine for so swiftly casting him off in favor of marriage to Cecco. She had agonized over the letters he wrote, which Lorraine either glanced at or sometimes didn't bother to open.

Bea had written to him herself so that he'd get letters from home. She had written when old Shadders died; she had written when, as everyone had long expected, Miss Dotty, the doctor's office nurse, gliding silently along a country road on her bicycle without reflectors, had at last been hit by a car. For a long time after that Miss Dotty was rather subdued and very careful about her bicycle riding at night. Rufe had answered all of Bea's letters and had never asked about Lorraine.

When he came home from Vietnam he seemed much more mature, so much older that Bea was at first shy and felt herself awkward again and childish. But he came to the house to talk to the judge and Clara, and then, gradually, he began to come frankly to see Bea. They would go to a movie, or just for a drive. He told her of his desire to go into the Foreign Service and why. Even in the beginning, she knew that he was dedicating himself to something which he believed might help the cause of peace in the world.

She remembered the first time he had kissed her; it was in the late fall, with a cold hunter's moon, and they were standing on the steps of the terrace. Rufe had been home for a few days and she had cherished every minute of their time together. They had gone to a movie, and she was about to go into the house when Rufe had pulled her coat collar closer around her throat and then, unexpectedly, almost as if he didn't mean to yet couldn't help himself, leaned over and kissed her. Then he had kissed her again, and they were in each other's arms. The world changed for her. The hunter's moon was white and the world was magic.

But he hadn't mentioned marriage until he was home again for a few days at Christmas time, and then it was in the most casual way in the world. They were skating on the little pond, and he had said in the middle of a conversation—"so when I get an appointment we can be married."

Married. Again the world became a magic place and life was full of meaning. They had skated on for a while. Then, when he helped her off with her skates, he said, "I didn't make a very romantic proposal, did I?"

She had laughed and said truthfully that he needn't be romantic.

No, there was nothing dramatic, no sweeping, earth-shattering romance, but she had always felt theirs to be an inevitable love, something they could count on all their lives.

She had struggled with German and French, as had Rufe; she had a little advantage on him in French because she had learned the rudiments in school. Rufe had the advantage in his aptitude for learning any strange language; he picked up grammar and accent more easily than she did. He had worked hard; the requirements for the Foreign Service were exacting. He had gone to law school but had interrupted his education when he went to Vietnam; when he came home he decided to train for the Foreign Service. Seth had not discouraged him; he only said that it was a hard course, and he too had helped him. Seth was a lawyer but he also had a specialized knowledge of international problems, for long ago he had turned from his law practice to politics and now was a senator.

Surely nobody could say that Rufe had anything to do with the judge's murder. Meeth had killed him.

The capsule the doctor had given her had blurred the edges of her mind. It struck her in a distant and half-dreamy way that the past was always amidst the present. Another judge—younger, vigorous, indulgent —seemed to walk through the present; yet in fact the judge had changed recently. He knew it too; he had resigned from the bench before the required age of seventy, saying impatiently that he preferred to resign before his ability for careful reasoning and judgment was impaired and the Bar Association was obliged to ask for his resignation. He had been right to resign, and Bea knew that Clara accepted it. At times he was perfectly lucid and natural, but in a second he could change into an unreasonable and querulous old man, touchy to the point of irrationality. The doctor had told Bea and Clara that there was no firm dividing line to define his mental state; they must simply be patient and not permit him to fall into a rage.

The last had been impossible; no one knew what might send the judge into a burst of flaring, violent temper. She had done so that night, sitting at the dinner table with him after Clara had taken herself upstairs to her Western. And when he had flared up, Bea had been fiery and defiant, too. What was done was done; she couldn't have stopped herself. However distant, she was of the judge's blood, and she was young and had strength and passion. Out of gratitude and a real affection she had trained herself to be calm and obedient, but there were some things the judge could not demand of her. She would have liked his approval of her marriage, but she could do without it. She could do without anything, she had thought in sudden blazing anger, except for Rufe. Yet surely the judge had guessed how things stood between her and Rufe? She wondered if that was one reason why he had been so intent and helpful about Rufe's training. He must have known that Rufe would receive only a minor appointment. The judge could have reasoned slyly that Rufe would be sent far away from

Bea, and that for a long time he wouldn't be able to afford to support Bea in—the judge was right when he called it luxury. But now her own love for the judge and her own reason tried to deny that suspicion.

Until her quarrel with the judge, it had been a great day. Rufe had come that morning to tell her the news that he had passed his final oral examinations. They had walked away from the house, past the old red barn which now served as a garage, and along the path to the pond, through the spring woods. A few swamp maples were flaming red; there was a golden haze around the willows. "I'm still shaky in French," Rufe had said. "German was all right. Duties requirements, those were all right, and so were tactics and strategy in the event of war."

"War?"

"Required instruction. 'War is a projection of policy when other means fail.' "

It was obviously a quotation. "Who said that?"

"One of our greats, Robert Murphy. What a Foreign Service officer hopes and tries to do is prevent failure."

After a moment she said, "Where are they going to send you?"

"Where are they going to send us, you mean. Oh, Bea!" Rufe had laughed exultantly. "We'll hear soon, I expect." He sobered. "It's what I've wanted to do ever since I was sent to Vietnam. If this world is to be saved, it's by communication. We've got to learn to talk to one another, to understand one another. It can be done by Foreign Service officers, by diplomacy. We've got to understand one another—nations, I mean—as people."

"I know." She had heard him talk like this many times. It was as if his experience in Vietnam had opened his vision; he was dedicating his life to the hope of being even a small thread in a mesh that could help bind the world of nations together in friendship and common cause.

The Foreign Service was strict in its demands, but surely the fact that Rufe's intended wife's great-uncle—so remote an association—had been murdered could not possibly endanger his career.

Suddenly she realized that a long time had passed since she'd come upstairs. She wondered what the police were doing. She started as someone knocked at the door and then opened it. "Seth!"

Seth was tall and lean, like Dr. Thorne; he had a long face with sharply aquiline features, a Yankee face, although it always seemed to Bea that in a portrait his neck should be surrounded by a ruff, like a Spanish grandee.

But no Spanish grandee would wear such old and baggy tweeds. "Dear Bea, I'm so sorry."

"Seth, I quarreled with him tonight! Seth, can this possibly hurt Rufe's career?"

"No!" He said it too vehemently, in his strong orator's voice, the voice that had helped him in his own career. Apparently he heard himself, for he added quietly, "Don't think of such a thing! How could it hurt Rufe? He had nothing to do with this."

"Was it Meeth?"

"They're trying to find him. Now, Bea, listen to me. The police have a warrant. They've searched the whole place—the judge's study, everywhere. They want you to tell them how you happened to find him, but tell me first."

She gave a careful, brief recital, and as he listened his angular face cleared. "All right. They'll make a record of everything you say, you know. I just wanted to be sure there was nothing that you—oh, that you might later wish you hadn't said. Stick to the facts and you'll be all right. Obrian is down there, and you're not afraid of him, are you?"

Obrian, the chief of the Valley Ridge police, had known Bea since her childhood; indeed, he had once caught her sailing full tilt down Main Street on roller skates. She couldn't remember how she had got there undetected, for the Salcott place (Clara's property, which in spite of her marriage to Judge Bartry was still called the Salcott place) lay over two miles from the quiet little village of Valley Ridge. Unluckily, Mrs. Benson had emerged from Bellow's Fancy Fruit Store just as Bea shot past. But she didn't shoot past; she butted full speed into Mrs. Benson. Even more unluckily, Mrs. Benson was wearing an immaculate white linen dress and fell into a tray of blueberries and red raspberries. Mr. Bellow had burst from the store; Obrian, already chief of police, had heard the commotion from his office and had taken Bea home after administering a sound whack to the seat of her blue shorts. Nobody was supposed to rollerskate down Main Street. The judge had been most apologetic to Mrs. Benson and had scolded Bea, but there had been a twinkle in his eye. Mrs. Benson was not one of his favorites.

Seth said, "Now then, wash your face; you'll feel better."

She did feel better after splashing her face with cold water. "Comb your hair," Seth directed when she emerged from the bathroom, and obediently she did that too, unable to repress the thought that Seth thus carefully advised clients before their appearance in a courtroom.

Seth stood behind her and watched in the mirror as she brushed her hair. "You're a beautiful child," he said unexpectedly.

"Me!"

"Look at yourself. Dark-blue eyes—but they can flash with anger. Hair like silk, sort of brown and gold. When you were a kid you had great golden curls. Your face was rounder then; now it shows character."

"Seth!" But she eyed herself in the mirror, momentarily distracted.

"Black eyelashes, black eyebrows, good strong nose and— Oh, don't look so surprised, Bea, you must have seen yourself. Rufe is a lucky fellow. A beautiful wife, and one with character. Soft on the outside," Seth said. "Concrete inside. Well, perhaps that's not very flattering. Marble on the inside."

"You're trying to stiffen my backbone."

"I don't think it needs stiffening. All right now, come with me—"

"Oh, Seth—" She rose.

"You'll have to talk to them. Just be yourself and— Control yourself, Bea, don't let them work on your emotions."

"No." She rose. "Seth, the doctor said they had called the state police."

"Oh, yes. They've been conducting the search."

"Two of them were here in my room."

'They haven't found any intruder—Meeth or anybody. The territory is hard to search. There are all the woods belonging to Clara's property, and those of the Ellison place on one side and the Carters' on the other. The Carter place hasn't been occupied since old Mrs. Carter died. The Ellisons are away and there's only a caretaker there. It's easy for somebody to hide. They've tried to find and identify tire tracks along the public road, but I don't think they found anything. The medical examiner came, he's gone now. He says he'll have a full report in the morning, but there's no doubt that the judge was shot. He says the bullet entered by the shoulder just above the heart, but too close. He called it the anterior chest wall." Seth's voice took on a sharp note. "He says . . . Well, you'll have to know. The medical examiner insists that whoever shot him tried and probably succeeded in removing the bullet from below his shoulder blade. I don't know how he can be so sure, but that's what he says. You'd better sit down!" He pulled Bea toward a chair barely in time. "Put your head down. I thought I'd better tell you here."

A dizzy swinging sensation descended on her like a curtain. "Did the judge know that? Was he conscious? How long could he have lived?"

He shook his head. "I doubt if he was conscious at the time the bullet was extracted—if it was extracted. I really don't think he suffered, Bea."

"He was conscious for a moment, just long enough to tell me to send for you and the doctor—"

"That's all he said?"

"That's all, Seth. There's simply nothing I know that could help the police. Nothing!"

"Well, then," Seth said, "take it easy. They won't know whether the murderer really succeeded in getting the bullet out until the medical examiner has made X-rays. He may be all wrong about the bullet being extracted. As a matter of fact, it seems to me they're being a little too fast about calling it murder. The judge was shot, yes, but knowing him and knowing that he was aware of his own physical condition, he just might have shot himself."

"But the bullet—"

"Could have gone straight through his body and is somewhere in the ground. If the medical examiner should be right, of course somebody must have shot him and believed the bullet could be traced. But suicide seems to me more likely."

"Not the judge."

"They found a gun near him. It may prove to be his."

"I didn't see a gun."

"You weren't in a state to see anything. Come, Bea—"

"He wouldn't have killed himself! Not the judge!"

"They'll try to trace the gun they found. We'd better go down. There's a lieutenant of the state police. The medical examiner let them take the judge away after he'd seen them; there was an ambulance. There are two detectives, men in plain clothes. Don't let anybody frighten you. Tell them what you told me, but don't say any more than that."

There was a significance in his words that she had to search out. "What do you mean, Seth?"

"Murder is a capital crime. The police never give up on a murder case."

"You mean more than that."

"I mean that one never knows just how entangling the evidence in a murder case can be. It's a good rule to say no more than you have to say and stick to it. Now don't look at me like that, Bea. You and Clara—good heavens, nobody will suspect either of you! But just do as I say. Talk to them as you talked to me, but not another word."

Rufe knocked and opened the door. "Bea, they want you to tell them how you found him."

She took a long breath and went down the stairs, following Seth, Rufe holding her hand firmly. In the study there was a group of men, some state policemen, some in the blue uniform of the village police, and, as Seth had warned, two men in plain clothes stood beside the desk. All of them turned as she came in, and Seth introduced them. The lieutenant's name was Abbott; she didn't hear the other introductions.

Chief Obrian surged heavily out of an armchair. "I'm sorry about this, Bea," he said. He was trying to put her at ease. "Now, these officers want you to tell how you happened to find the judge."

Lieutenant Abbott stepped forward, and politely, as if he had memorized an exact formula—as indeed, she thought vaguely, he must have— gave her a formal warning to the effect that as a witness she must be willing to make a statement. Another policeman took out a stenographer's pad and a pencil. She told her story, aware of the alert eyes and ears around her and of the swiftly moving pencil of the man taking notes.

When she finished, Seth said in a low voice, "It will be typed up and then you'll be asked to sign it. All right?"

Bea nodded as they began to question her. She knew that her answers were being added to the notes.

"Now this burglar alarm," one of the men in plain clothes said, "I've seen many of them. It goes off when a door or window that has been bugged is opened. You say this door"—he jerked his head toward the terrace door—"was open when you came down. How much time elapsed while you and Mrs. Bartry talked up there in the hall before you decided to look for the judge?"

"I don't know; only a few minutes. The alarm makes such a noise. I got into a dressing gown and slippers, and when I came downstairs the judge wasn't here—"

"We understand that. But the medical examiner says that whoever killed him had to have time to dig out that bullet. Now, if the judge had gone outside after Mrs. Bartry set the alarm, it would have sounded then."

The second man in plain clothes cleared his throat. The other nodded. "Yes, I'm coming to that. There's a caretaker on the Ellison place next door. Name is Griffin. He heard and saw the police cars and came forward with some information."

Willie Griffin, Bea thought; she knew him. Any information he had to give was probably accurate. It also proved to be difficult to understand.

"He says," the first detective went on, "that he heard not just one shot but two shots. Heard them distinctly. After that, he is sure that it was maybe ten, fifteen minutes after the two shots that he heard your alarm go. Any answer to that, Miss Bartry?"

Bea shook her head. "Two shots?"

"So he says. We found only one gun. It had been fired once as far as we can make out at this time. You're sure you heard no shots at all?"

"No, no, I told you—"

"If this man Griffin is correct, then the judge must have gone outside before the alarm was set. So it looks as if whoever shot him had time first to dig out the bullet and then come back in the house, setting off the alarm. The judge—or the murderer—apparently closed that door when the judge went out. After that the alarm was set. When the murderer came back to the house and opened the door, the alarm started. At least that's the way it looks now."

All of them seemed to conclude that it was murder; nobody even mentioned suicide. But then Bea herself wouldn't have accepted suicide.

The detective asked thoughtfully, "Why would anyone come back into the house? It was a terrific risk. What could anybody want? Money?"

"We never keep much cash in the house."

"Jewelry? Did anybody have time to do any rummaging around for jewelry after you and your aunt heard the alarm?"

"No."

"Well, whoever killed him wanted something from the house pretty badly."

THREE

"But there isn't anything," Bea said.

There was a long and thoughtful silence. It struck her that there was a faint, grimy dust over almost everything in the study, particularly on the judge's desk; it must have been to get fingerprints. Rufe took her hand and pulled her down into a chair. Finally the lieutenant said, "There's another consideration. If that bullet was removed, whoever dug for it must have had some kind of surgical experience. He'd have to know where to dig and how, in the dark—"

Dr. Thorne was sitting in a chair in the corner; Bea hadn't seen him till he spoke. "I have certainly had medical, even some surgical experience, but I assure you I didn't shoot the judge."

Rufe said suddenly, "That bullet would have had to come from a thirty-two, wouldn't it?"

All the men looked at him sharply.

Rufe said, "Well, it stands to reason. A forty-five would have been too destructive. A thirty-eight would probably have gone through the body. A thirty-two is my guess. My father's gun is a thirty-two. You can look at it yourself. He always keeps a gun in his car—"

"Why?" the lieutenant said, surprised.

Dr. Thorne answered, "Because I'm a doctor. I make night calls. The country is different now—you never know. Well, I have a permit, and you can examine the gun. I don't think it's ever been fired, thank God."

"He hasn't even cleaned it," Rufe said. "Believe me—"

"You pointed out the fact that the gun that killed the judge was likely a thirty-two," one of the detectives said slowly. "Now, if the judge had worn that coat of his"—he nodded at the heavy, shabby tweed jacket which now lay neatly folded over a chair—"the bullet probably wouldn't have gone so far through to enable anybody to try to extract it from his back. You've had army experience, I understand?"

Rufe replied shortly, "Of course."

"I expect you have a gun."

"I had one. I turned it in with the rest of my gear when I got out of the service."

"What did you do in the army? I mean your special job."

Rufe's face became the reserved mask which was partly natural and partly cultivated since he had been training for the Foreign Service. He replied agreeably, "I was a medical corpsman for a while."

The lieutenant's face sharpened. "How did that happen? I understood from Obrian that you had studied law."

"I did. But my father's office is in our home, and from time to time since I was a kid I'd hang around and give him a bit of help now and then. Anyway, I knew something of first aid, so they made me a corpsman. Of course, they gave me some training."

"You'd know how to dig out a bullet," one of the detectives said almost to himself.

Rufe remained agreeable. "I've dug out plenty of bullets. Made plenty of splints and all that, too. But I had help—lights for one thing, and assistance."

There was another long silence. Everyone was wondering how anybody could successfully extract a bullet in the dark shadows of the laurels. Finally one detective, small, thin, gray, put another question to Rufe. "You were a corpsman all the time you were in Vietnam?"

"No. I was transferred to another outfit. They called it intelligence. I was new at it and green. Mainly I only had to interview prisoners or villagers, try to get at the truth of things."

"But did you understand their language?"

Rufe looked rather grim. "No. You understood—oh, other things. Gestures, attitudes—I can't explain it. I picked up a few words."

Seth said, "He was good at it. His commanding officer gave him a fine recommendation for Foreign Service training."

The detective looked soberly at Seth and then back to Rufe. The lieutenant fingered his own polished holster from which protruded a businesslike revolver. "But you know something about guns."

"Quite a number of young men know something about guns," Dr. Thorne said wearily.

Seth said, "Can Miss Bartry leave now? She's had a frightful shock. She'll talk to you any time. But tonight . . ."

Obrian's face seemed relieved at the idea of a respite. He heaved himself out of his chair. "I do advise that, Lieutenant."

Rufe said, "When did you get the alarm at the police station, Mr. Obrian?"

He turned a fat face toward Rufe. "I'm not sure. Tony!"

Tony Calinas stepped forward. "Yes, sir."

"When did that alarm come on?"

Tony replied promptly, "I was in the patrol car, and we got the alarm from the police station at ten forty-five almost to the second. I made a record of it."

"There'll be a record at the station too. What's on your mind, Rufe?"

"Whoever came into the house and set off the alarm must have got out fast."

"The alarm scared him away," Obrian said. "At least that's what it is supposed to do."

The lieutenant said, "We've got to find out when Mrs. Bartry set the alarm—"

Dr. Thorne interrupted him. "You cannot question Mrs. Bartry tonight. If you insist on it, I cannot be responsible for the consequences. You can get her statement tomorrow."

There was another pause; then one of the men in plain clothes spoke. "The point is, what did the murderer want?" He eyed the three steel filing cabinets that stood behind the judge's big desk.

Obrian looked from the files to Bea. "You acted as your uncle's secretary. Do you know of any record or anything that somebody might have wanted?"

"No. Only the usual letters and accounts. And he was working on his memoirs."

The little gray detective turned to her, his ears seeming to prick up. "Memoirs?"

Obrian's plump face tightened. "His autobiography?"

"They're in the files. He'd talk into the dictating machine and then I'd transcribe the tapes." She thought of all the pages, most of them flat and dull, which she had laboriously typed out to the accompaniment of the judge's rather harsh voice on a tape. "You can look at them—they're in the files. But I'd remember anything that—that anybody might want. There must have been some other reason for the murderer to come into the house. We didn't hear or see anybody." Her voice rose unsteadily.

"It's all right, Bea," Seth said.

The lieutenant tapped his fingers lightly on his revolver holster as if he were playing some tune which only he could hear, and addressed nobody in particular. "Now, the time the alarm came in at the police station was, say, a minute before the alarm reached the patrol car. So whoever came into the house had to be here before ten forty-five but after Mrs. Bartry set the alarm. So"—he addressed the ceiling—"if this fellow Meeth should happen to have an alibi for that time . . ."

He paused, and after a moment Obrian said heavily, "Then we'll have to look elsewhere."

"That's our job," the lieutenant said shortly. Having got that off his well-tailored chest, he seemed to feel better and stopped playing tunes on his holster.

The detective with the gray suit, gray hair and grayish face said, "The judge had a gun, Miss Bartry?"

She nodded.

He said, "Could you identify it?"

"No. But he had it registered."

"You've seen it?"

"Yes. He showed it to me."

"When was that?"

"About a couple of weeks ago."

"Any special reason for showing it to you?"

"Yes. He'd had it for some time, but he never wanted my aunt to know about it. She's nervous about guns and she was upset because Meeth was about to be released from prison. That's why we had the burglar alarm installed."

"Why did the judge show you his gun?" said the detective.

"He told me how to load it and where he kept it."

"But why? Was he afraid of something—or somebody?"

"He said that I ought to know he had it, that was all."

"Was it loaded when he showed it to you?"

"Yes. He said there was no use keeping a gun around unless it was loaded."

"Was he afraid of Meeth?"

"No! He said once that if he were afraid of everybody he sentenced, he'd never have an easy moment."

"Where did he keep the gun?"

"In a desk drawer."

"Which one?"

The detective's voice was quiet, yet there was tension in the room when Bea went to the desk and pulled open the third drawer from the top. The police seemed to crowd around her, but it was Rufe who said quietly, "It's not there. Maybe he changed the place. Look in the other drawers."

The gun was nowhere in the desk.

"How about the files?" the lieutenant said.

One of the detectives shrugged and pulled open the top drawer of the nearest filing cabinet; it slid out easily and heavily, disclosing labeled, packed papers. He gave a look of dismay at the others, then quite openly glanced at his watch.

Abbott seemed to sigh. "We can't go through all those tonight. What about the rest of the drawers?"

Bea said, "They're almost full, too."

Obrian said thoughtfully, "I guess as people get older they save more and more. No sense to it, but they do."

Bea pushed her hair up from her temples wearily. "There are tax records, bank statements, my aunt's brokers' statements, letters—quite a number of them, both copies of letters he sent and the replies. There are the records of insurance premiums paid, and he kept paid bills for five years. His notes for the memoirs are in the lower file drawer on this side—"

Obrian said, "Now, these memoirs—"

Bea understood him and said firmly, "There was nothing in the judge's memoirs that could hurt anybody. It gave him something to do." She remembered how often she and Clara would hear the judge's voice, not as resonant and commanding as it once was but still with a certain authority, rumbling along at all hours; they would exchange a kind of conspiratorial glance which said "It keeps him occupied."

Obrian's great hand closed the packed drawer of the filing cabinet. "The point is, the judge couldn't have shot himself and then tried to dig out that bullet."

The little gray detective said in a tired voice that they could check to-morrow on whether the gun they had found belonged to the judge.

The other detective heartily agreed with him. "We can't do any more just now. Have to find this man Meeth, take a look through the judge's desk and files. That'll take time."

The lieutenant said, "We haven't taken Mis Bartry's fingerprints."

The second detective grunted. "She's not going to run away. But I'd suggest leaving a man here in the house who'll keep an eye on"—his gaze went to the filing cabinets—"things," he finished, his underlip protruding.

"I can't spare a man. God knows what's going on right now at the bar-racks. But—" The lieutenant made up his mind and turned to Obrian. "Have you got a man you can leave here tonight?"

Tony stepped forward smartly. "I can stay, sir."

Obrian frowned. "That'd be overtime for you. Sure you don't want me to get someone else?"

"No, sir, it's all right."

The lieutenant seemed unhappy but yielded to the pressure of time and to the obvious desire of the two detectives to depart. "All right." He gave Tony a severe stare. "Just don't go to sleep. Keep your eyes open. Now then, men—"

They were leaving. The young policeman with the stenographer's tablet put it carefully in his pocket. Bea saw that the small gray detective was carrying her dressing gown over one arm.

There was the measured tread of feet along the terrace, then the roar of cars starting up in the drive. Nobody spoke until the thud of the engines had diminished down the drive. Then Dr. Thorne took up his medicine bag. "I've got to get home to check my answering service. Bea, if your aunt wakes and gets restless I left two capsules on her bedside table. Give her one. Coming, Rufe?"

"I think I'll stay here tonight, Pa—that is, if Bea wants me."

"Yes—" Bea began, but his father interrupted, "Of course. Well—" He put a hand on her shoulder in a gesture which was meant to be comforting. "The judge couldn't have recovered, Bea. He was getting worse all the time—everybody knew it. He'd get something on his mind and brood over it and build it up and . . . It must have been very difficult for you and Clara. He was a proud man. Wouldn't surprise me at all if he used his own gun to—"

Rufe shook his head. "He *couldn't* have dug out the bullet, Pa."

"But suppose the medical examiner is wrong. He's new here; I don't know much about him. Suppose the judge killed himself. I'm not sure I could tell whether the bullet was extracted or whether its velocity had torn the flesh."

"You could tell," Rufe said.

Seth said thoughtfully, "When I used to go hunting, I'd sometimes dig out a bullet, but I'm not sure I would have known afterward whether it was dug out with a knife or whether it just came out. It was a messy business, anyway."

"Don't—" Bea said in a small voice.

"Try to sleep, Bea," the doctor said and went out the terrace door.

Seth said, "I'll be going too. Unless you want me to stay."

Bea saw his own weariness; his aquiline face seemed to fall into sagging lines, so that his tight iron-gray curls looked even crisper than usual.

"No, Seth, thanks."

"I'll come by tomorrow. There's his will, you know. He had me draw up wills for himself and Clara when I was home last fall. They fixed it so everything Clara and the judge had is to come to you eventually—"

"To *me!*" Bea stared at Seth. "But I— That's not fair!"

"It's the way he wanted it. I'll explain it tomorrow—"

He broke off, for at that moment the terrace door flung open and Lorraine swept into the room along with green chiffon, sables and perfume. Afterward it seemed to Bea an almost shocking example of Lorraine's gift for timing that she should arrive at the precise moment when Seth was talking about the judge's will. But in her astonishment she said only, "You can't be here! You're in Italy!"

"In Italy? What do you think? Darling Seth! I hear you're still a sena-tor. It must be almost your third term. You don't look a day older! Just as handsome as ever. More so!" She swept over to Seth and kissed him warmly. Then she swirled around to Rufe and embraced him warmly too. Altogether too warmly, Bea thought.

Lorraine had been her rival for years—no, Bea had to amend that, for the fact was that though Rufe had once been in love with Lorraine, it was a long time ago.

Lorraine perched on the corner of the desk, her slender white hand on Rufe's shoulder. "And they tell me," she went on, "that you're going into the Foreign Service, Rufe. You'll be a great man. It's wonderful."

"I didn't know you were here," Bea said lamely.

Lorraine gave a high-pitched, shrill laugh, like a bird's song—but a glit-tering, flashing, predatory bird. "I've been here two days. I'm staying at the Bensons'."

"The Bensons'! Why on earth?"

"Oh." Lorraine laughed lightly again. "I knew the judge wouldn't wel-come me here. I thought I'd take a few days to see how the land lay—that is, if there was a chance of softening him up. He told me never to darken his door again." She giggled. "He really said that, just like a stern father in some old melodrama. All because I wanted to marry Cecco. That is"—she caught herself and seemed to snuggle her lithe body toward Rufe—"I *thought* I wanted to marry Cecco. I wouldn't have done it if the judge hadn't opposed the marriage. I couldn't let him bully me. But it happens that the judge was right. I've left Cecco. Will you help me get a divorce, Seth?"

Seth said soberly, "Don't you know what happened tonight?"

"Oh, of course. That's why I came. I was at a dance at the club with Ben Benson. Somebody heard the news and told us, so I got Ben to bring me here and . . . here I am." Her eyes danced toward Bea. "My clothes are at the Bensons'. We'll have to get them tomorrow. I'll stay here now, of course. Aunt Clara will want me. Aunt Clara always loved me. It was the judge who got upset about my marriage. Too bad he'll never know how right he was." Lorraine laughed again and tossed back her head so that the black locks of thick hair framing her narrow, heart-shaped face displayed her high cheekbones, her bold white forehead, slanted black eye-brows and red lips to advantage. The gesture was so graceful that it seemed practiced; nevertheless it was attractive.

Rufe's face showed neither pleasure nor surprise as Lorraine leaned against his arm.

Seth said, "Are you sure Clara will want you here, Lorraine?"

"Oh, yes!" Lorraine said confidently. "I'm her niece, her only blood relative."

Seth said, "I'll be going. Try to rest, Bea."

"Seth, wait," Bea said quickly. "What will happen now?"

"An investigation. An inquest—"

"When?"

"Possibly not for some time, and unless they have very strong evidence, the inquest may be adjourned or there may be a verdict of murder by a person or persons unknown. After that," Seth sighed, "well, if they can secure strong evidence against some person, there'll be a warrant sworn out, that person will be taken into custody and then the evidence will be presented to the grand jury."

"And after that?"

"If the grand jury brings in a true bill—that is, indicts someone—there may be bail set, later a trial . . . Oh, don't think about all that now, Bea. Besides, I still don't see how the police can jump so fast to the conclusion that it's murder. I suppose that Meeth's threats set them off. That, and this medical examiner saying the bullet had been dug out. Still, this talk about murder isn't really conclusive. Of course, they have to consider it and investigate—that's their duty. But I'm not sure—" He shook his head.

He was certainly not as handsome as Lorraine had proclaimed but he did have a distinguished air in spite of the baggy clothes he wore, which Bea always suspected were assumed to fit his political image, that of a New England lawyer from a small town. Yet it was like Seth to refuse to put on airs.

Tony had removed himself unobtrusively to the corner by the door. His dark face was lowering and angry. Why? Then Bea remembered that he had been with Rufe in Vietnam; he must know of the many letters Rufe had written to Lorraine, and of Lorraine's failure to reply to them. Out of sight, out of mind must have been one reason for Lorraine's swift rejection of Rufe, but another was because she had met Cecco. Tony gave Lorraine a baleful glance, which she noted instantly. Sliding off the desk, she went over to Seth and lifted her charming face again. "I never knew a senator could be so handsome," she said softly. "But then, you always were handsome, Seth—"

Seth gave a short laugh. "I'm working up to fifty, Lorraine. No blandishments, if you please. Better ask Clara what she wants you to do." His glance took in Bea and Rufe. "I'll see you," he said, and left.

"*Ciao,*" Lorraine called after him, and then turned back to Rufe. "Goodness! I always thought of Seth as being ancient. Forty-five or whatever isn't too old. Did he ever marry?"

"No."

"H'mm." Lorraine was thoughtful. "Living in Washington, knowing all those famous people. Why, he really needs a wife, a hostess."

Tony abruptly and unexpectedly changed the subject. "Now don't worry, we'll see to things, Miss Bartry."

"You're not married either, Bea?" There was a teasing quality in Lorraine's voice. "And so many men around! Why, I thought you'd have been married long ago."

Tony moved restlessly, watching Rufe from the corners of his dark eyes.

Lorraine gave that graceful little toss of her head again. "Well, it was smart of you to make yourself useful to the judge and Aunt Clara. She's so rich!"

"Lorraine, it's been a dreadful—" Bea's voice broke a little.

Rufe made a move toward her, but somehow Lorraine was between them, stooping to pick up the sable stole she had dropped at his feet.

Bea went on, "I think that Aunt Clara would want you to stay here. I can give you a nightdress. Is Ben waiting for you?"

"Oh, no, I told him to go home before his mother got upset and began to phone all over the place." There was an edge to Lorraine's voice. "If ever anybody was tied to his mother's apron strings, it's Ben Benson. Of course, I'm very sorry about the judge, but Ben did tell me that he had been ill, so possibly he just decided to kill himself," she said airily. "I don't see how they can possibly be sure that somebody shot him."

"They can be," Rufe said shortly. "Take it easy, Bea. I'll stay down here with Tony." He came to her, lifted her face and kissed her.

Over his shoulder Bea saw Lorraine looking knowing and a little amused. "Come on, Lorraine," she said, breaking away from Rufe. "We'll have to be quiet. The doctor gave Aunt Clara something to make her sleep."

But Lorraine had not finished. "Tony!" she cried with delight. "Why, of course! I knew that I ought to remember you. You used to work at the filling station on Oak Street."

Tony nodded.

Lorraine swept on, apparently overcome by rapturous admiration. "And now you're a policeman!"

"Yes," Tony said. "And I was told to stay here tonight."

Something in his voice and lowering face put Lorraine off her stride. "Oh, well. That's very good of you. And you, Rufe. We'll feel so safe. I'm coming, Bea."

Tony's adamantine face was a small triumph; Bea could have kissed him. She led the way, Lorraine's sables brushing against her arm, up the stairs, lightly, in the hope of not rousing Clara. It seemed remarkable that nothing in the house had changed. The lower hall was wide and gracious; the big mirror above the table reflected the two young women, flashes of green chiffon and black hair, flashes of herself, pale and tired-looking, in her brown sweater and skirt. Nobody, not Seth or even Rufe, could think her beautiful now. She had always felt gawky and pedestrian in Lorraine's presence, but now she felt it acutely when they entered her room. She took out a nightgown for Lorraine, who laughed, but checked it when Bea put her finger to her lips. "It's the nightgown," Lorraine whispered. "Nobody wears nightgowns!"

"Well, don't wear it if you don't want to. Nobody cares!" Bea snapped.

Lorraine eyed her. "What's all this between you and Rufe?"

Suddenly Bea's fighting blood surged up. She said forcefully, "We're engaged. We're going to be married as soon as Rufe gets his appointment."

"Oh, are you?" Lorraine smiled. "You've taken my room, and apparently you've tried to take my place with Aunt Clara as well as with Rufe. I'll go to that big guest room."

She seemed almost to dance out of the room. If anybody regretted the judge's death, it wasn't Lorraine. Exultance was in her every move and word.

Bea pulled her sweater over her head and paused to look at herself again in the mirror. There were shadows under her eyes; her face was pale and seemed oddly determined. Seth had called her beautiful either to distract or encourage her, but now she told herself to accept his compliments and proceed as if they were true. Lorraine was no ordinary rival.

Sometimes Rufe had said something flattering, and even the judge sometimes had given her a swift, hard look, usually over the dinner-table candlelight, and said that she was *en beauté* that night. It was one of his fancies to use French or Latin phrases. Apparently it hadn't occurred to him that if there was a special sparkle in her face, it was because of Rufe.

But the judge was perceptive. He couldn't have been as surprised as he pretended to be when she told him that she and Rufe were going to be married as soon as he got an assignment. He had been pleased when she'd told him the good news that Rufe had passed his last tests, but he had taken that as a credit to himself and whatever assistance he had given Rufe. Yet she could not reasonably ignore the fact that the judge simply preferred to keep her at home because she was useful. Clara had plenty of money; even now she could have contrived to employ a chauffeur, a secretary for the judge and a housekeeper; instead there was only Velda Mathers from the village who came in by the day. Somehow she kept the big house in order with Bea's help. Sometimes Clara deplored this, but not often, for the judge's wishes came first in her life.

Bea was sure she couldn't sleep. She was tired to the bone, but not sleepy-tired. Lorraine had said something about divorcing Cecco. Obviously it wasn't because of his lack of money. She remembered the rings flashing on Lorraine's white hands, the sable stole she had dropped on the floor as if it were a rug, the adroitly designed green chiffon dress. Perhaps Lorraine had simply tired of him.

Certainly she had taken a swift interest in Seth, a long-time senator who, Lorraine had said, must need a wife and hostess for all those important people in Washington. But she had also instantly flirted with Rufe. Did she feel sure of getting him back again?

But naturally Lorraine would feel sure of getting anything she wanted.

Eight years older than Bea, Lorraine was the daughter of Clara's only sister, who had divorced her husband and remarried. Then her father had remarried too. Bea had never heard the entire story, but she did know that Lorraine had been welcome in neither household and that Clara had lovingly offered her a home. She must have been about twelve or thirteen when Bea herself was introduced into the household, but even then Lorraine possessed a certain sophistication. She hadn't paid much attention to Bea; she wasn't interested in small children. Later on, though, she had permitted Bea to watch while she prepared to go out with some boy. She would fix her hair in this arrangement or that; put on lipstick and then wipe it off to try another color, leaving her lips bare but inviting; would let Bea watch her try on her dresses.

Bea didn't know when it was that she began to recognize Lorraine's facility for lying, but was always astonished at the way she could coolly lie to Clara or the judge.

Bea was also very much aware of the progress of her cousin's interest in

Rufe. Lorraine would laugh in a satisfied way and tell her how Rufe adored her, how he felt that she was the only woman for him!

Bea didn't know how much she had believed as a child, but certainly Rufe's behavior had confirmed at least some of Lorraine's smug statements. He was always underfoot, the judge had said once testily, but Clara had intervened. They had known Rufe all his life, and they couldn't find a better husband for Lorraine.

Lorraine had looked rather sulky at that and said she didn't need to have anybody find a husband for her; she could do it herself. This bothered Clara, whose faint eyebrows drew together over her troubled pale-blue eyes. Clara had taken a motherly interest—almost too great an interest— in Rufe since his own mother had died many years before. Rufe had complained once, but laughingly, saying that Aunt Clara would still have him in long woolen underwear if she could. But he loved her and called her Aunt, a courtesy title.

Yes, both Clara and the judge would have accepted him as Lorraine's husband. But then Rufe had gone to Vietnam, Cecco had arrived on the scene and Lorraine had fallen for him—or perhaps vice versa. In any event, the judge had opposed their marriage so violently that in the end they had eloped and gone to live in Italy.

Gradually as Bea grew older she had become like a daughter to both Clara and the judge. She knew that they loved her, knew that they had grown to depend on her, and so she had made it her task to take on more and more responsibility.

Long ago Rufe had taught her to skate on the pond down by the woods; he had romped and run with old Shadders, the dog the judge had given her, a stiff-legged Airedale whose manners were also rather stiff at first acquaintance. But he had loved Rufe, and Bea had loved Rufe too, counting the days to his vacations even though she knew that he would be coming to the house because Lorraine was there.

But then, years later, Rufe had come home from Vietnam and went into the arduous training for Foreign Service, and he and Bea were now engaged to be married. She held that fact close; Rufe wouldn't be taken in again by Lorraine.

Or would he?

Now the shadow of the judge's death fell over her again. How could she think of anything else! She debated briefly whether to reset the burglar alarm; all she had to do was go to the linen closet where the tiny panel

was set into the wall. There were two small lights in the panel and a
smaller push button; if the bugged doors and windows were properly
closed, a white light showed; if not, there was no light at all. When the
white light showed, one push of the button would switch it off and turn
on the red light, showing that the alarm was set.

She decided against setting the alarm. Tony or Rufe would be strolling
around the house and might open one of the doors. She was thankful for
their presence; she would go to sleep safely. But her mind was like a pin-
wheel whirling around and around, shooting off sparks: the judge's death,
the gun, a police inquiry. Hadn't Seth said something about the judge's
will, something that affected her?

The spark of consciousness floated off and vanished into darkness. She
went to sleep as if she had taken some of Clara's medicine, drugged into
insensibility. Yet she dreamed; she was telling Lorraine again that she and
Rufe were going to be married, and Lorraine was looking at her with brilliant green eyes and saying again, not quite restraining laughter, "Oh, are
you?"

A sound aroused her; she sat up, wondering what burden had fallen on
her and at once remembered. It was a dull day; gray light came through
the curtains. Somewhere there were voices. Lorraine was saying, piercingly
and sweetly, "Darling Aunt Clara! Of course I came at once to be with
you," and a man's voice murmured in a low tone.

FOUR

So the day began. After a quick shower Bea dressed in her usual casual
fashion, but she brushed her hair into a shining mass, even though she
knew it couldn't rival the dramatic effect of Lorraine's hanging black frame
of hair. As she walked down the hall she saw that Clara's door was open;
Lorraine was there, still in her green chiffon, perched at the foot of Clara's
bed. Seth was there too, lanky and sober, sitting on a straight chair. "—no,
his will doesn't have to be probated at once, Clara," he was saying as Bea

paused in the doorway. "I'll stay home as long as I can. But the sooner you get all the business details over with, the better."

Clara had a breakfast tray across her lap. Her hair was neat; her face a little pale but firm; she wore a fluffy, coquettish bed jacket and eyed Lorraine with a troubled gaze. Lorraine waited, as still as a cat about to pounce upon a mouse.

Then Clara's worried gaze caught Bea, standing in the doorway; she smiled. "Come in, dear. This concerns you, too. Tell her, Seth."

Seth politely offered Bea his chair. She shook her head and went to the other side of Clara's bed, taking the same position as Lorraine, but in her yellow sweater and blue tweed skirt Bea looked, she was sure, anything but glamorous.

Seth wriggled his angular body back into the small chair. "I started to tell Bea last night but I don't think she paid any attention. It's the judge's and Clara's wills."

Clara touched a lacy napkin to her lips. "Explain it to Bea, Seth."

"Yes. Well, in a way it's unusual, yet the judge wanted it this way and Clara agreed."

Clara gave a little nod. Lorraine sat statue-still and seemed to be holding her breath. Seth locked his hands together and looked at them as if he were consulting a brief. "I drew up both documents. The judge asked me to do it; he and Clara have separate wills of course, but they amount to the same thing."

Lorraine did move then. She put out one white hand on which diamonds flashed. "But you're still a senator!"

"I've always kept up an office here. Joe Lathrop sees to things, real-estate transfers, title searches, that kind of thing. But once in a while an old friend asks me to do something as the judge did. I wasn't sure it was a wise move on the judge's part but it wasn't my business to advise. Anybody can do anything he wants to in a will. And Clara agreed—"

Clara said, "Of course I agreed."

"Naturally," Seth said rather dryly. "You always agreed with the judge. The point is this, the wills are so written—" He turned to Bea. "If the judge predeceased Clara—as tragically he now has—then her property as well as his own were to be made into a trust for Clara's lifetime. After her death the whole of the property, Clara's portion as well as the judge's, was to come to you, Bea."

"That's what you meant," Bea began in astonishment. Yet she had taken in enough the night before to say that it wasn't fair. She said it again. "But that's not fair to Lorraine."

Lorraine made no sign that she even heard Bea. Seth said, "As you know, Clara has a great deal of property and money. She was content with the judge's arrangement—weren't you, Clara?"

Clara eyed her empty coffee cup and nodded.

"The fact was, I suppose, that the judge didn't quite depend upon Clara's judgment about business." Clara's eyes went up to Seth's face and a slight smile touched his lips. "I can't say that I agree with the judge. This kind of arrangement—that is, Clara's care of her own property, to hinge on the judge's predeceasing her—is unusual but it's perfectly legal. Nothing I could do to stop it as long as Clara agreed. But Clara always wanted to please him. Now, as we all know, the judge had not been himself recently; he was very uncertain in his mind. He would get—notions," Seth said gravely. "And nothing in the world could change his decisions. So I drew up the wills. He and Clara signed them. Joe Lathrop and the office girl he occasionally employs both witnessed them. The original documents are in my office safe. I expect the judge put copies in his safe-deposit box. Unless they are in the files in his study—" He looked inquiringly at Bea.

She shook her head. "No, I'd have seen them. That is—well, I'm not sure. If I had just gone about the usual filing routine I might have missed them, I mean the judge might have slipped them into the files under some other heading, something I would not have been likely to notice. But I'd remember it if I had seen them."

"It doesn't matter. The point is the judge's will must be probated and I want Clara to tell me whether she wants the original arrangement, the trust fund, to stand or whether she wants to make another will. You don't have to make up your mind now, Clara."

Clara crumpled her lace napkin and dropped it on the tray. "I'll think about it."

Bea felt Lorraine's sudden movement and heard what sounded like a sigh of relief.

Seth rose. "Now if there's anything I can do, Clara—"

Clara's little hands fluttered. "The obituary, Seth. It's got to be right."

"I'll see to it."

Lorraine pushed back her hair. "I saw the morning *Times*. It was delivered just as Tony and Rufe were leaving. I was downstairs and—dear

Aunt Clara, the account of the judge's death is in it. Short. Somebody must have phoned it in late last night."

Seth said comfortingly, "It was news. There are always reporters interested in anything that goes on at the Welbury barracks. They must have got the facts from somebody. I saw the account, too. It is brief and—no sense looking at it, Clara."

Clara looked up in a composed way. "But he was a well-known man. I expect there'll be a great deal in the papers. But first— Let me see, this is Saturday. You can phone in his obituary in time for tomorrow's papers. You write it, Seth. You know about the judge."

"You'll have to help me. My memory may not be as accurate or as complete as yours."

"Of course. What about a photograph?"

"Oh, I expect there'll be a photograph in the morgue."

Clara's eyes opened wide. Seth added hurriedly, "I mean the file the newspapers keep on well-known people. I'll go downstairs now and work on it. The police will want you to make a formal statement, Clara. I'll stay with you. Probably once they know you are here, Lorraine, they'll want a statement from you. Oh, yes. There may be reporters around, too. I'd only advise you to remember—well, since the police think it is murder, the least said the better just now."

His lanky figure in its baggy and unpressed tweed slacks and jacket went out. Lorraine said softly, as if to herself, "He really does need a wife to see to him. His clothes! Aunt Clara, I'm so thankful that I happened to be here just now when you need me. That is, darling, if you do need me, I want to stay."

Clara's little hands went out lovingly toward Lorraine. "I want you to stay. Where else would you go? I'm so thankful that you have left that dreadful person, Cecco. Bea, will you take Lorraine to the Bensons' and get her clothes now?" She moved to get rid of the tray, and Lorraine sprang up, took it from her and put it on a table. "Now, you girls run along. I'll be dressed by the time you get back."

Lorraine's green chiffon swished softly as they went down the stairs. The keys for the car were on the hall table. Bea took them and opened the coat closet. "It's foggy. Here—" She handed her own raincoat to Lorraine, who took it without thanks; Bea put one of Clara's coats around herself. At the front door both girls stopped abruptly, for there were three cars in the drive, and the instant the door opened men tumbled out. "It's the reporters!" Lorraine cried, and stopped to pose, her head up.

"Oh, come on. We've got to get past them to the garage." Bea hurried on, but could not evade the two reporters who bounded up at her elbow and asked if she was Miss Beatrice Bartry.

She said something, anything, and hurried to open the two halves of a door of the ancient red barn which had been turned into a very outdated garage. The doors were fastened together with only a bolt, which one reporter obligingly pushed upward for her. "Miss Bartry—"

"Not now. Please." Bea slid into the judge's gleaming Mercedes, which he usually had permitted only Bea to touch and only when he wished her to drive for him. Household errands were accomplished in a tiny, rather shabby and unreliable car that stood humbly beside the Mercedes. She heard Lorraine's high voice, sweet and sorrowful as she told somebody that it had been a tragic shock, yes, and she was Mrs. Bartry's niece—

Bea started the engine, its roar shutting out whatever else was said. Lorraine appeared then and leaped into the seat beside her. Bea thought that a reporter had to spring out of the way hurriedly as she backed out of the garage. She went as fast as she dared past the cars parked in the drive, aware of poised cameras as they went.

Salcott Road (named for the ancestor of Clara who long ago had had the perspicacity to buy two hundred acres near Valley Ridge, then really a village) wove its way around curves and over bumps. Clara had kept the entire piece of Salcott property intact in spite of many offers to buy with the intention of cutting it up into two-acre tracts and building houses. The judge had agreed with her, although he had looked rather serious when he figured just how much money that two-hundred-acre tract would now represent.

They turned on Stony Road, passing Seth's ancient little house, which his father had used as a summer place until he retired and spent the rest of his life there. Seth Hobson had continued to use it as his only home even though he spent so much time away from Valley Ridge. They went on to the Bensons', where Mrs. Benson greeted them coldly. She was a tall, stately woman who, Bea suspected, had never forgiven the blueberry, red-raspberry incident of Bea's childhood. Her long face lighted a little, not much, when Lorraine explained that Aunt Clara wanted her to stay with her and she wished to get her clothes.

"You ought to have gone there in the first place," Mrs. Benson said. "I can't imagine why you didn't. But of course, when Ben explained that you wanted to stay with us for a few days, you were very welcome," she added, lying in her very white false teeth. "You know the guest room.

Now, Bea, what is all this I hear? Is it true that that awful man Meeth shot the judge?"

It was true that the judge had been shot, Bea told her.

Mrs. Benson's gaze sharpened. "Aren't they sure it was Meeth?"

"I don't know."

"I see. I suppose the police don't take you or Clara into their confidence." She thought for a moment. "Someone told me once that the judge had been writing his memoirs."

"Yes."

"Had he finished them?"

"No."

"You seem to know— But of course, I remember, you did all his secretarial work for him."

"Yes." Bea wished Lorraine would hurry.

Mrs. Benson thought for another long moment. Then she said, "Was there anything in his memoirs that would—oh, give you an idea about a— a—" She stuck there.

Bea said wearily, "A motive for killing him?"

"Well, I—yes, I suppose that thought crossed my mind."

Bea did not reply, for Lorraine came running down the stairs. She had changed out of her green chiffon and into black slacks that fit as if molded to her handsome legs, and a dark-green turtleneck sweater which brought out the emerald gleam in her eyes. Mrs. Benson said goodbye, something intent and baffled in her light-gray eyes. She pointedly did not ask Lorraine to drop by sometime.

Lorraine giggled as they got back in the car. "She thinks I'm after her Ben!" she said with scorn.

When they returned to the Salcott place the reporters were gone. "I expect Seth got rid of them," Bea said as she stopped the car. "I'll park here in front of the house."

"I'm hungry." Lorraine lugged a large suitcase up the steps. "There's a servant of sorts, isn't there? At least a female in yellow-and-green plaid brought Aunt Clara's breakfast. Why not a uniform?"

"She wouldn't think of wearing a uniform. And don't let her hear you call her a servant."

"What *do* you call her?"

"Velda. Velda Mathers."

Lorraine tugged at the suitcase, and Bea let her tug; however, she relented sufficiently to hold open the big front door so Lorraine could deposit the suitcase in the hall. Lorraine shook back her hair. "I've got to have breakfast."

For once Bea agreed with her. Velda, summoned to the dining room, did not. "Don't you know it's nearly eleven—" Her gooseberry-green eyes focused on Lorraine. "Why—why, it's the niece! Mrs. Bartry's niece! Now I know who you are—you're the one that married that Italian fellow. People said he was a count or something and—"

"Coffee," said Lorraine tersely. "Orange juice and an egg, three minutes."

Velda flared in instinctive rebellion. "I got breakfast for Mrs. Bartry and somebody had fixed coffee and things in my kitchen early this morning before I got here." Tony, Bea thought, and Rufe.

Velda said, "Not that I was on time. Mr. Obrian came to my house early this morning and I had a long talk with him." Her manner was sinister with heavy implication.

Obrian? Bea thought. What could he and Velda have had a long talk about? The obvious answer was that he wanted information about the judge or about anything whatever in the Bartry household. Bea thought uneasily of her quarrel with the judge the previous night. Only the night before, and now the judge had been killed!

Velda, eying Bea, suddenly relented. "Oh, all right. I'll fix you something. But stay out of my kitchen."

This was contrary to the rule; usually Bea had breakfast at the kitchen table while she and Velda planned meals and shopping for the day. Clara peaceably, Bea prudently, even the judge, on occasion, accepted Velda's demands. The judge had been inclined to be impatient with her assumed authority, but both Clara and Bea knew how nearly impossible it was to get anything remotely resembling a servant.

Bea got place mats and silver from the enormous buffet, wondering what Velda had told Obrian. Lorraine sat down at the table. "Why, when I was young we had two gardeners, I remember. A cook—and a good one —and I think two housemaids floated around—"

"That was some time ago. Things had begun to change before you eloped with Cecco."

"Really, I don't remember."

"Well, I do." Bea plunked silver down before Lorraine. "I was lucky to get hold of Velda. Don't hurt her feelings. She says she's very sensitive—"

"Sensitive!" Lorraine's eyes flashed. "I promise you, now I'm home to stay we'll have some decent servants—"

Unfortunately Velda, bearing coffee, came in through the pantry in time to hear. "Decent! I'll have you know I'm a decent woman. All Valley Ridge knows me. I think I'd better leave now, Miss Bea. I didn't undertake to cook for anybody who says I'm not decent. I'll leave this morning."

Lorraine gave a genteel snort. Velda's angry gaze zeroed in on Bea. It had been the judge who thundered at Velda, ordering her to say Miss Bea; at first, with fine democracy, Velda had addressed her merely as Bea.

"Please don't think of such a thing, Velda. You know how much we need you. Especially now. It's so terrible. The judge—" Bea shuddered as she thought of the horror of the night before and heard the renewed sense of shock in her voice.

Velda softened. "Well, all right. Seeing how Mrs. Bartry needs me right now." She flounced off into the pantry.

Lorraine said, but this time in a whisper, "She wouldn't leave for anything. Just think how she can report everything to the village!"

Velda could gossip. Bea knew that. But surely there was nothing to gossip about that all the village did not, probably, know by now.

The pantry door swung open again. Velda's pale face and pale hair and pale but avid eyes appeared. "I'm really sorry, Miss Bea. But Obrian said I had to tell the truth. He's the law."

"Tell the truth—"

"About your quarrel with the judge last night." Velda did look embarrassed. "I was here in the pantry, doing the silver. Could I help it if I heard every word you and the judge said? Both of you shouting like that. That is, the judge was shouting. But you were holding your own, all right. I never heard you talk like that. You must have been good and mad. I heard the judge say you'd have to marry Rufe over his dead body. Oh—" Velda turned an even pastier color. "I didn't think of *that*."

Lorraine's black head jerked up. "He said *that*?"

Velda nodded, cast Bea a worried but sharp look and vanished again.

Lorraine turned to Bea. "I didn't hear about this."

Bea poured coffee into Lorraine's cup and her own. "The judge didn't want me to marry. He had nothing against Rufe. You haven't been here, Lorraine. You don't know how the judge had changed. He was different."

"He didn't want me to marry Cecco either! But I went right ahead just the same. I must say I wish I hadn't. Why did the judge object to your marrying Rufe?"

"Because he didn't want me to." She couldn't say it was mainly because he wanted his own smooth way of life to continue. "He said that we should wait. He knew that Rufe's salary wouldn't be large enough at the beginning."

Lorraine seemed deep in thought as she sipped coffee. Velda brought in toast and orange juice and whisked out again. Lorraine said finally, "Over his dead body! Dear me! I wonder what the police will make of that."

"Nothing can be made of it." Bea hoped that she was right. "The judge was angry. He had moods like that. Explosive—"

"Over his dead body." Lorraine bit into toast with a snap of very small, very sharp white teeth and chewed meditatively.

A car came up the drive. Another car followed it. Doors were banged. Lorraine turned to look toward the hall. The front door was closed and there was the sound of feet marching along the terrace. "They're going to the garden room. It must be the police."

Bea's heart went down in spite of herself and in spite of the fact that she had of course known the police would return.

It seemed odd, now, for Lorraine to call the judge's study the garden room. It had been the garden room when Lorraine eloped with Cecco. After the judge retired he had chosen it for his study; he said, truly, that the library was dark and dismal. So he had had his filing cabinets, a type-writer for Bea, his big desk and chair, his dictating machine placed where he wanted them. The office furniture looked out of place among the wickers and rattans of the big room with its long windows looking out on the lawn and, further, the garden. But the judge liked it, so the change suited Clara.

As Bea was finishing her breakfast, Seth appeared in the dining-room door. "It's the police," he said unnecessarily. "They want your finger-prints, Bea, and yours too, Lorraine. It seems that Tony reported your arrival last night, so they want to question you, too. Oh, yes, and they want Velda's fingerprints."

Velda was close to the pantry door and she popped it open; her face was pale and apprehensive. "My fingerprints! I'll let them have no such thing. Senator, can't you tell them to mind their own business?"

"This is their business, Velda." Seth's voice was soothing but definite too. "They took fingerprints from every surface in the judge's study last night."

Bea remembered the film of faintly grimy dust. Seth said to her, "You and Clara were upstairs. But they took Rufe's prints, the doctor's, mine. Now they want yours, Bea, Clara's, Velda's. Yours, too, Lorraine, now they know you were in Valley Ridge last night. It's only to eliminate."

"Eliminate?" Velda was suspicious.

"I mean if your fingerprints turn up on, say, his desk, they'll be able to segregate your prints from any others that are there. You'll have been dusting, a perfect reason for your fingerprints. Understand?"

Velda understood perfectly. "Why, certainly, Senator. I'll come right away."

"No need for that." Seth turned as two men in uniform came from the hall. "All right, here are the two young ladies and Velda Mathers. I'd suggest the pantry . . ."

It was a rather gruesome little ceremony, but Velda seemed to be pleasantly interested in seeing her own fingerprints, black little marks. Afterward one of the policemen obliged with a fluid to remove the ink from their fingers. This didn't satisfy Velda, who instantly scrubbed her hands thoroughly at the pantry sink and then handed the soap to Lorraine and Bea.

"If you've finished breakfast," Seth said, "the police want to talk to you, Lorraine, and you too, Bea."

About my quarrel with the judge, Bea thought, and then thought of the gun they had found beside the judge. "Seth, did they find my fingerprints on the gun?"

"I don't know."

But they *had* found fingerprints on the gun. She could see that in the faces of the two young policemen who were neatly storing away all those tiny black and identifying curves. "They found mine," Bea said. "I touched it. The judge put it in my hands when he showed it to me and told me how to load it and—"

"You already told the police about that," Seth said as he swung open the pantry door.

Lorraine went ahead. The two young policemen followed them into the study, where the lieutenant and two men in plain clothes waited, where Clara sat and looked calmly at Obrian, who knew that Bea had quarreled with the judge and that the judge had said "Over my dead body."

Clara was composed. "They've asked me to tell them everything I know," she said. "What time I set the alarm, everything. They were very polite. They asked me if I was willing to make a statement and of course I said yes. Somebody took it down. But there wasn't much I could tell anybody about last night." She folded her hands quietly, with an air of having finished with the police.

Lorraine went to stand beside Clara. Bea went to a chair, to hold its back and brace herself for what she knew was coming. It came at once. Obrian said, "First I have to tell you that there is no question of its being suicide. The medical examiner is absolutely certain it was murder. So we have to proceed on that basis, no doubt about it." He turned to Bea and went on with a shade of apology in his attitude. "I guess you know I talked to Velda Mathers. Now she thinks you had a quarrel with the judge last night. She says you sounded very angry. That right?"

"Yes," Bea said helplessly.

FIVE

But they couldn't believe that she had murdered the judge. It wasn't possible. She looked up gratefully as Seth's lanky figure moved to stand beside her. "Did they find any fingerprints on the gun?" he asked directly.

The lieutenant's head jerked up; he was about to speak when Obrian said, "Yes."

"Whose fingerprints?"

"Now, Seth, you needn't act like a lawyer—"

"I am a lawyer," Seth said. "If you found Bea's fingerprints on the gun, she has already explained how they got there. The judge showed her the gun, gave it to her to tell her how to load. Naturally there could be her fingerprints—"

Obrian eyed the ceiling uneasily. "The gun has been fired recently. Last night, they think."

The lieutenant shot a glance at the two detectives, neither of whom moved.

Obrian spoke again. "There were her fingerprints, yes. There were some smudges too—" He gave the lieutenant a warning look as if he dared him or either of his men to interrupt.

"There were smudges all over it. You can't tell, fingerprints or even gloves or— But the point is," he went on hurriedly, as if the lieutenant or one of the detectives might try to stop him, "they did the autopsy. Whoever killed him got the bullet out all right. Remember Griffin heard two shots. The judge's gun has been fired only once."

"So," Seth said, "you can't be sure whether the judge was shot with his own gun, or another gun was used and taken away by the murderer."

Obrian shook his head. "Whoever it was took a chance, digging out that bullet, working so fast. The medical examiner said it wouldn't be difficult to get out the bullet; it could have popped right out under a knife. But he's sure that the exit wound was made by a knife. The murderer might have had a flashlight, but he took a big chance. Maybe he used the judge's gun and then left it there, but it doesn't seem likely."

"He *could* have just forgotten it," the lieutenant said.

One of the detectives, the one in the gray suit again, said gently that was how murderers were caught; often they simply forgot something. "If they were really intelligent, they wouldn't murder," he added dryly.

"Never mind all that. We'll find whatever gun was used to kill him," the lieutenant said shortly.

Obrian sagged down into the judge's big chair and looked at Clara. "Mrs. Bartry, we haven't told you. We—rather the state police—got Meeth. He was here last night. Admits it. But says he didn't hurt the judge, didn't even talk to him."

"Meeth!" Clara's calm deserted her.

Once more the little man in gray took over. "Picked him up in a rooming house where he'd lived before the judge sent him to prison. Admits he borrowed a car from a friend and drove here last night. Parked out in the road. But he says he didn't intend to hurt the judge; he'd got all over that idea. He did want to give him a piece of his mind, though. And it's a fact that people did think the judge was a little harsh—didn't direct the jury, couldn't of course, but just as good as told them to give Meeth a stiff sentence."

Lorraine said, "Who's Meeth?"

Clara replied quickly, "He's a man who murdered his wife. The judge was convinced he was guilty—first degree. Made it quite plain to everyone. That was before he retired. The jury sentenced Meeth to a long prison term. But then recently Meeth was paroled. The prison doctor and a psychiatrist said his wife's murder was not premeditated, and the parole board voted to let him out on probation. I knew he'd come straight here. He was beside himself when he was sentenced. He swore he'd kill the judge. You may believe that he came here with no intent to kill the judge, but I say he did!"

Lorraine slid down to the arm of Clara's chair. "But I never heard a word of all this."

"Naturally not. You were in Italy with that dreadful—I mean with your husband. I don't know how Meeth got hold of the judge's gun," Clara said firmly. "But clearly he did. And then . . . then he got out the bullet and then . . . well, forgot the gun. What have you done with Meeth?"

"But there were two shots—" Obrian began.

The lieutenant interrupted. "We're holding him now as a material witness. He had quite a story to tell." He glanced at the detective in gray, and for the first time Bea heard his name. "Smith, maybe we'd better get young Thorne to hear Meeth's story."

Smith said, "Yes, I agree. Where is he?"

"He stayed here all last night," Bea heard the unsteadiness in her voice. "He went home early this morning—"

Why did they want Rufe to hear Meeth's story? What was his story? She had not seen him the previous night; she had never seen him. She had heard little of Meeth's case in fact, until recently when the judge had learned and strongly disapproved of the decision of the parole board.

The lieutenant turned snappily toward the terrace door and as snappily another policeman in uniform came into view on the terrace. "Get that young fellow Thorne, lives across the road—"

"Yes, sir."

Clara put her small hands tightly together. "I don't know what Meeth said, but Rufe had nothing at all to do with the murder of the judge."

Detective Smith opened the drawer of one of the filing cabinets, gave it a rather despairing look and turned to Bea. "Did he use this dictating machine much?"

"Oh, yes. Letters and his memoirs and things."

"Where are the tapes?"

"In that cupboard, in the corner behind the door." She nodded.

Smith walked over to the cupboard, opened the door and gave the boxes a long look. "All those?"

"Yes," she said, but hastened to add, "The tapes now mainly have my own French practice on them. After the judge had used them I used the same tapes; they erase as you go, and I put on the new—"

"I know." Smith nodded shortly and then looked puzzled. "What's this about French?"

"I practiced and then listened to myself. I was trying to learn to speak it more fluently."

Obrian said, "She and Rufe Thorne are going to be married as soon as Rufe gets his appointment. I expect she wanted to learn languages. Rufe has been training for the Foreign Service." He paused, brushed his chin nervously and added, "As you know."

The lieutenant nodded at a policeman who had a pencil and pad of paper ready, and addressed Lorraine. "We'd like a statement from you if you are willing to give it."

"Certainly," Lorraine said promptly.

"I understand you arrived in Valley Ridge two days ago, Mrs. di—di Pall—"

"Pallici," Lorraine said. "Yes. I stayed at the Bensons'. Last night I was at the club dance with Ben Benson."

"How did you learn of the judge's murder?"

"Ben—Mr. Benson and I had left the club. It was a warm evening, so we drove around a little. Then we dropped back at the club for a nightcap. By that time someone had heard of the murder or seen the police cars or something. Anyway, they were talking about it, the people who were still there. I was very shocked. I didn't quite know what to do. My aunt didn't know that I was in Valley Ridge—"

Detective Smith interrupted smoothly. "Why didn't your aunt know of your presence?"

"Because I didn't tell her," Lorraine replied as smoothly, but added with candor, "The fact is, I wasn't sure that the judge would welcome me. I thought I'd stay at Mrs. Benson's a day or two and find out just how the land lay, so to speak. That is, if the judge had forgiven me—"

"For what?" the detective said smoothly again.

"For marrying my husband. I thought I'd see my aunt alone and— But I hadn't yet."

"So when you heard of the murder, what did you do? I understand that you arrived very late, after we had gone."

"I suppose Tony reported it. However, you'd have soon heard of my arrival. Well, I was very shocked and, as I say, I didn't know what to do, so Ben drove me around again for a while, a long time, I think, and then we decided that my aunt would want me here. So I came."

The lieutenant glanced at the detective, who returned his look; they might as well have said audibly: We'll talk to Ben Benson and see if he agrees with your story.

Clara reached up and took one of Lorraine's hands in her own, lovingly. After a short silence the detective said, "May we see your passport?"

"Certainly," Lorraine replied again with great promptness, flashed out of the room and up the stairs. In a moment she returned and handed over her passport to the detective, who said he would return it to her soon, and put it carefully in his pocket.

There was another brief silence while the two men, as if overwhelmed by the long task awaiting them, opened and studied the contents of one file drawer after another. There was nothing there, Bea knew, that would serve the slightest purpose in their search for evidence. Smith moved away, eying her as if she were responsible for that mass of papers. "Are all those boxes of tapes jammed full of French lessons?"

"I think so, yes."

The detectives exchanged sadly resigned looks. The lieutenant at the terrace door seemed to stiffen in a military way. "Here he comes."

Rufe came in; he was dressed casually, but he had taken time to plaster down his rebellious hair. He had also taken time, Bea thought, half amused even then, to assume a very dignified and quiet expression. A Foreign Service officer must never seem troubled and nervous, Rufe had told her, laughing. Now there was a serious need for self-control. He said a general kind of good morning, which included Clara and everyone in the room, shot a swift glance at Bea, who nodded as if to say she was all right, and then said pleasantly, "All right, Lieutenant. Your men tell me you want to question me."

The lieutenant gave Smith an admonitory jerk of his chin. Obrian sank further back in his chair and looked at his sturdy shoes. The policeman taking notes adjusted his pencil and paper. Smith sighed. "It's this way, Mr. Thorne. Did you know of the judge's will? And of Mrs. Bartry's will?"

"Yes," Rufe said coolly.

"Who told you?" Smith seemed to have taken over the proceedings.

Seth stirred, putting one long leg over the other. It was like a warning gesture, but Rufe ignored it. His chin stuck out in the way that Bea knew was indicative of controlled anger. "The judge told me."

Clara guessed what was coming. "Oh, no! No, Rufe!"

Rufe smiled at her reassuringly, but said to Smith, "Apparently you know that I came here to see him last night after dinner."

Seth unfolded his legs and rose. "Now, Rufe—"

Rufe gave another casual smile, this time at Seth. "They'll find out.

They already have found out, apparently. Yes, I came here last night. I thought I could talk to the judge. I guessed that he wouldn't want Bea— Miss Bartry—to marry and leave him. He was always a good friend of mine but he was also interested in his own comfort. Miss Bartry was like a servant here—"

"Rufe," Clara said quickly, "the judge was very grateful for all of Bea's help, so was I. But"—she shook her head reprovingly—"Bea has never been like a servant. You should know that."

Rufe was apologetic. "No, of course not! I didn't mean to say that. But I knew that the judge wouldn't approve of our marriage. I thought if I could talk to him— But I couldn't, he wasn't—" Rufe paused and added wryly, "Talkable."

I couldn't, he wasn't—" Rufe paused and added wryly, "Talkable."

The lieutenant frowned. "Talkable?"

"He was already seething. Miss Bartry had told him he intended to marry as soon as my appointment comes. He was already like a firecracker ready to go up. And the minute he saw me he exploded."

There was another silence, but a short one. Smith asked, "What did he say?"

"What didn't he say! Among other things, he accused me of wanting a rich wife. Or one who would some day be rich. He said a rich wife is a great help to a poor young Foreign Service guy. About then he turned so purple that I was afraid he was going to have a stroke. He hadn't been well, you know, lately. He'd get moods like that and—"

Smith broke in. "He told you about his will?"

Rufe nodded in an unperturbed manner. "The judge's will and Mrs. Bartry's will. He said that if he predeceased his wife, she would probably alter her will so there wouldn't be a trust fund at all but everything both of them had would go to Bea. At least he told me that I must be counting on that. And then he said—"

"Rufe!" Seth Hobson went to him and took his arm.

Rufe shook off Seth's hand good-naturedly. "Keep your cool, Seth. The judge said the shock of his death would undoubtedly kill his wife—"

Clara said firmly, "It didn't."

Bea wished that Rufe would not keep his own cool with such infuriating —and dangerous—candor. He went on calmly, "So I left. There was no use in trying to talk to him."

The lieutenant glared at the two men in uniform who had gone to get

Rufe and who now stood behind him, near the door, as if to prevent his escape. "So you had to tell him what we wanted him for!"

Rufe intervened. "Certainly not! Neither of them said a word except to tell me that I was wanted for questioning. It wasn't hard for me to guess why. I suppose someone saw me and it's possible that same someone heard our conversation. The door here was wide open. It was a warm night. Someone could have stood outside on the terrace. Who was it?" Rufe asked in a conversational way.

Both detectives looked at him very sharply. Clara said, "They've found that man Meeth. He was here last night."

That did surprise Rufe. "Meeth! But I didn't see him!"

Smith took over again. "He parked his car down in the road. He came up here and saw the lights in this room and saw the judge. He saw you and heard you. Said the door was open. He heard every word."

"Oh, Rufe!" Clara pulled her hand from Lorraine to put both out beseechingly toward Seth. "Seth, stop him."

"I tried to stop him. But it's true, Rufe. They got that story out of Meeth, and a fishy story I'd have said. But—" Seth turned toward the detectives and the police lieutenant. "That's all Rufe is going to say. I doubt if you find it strong evidence for a warrant. And I doubt if the grand jury would call it evidence for arraignment."

"But Thorne has confirmed it," Smith said gently. The lieutenant took his gun from its gleaming leather holster and looked at it reflectively.

Rufe said, "Was it the judge's gun you found?"

Obrian answered. "Yes. He had had it registered."

"What about the bullet?" Rufe asked. "Did the medical examiner find that?"

Obrian shook his head. "No. It was gone, all right. Cut out sort of botchily with a knife. That's what the medical examiner says."

He remembered Clara's presence and gave her an apologetic glance, but Clara was unmoved. Seth said, "Who is this medical examiner? He must be new here. How can he be so sure?"

"Oh, he's sure," Obrian told him. "He's new here, yes. But he's had considerable experience. He was a naval surgeon all during World War Two. Says he can tell the difference between— Well, if you don't mind, Mrs. Bartry—"

"Go on," Clara said firmly.

"He said between a hurried botchy kind of job done with a knife and a normal exit wound a bullet would make. I believe him, Seth. A jury will believe him. However, there's no bullet, so there's no way to prove it did or did not come from the judge's gun."

For the first time a trace of steel seemed to underlie Rufe's almost casual manner. "So either it came from the judge's gun or it came from some other gun. You have your work cut out for you, Lieutenant."

Obrian stirred in a worried way. "Now, Rufe—"

The lieutenant eyed his revolver almost affectionately, certainly wistfully, it occurred to Bea. Seth apparently shared her feeling, for he said, "Obrian, surely you're not going to accuse Rufe on such flimsy evidence as this! That man Meeth would say anything to clear himself after all the threats he made against the judge's life."

Obrian rose ponderously, debated for a moment and said, "I don't know what the state police will say. I for one would like to have some good hard evidence."

"Right." Seth nodded. "Of course you want firm evidence! In my opinion you haven't got it."

"Now, Seth," Obrian began, "don't try any of your orator's tricks on us—"

"I wouldn't think of such a thing!"

But Bea knew that was exactly what Seth was going to do; his voice was his talent both in law and politics. As he spoke she could almost feel the adamant attitude of the two detectives and Lieutenant Abbott weaken. "Now, this boy isn't going to run away. I'll answer for that. But the point is you wouldn't want to ruin his career by charging him with murder—on the say-so of a man who *is* a convicted murderer. An arrest now—when this boy has just passed his Foreign Service examinations, a boy who had a fine record in Vietnam, a young man respected in this community! Why, his father has the respect and love of everybody in this town. You wouldn't want to make a mistake like that, one you'd regret always."

"They tell me," Smith said softly, "that you could have been one of the best defense lawyers in these parts, Senator, before you went into politics."

Seth said frankly, "I still could be, I think."

The lieutenant's mouth opened and shut. Obrian, liking Rufe, liking Bea, said, "Something in what he says, Lieutenant."

The lieutenant thought hard. "But there's a motive."

"Motive?" Seth appeared to consider it. "Well, call it that. Far-fetched, though, isn't it? Nothing to keep Miss Bartry and Rufe here from going off and getting married any time they wanted to. Now my guess is that

Miss Bartry talked to the judge about her marriage because she was fond of the judge, she wanted his approval. Same reason Rufe tried to talk to him. Everybody in town, though, knows that the judge hasn't been—"

Obrian interrupted. "He's been off the beam. Begging your pardon, Mrs. Bartry. People respected him and made allowances, but that's the fact. No telling what's in those memoirs of his—facts or nonsense."

"But I told you," Bea said, "there is simply nothing that could hurt anybody."

"All the same," Obrian said, "let the judge get some notion in his head and *whoof*—fireworks! Like you said, Rufe. I agree with you, Seth. Better take some time than make a howler of a mistake, Lieutenant."

The lieutenant's jaws worked rather in the exasperated manner of a hound who sees his rabbit dashing into a briar patch, but he nodded. "All right. But don't try to leave, Thorne. Smith, Whipple—"

Whipple, then, was the name of the other detective, Bea thought.

Smith took off his coat, obviously preparatory to tackling the files. Clara rose. "Rufe, nobody believes for an instant that you killed the judge."

Smith's eyebrows rose. Whipple sighed and stared at the filing cabinets. The lieutenant touched his gun, wistfully again. Clara went on in a cool and motherly manner, "You go on home, Rufe, and get a shave. Dear me, your chin— And I expect Miss Dotty will want to give you some more breakfast."

Miss Dotty was not only Dr. Thorne's office nurse; in fact she was everything—nurse, housekeeper, and, some said laughingly, keeper, for Dr. Thorne was getting older and more forgetful. Miss Dotty was a firm and formidable woman.

Clara said, "Now, if that is all, Lieutenant, I wish to talk to the senator about—about the judge's obituary." Her firm voice did falter then.

A rather troubled and sheepish look came over Obrian's face. The lieutenant didn't look sheepish but he did bow in a polite fashion and slid his revolver, regretfully, Bea was sure, back in it holster. He and Obrian left together.

Rufe lingered for a moment. "Anything I can do, Aunt Clara?"

"Not now, Rufe. I think the judge would want you to be one of the pallbearers. I do want everything about the services for him to be just as he would want them. When can we hold the services, Seth?"

"I'd say about Tuesday. I'll talk to the police about it."

Rufe gave Bea a look of, she thought, reassurance, waved his hand with admirable nonchalance and went away too.

Lorraine gazed after him, sighed and said, "Dear me, he certainly is attractive."

Seth eyed the two detectives, who were starting to work on the masses of papers in the files. "Do try to get things back in the right order."

Whipple gave him a reproachful glance. "This is part of our business."

Clara said, "Come into the library, Seth. Bea dear, there are people who ought to be told about the judge's death—not read it in the papers first. I'll give you a list."

The day turned suddenly from a police inquiry about murder into a conventional routine of which Velda showed she knew every nuance of etiquette. When callers began to come, it was Velda who brought out sherry and small cookies and emitted an occasional lugubrious sniff which obviously she felt was appropriate.

Between visitors and frequent telephone calls Seth and Clara wrote the judge's obituary, and Seth telephoned it to Joe Lathrop in his office, who in turn was to telephone it to the *Times.* "And the Bridgeport papers," Clara told Seth. "And Hartford. After all, the judge was well known."

Bea spent most of the day in the dismal library working on the little personal notes Clara wished her to write; some of the messages went at Clara's wish by telegraph. "And be sure," Clara said, "to try to find out who is coming to the services."

Seth talked again to Obrian, who conferred with the state police, who apparently said that the services could now be arranged at any time. Bea telephoned the Reverend Cantwell to arrange for the church services and to set a time, which was two o'clock Tuesday afternoon. She hurriedly began to add that to her notes and telegrams. Seth sat in the judge's study while the two detectives minutely yet rather speedily too, as if well accustomed to their work, went through all the judge's files. Seth did some of the telephoning for Bea, as Clara's friends came in a decorous stream to make their calls of condolence.

All this was in the Valley Ridge tradition, and it was a heartwarming tradition, Bea thought, as she interrupted her task time and again to speak to each caller briefly and listen to their expressions of sympathy.

Rufe did not return, as Bea half expected him to do. Seth and the detectives were still in the study when she gathered up all the little notes, put on a coat and took the car quickly past the other cars in the drive and then on to the village post office in time to catch the last mail. Even so, of course, it being Saturday, none of the notes would reach their destination before Monday, but in any event that gesture of amenity had been made.

It seemed strange that the main street, the red-brick post office were just the same. She did think that people on the street eyed her rather closely, but she shrugged that off as imagination. By the time she reached home again, the living room was empty, the detectives and Seth had gone and there was the rather brooding silence in the house which follows a storm. She trudged upstairs, feeling tired and dirty, took a long hot shower and changed her clothes.

She was fastening her dress when Lorraine came in. "The reporters have all gone. Seth wouldn't let me talk to any of them. Where is Rufe?"

"At home I suppose. He was up all night."

"Are we going to be alone tonight?"

"I hadn't thought of it."

"I can't say I like the idea. Of course, Rufe wouldn't hurt *me*. Or you."

"Rufe!"

"He did know about that will of the judge's and the one Clara made. And the police seem to feel it does provide a motive. Aunt Clara has complained about her heart ever since I knew her. A shock like the judge's murder—"

Bea restrained a desire to reach out and pull Lorraine's hair viciously, but borrowing a leaf from Clara's book, she said quietly, "But she didn't die. She's taking all this very well."

Lorraine's green eyes glinted reflectively. "She acts almost as if it's a relief, really. Living with the judge all these years, especially since he's been out of his head, can't have been much fun."

"He wasn't out of his head. He was only . . . he only had moods . . . and Aunt Clara adored him."

"I expect she did. In her way. You know, it never struck me until today that Aunt Clara has a very strong character. Of course, she'd have to be pretty firm, trying to cope with the judge. But still, I wouldn't have expected her to react as she has. Calm as all get-out. Not a tear."

"She's not the weeping kind."

"Nobody around this house appears to be the weeping kind." Lorraine lifted slim black eyebrows. "I haven't seen you dissolving in grief."

"There's been too much to do. And too much—"

"Yes. Police. They're not through yet either. I heard the judge say one time that a murder case is never closed until they nail the murderer. Isn't that right?"

"I think so."

"It really would be too bad if they arrested Rufe. Even if later he was proved not guilty, he'd never get a job in the Foreign Service. They go through everybody's records. Why, if he'd even so much as been fined for speeding, it would count against him. I think." Lorraine added frankly, "I don't really know much about it."

Someone knocked on the door and then opened it. Velda stood there. She was no longer lugubrious and long-faced; her gooseberry eyes were shining at Lorraine. "There's somebody to see you. He says he's your husband."

Lorraine shot up, straight and tall. "Cecco! Oh, no, no!"

But it was Cecco. He came up behind Velda, moved her to one side and smiled at Lorraine. "Glad to see me, darling? I heard of the murder. I felt my place was at your side."

"But you can't be here!" Lorraine cried, much as Bea had cried on seeing Lorraine. "You're in Italy!"

"You left me there, darling. But now I'm here. And this is little Bea, quite grown up. Dear Bea—"

He took Bea's hand, bowed and kissed it. She had a fantastic impulse to count her fingers; somehow one did count her fingers after Cecco di Pallici kissed them. Cecco himself was the very picture of an old-time Italian nobleman, tall, slender, his dark features aquiline, dark eyes dancing, his white teeth shining.

Lorraine said, "You can't stay here. I'm getting a divorce."

Cecco smiled, showing all those white teeth. "I think I'll be the one to get the divorce, darling. Unless of course you wish to change your mind."

SIX

There was a slight rustle in the doorway where Velda stood riveted, watching the scene. Bea could do nothing about that, or the fact that Cecco so openly implied his knowledge of something which, Bea thought wildly, could show Lorraine in a very poor light. She really shouldn't mind Lorraine's being shown in a bad light, Bea told herself firmly, yet she could not help feeling a tug of the family tie, a desire to protect the other girl. Although not related by blood, she and Lorraine had grown up as cousins in the same household, and she couldn't deny that bond.

Lorraine, however, seemed to need no defense; she said coldly, "Why did you come here?"

"I told you. When I heard of the murder I rushed to be at your side—"

"You couldn't have come here from Italy. You were in New York!"

"Well—"

Lorraine's eyes flashed fire. "Or right here in Valley Ridge!"

Again Cecco bowed suavely.

There was something about him—his high cheekbones, high thin nose and forehead—which for a fleeting second reminded Bea of Seth's New England face. But Seth would never be done up in a natty, broad-shouldered pin-stripe suit and glistening oxfords with very thin soles; Seth wouldn't have been caught dead in a fantastically colored tie of geometrical design and a turquoise pin in it.

"The taxi is waiting," Cecco said. "He wants money!" He shrugged in an entirely Latin gesture.

Again Lorraine's eyes blazed. "Do you mean to say—"

"I managed to have a little money you couldn't touch."

"I suppose you got another mortgage on that decrepit rock pile you call a *palazzo*?"

"Now, now, darling!" Cecco shrugged, a ripple right down his spine. He spread out his hands and a rather dubious-looking diamond flashed on one finger. "There was only enough money for my plane fare. And I had enough left over from that to come to Valley Ridge by train. But not enough to pay for my hotel bill and not anything at all for the taxi driver, who may be getting a little restless."

"Hotel?"

"I think they call it the Valley Inn. Small place but pleasant."

"So you arrived last night. You went to the Valley Inn."

"Where could I go? I didn't think you—or at least the judge—God rest his soul," said Cecco and this time bowed presumably to the judge's soul, "would give me a welcome here. Or Ben Benson—"

"Here! Wait—" Lorraine ran out of the room.

Cecco glanced at Bea; there was a merry twinkle in his dark eyes.

"I suppose you always get what you want," Bea said tartly. "She's probably gone to get some money to pay off the taxi. Our American cabbies are a little emotional about not getting paid."

Cecco nodded graciously. "But I knew Lorraine would pay him. Couldn't have talk around town, you know. Cecco di Pallici without enough money to pay a taxi! Ah—"

Lorraine flashed in again, a handsome black handbag under her arm. From it—the jewels on her fingers glittering (not dubious jewels, those, Bea thought)—she extracted some bills. "Pay for your taxi and go back to Valley Inn and pay your bill there, and then take the train to New York. After that I don't care what you do, but stay away from me."

The bills flicked out of sight and into Cecco's pocket so swiftly that Bea scarcely saw the motion.

Cecco looked at Lorraine and said, a tone of mock-sadness in his voice, "No, darling. I wouldn't think of leaving you just now. The tragedy of the judge's death—murder— Oh, no, my place is here with you. I'm sure your aunt will agree."

Velda, still in the doorway, made a sound not unlike a robin choking on a particularly active worm.

Bea looked at her. "Velda?"

"He's right, Miss Bea. Mrs. Bartry will want him to stay until . . . well, until . . ."

Velda could be trying at times but she had her very good points too, and one of them was a sure sense of Valley Ridge propriety.

Bea nodded. "Aunt Clara will want him to stay here, Lorraine. Until . . . well . . . for a while. You see, everybody in town would know that he was here and didn't stay and—"

Cecco's eyes gleamed merrily. "You see, Lorraine darling. Your aunt would not like any talk."

Lorraine seemed to debate with herself for a moment, then said, "All right. If Aunt Clara says you can stay. Have you got any baggage with you?"

"One small bag in the taxi. A couple of others at the inn."

"We'll get those later. Now pay the taxi man and bring your bag up here—"

Clara said from beside Velda, "There's a taxi waiting outside but I didn't see anybody— Oh!"

"Madam—" Cecco again performed his lithe and graceful bow. He took Clara's astonished hand and kissed it. And, Bea thought with a quiver of laughter, Clara too looked at her hand thoughtfully when he released it, exactly as if she also had an instinctive impulse to count her fingers. There was simply something about Cecco which induced suspicion.

"You," said Clara inadequately.

Velda spoke from the doorway. "He was at Valley Inn last night, Mrs. Bartry. I was sure that you'd want him to stay here—at least just now. I mean you wouldn't want people to talk—"

Clara had got her breath back. "You are quite right, Velda."

Suddenly, irrelevantly, Bea thought: But Velda could be very wrong too; it was she who had blurted to Obrian about Bea's fiery quarrel with the judge. At this moment Velda caught her eyes and apparently read her thoughts, for a pinkish flush crept up into her face.

Cecco, secure now in his position, smiled graciously all around, then went swiftly out and down the stairs. Lorraine watched him go, fury stamped on her face. Then she, too, left. "He can't stay in my room," she said over her shoulder, and disappeared.

Velda turned to Bea and said earnestly, "Miss Bea, I did tell Obrian about your quarrel with the judge. I shouldn't have, I know. I didn't mean to get you into trouble. He got it out of me before I—well, I was shocked, you see. I hadn't known a thing about the murder. Obrian arrived before I'd so much as had a cup of coffee, and before I knew it— well, I'm sorry. But it really didn't do you any harm, did it?"

"I don't know. That is— Oh, it's all right, Velda. I see how it happened."

Clara, who had been standing quietly, seemed pleased that Bea had accepted Velda's explanation. Now she turned almost eagerly to change the subject. "Put Mr. di Pal—mal— Oh, put his things in that other guest room, Velda. Show him where it is."

Velda nodded. "They used to say that he's a count. Doesn't look like it to me."

"You may be right," Clara sighed.

Velda made for the stairs to meet Cecco and steer him to his room.

Clara, still sighing, said, "I can never get his name straight. But then, I've had so few letters from Lorraine. In answering them I always had to look in my address book to get the name straight. No, I suppose he isn't a count. I wonder how anybody got that impression—unless from Cecco himself. In fact"—Clara frowned—"I can't even remember who brought him here to Valley Ridge. I do remember that there was a sort of impression that he had money and a fine *palazzo*—is that what they call it?— in Italy. But Velda is right about these things. She's lived in Valley Ridge all her life. As I have. There's enough for people to talk about; let's not add to it. Seth's gone. The men in the study have gone, too."

"They couldn't have found anything of interest in the judge's papers. If there were anything, I'd know," Bea said.

"It was Meeth." Clara spoke with simple obstinacy. "I don't care what anybody says. He waited around till after Rufe had gone and then he got into the study and the judge got out his gun. Meeth took it from him and he made the judge go down to the road—outside the house so we wouldn't hear him—and then he . . . then he shot him."

"When did you set the alarm, Aunt Clara?"

"It was during the commercial. The ten-thirty one. I told the police about it. I thought the judge was upstairs, so I came out and touched that little button, then I went back and listened to the program for a few minutes. I had turned off the program just before the alarm went. The police say the report of the alarm came in at close to a quarter to eleven. That would be about right. Oh, Bea, if I hadn't had that program going I might have heard the gunshots. But there were so many gunshots . . . I mean in the program . . . and I'm a little deaf. The judge always said I turned my programs on so loud he could hardly hear himself think, let alone sleep."

"You couldn't have stopped anything, Aunt Clara. And it does seem reasonable," Bea said slowly, "that Meeth did exactly that. Somebody had to get hold of the judge's gun, so the judge himself must have taken it out of the desk drawer. And somebody could have forced him to go out toward the road, away from the house."

"That's the way the police will see it," Clara said firmly. "They just need a little time to do all the things they're supposed to do. Police routine, the judge used to call it. I see you've freshened up for dinner, dear. That's right. We really must go on as we always do. That's another thing the judge used to say. Conventions are made for emergencies. But I do wish that dreadful man Cecco hadn't followed Lorraine here."

At that moment Cecco came bounding lightly up the steps; he was carrying his own bag. Velda followed him, gave a firm wave of her hand toward a guest room beyond the one Lorraine was using, and said, "I've got to see about dinner, Mrs. Bartry." She rustled back down the stairs.

Cecco gave them both a flashing smile as he went to his room. Clara sighed again, then said she, too, would change for dinner. Bea watched her go, her pretty head held high, into her own room, and then went downstairs to help Velda, who accepted her aid with a grunt. "Not a very nice dinner. Can't help it. I've had a busy day. You better mix some strong cocktails, Miss Bea. Your aunt is bearing up very well, but I can tell, she needs a drink. If you can't keep your spirits up," said Velda rather surprisingly, "put some down."

Bea made martinis as the judge had taught her, and as Velda advised, a large and strong quantity.

"Where's that Rufe?" Velda asked, watching as Bea stirred the contents of the tall pitcher.

Velda might permit herself to be browbeaten by the judge to the extent of saying Miss Bea—or Miss Lorraine—but never would she have referred to Rufe as Mr. Rufe, not the doctor's boy whom she had known more or less all his life.

"I don't know. I expect he had to sleep some. He and Tony were here all last night."

"Oh, I know that. Rapping away all night, I suppose."

Sometimes Velda was startlingly *au courant* in her way of picking up the latest slang.

"I suppose they were. They must have had a great deal to talk about."

"Got into my refrigerator. All that pie is gone. We'll just have to have ice cream out of the freezer tonight. You don't think your aunt will mind not having soup."

"She'll not notice." Bea tasted her martini mix, blinked and shoved more ice in it.

When she carried it and glasses on a tray to the living room, Lorraine and Clara were already there. Lorraine took over the chore of pouring the drinks. Cecco came gracefully into the room in time to take the first glass from her hand and present it, with another spine-wriggling bow, to Clara.

Clara eyed it rather doubtfully, as if he might have dropped in a touch of cyanide, Bea thought with a hysterical little quiver of mirth, but took it. At this point Rufe arrived, this time an orderly, brushed and indeed almost dressed-up Rufe. Clara's face brightened. "Oh, Rufe! I hope you've come to dinner. We've had such a day—"

"I know. I saw all the cars. Thank you, Lorraine, I can do with that." He took the pitcher, saw that Bea had a glass in her hand and poured one for himself. A good thing I made enough, Bea thought. Rufe pulled up a footstool near Bea, balancing the martini glass neatly, and sat down. "I've got to go to Washington on Monday. Somebody phoned me today. Is that all right, Aunt Clara?"

"Of course, Rufe. But you must be back for the services Tuesday."

"I'll get back Monday night or at the latest Tuesday morning. Miss Dotty told me the time. I've phoned Obrian to ask if it's all right for me to go to Washington for the day. I explained it to him. He said sure, go ahead, and then my father got on the phone to find out what the police are doing."

"Is there any special news yet?" Clara asked quickly.

Rufe shook his head. "Nothing new."

"Oh, I think I'll just have another martini, Lorraine."

But Cecco, who had been sitting thoughtfully in a corner, rose swiftly to take her glass. Rufe apparently had not seen him, for he jerked around on the footstool. "Why—why, I didn't know anyone else was here! That is—"

Lorraine didn't quite bite off the words, but almost. "My soon-to-be former husband. He arrived in Valley Ridge last night. Stayed at the Valley Inn."

"How do you do," Cecco said happily. "So you are my defeated rival. Ah, yes. You had gone to Vietnam, wasn't it, when I came to Valley Ridge?"

"It was Vietnam." Rufe stood; the two men shook hands. "Well, well." Rufe eyed his victorious rival. "You weren't expected here, were you?"

"A happy surprise to my dear wife." Cecco's white teeth gleamed.

Lorraine uttered something which perhaps fortunately was not entirely audible.

Velda came to the door and said, "Dinner!" as if she were firing a cannon.

Rufe collected the martini pitcher, still not quite empty. "May I bring this to the table, Aunt Clara?"

Velda gave him a swift glance. "Might as well stay here and finish up those good martinis. I wasn't expecting you, Rufe. I'll have to put on another place. That is, if you're here for dinner."

Clara replied serenely, "Oh, yes, Velda. You know he's always welcome."

"It's not much of a dinner," Velda said. "But it's better than what Miss Dotty would give you." Velda did not like Miss Dotty, who, Velda said, put on airs.

Cecco deftly took the pitcher from Rufe, and assuming the air of the man of the house, the host, poured more drinks. Lorraine's eyes glittered viciously at him; her jewels glittered too, a bracelet, rings, a stunningly huge diamond clip. Bea wondered briefly how Cecco had got the money to pay for all those jewels. Lorraine had not changed into a dress; she still wore her skintight black slacks and dark-green sweater, but apparently considered the display of jewels sufficient for a home dinner—and indeed, Bea thought tartly, the jewels would have been sufficient decorations for a ball.

Clara told Rufe of the callers that afternoon. Cecco brought Bea another martini, which she took, and then wished she hadn't, for she began to feel distinctly dizzy. Luckily Velda appeared again and they went in to dinner.

It wasn't a very good dinner. Perhaps Velda had had an ulterior purpose in speaking so encouragingly of martinis, hoping for their euphoric effect. Clara obviously was affected by her unusual double dose of drinks, for as she speared a mushroom she said, "It's a good thing we keep a store of canned mushrooms and things," and then added unexpectedly, "Soup."

Velda had been hovering at the pantry door. She stuck her head in. "Soup, Mrs. Bartry?"

Clara shook her head. "No, no. I was thinking of something else. How do you manage?" She said to Lorraine, "I mean doesn't your hair sort of get in the way when you have soup?"

Lorraine looked up with a gasp, shoved both heavy curtains of black hair back, anchored them behind her ears and said sweetly, "That's how I do it, darling Aunt Clara."

But Clara was still doubtful. "Your uncle wouldn't have liked your hair, dear. It doesn't look tidy."

Rufe choked. Velda disappeared into the pantry and brought out the coffee tray, which she carried into the living room. Cecco's black eyes danced but he said nothing. By the time they had finished Velda's hastily concocted dessert of ice cream and pound cake—at which Lorraine looked with marked distaste—and returned to the living room, Lorraine had recovered her poise. She seated herself, the daughter of the house, behind the coffee table and began to pour. "I'll cut off my hair, darling Aunt Clara," she said sweetly. "If you don't like it, certainly I'll have it cut."

Clara was troubled. "Dear Lorraine, it's your hair. And beautiful too." She seemed to brood for a moment, then put down her cup and added, apologetically, "But you might just do it up for the services, Lorraine. Everybody in town will be there."

Cecco's eyes met Bea's; she turned away from him, but he said, smiling, "Little Bea has grown up so properly. No longer braces on her teeth, an excellent coiffure and, may I say, a figure—"

"I'll have more coffee, please," Clara said sharply.

Rufe said, "Come walk with me, Bea, unless of course you'd like me to stay here tonight. If you do—"

Cecco again took on the position of the man of the house. "Not at all, my dear fellow. Not at all. I am here."

Perhaps it was the unaccustomed martinis that still affected her, or perhaps it was the firm calm which Bea was beginning to observe was a part of Clara's nature that during the judge's lifetime she had somehow contrived to conceal. Whatever the source of her poise, Clara told Rufe he need not stay. "Thank you, though. It's like you. But if anything should happen, we'll call you. And we'll set the alarm." There wasn't even a quiver in her voice as she mentioned the alarm, the alarm that had announced the murder of the judge. Yes, Bea thought, Clara had a courage and strength which in deference to the judge, Clara must have tactfully concealed during their life together. She would never have opposed the judge about anything. Even about their wills.

Bea went with Rufe. When they were outside, on the terrace, he suddenly laughed. "So that's Cecco! You wrote to me about that time, when he came here. Who introduced him?"

"I think it was Ben Benson. I don't remember. Just all at once Cecco and Lorraine eloped. The judge didn't want her to marry him. But not for the same reasons he didn't want me to marry you."

"To think that once I was desperately jealous of him!"

"Lorraine says she's going to get a divorce."

"A good idea," Rufe said in an absent way. "Funny though. Cecco seems to speak English very fluently, no trace of an accent."

"I believe he went to an English school."

"Doesn't have that kind of accent either. I'd be inclined to think—" He paused. They strolled on down the drive. Finally Rufe said, "Are you sure that was his first visit to America? I mean when he came here to Valley Ridge and got acquainted with Lorraine?"

"Why, I—I don't know. I just assumed it was."

Rufe walked on in thoughtful silence for a moment; then he said, "You were in your teens when Lorraine met and married him."

"Yes, of course."

There was another thoughtful silence on Rufe's part. Finally he said, "How did he get to know Ben?"

"I don't know that either."

"Miss Dotty said that the news of the judge's murder was on the radio today. Every local news broadcast. I suppose that's how Cecco knew of it. That, or someone at the inn told him."

"Rufe!" Bea stopped abruptly to look up at him. "Could he have killed the judge?"

"I didn't say that."

"No, but—could he?"

"I doubt it. He doesn't strike me as a very violent man. Besides, if Lorraine is leaving him, how could he possibly expect to gain anything by the judge's death?"

Bea thought for a moment, then said slowly, "Suppose he believed that Clara's heart is really so bad that the shock of the judge's death might kill her too. Suppose he thought that Lorraine, Aunt Clara's only blood relation, would inherit from Aunt Clara. Suppose he relied on his charm —I suppose you'd call it that—to get Lorraine back again."

"That's quite a bit of supposition." Rufe took her hand and held it tightly. "Let's forget Cecco. I really don't think he murdered the judge. And I think it's safe to let him stay in the house. Only remember, Bea, it was murder."

"Aunt Clara is sure that Meeth shot the judge. She says he must have waited until you left and then came in the house, the judge got out his gun and Meeth got it away from him—the judge was rather feeble in a way, you know. She says Meeth made him go outdoors and down by the wall and—"

"I know. Apparently the police think that's a possibility too, otherwise they wouldn't hold Meeth as a material witness. I didn't see his car parked in the road when I left. But I wasn't paying much attention to anything then. I do remember, though, a car came along, going in the direction of Valley Ridge just as I was crossing the road. Lights came full on me. So I was seen all right. But the car went on. It could have been Meeth's car and he's not saying anything about it. It would put him on the spot as I was leaving. He says he had gone before I left. It's possible that he shot the judge. That coat of the judge's bothers me though."

"Coat? Oh, the old tweed one that was on his desk?"

"Yes. Nobody can avoid the fact that a thirty-two—if that was used and I think it must have been—wouldn't have had the force to go right through that thick tweed and the—the judge, and then reach a spot in his back from which it could be readily extracted. So how did the judge happen to remove his coat?"

They turned and started up toward the house again. Gravel crunched beneath their feet. "It was a warm night. It turned suddenly cold later. But it had been too warm for this time of the year," Bea said at last. "He may simply have taken it off because of that."

"He was wearing it when I talked to him. I'm certain of that. The judge was a kind of—oh, formal man in his way."

"But the coat was there, over his desk."

"But, Bea, who could have induced the judge to remove his coat?"

"Maybe the murderer got the judge's gun, knew he'd have to get the coat away from the judge and just—just did it."

"By force? Holding the gun at him? No. The judge was no fool. Remember Griffin says he heard two shots. I don't think the bullet that killed the judge came from the judge's gun. I don't think the police believe that either. It's the same question. Why dig out that bullet, taking such a chance, and then leave the judge's gun? The police checked on my father's gun. I was right. It hadn't been fired, hadn't even been cleaned lately. They searched through his surgical instruments, too."

"His surgical— Oh, for the knife that was used to extract that bullet. Do you mean to say that Miss Dotty allowed them in your father's office?"

Rufe chuckled. "Yes. I was surprised she didn't take a knife to the lieutenant."

"Rufe, I've been wondering. The judge must have made other enemies besides Meeth. He had a long career on the bench. First as judge of the juvenile court, then the superior court."

"You typed his memoirs. You ought to know."

"There really wasn't a thing that could indicate any danger to him except Meeth's threats."

"Something may develop. There's not been much time for the police and the detectives."

They had almost reached the steps to the terrace. Bea put her hand on Rufe's arm. "Rufe, this trip to Washington. Why? What do they want?"

"I don't know. I was just told to come."

"Is it about"—Bea swallowed hard—"the judge's—the murder—"

"Why should it be?"

"They must know about it. They seem to know everything about you."

"Well, then," Rufe said cheerfully, "they'll know I didn't murder the judge."

"I do wish you hadn't admitted coming here and talking to the judge. You could have let them think that Meeth was lying."

Rufe laughed shortly. "Darling, how could I tell a lie!" He sobered. "No, I wasn't so hell-bent on telling the truth as it seems. I remembered those car lights. I'm sure that sooner or later somebody will come forward and tell the police he saw me crossing the street. I thought I'd better get my story in first."

"But nobody has told the police that he saw you."

"No. And that is rather odd in a way. However—"

"Rufe," Lorraine called from the terrace. Bea turned. She couldn't see Lorraine's face; the light from the open door was behind her. But she could see her lovely figure outlined against the light. Lorraine came down the steps, and ignoring Bea, put out her hands in a pleading gesture to Rufe. "Oh, Rufe! If only you hadn't gone to Vietnam just when you did. We were so much in love with one another. I was a fool to marry Cecco. I don't know how it happened!"

"Because you wanted to marry him, of course," Rufe said pleasantly. Bea could now see Lorraine's face, for she had moved closer to Rufe. She was lovely in that half-light—or in any light, Bea admitted in honest appraisal.

Rufe said, "Goodnight, Lorraine." Then he turned and bent over Bea and kissed her, but rather lightly. He went off quickly down the drive. Lorraine looked after him and then at Bea. "How easy it will be to get him back! That is, if I want him."

SEVEN

"You needn't be so sure of that!" Bea spoke with assurance, but she could not help but feel that it could be easy for Lorraine to get any man—if, as she said, she wanted him.

No, Bea told herself. Not Rufe!

Aunt Clara had already gone upstairs. Cecco was still there, smoking one of the judge's cigars. He went with Bea as she made a little tour of the house, shutting doors and windows. Velda had gone long ago, leaving a sparkling clean kitchen and the back door unlocked. Bea locked it.

Both Cecco and Lorraine watched over Bea's shoulder as she set the tiny button on the burglar alarm. Cecco said thoughtfully, "Oh, I see how it works. That white light shows that the doors and windows that are bugged have been closed. Then you punch that little button and the red light comes on, instead of the white. After that—"

"After that," Lorraine said sharply, "don't even go down the stairs, Cecco. Front stairs or back stairs. Isn't that right, Bea?"

"Oh, yes. It would set off the alarm."

"Loud?" Cecco's eyes were intent.

"Loud enough to wake the—" Bea caught herself.

Lorraine finished for her. "To wake the dead. Except it didn't."

"He wasn't dead then. He died— Oh, please don't talk about it."

After she had got into her own room and closed the door, Bea went to the window. In the summer the heavy foliage of the woods shut off lights even from nearby houses; now in the early spring, she could see a faintly yellowish area reflected in the haze above the village streetlamps. She could imagine—almost hear—how the whole village must be buzzing. Murder in Valley Ridge just did not happen, yet—knowing the town and its people, Bea guessed that those men who had guns had taken them out and loaded them. And those who had no guns had probably spent the day driving to Stamford or Bridgeport or even to New York in order to buy them. And she was sure there was a rash of orders for burglar alarms.

The news had undoubtedly spread that whoever shot the judge had extracted the bullet. She shuddered as she thought of it; it seemed almost worse and uglier than the fact of murder itself. She could hear the speculations, the belief that only someone with surgical or some kind of medical experience would have had the skill to extract that bullet—in the dark, hurriedly but efficiently.

But here the repeated question arose. If the murderer had meant to remove the bullet in order to prevent its identification as a bullet coming from the judge's gun, why leave the gun? If the judge's gun had been fired recently—and the opinion of the police that it had been fired the night the judge was shot was almost certainly accurate—then who, if not the murderer, had fired it? But then why take such pains to remove the bullet?

Almost more important than anything else was the fact that someone had entered the house, setting off the alarm, after the judge had been shot—why and what had that person wanted?

She couldn't answer anything, Bea told herself as she turned wearily away from the window. I must try to sleep, she thought—and she did, although troubled thoughts woke her frequently, thoughts of Rufe, Lorraine —and the judge.

Early the next morning the police came to question Cecco. There was an excellent grapevine for news in Valley Ridge. Cecco's presence was known immediately. They talked to him in the judge's study. The whole thing took only a short time, and when they left they were apparently satisfied with Cecco's replies.

Cecco came back up the stairs and met Bea. "Nothing to it," he said airily. "They looked at my passport. Took it away with them. They know when I arrived in New York. They understood my reason for coming to Valley Ridge. They had inquired at the inn. I have an alibi. I didn't leave my room that night. Someone would have seen me. They understood perfectly why I didn't come here until yesterday evening. I didn't hear of the murder until noon, I slept late. And when I did hear of it, I had to debate about coming here. I wasn't sure of my welcome—that's easily understood. But then I decided that my place was at Lorraine's side. Oh, they were most understanding about it. I believe," Cecco added, frowning slightly. But then his face cleared. "However, I do have that alibi. Not that I need it."

Lorraine was standing in the open door of her room, a dress hanging over her arm. "Alibi!" She thought for a moment. "Come in here, Bea. I want to talk to you. You too, Cecco."

Cecco followed Bea into the room and settled down on the chaise longue, languidly. He got out an ivory holder and inserted a cigarette in it. Lorraine gave him an angry glance. "Bea," she said directly, "will you promise me something—"

Cecco said lazily, "I wouldn't, Lorraine."

Lorraine shot a swift look at him. "I can count on Bea."

Cecco lifted his thin black eyebrows. "I wouldn't count on anybody when it's an alibi for murder."

Lorraine didn't quite snort, but almost. "That's all right for you! You can prove that you came out on the eight-ten train, went by taxi to the inn and spent the night and most of yesterday there." Cecco nodded. "But I wouldn't put it past you to sneak out some way and do anything you wanted to do, except"—Lorraine grudgingly admitted—"you couldn't have managed to dig out that bullet!"

Cecco's eyes went to Bea. "I couldn't have done that. She's quite right. I'm afraid of blood. Gives me the creeps. No, I didn't kill the judge. Besides, I had no motive. My wife is divorcing me! Why, even if the judge had left her money or she hoped to get it from her aunt, I wouldn't have profited."

"But you were here," Bea said so accusingly, she surprised herself. It then occurred to her that, oddly, Cecco and Lorraine seemed on slightly better terms. She didn't know why it had struck her and she couldn't be sure of it. But there seemed to her an air of complicity about them, as if they had come to some sort of understanding which neither of them liked but which might be expedient.

Lorraine said, "Oh, that doesn't matter! Nobody is going to blame you, Cecco! But I— Once they know about the judge's will and that Aunt Clara is going to write a new one—"

"Are you so sure of that, darling?" Cecco waved his cigarette gracefully.

"She hasn't said so definitely. Yet. But I'm her only blood relation. She knows the arrangement the judge made her agree to isn't fair. She wants me to stay here. She loves me. Oh, yes, she'll make a new will and she'll put me in it."

"How nice to be sure of that, darling."

"I am sure. I told you—that is—"

Again the notion of some sort of guarded agreement between Cecco and Lorraine flashed across Bea's thoughts. She said, however, "What were you going to ask me to do, Lorraine? You spoke of alibis. I can't possibly give you an alibi. You weren't here. I didn't even know you were in America."

Lorraine bit her lip. "Well, you could try, couldn't you? I mean, couldn't you say—oh, that you'd forgotten but that I was here with you—"

"Oh, Lorraine!" Cecco almost laughed. "Bea has already given her evidence to the police. So have you. Neither of you can change your statement now."

Lorraine debated. "You can, Cecco!"

"No," said Cecco.

"Yes, you can. You can say you phoned for me—or somehow got the notion that I would be at the club dance. Yes, that's it. Then you came and met me and we talked. So easy for you, Cecco."

Cecco shook his head. "I've already told the police where I was."

"But, Lorraine, you said you were with Ben, dancing or driving," Bea wished wistfully she and Rufe had been dancing at the club at the time of the judge's murder.

"The fact is, I wasn't. Not all the time. I don't have any sort of alibi for at least an hour and a half. It's all Ben Benson's fault."

"Ben's?"

"Because he dances like a cow. I couldn't bear having my feet stepped on any longer. So I pretended to go to the ladies' room and instead I went off and sat in a corner of the veranda, that long one near the bar. I thought somebody might come in the bar, somebody I knew, and would be a better dancer than Ben. But I'd been gone too long. Nobody I knew came, or at least nobody I wanted to get chummy with again. All of them have married and got fat," she said viciously. "I could hear their talk. Nothing but stocks, gold and babies. The window was open."

"But didn't anybody see you?" Bea asked.

"Nobody. I finally gave up and went in and danced with Ben a few times, and when my feet really couldn't take it any longer, I suggested we take a drive in his car. So we did. That much is true. Later—this is true, too—we dropped back at the club for a nightcap and heard the news. Then I couldn't decide what to do, so we drove some more—"

"Until—what time was it?—three in the morning or thereabouts?" Cecco asked, smiling.

"It doesn't matter what time it was, or where we went or—"

"Or what you were doing?" Cecco was still smiling.

Lorraine snapped, "Or what we were doing. Actually, we weren't even talking much. At least I wasn't. I was shocked at the news. And Ben Benson is about as thrilling an escort as he is a dancer. I don't remember. Was he always like that, Bea?"

"Oh, I don't know. Ben's all right. Ben's of the older crowd. But he's almost the only bachelor in town except Rufe and Seth, so he does get invited everywhere."

"Quite a catch," Lorraine said bitterly. "And I've got bruised feet to prove it. Old Mrs. Benson didn't really want me as a guest. I could tell that when I proposed myself. But she gave in. I suppose she thought I was after her darling Ben. Not me."

"Flying for higher game?" Cecco said sweetly.

Lorraine was taking a dress from her suitcase; she whirled around and flung the dress at Cecco, who dodged, gathered it up and eyed it. "You must be more careful of your dresses, darling. I believe this is a Dior—

something I couldn't pay for, no doubt. I hope someone paid for it."

"Never mind who paid for it." Lorraine's cheeks had sudden flames of red. "You go straight back to the inn, or for that matter, go——"

"Now, now, Lorraine. Enough of that!" Cecco dropped the dress over a nearby table and took up a small lacy pillow which he placed under his handsome head.

Lorraine opened her mouth, seemed to think that whatever she had intended to say wasn't sufficiently insulting, and closed it again.

Bea said, "Aunt Clara wants him to stay here. For the time being."

Cecco laughed. "We're all agreed that there would certainly be talk if it were known that I was staying at the inn, clearly unwelcome to stay with my wife. And I'm sure Lorraine agrees too."

Lorraine turned around toward the closet swiftly, as if Bea might catch some expression in her face which Lorraine didn't want seen.

Or am I imagining this? Bea thought. If there is some sort of pact, some sort of arrangement between them, that's their business, not mine. Isn't it? But she wasn't sure of anything any more.

Lorraine said from the depths of the closet, "I don't care what Cecco does so long as he stays away from me!"

"Darling!" Cecco chuckled. "Don't be fatuous. Besides, your dear Ben has certainly by now backed up your story."

With a feeling that in another moment Lorraine was going to hurl everything she could find at Cecco's head, Bea went out of the room.

It was Sunday, but Velda, contrary to her custom, had arrived early, prepared breakfast and a salad for supper or lunch and then apparently gone again. Bea went to the study to find Clara. Through the open door she caught a glimpse of two men in uniform crouched down under the laurels, apparently searching all through the leaf mold of the previous summer. Searching for the missing bullets? Searching for a knife? There were far too many places in the woods to hide either or both.

She found Clara in the library. It was always a dismal room, as the judge had said. It had been furnished at some time with glass-enclosed bookshelves holding volumes of books, enormous chairs and a great mahogany table in the middle of the faded Brussels carpet. The windows were small and half covered with ivy, so there was only a gloomy light filtering through. Bea had loved its seclusion for reading. Clara had loved the room as it was, and when the judge had suggested a change, Clara had turned stubborn. What was good enough for her father and grandfather was good enough for her. Now Clara had the Sunday *Times* spread out and was clipping the judge's obituary with steady little hands. She looked up as Bea came in. "Good morning, my dear. They've made a few mistakes, but not many."

Bea read the clipping Clara held out to her.

Cecco came strolling in and looked at the obituary over Bea's shoulder. He used some sort of cologne, which wafted unpleasantly around him. "I didn't realize the judge was so well known," he said. "That photograph is very fine."

Clara glanced up. "It was taken some time ago. But it is like him—as he once was."

Not as he had been of late years, Bea thought. But he had once been a handsome man and even lately he had a distinguished appearance. Tears came to her eyes suddenly as she looked at that early photograph. Once when the judge had found her in tears over some childhood mishap, he had told her soberly that ladies, even very young ladies, didn't cry. And it was after the incident of Mrs. Benson and the blueberries that he had brought Shadders to her, the long-legged, frolicking Airedale puppy. When the dog had fought his last fight and she had written to tell Rufe, Rufe had said to have him buried on the place, and she herself had dug the grave, down near the pond, below some willows. She wouldn't cry now; she felt almost as if the judge were watching her.

Clara was saying, "It's a good obituary. They left out a club—no, two clubs—and his term as judge of the juvenile court. It was his friend, former Governor Joe Collins, who got him moved to the superior court. Of course, the state legislature always must approve an appointment." Clara took the clipping and started to fold it up.

Lorraine came in then and said, "Aunt Clara, do you have a black dress?"

"Black—" Clara looked stricken. "No! I never thought of that. Why, I haven't got a black dress to my name. The judge liked light colors."

"But you'll have to have a black dress for the services," Lorraine said. "And a black hat, too."

Bea thought swiftly through her own clothes. "I have nothing black either. We can't do anything about it today, but tomorrow I'll go to New York and find dresses for us."

"I have a black dress," Lorraine said smugly.

Clara gave her a worried glance. Lorraine added quickly, "Long sleeves, high neck. Quite proper, Aunt Clara."

*   *   *

"Then you can drive to New York with me," Rufe told her that afternoon when she said she was going to the city. "I had my old car tuned up last week. It runs all right."

It was by then late in the evening. After a rather scrambled lunch, which Cecco had unexpectedly helped Bea to serve, both Lorraine and Cecco had disappeared and Clara had gone to her room to rest. Bea was sitting in the study, once more reading the judge's obituary. It stated only that the judge had died suddenly in his own residence. The front page had an account of the murder; and there was a headline: Prominent Jurist Shot. The account was long and was continued on a back page, but there was no mention of Rufe. Bea had looked with a feeling of incredulity at her own name: ". . . the body was found by Miss Beatrice Bartry, a niece and ward of Judge Bartry."

Rufe had come in through the terrace door and taken the paper away from her. "Don't keep reading it."

"Rufe, it didn't mention you. That's good, isn't it?"

"This has nothing to do with my job. My prospective job, I should say."

"Tomorrow will you know more about where you are to be sent?"

"I don't know. It's possible."

Bea thought of her last stormy talk with the judge. Among other things, he had said that Bea would have to act almost as an unpaid servant to, say, the ambassador's wife. "No," Bea had told him hotly, "all that is changed —if it ever happened. The wife of a Foreign Service officer, so matter how minor an officer is at the beginning, is supposed to be a private citizen." There was an added consideration, however. She said now, "The wife of a Foreign Service officer is supposed to behave in every way in a manner suitable to the—the dignity of the United States. Being associated with murder isn't exactly dignified."

"Oh, Bea!" Rufe took her hands. "You couldn't help this—this dreadful thing. Nobody can possibly feel that you have behaved badly. Don't be such an idiot."

"But it means so much to us both."

"Listen, darling, I may be the third undersecretary of the third undersecretary down in the third cellar. I have no dignity or status to maintain."

"But you will have. And this horrible thing! Nobody knows where a murder case can begin or end, and nobody knows how many people can be involved in it."

"You're quoting the judge."

"Perhaps I am. But he spoke the truth. The police even questioned Cecco this morning."

"He was in town. Supposedly at Valley Inn—"

"They checked that. The people at the inn said he was there."

"Those windows are low. He could have simply dropped out and come here—"

"How would he get the judge's gun?"

Rufe sighed. "How would anybody get it? Do you suppose Lorraine has induced your aunt to make a new will yet?"

"I don't know."

"She will."

"Naturally. Lorraine is really her niece."

"Aunt Clara will marry again," Rufe said casually, picking up a cigarette box and looking at it as if it were important.

"Aunt Clara!"

"Why, of course."

"But she was devoted to the judge, she gave in to him about everything, she—"

"She put on quite an act, Bea, of being the cozy little-woman type. In fact, I've always known that she had a will of iron. She's much younger than the judge. She can't be more than fifty or thereabouts—"

"Fifty-two."

"There, you see. Mark my words. She's honestly grieving for the judge and will for some time. Perhaps later she'll travel. She'll do something. And believe me, Bea, it won't be long before she marries again. A good-looking rich widow— Now, don't glare at me like that! It's the natural thing to happen. She'll have time to make a dozen wills."

"But her heart—"

"I'll bet anything you like that her heart is really as good as yours or mine. My father doesn't get very upset about it, believe me. And it seems to me that it's just possible Aunt Clara had a heart attack whenever she wanted to get out of something."

"You're not to speak like that about her—"

"Oh, Bea! I love her. I've always loved her. But I think I see her more objectively than you do. This is all beside the point, anyway."

"Rufe, wouldn't you really rather have a rich wife than a poor one? The judge said that in the Foreign Service—"

"The judge said a great many things. He was an opinionated, selfish old man. Don't quote *de mortuis nil nisi bonum* either. People don't change because they've died. He simply didn't want you to leave him, didn't want to lose all that attention he could count on from you. Let's not quarrel about the judge, Bea. Or about a rich woman or a poor woman—"

Lorraine again showed her talent for appearing at the wrong time and, as far as Bea was concerned, the wrong place. Now she sauntered into the room. "Oh, I wondered where everybody was. I just got back. I took Cecco to Valley Inn to pay his bill and pick up the rest of his luggage. I left the car in the drive, Bea. It's all right there, isn't it? I wasn't sure I could make that curve into the old barn."

"Bea is just going to bed," Rufe said. "We'll have to be up early. I'll toot outside for you about six. All right, Bea?"

"All right."

Lorraine eyed her. "Are you going to Washington with Rufe? What about those black dresses?"

"I'm just going with him as far as New York," Bea said shortly. "Goodnight, Rufe."

He pulled her toward him, kissed her, said goodnight and was quickly off down the drive. Bea wished his kiss had not been quite so brief. But then, Rufe had a strong sense of privacy; he wouldn't have wanted Lorraine—and Cecco, who now stood in the doorway behind Lorraine—to witness any display of emotion.

Feeling let down, Bea arranged the papers on the desk and folded away the account of the judge's murder. When she looked up, both Lorraine and Cecco had gone too.

She closed the terrace door and bolted it. Then she went through the living room and the hall. The front door stood open and lights from the hall were reflected on the shining fenders of the judge's car. He would never have permitted it to stand outside even on a warm spring night.

After a moment she went outside. Lorraine had left the keys in the ignition. Bea started the car, wondering how long she and Aunt Clara would still feel themselves obliged to follow every admonition, every like or dislike of the judge's.

Bea negotiated the abrupt curve into the garage.

It had been an enormous barn; the stalls and feeding troughs had been removed to make space for the two cars, but the ancient beams and the old tack room behind it still remained. Whenever it had to be repainted,

Clara had insisted on the original faded-red. There were two doors. Each one was twofold, the leaves latched back. There were bolts on the outside of the leaves fastening them together, but no lock.

She drove as carefully into the slot for the judge's car as if even now he were standing outside, watching her progress sternly. She turned off the engine and lights.

She was getting out of the car when the two leaves of the door behind her swung quietly together.

EIGHT

The doors had blown shut, of course. Someone had failed to hook back the two leaves. It was very dark, and in the darkness the place smelled so like a barn that she almost expected some long-ago horse to whinny.

She felt her way along the car to the door behind it. She tried to push it open. The leaves rattled but held firm. It was with a sense of shock that she realized they must be firmly bolted on the outside. The wind couldn't have done that.

She pushed and worked at the door; the bolt held. She felt her way to the door behind the small car which she usually drove. It was, as she expected, tightly bolted on the outside, too. She was sure she encountered a cobweb, and brushed her hand on her skirt with an odd tingling of nerves. She tried to calm herself. She had turned off the engine; there would be no chance of carbon monoxide even if she couldn't make anyone in the house hear her.

She had a sudden thought. There was a sure way of making herself heard. She groped her way to the judge's car again, leaned into the seat and found the horn. Its wail echoed wildly in the enclosed space of the old barn.

They made solid barns in the days when this one had been built, solid enough to protect animals from New England winters. But surely someone from the house would hear her. She leaned on the horn until her own ears seemed to rattle.

Clara could have turned on her television, and turned it up very loud, as she always did. But surely Lorraine or Cecco would hear and come to her aid.

Big as it was, it wouldn't be very comfortable if she had to spend the night sleeping in the judge's car. Besides—besides, she didn't like the idea of being alone in the big, dark old barn, accessible from the outside.

Suddenly she remembered that at some time they had put an electric light in the barn. It was rarely used. She felt her way back again to the doors; she had a vague memory that the switch for the light was just inside the doors and that there was one big light hanging on a wire from a ceiling beam.

She found the switch after another unpleasant encounter with a spider web, but no light came on. Perhaps the bulb had burned out and never been replaced; since the judge had retired, no one ever used the garage at night.

She tried the horn again. It sounded deafening to her, but still no one came.

It simply wasn't possible that someone had intentionally shut her in the garage. There was no reason for it. All the same her heart gave a choking leap at the thought. Whatever had happened, she didn't intend to stay there all night. She pressed the horn in a series of furious blasts.

Quite suddenly she felt a current of fresh, cool air on her face. She heard one of the halves of the door swing creakily open. She could see the dimly lighted rectangle behind the car. Someone said, "For God's sake, who's that? Take your hand off the horn."

It was Cecco. She took her hand off the horn. No matter what her feelings about Cecco, at that instant she could have kissed him. "It's me," she said rather faintly.

He flung aside the other half of the door; she could see his tall figure dimly in the gloom. "Do you mean— Is it little Bea?"

"Oh, yes!"

He came closer. "What's the matter?"

"N—nothing. That is—the doors closed." She was recovering a semblance of control. "They must have blown shut just as I was putting the judge's car away."

Cecco came closer; he was between her and the door, and for a brief moment she had a sense of being trapped. A faint odor of cigar smoke came with him and, oddly, steadied her wild fancy.

He said, though, "But, dear little Bea, there's no wind."

"It doesn't matter. It was an accident. Let's get out of here—let's go to the house."

He waited a second and then obediently turned. She took a long breath and followed him out of the garage. Cecco drew the two leaves of the door together. She said, "There's a bolt."

"Yes, I found it."

There was something rather thoughtful, even evasive in Cecco's voice. Bea told herself that she imagined that. Cecco wouldn't have bolted the doors and then after so long a time come back to let her out. Probably the time in the garage had not been as long as it seemed to her.

After a moment Bea said again, but with a strangely tight kind of feeling around her throat, "Accident," and started along the graveled drive toward the house. Cecco said nothing, just walked along with her. When they reached the terrace he said, "Lucky I heard you. I had been out strolling and smoking."

Bea said abruptly, "Where were you walking?"

"I don't know, really," Cecco replied promptly. "There's a kind of path. I could barely see it. It seems to go through the woods. I remembered that there is a lake down there somewhere. Anyway, I only wanted to take a walk. Aren't you glad I released you, little Bea?"

"Somebody would have come," Bea said, and then repented and added, "I'm glad you came. Thank you, Cecco."

He took her hand and kissed it in his caressing way. She said, "Is there a policeman on the place tonight?"

"Why, no. At least I have not seen a policeman. I think it is unlikely—"

They walked in at the big front door, which she bolted behind them. Cecco followed after her as she went through the dining room and pantry back to the kitchen door. He watched as she closed it and put on the chain bolt. He followed her back to the hall; she turned out lights as she went. When they reached the hall Cecco said, "Aren't you going to set the famous burglar alarm?"

"Yes." Bea felt him walking softly behind her all the way up the steps and it was as if a very handsome, strong panther were treading on her heels. That was *really* preposterous, she told herself. And again he watched, his gaze bright and lively as she set the alarm.

"I hope Lorraine is in the house," he said. "If not—"

"Oh dear, I forgot Lorraine." Bea went to Lorraine's door and knocked.

Lorraine called out almost immediately, "Cecco, you have the other guest room! I told you—"

"It's not Cecco, it's Bea. I only wanted to be sure you're upstairs. I'm setting the alarm."

"Go ahead. If Cecco gets caught outside, it will serve him right. I don't know where he is."

Cecco laughed. "I'm right here, darling. Don't concern yourself about me." He spoke in melodious tones, as musical as Bea had ever heard outside an opera house.

Lorraine's reply was short. "I'm not concerning myself about you!"

Bea said briefly, "Goodnight."

Clara's door was closed and there were no sounds of the television; apparently she was asleep. Conscious of Cecco standing politely in the hall, waiting for her to close the door, Bea shut it hurriedly and with rather a bang.

Somebody had thoughtfully turned on her bedside lamps and her desk lamp. Clara? It would not be like Lorraine to think of it.

The night was quiet. Yet nobody had heard the horn she had sounded so loudly and so long. Cecco had been in the vicinity; Cecco had heard it. Cecco had come and unlocked the bolt.

Bea went to the closet to get out a dressing gown and remembered with a chill the other gown, stained and blotched with blood, which the police had taken away with them. Nobody had questioned her about it; perhaps its true significance was clear. As she reached into the closet she noticed that dresses were hanging in odd confusion, as if they had been pushed this way and that, all askew.

Lorraine? But Lorraine respected and liked clothes; she wouldn't have shoved them all awry on their hangers. Bea reached out and straightened several of them. Mere curiosity could have led Lorraine to explore while Bea was outside—shut in the garage. Or possibly there was some article of clothing Lorraine merely wished to borrow.

But Lorraine wouldn't have bolted her in the garage for such a reason; all Lorraine would have had to do was say that she forgot to pack this or that.

The question was: Who had bolted her in the garage, and why?

She began to wonder whether Cecco had a perverted sense of humor, enjoyed playing crude practical jokes. Certainly he had been somewhere near the garage. She couldn't avoid that fact.

She had dropped into a tired sleep when something seemed to nudge at her, half rousing her: the thought that her closet had looked as if someone might have pushed aside the dresses in order to hide there.

But why—who? There was nobody in the house who would have reason to do that. The whole thing was like part of an uneasy, troubled dream—but a dream. She dismissed it.

She woke from a troubled sleep well before six o'clock. Sleepily she looked at the little French clock on her bedside table, thought it was six and scrambled out of bed so fast that the small rug skidded over the highly polished floor, threw her back on the bed and jolted her into taking a second look at the time. It was only five o'clock, so she had plenty of time to dress. She turned off the alarm, went down stairs and made coffee and boiled an egg. Then she sat so long, pondering recent events, that she heard the light toot of Rufe's car before she was prepared for it. She dashed upstairs, snatched up her big handbag and a coat and ran downstairs again. Dawn was cool and slightly misty. They took the winding road across to the main road going into Valley Ridge. They passed the Congregational church with its white steeple pointing skyward; its bell was just tolling the gentle strokes of six.

They had almost reached the wide approach to the Merritt Parkway before Bea could make up her mind to tell Rufe of the unnerving—yet, in the end, harmless—happening of the previous night. When she did tell him, she made it light and casual. The barn doors had been closed, she said. They had been bolted. Cecco had let her out.

Rufe's face took on the closed expression which she recognized as his way of wearing a mask while he was thinking very troublesome thoughts. "There was no wind last night. Besides, that bolt needs hands. So who did it?"

"I don't know. But it really wasn't anything. I put my hand on the horn and held it there, and then, I told you, Cecco came along and let me out."

He turned onto the Merritt. Even at that time of day, there was a stream of cars, speeding toward New York. After a while he said, "I wonder if that could have been Cecco's idea of a rather mean joke."

"I thought of that, too. But he— No, it didn't seem like that. I really think he was just strolling along that path down toward the pond and heard the horn."

Rufe was silent for what seemed a long time. Then he said, "Bea, if there is the slightest thing you know which might give the police an idea about the murderer, you'd better tell them."

"I don't know anything."

"Somebody had to bolt that door. I can't see why unless—to frighten you, do you suppose? That doesn't seem likely. Was anything at all dis-

turbed in the house when you came back with Cecco? Did it look as
though anybody had been, say, prowling in the judge's study?"

"No. The terrace door was closed. The front door was open. I bolted it
and the kitchen door. Cecco trailed along after me. There wasn't— Well,
yes, somebody had been in my room. That is— Oh, it can't be important,
Lorraine or Aunt Clara did it, but the lights had been turned on in my
room. And the dresses in the closet looked as if they had been pushed
aside. Leaving a place big enough for somebody to hide in," she added.
"But why?"

"Because someone may have come along the hall, and whoever was in
your room didn't want to be seen and have to explain it."

"Only Aunt Clara and Lorraine were in the house."

"The front door was open. The kitchen door was probably unlocked.
Anybody who wanted to could have got into the house. So who?"

"Nobody! There's nothing I know that could hurt anybody."

He considered that for a while, too. "It could be something you don't
know you know, if you understand me."

"Of course I understand you but—no."

"We'll tell Obrian about the garage doors. I hope to get back tonight.
I'll take the shuttle from La Guardia. If you'll drive back to New York
and park behind my club—there ought to be plenty of parking spaces in
the early morning—then I'll get back there by, say, four, earlier if I can
make it, or if I'm held up until tomorrow morning, I'll send a message.
Ask the doorman at the club for it."

There was a shuttle flight to Washington loading when they arrived at
the airport. It was still so early by the time Bea reached New York that
the stores were not yet open. She parked in the space behind Rufe's club
and went to St. Patrick's, and to the lovely solemnity of the Lady Chapel.
She sat there for some time, thinking of the judge. His loving kindness
over the years seemed to blot out the querulous, erratic man he had become. When she left, it was with a sense of comfort, as if she had said
her own private funeral service for him. She couldn't remember much of
her own father; his place had been taken by the judge.

It was a curiously normal day. She found a dress for Clara; she found
a hat which she was not pleased with but bought because she could find
nothing she was sure Clara might like; she found a veil, a thin shoulder-
length veil bordered with black ribbon; Clara—or the judge—would have
wanted that. She remembered black gloves. She lunched late at a convenient Longchamps, then went back to Rufe's club, where the doorman

had a message for her. Mr. Thorne had phoned. He said to tell Miss Bartry he couldn't get home tonight. The doorman relieved her of her packages and added, "He said something else. He said don't go to the garage again. Was that right, Miss Bartry? I wasn't sure I heard him correctly."

"Oh, yes. That was right." She thankfully permitted him to carry her packages out to Rufe's car and get her started on the way home.

Her heart felt like a lump of lead; she knew exactly what Rufe had meant by saying not to go to the garage. Somebody wanted to harm her. But why? There was no reason for it.

She had hoped to escape the late-afternoon traffic. But early as it was, there were several bottlenecks of traffic. It was almost six o'clock when she reached home. Chief Obrian was sitting in his car watching two policemen who again were searching the lawn down by the shrubbery where the judge had been shot, searching it inch by inch on their hands and knees.

Nobody was at home, he told her, not even Velda. He himself had questioned Willie Griffin again. "He still insists that he heard two shots the night the judge was killed and at about the time he must have been shot. He isn't sure of the time, but it was after ten o'clock, maybe nearly eleven. After the shots, he heard the burglar alarm and then the police car. He says he had gone down to the Ellison gate across the driveway to make sure it was closed. He said that young people had begun to drive in and park there and he was going to put a stop to it. He swears up and down that there were two shots." Chief Obrian eyed the packages beside her, crawled out from behind his wheel and lumbered across to her. "I'll carry these. You look pretty tired out. I hope you don't mind if I ask you again—but are you sure you didn't hear any shot at all?"

"Oh, I'm sure. But what do you think it all means? Do you think the judge himself shot at somebody? And that's why his gun had been recently fired?"

The chief went into the house with her, deposited the packages on the hall table and chair, sat down and sighed heavily. It was obvious that Chief Obrian was taking the judge's murder very hard; there was a sagging worry in his face; usually, no matter what, he had a cheerful way of looking and speaking. He said, the troubled lines deep in his face, "I wish I could answer all that. The men are down there again, looking for those two bullets. And a knife. Not much chance of finding anything. All these woods around. Well—"

She said thank you as he went out again. After a moment she went up the stairs, thinking of a shower and fresh clothes. At the door of her room she stopped—even at a glance, she could see there was something wrong with it.

NINE

There were several things wrong. She stood in the middle of the room and looked around.

Clara had trained her as a child to neatness and order. The judge had declaimed frequently to the effect that everything had a place and everything should be in that place. The judge didn't subscribe to that notion himself but he expected it of Clara and Bea.

As was her habit, she had made the bed that morning before going downstairs to breakfast. It was now slightly wrinkled and the pillows were not in their usual order: the two plump pillows below, the tiny pillow she actually slept on, on top. Now the small pillow lay at the foot of the bed.

She had seen to the care of her room since she was old enough to do so. Velda would never have touched anything in it.

A drawer in her dressing table was half out, at an angle, as if it had been opened and then closed so hurriedly that it stuck. Objects on her small writing table were just a little displaced; the Irish glass and silver holder for pens and pencils stood at the left instead of the right, as if it had been pushed aside in order to permit someone to examine the big closed box where she kept her correspondence. Her small French clock lay face down on the rug. Someone had been in her room, searching for something. Lorraine? Not likely. Cecco? Not likely. After a stricken moment, she thought of the chief and ran downstairs. He was sitting on the terrace steps. He rose, listened to her hurried story and went swiftly upstairs with her.

He looked about for a few minutes, passing his hand worriedly over his lined face. "Are you sure, Bea? You left in a hurry this morning. Perhaps you weren't as careful as your usually are," he said finally.

"I'm sure. I know everything was okay when I left."

"Well, then—is there anybody who would do this to you just out of spite? Something like that?"

"Somebody shut me in the garage last night! Sunday night!"

He listened again while she told about it, now thoroughly frightened. "And there was something else," she finished. "I told Rufe about it. It seemed unimportant then, but now—"

"What else?"

"When I got to my room last night, after Cecco let me out of the garage, my dresses were pushed aside in the closet. As if"—she swallowed hard—"as if somebody might have hidden there."

Obrian didn't like any of it, obviously. "This Cecco fellow, he let you out of the garage?"

"Yes."

"H'mm. Let's see what Velda Mathers has to say. If somebody was here this afternoon—"

"I know there was!"

"Let's talk to Velda. She doesn't miss much. What's her phone number?"

Bea took him to the extension in the judge's study and listened while he dialed. Presently Velda answered.

"Velda, where is Mrs. Bartry? . . . Where's the rest of the family? . . . Yes, I know, but she's just got home." Velda talked for a long time. Finally he thanked her, hung up and turned to Bea. "She says the parson came to see Mrs. Bartry and then took her to view the—remains," he said delicately and probably in Velda's very words. "Then he was going to talk to her about the hymns for the services and then take her to see that everything is in order in the Salcott lot out at Old Cemetery. Velda said that Lorraine and her husband had gone somewhere in the Mercedes, she didn't know where. She said there had been so many telegrams phoned in, she finally asked Western Union to deliver them instead. Some of them are from people who are coming to the services tomorrow."

"I do hope you'll come back to the house after the services. You've known the judge a long time."

"Thank you," Chief Obrian sighed. "I always liked the judge. Although he was pretty harsh lately, changeable and—well, you know, not himself. But let's get back to business. I don't like what's going on, Bea. But maybe your cousin, Lorraine—"

"No," Bea said positively. "It wouldn't be like Lorraine. If she wanted anything she'd come straight out and ask me for it."

Obrian eyed her shrewdly. "Not if it was something personally important to Lorraine."

"I have nothing important to Lorraine," Bea said flatly.

"Then what about that husband of hers? He might be snooping around."

"He might be but— Oh, I don't know, I don't think he'd do it just that way. I mean, he acts and moves as softly as a cat. I think he'd leave everything exactly as he found it. Besides, it was Cecco who let me out of the barn Sunday night."

"How long were you shut in the barn?"

"It seemed ages. But I— No, I really don't know. Perhaps fifteen minutes. Or longer. I can't be sure."

"Long enough for somebody to get into your room and then hide in the closet if he heard somebody coming. Then this Cecco strolls along and lets you out."

"I suppose it's possible that Cecco heard the horn and just simply didn't come at once to open the door. Oh, anything is possible!"

Obrian nodded, then said after some frowning thought, as though checking out all possibilities, "Mrs. Bartry? No. Velda—"

"No!"

"If somebody was there in your room—"

"Somebody was there."

"Whoever it was didn't do a very good job of covering his tracks. So it wasn't one of the state police. Besides, I think I'd have been told."

"I never thought of the police."

"You'd never have known it if they had been here."

"No—" Unexpectedly Bea thought of Seth, shambling around in his untidy way, leaving a drawer askew.

She said, "Where's Seth today?"

"Seth!"

"I only wondered . . . I don't know what to think any more. I mean— oh, Seth is careless about things."

"What would Seth want in your room? I think you're imagining too much. Besides, he's in Bridgeport. I think he said he was going to do a little fence-mending."

"I just don't see why anybody would search my room," she said wearily.

Obrian sighed. "Somebody must have known the house was empty. I hadn't arrived yet, so no policemen were around and whoever it was took the chance of getting into the house. He must have known which room is yours." He sighed again. "We'd better take a look through the rest of the house. See if he got into other rooms."

Apparently "he" hadn't. Clara's room was neat and fragrant and orderly. Lorraine's was orderly enough and reeked of perfume. Cecco's room was littered with magazines and smelled of cigar smoke and after-shave lotion.

"This is the judge's room." Bea opened the door. Someone, Velda probably, had closed the shades, so it was dimly lit. She snapped on a light. But here, too, there was nothing out of place. It seemed so full of the judge's personality—with its heavy table for books and its pipe rack and jar of tobacco, its heavy mahogany chairs and chests of drawers that had been selected by one of Clara's forebears, but which in this case (as not in the library) the judge had liked—that Bea almost expected the judge to come in and impatiently demand what they were doing there.

"Nothing out of the way here." Chief Obrian frowned. "Looks as if whoever it was singled out your room. To tell you the truth, I can't make any sense out of it at all."

He went out of the room. Bea followed him down the sairs. At the door he glanced down at the men still crouching under the shrubbery, and said, "Lorraine can't like you very much now. At least until your aunt changes her will, as I expect she'll do. But I agree with you, I can't see why Lorraine would hunt through your room or shut you in the barn. Maybe to scare you—but why?" He hesitated; there was an odd look of indecision in his face. Bea had a brief notion that he was debating about something he only half wanted to say. If so, he decided against speaking and got in his car, turned it and called to the men in the shrubbery to stop the fruitless searching. After a short colloquy both of them got into the chief's car. The gravel rattled as it went off down the driveway.

It had turned into the public road and disappeared behind firs and shrubbery when the telephone rang. Bea answered it in the judge's study.

It was Rufe calling from Washington. He wanted to be sure she had got his message, had reached home safely and his old car had not broken down somewhere. He would be home the next day in time for the services. About then he must have sensed something in her voice that wasn't right, for he broke off abruptly. "Are you all right? Has anything gone wrong?"

She decided not to tell him then about the unnerving evidence of a search of her room. There was nothing he could do about it and she had already reported it to Chief Obrian. Also, there could readily prove to be some simple explanation. "Obrian and two men were here, still looking for one of those bullets."

"Yes, I keep thinking tbout those two shots Willie Griffin heard. I believe him. I suppose the police have covered all the possibilities. But I wonder if whoever killed the judge meant to suggest suicide—you know, firing the judge's gun into, oh, anywhere, into the shrubbery or the woods? Then leaving the judge's gun— No," he caught himself up. "That can't be right; if he had done that he wouldn't have removed the bullet. No, the bullet that killed him must identify the murderer. We can't get around that. Don't go out tonight. Don't go near the garage."

"I won't. Rufe, what about today? What did they want? Is everything all right?"

"Oh, sure. That is—yes. I'll tell you tomorrow."

After she had hung up, the house seemed very empty and subtly threatening. She felt a tingle of something like apprehension. There wasn't a sound, not a footstep, not anything. But nobody could be there! She and the chief had tramped all over the place—bedrooms, kitchen, everywhere.

No, nobody could be in the house. Thinking it over, she decided that there just had to be some small and unimportant explanation for the apparent search in her room. Clara had wanted something; Lorraine had wanted something—

In any event, she began to feel foolish; she had let her imagiantion gallop away with her. She would go upstairs, ignore the tiny disorder in her room, take a shower, try to recover some semblance of common sense. Clara would be returning soon. The peepers down near the pond were beginning their nightly music.

She went into the hall and stopped at the table where her purchases lay. As she gathered up the packages and her handbag, she glanced automatically at herself in the mirror above the table—and it moved.

It didn't actually move; it couldn't; it was fastened firmly to the wall. Something had moved in it, behind her. She whirled around, her heart thudding like a drum. She faced the open door of the library, shadowy now. There was nothing there.

But something *had* flickered for a second in the mirror behind her, and then vanished.

She should look in the library, she told herself. But overcome by panic, she knew she couldn't do that, not by herself. She had only one thought now—she wasn't going to stay alone in that empty house. She almost stumbled down the steps and all at once she was in Rufe's car, thankful that she had snatched up her handbag with the keys to the car in it.

She'd take the car home and she'd see Dr. Thorne and she'd stay with him until she was sure that Clara and Cecco and Lorraine had returned. She backed and turned and went down the driveway at top speed. She did have the presence of mind to brake before she entered the public road. The stone wall was high; the thick shrubbery shut off the views right and left. The road was empty; she shot across it, down to the Thorne drive and into it. There she stopped and took a long breath. Was she running from a fancy? *Could* someone have been in the library? It had to be. She could still see that shadowy flicker in the mirror.

She got out of the car as soon as she could control an unsteadiness in her knees and took the narrow walk that led from the drive to Dr. Thorne's consulting rooms. There was a bell; she pushed it, over and over again.

She could hear it pealing away somewhere within the depths of the house. It seemed a long time before Miss Dotty came to open the door. She had an apron over her white uniform and a small, very sharp carving knife in her hand. She clearly didn't welcome a caller just then. Her bushy black eyebrows drew together; her mass of untidy black hair, usually neat under a white cap, seemed to bristle. "Oh, it's you! Trouble with your aunt, I suppose."

"No. I just brought back Rufe's car. It's out there in the drive."

"He's not coming back tonight, then?"

"No. He phoned me just now. He'll be home tomorrow."

"Oh—well, thanks," said Miss Dotty grudgingly. "I'll tell the doctor. He's working himself to death. Can't stop him. Can't do anything with him. He's taken the judge's death very hard."

A slight odor of scorching food wafted from the back part of the house, and Miss Dotty started to turn away from Bea. "I've got to go. I'm frying some chicken for the doctor's dinner. He never sees to himself."

Her martyrlike air stung Bea unexpectedly. Miss Dotty enjoyed her grim authority over the doctor too thoroughly. Bea said, "We really should see to it that the doctor has a housekeeper. Of course," she added quickly as there was an ominous flash in Miss Dotty's black eyes, "you are very good to him, stay after hours, see to most of his meals I expect—"

Miss Dotty cut in savagely, "Your Velda wouldn't do what I do! Naturally! She couldn't! She's not a nurse. But if I say it myself, I don't see how the doctor could get along without me." She eyed Bea with a sudden spark of curiosity. "You look scared. What's the matter?"

"Oh—my aunt is gone and Velda went home and the house—" Under the piercing gaze of Miss Dotty's black eyes she couldn't say that she was frightened and had fled. She said instead, "I'd like to stay here till my aunt gets back—"

Miss Dotty turned around and headed for the kitchen. "Stay as long as you like," she called back over her solid shoulder. "I can't stay here chattering—"

A door closed with a hard bang. So all I've done, Bea thought dejectedly, is nearly quarrel with Miss Dotty and ruin the doctor's dinner.

The door to the patients' waiting room was firmly closed. She didn't dare follow Miss Dotty to the kitchen. As she stood debating what to do, she heard a car coming slowly along the road. She was sure that it turned in at the Salcott place, so she went out again. She took the keys to Rufe's car along with her, however; she couldn't face Miss Dotty again to hand them over to her.

Bea walked down the driveway, under the canopy of old maples which were now beginning to show a thin green foliage. As she reached the drive to the Salcott place, a car was going out, slowly and cautiously. The driver wore a clerical collar and contrived to bow to her with the correct measure of kindness and sympathy even while remaining nervously intent upon his driving. Everybody knew that when the Reverend Cantwell came along in his eccentrically guided car, it was well to take cover.

This time he negotiated the turn into the public road without running into the stone wall, as for an instant seemed to be his intention, and Bea went on to the house to find Clara sitting in a chair in the study, still hatted and gloved. She lifted her head toward Bea and said, "Everything is all right, I think. I couldn't be sure what hymns the judge would have liked; you know he was never much for church, so I selected some of my favorites. They—they made him look so lifelike." She didn't have to say who. "But the judge himself— Oh, Bea, he's gone!" There were no tears in her eyes but there was an acceptance of mortality and a desolation in her face that went to Bea's heart.

"Dear Aunt," she said. "He loved you. You were always so good to him."

"But he's not here," Clara said. Then she braced herself and went on, "Did you get my black dress? I'd better try it on."

There was the sound of a car, the bang of doors, the murmur of voices in the hall. Lorraine appeared in the doorway of the study, carrying a

88   ✱   *Mignon G. Eberhart*

dress box. Suddenly Cecco called sharply from the hall, "*Little Bea—little Bea—*"

There was a note of urgency in his voice. Bea, with Lorraine and Clara close behind her, hurried to the hall. Cecco stood at the library door. "Who got in or out of that window, I wonder?" he said, pointing.

TEN
_____

All three women went closer to look.

Cecco gestured toward the window. "Screen not on yet; I expect it's too early. But the window is open, and see that—" He pointed. Torn strands of heavy ivy dangled along the window sills.

"I don't want to frighten you. But it really does look as if someone got in that window—and went out the same way."

So someone *had* entered the house, and escaped by that window. There *had* been a flicker in the mirror, the suggestion of motion behind her. It just might be, Bea's reason said, that it was a good thing for her she hadn't at that moment summoned up the bravery to explore the library.

Lorraine said, "Velda must have been cleaning in here, airing the room. She probably forgot to close the window."

Clara gave Lorraine an impatient glance. "Velda hasn't touched this room or the living room since—since the night the judge died. I meant to speak to her about it. But she's had so much to do."

Cecco's eyes were narrowed in thought. "Perhaps it would be a good idea to close and lock it now." His slender fingers worked at the lock; then he turned with an air of triumph. "There we are! Now then, shall I mix the cocktails, little Bea?"

Bea's nerves snapped. "If you don't stop calling me little Bea I'll—I'll—"

"Drop a pinch or two of arsenic in his cocktail," Lorraine said. "Not," she added, "that it would affect him."

"*Girls!*" Clara was reproving.

They all started up the stairs, quiet now, each seemingly engrossed in her own thoughts. When Clara went into her room, Bea and Lorraine followed her, almost automatically. Bea, unable to contain herself, faced them both and blurted out what was uppermost in her mind. "I think that someone was in my room while I was in town. Was it either of you?"

Clara shook her head and looked hurt at the very thought. Lorraine eyed Bea narrowly. "Do you mean to say you think somebody really got into the house and out again by the library window and was in your room? Did you miss anything?"

"No. But if there was somebody—"

Clara took off her hat and pushed at her hair. "I'd better take a look in the safe. That is, if—" Her voice trailed off, as though she did not really want to admit even to herself that the house could have been entered. But she went into the judge's room, where there was an antiquated wall safe. Lorraine and Bea followed.

Clara's little hands moved efficiently over the dial of the safe, opened it and took out, one after the other, her store of rings, bracelets, necklaces— most of them heirlooms, which her grandfather and probably her great-grandfather had presented to their wives. She loved best the jewels the judge had given her, and Bea's throat ached with pity as she watched Clara lovingly, slowly, count over the several rings, the bracelet, the pearls.

Bea glanced up at Lorraine and caught the smug smile on her face as she eyed her own massive bracelet and sparkling rings, far more expensive than anything Clara possessed.

Clara replaced all the boxes. She looked at the few trinkets which belonged to Bea and counted them too. Then she swung back the door of the safe and twirled the dial. "Nothing gone. Whoever it was must have been disturbed before he could work on the safe. Or perhaps there really wasn't anybody."

Lorraine wouldn't let it go like that. "Why did you think someone had been in your room, Bea?"

"Oh, nothing much. That is, small things. Not in their usual places."

"Is that all?"

Bea nodded.

Lorraine thought it over briefly. "I don't see that that is anything to suggest a thief. You and Cecco seem to be trying to frighten us, really. Cecco's talk of an open window. A few things in your room out of place, you say. I don't think we need worry about that, Aunt Clara."

"Please, girls, let's think of other things now," Clara said. "I'll try on the dress Bea bought for me."

"I bought one too," Lorraine said sweetly. "I got to thinking of my black dress and it— The fact is I don't think it would have been suitable for the services tomorrow. It—clings."

Clara gave her an absent but approving smile. "I'm sure you're right, dear. Where did you get the new dress?"

"I took the big car. Cecco went with me, he wanted a haircut. We went to Stamford. It took forever. He spent most of the afternoon at the barber shop. Did you get something for yourself, Bea?"

"Yes. I'd better go now and take it out of the box— See you later."

Once in her own room, she picked up the little French clock and straightened the bed. She believed Clara, she believed Lorraine. She wasn't so sure about Cecco. Had he spent most of the afternoon in a Stamford barber shop?

She hung up the new black dress, washed and changed from her suit into a dress. By the time she went downstairs Cecco was pouring cocktails. He told her proudly that a casserole Velda had prepared was heating in the oven. He had put it there himself. If all else failed Cecco, it occurred to Bea that he might enter upon a promising career as a chef.

The cocktails were excellent. However, tonight Bea carefully limited herself and so, she noted, did Clara. Halfway through dinner a boy came from the Western Union office and delivered a thick sheaf of telegrams to Clara, who spent the rest of the dinner hour reading them aloud, telling just who was coming to the services and how many people should be invited to the house afterward. Cecco listened soberly, his fine-featured face intent. Only once did he half smile, and that was when Lorraine's hand, reaching for another helping from the huge casserole, caught Clara's eye. Or rather Lorraine's jewels, blatantly flashing, for Clara said absently, "You really ought to put your jewels in the safe, too, Lorraine. So many of them and so beautiful!"

Lorraine said nothing. Cecco, his face amused yet sardonic, asked Lorraine solicitously if she wished dessert.

The lists occupied yet an hour after dinner; Clara then rose, said she was tired and went to bed. Bea set out to tour the lower floor of the house as usual; Cecco accompanied her again like a sleek, silent tomcat.

Tomcat, Bea thought, panther? In any event, he had stopped calling her little Bea.

Lorraine had disappeared by the time she went upstairs; Cecco waited again while she set the alarm, then said goodnight politely.

There was nothing she could do now about it. However, questions nagged at her; she could see that someone might have entered the house without being seen; there were the woods around the house, some of the pines and clumps of shrubbery were very near the house, especially those which all but covered the library windows. There was the back door which even now Velda rarely remembered to lock when she left. The door had a lock and Velda had a key but locking doors was not—or at least never had been—a custom in Valley Ridge. That habit might be changed now. Some one could have entered the house, even when Obrian and his two men were at the front. Someone could have escaped through the library window; she still felt that she had caught some movement in the mirror. The torn ivy certainly suggested that. She had heard no car leaving the place. But then anyone entering the house could easily have driven a car into the Ellison drive or the Carter drive (more likely the Carter drive since the Ellisons' caretaker lived on the place), and come from there, quickly and easily through the woods, taking advantage of the pines or laurels as shields. He could have escaped by the same route.

It was not altogether necessary for him to have parked a car somewhere out of sight. Lorraine had said that Cecco had "taken forever" at the barber's getting his hair cut. Cecco *could* have taken a taxi from Stamford back to the house; Cecco *could* have pretended to discover the open window in order to shield himself from any questions.

Anybody, knowing the house, could have entered it. Whatever that searcher had wished to find, it had to be something small—small enough to be contained by her box of correspondence or the drawer filled with writing materials. So then what?

She had few jewels, nothing of importance, and what she had was still in the safe. It was Lorraine who had the valuable jewels. Cecco had openly hinted that someone, not Cecco, paid Lorraine's bills; Cecco professed himself to be entirely without money. At the same time there was Bea's curious notion that while they insisted they were enemies, Lorraine and Cecco had come to some kind of understanding. That was only a notion of her own, Bea told herself. There was nothing to substantiate it.

Clara would not like the idea that someone else—Bea put it to herself vaguely—had been buying jewels, clothes, furs, for Lorraine. Naturally, though, that man—if he existed—was the reason for Lorraine's insistence upon a divorce from Cecco. Yet again Bea could not dismiss her impression that somehow, in some way, Cecco and Lorraine were in a guarded agreement.

Through the open windows she could hear, off in the distance, near the pond, the peepers shrilling in the night. She remembered her childhood days, when there were gardeners about the place; one of them, wise in the ways of nature, had talked to her of the peepers. "They come out once, then it turns cold and they go in again. They come out a second time; same thing happens. But the third time they stay out, it's going to be spring."

The next day Rufe arrived home in the morning but Bea did not see him until he came slowly down the church aisle along with the pallbearers, Joe Lathrop, Ben Benson and the others. There was Tony, too, almost unrecognizable in his sober dark suit.

The church was filled mainly by old friends; murder was one thing and terrible, but the death of a well-known and respected friend was quite another thing. If there was a special something in the air, a kind of tension and half frightened anger, Bea sensed it only in the utter silence of those around her. She doubted if anyone at all had come to the church from motives of curiosity. Everything was done as the judge would have had it. In Old Cemetery the rites were also orderly and dignified. Clara was completely composed; Dr. Thorne stood at Clara's side with her black gloved hand on his arm. Seth stood just behind her.

Dr. Thorne was very neatly dressed, unusual for him. Suddenly, even at this inappropriate time, Bea was again assailed with suspicion. The doctor knew Bea's room. He was one of the closest of the judge's and Clara's friends. Could he have been too close a friend of Clara's? Could the judge's murder have been the drastic climax of an elderly, but sad and now tragic romance?

The cool breeze touched her suddenly hot face and swept away her speculations. Not the doctor. Not Clara. She was thoroughly ashamed of her ugly, baseless thoughts. She took Rufe's arm as they left Old Cemetery.

The First Selectman, James Castleton, came to shake hands with Bea and say a few words of sympathy. He fell in beside Seth. "Good to see you at home, Seth. I expect you're busy politicking." He gave a decorous little chuckle. "You've always had my vote. Far as I'm concerned you'd be a good President! Why stop at the Senate!"

Seth gave a deprecating murmur. Mr. Castleman added, "Mrs. Bartry is holding up well. Of course the doctor is a great help to her."

He disappeared, and as Bea watched the doctor help Clara into the waiting car, a sudden and devastating notion flashed into Bea's mind. The judge's shabby old jacket had been left in his study. True, it was a warm night; he might have removed it and flung it over the desk himself. She had rarely seen the judge—a formal man—without a jacket, although if the doctor had happened in and taken the judge's blood pressure, the judge would have had to remove his jacket.

She could not help noting the solicitude with which the doctor settled Clara into the car. Again she felt a kind of hot wave of shame at the course of her own galloping doubts. No, she said to herself. No! Seth folded himself into the car with Clara and the doctor and managed to knock his hat off in doing so. Rufe picked it up and handed it to Seth.

The house was filled with people; Velda had known precisely what to prepare; coffee and tea with sandwiches and tiny cakes in the living room but drinks in the judge's study. The governor had arrived a little late; he was obliged to leave early for the drive back to Hartford. The state's attorney, his eyes alert, but questioning nobody, went with the governor. When they had gone, other people drifted away. Bea was aware of Rufe's helping with tea cups or drinks, as indeed did Cecco, looking all the time very intent, even fascinated by this evidence of American custom. She had no chance to speak to Rufe alone until everyone had left; Clara had gone upstairs and Velda was noisily gathering up glasses and plates. The house was too full of flowers and their sweet odors. Bea started out the back door, intending to walk down to the pond, through the woods, her favorite walk. As she left, Rufe called to her, "Wait, Bea. I'm coming too. Gosh, the air in there is like an oven. I thought people would never stop shaking hands and leave. Cecco is helping Velda with the dishes."

"Rufe, how did things go yesterday?"

Afterward it struck her that her question brought for the first time the faintest hint of some change in Rufe. At the time, though, he said, "All right. It was a—general sort of conference."

"Was anything said about the judge?"

"Yes. In a way. Nothing to worry about, Bea. Really." He hesitated. "Old Upson spoke of him, too. I had dinner with him. He was very shocked about it. He'd known the judge."

Upson was a congressman who had given Rufe a fine character reference. But there was something about Rufe that seemed, all at once, evasive and not like him.

They had reached the shallow, swampy edge of the pond. She said bluntly, "There's something wrong, Rufe. What did they say about the judge's murder?"

Rufe walked on for a few steps. "Oh, nothing much. That is, of course they had known of our coming marriage. That's the way things are. They had read the news of the judge's murder in the New York papers."

"They asked you just how much I might be involved in his murder!"

"Oh, Bea, forget it!"

"They don't want you to marry me. At least until this—this thing is settled and it is proved that I had nothing to do with this murder."

"I think that I am of more interest to the police than you just now," Rufe said shortly. "Oh, Bea, let it alone."

"No." They both walked on among the shadows of the pines. Finally Bea said, "We'll not be married until the police have found the murderer. If they ever do," she added.

He swung around. "Bea—"

"No." She meant it. "I'll not marry you and put any kind of doubt or smear on your name."

"Our name," Rufe said. "You didn't kill the judge. Neither did I."

"But it's got to be proved. We can't start out on your career with a— a—"

"Blot?" Rufe said with a short and rather grim laugh. "Don't worry, Bea. Things will straighten out. It's been only a few days."

Again, though, in spite of his words she sensed an evasiveness. Either his interview with his superiors had effected some change in him or—or perhaps Lorraine. Lorraine?

They turned back, past the willows, yellow now; past the thickets of laurel and pines toward the house. Rufe said suddenly, "These memoirs of the judge's. You say you typed all of them?"

"Yes. He would dictate and then I—"

"I know. Bea—" He stopped to face her. "Was there anything about my father in them?"

"Your father! Why, no! I'd remember."

"They're all in those filing cabinets?"

"Yes!"

"The police would have found something by now," Rufe said, as if to himself. "But still, if the judge put it in veiled language—"

"Rufe, what are you talking about?"

"A suit for malpractice."

"A suit—you mean, your father was sued!"

"And somehow the judge fixed it."

"But he—no, I'd have guessed! If there was anything like that in the memoirs I'd have recognized the circumstances."

They passed the big old barn. Lights were appearing in the house. Finally Rufe said, "How were those memoirs filed? Under what headings?"

"Oh, the usual. Childhood. School. University. Opening his law office. Then his term as judge of the juvenile court. His term as judge of the superior court."

"Nothing else?"

"Yes, there was one he facetiously called Extracurricular Activities."

"Personal affairs?"

"Yes, in a way. They were personal anecdotes, mainly things he did *ex officio*, so to speak. As you know, people still came to him when they wanted friendly advice, even after he closed his law office."

"Nothing about my father?"

"No! That is, not by name, Rufe. I'd remember that. But—your father! I can't believe it. A suit for malpractice!"

"Miss Dotty told me this morning when I got home. She had to make it quick but I think I've got the facts. There was some sort of accident on the road. My father happened to drive past, and of course he stopped and tried to help. The ambulance came and took the man to the hospital. He was unconscious. Something went wrong and in the end the injured man sued my father."

Bea swallowed her astonishment; if Miss Dotty had told Rufe, it was all true. "When did this happen?"

"Years ago. I was away at school. The point is everybody in Valley Ridge seems to have heard about the judge's memoirs. Miss Dotty got it into her head that the judge might have mentioned this—if not by name then in such a way that anyone reading it could guess quite accurately the facts. I don't know how the judge got Pa out of the thing, but he did."

Bea thought for a long moment. "We'd better look at the files."

"There's another consideration. Remember how the judge has been lately. Suppose all at once, after all this time, he got it into his head that Pa shouldn't be allowed to practice or that he ought to let people know about the malpractice suit. Remember how he was about the Ellison boys' still?"

She remembered all too well. The Ellison boys, as a lark, had built a still in the Ellison woods. The judge had sniffed it out, probably; in any event, he had reported it to the police. Mrs. Ellison had managed to get the still destroyed and the boys off to school, but after that, she refused to speak to the judge.

Bea said soberly, "People have gone. Let's look at the files now. The suit would be in his Extracurricular business."

Velda was still working furiously in the kitchen. She gave them a sharp look and said they were to have a cold supper. "Funeral baked meats," she added with gloomy relish. Velda had ways other than current slang to express herself.

When they reached the study they found that not only was his Extra-curricular file gone but also the file on his juvenile court term. "But they ought to be here! Right here!" Bea held the long drawer open so Rufe could see they were indeed missing.

Rufe sighed. "I suppose the police have them. Is there anything else gone?"

"No. But really, there simply wasn't anything in either of them that would interest the police." She paused, then said, "Rufe, I didn't tell you over the phone. Last night, I mean yesterday afternoon, when I got home somebody had been in the house and in my bedroom."

The curiously remote expression settled in his face which was in reality, she knew, an extremely sharpened interest. "Take anything?"

"No. But I'm sure that my room was searched." She told him what she knew. Obrian had been there, and had seen no one. But there was nothing she had which anyone else could possibly want. Later she had seen, or thought she had seen, a movement in the mirror; she had gone to Dr. Thorne's and talked to Miss Dotty. When she returned and Cecco and Lorraine arrived, Cecco had pointed out the torn vines and the open library window.

Rufe sat for a long time on the edge of the desk, looking at the floor. "And somebody shut you in the barn Sunday night and might have given your room a quick search then. There must be a reason. And somebody took those two files. If it wasn't the police it was someone who had good reason to think there was a secret between him and the judge. Of course, Miss Dotty would do anything at all to protect my father. She's had considerable experience as his assistant."

"Rufe! She didn't dig out that bullet!"

"I don't think so either. I only meant that she could have done it. My father could have done it for that matter. But he didn't. Let's have some of those funeral baked meats Velda warned us about."

Clara came down; she had changed from her black dress to a blue silk with a touch of white at the throat and a diamond brooch. She was attractive, Bea thought suddenly; she was very attractive. She had been deeply, sincerely devoted to the judge; but she was much younger than the judge, and Bea was beginning to get glimpses of that will of iron.

Lorraine, who had done her hair up neatly in a smooth roll for the services, came down too. Cecco joined them in time for more cocktails.

Supper was eaten in what struck Bea as a cold if exhausted silence. Afterward she had her second real shock of the day, for Ben Benson came to see her.

She had walked down the drive with Rufe and it occurred to her this time more forcibly that there really was a subtle change in Rufe. It wasn't owing to the story Miss Dotty had told him; he had been perfectly open about that, trusting her, telling her the whole of it. Whatever made an odd kind of barrier between them had nothing to do with his father. But it was there all the same. Was it a threat to his career? Or Lorraine? He kissed her goodnight in an absent way and started across the road. At that moment Ben Benson drove up, stopped his car, leaned out and spoke a few words to Rufe. Then Rufe went on; Ben drove toward the house and saw her, standing at the edge of the drive.

"Bea?"

She came forward. "Yes. Do you want to see Lorraine?"

Ben was a lawyer; he was the youngest member of the legal staff for a large city corporation. He had been born discreet, but had now grown pompous. He turned off the engine of his car. The dashlight shone upward into his plumply stolid face, which, though usually pink, seemed pale and flabby in that light. "The fact is I want to talk to you, Bea. You see—well —it's the judge's memoirs," Ben said in a burst.

"The judge's—" Did all of Valley Ridge know of the memoirs?

Ben said in another burst, "My mother—she's afraid everyone—she's afraid somebody—the police or— She knows that you typed them for the judge. She wants them back—that is, the part that relates to her."

"Ben! Your mother!"

Ben's stubby fingers grasped the wheel. "She—the fact is—there was a time when—" He removed one hand from the wheel and brushed his forehead. "She was a kleptomaniac," he said desperately. "She was caught. The judge fixed things for her."

ELEVEN

She stared at Ben's face; to her horror a wave of almost hysterical laughter caught her. Mrs. Benson a shoplifter! She had to get control of herself. She mustn't even let her voice quaver.

But then speculations began to whirl through her mind and her suppressed giggle suddenly vanished. Bea imagined her walking through the woods to the back door of the house in such a way that Obrian and the police would not see her. It was almost easier to fancy Mrs. Benson in the role of a kleptomaniac than to envision her crawling in and out the library window and searching Bea's room.

Bea said, "I can't believe you!"

"I'm afraid—yes, it's true. You see—" Ben gulped and went on, "My mother told me all about it last night. My father—well, not many people knew it; I didn't know it, although sometimes I wondered—but I was away at school and—" He seemed to realize that he was incoherent. He took a long breath. "My father was a periodic drunk. My mother did everything she could to stop it. She went through a time of terrific nerve strain. Somehow, nobody knows about these things; maybe a psychiatrist understands, I don't." He stopped himself, wiped his forehead on the back of his hand again and said unhappily, "Anyway, she began to—to shoplift. She said she didn't want the things she took, she had plenty of money to buy anything she wanted but— Anyway, to make it short, somebody caught her in the act. She got hold of the judge, and he fixed things up. Then he got her to go to a good psychiatrist, and he cured her—he and, I'm afraid, my father's death. It's all in the past, long in the past, but those memoirs—you see, the judge had changed so much he might have told the whole story or—oh, for God's sake, Bea, what am I going to do?" He checked himself abruptly as a car turned into the drive behind them. It puffed up the slight slope and stopped. "Hello, Bea," Seth said from the car. "Oh, it's you, Ben. Clara told me to come back tonight."

"She's in the study, I think."

"All right." Seth edged past Ben's car and went on to the steps. His car door banged. The shadows under the old maples and along the stone wall seemed heavy and quiet. Ben said, "You didn't answer me, Bea. What am I going to do?"

Bea replied flatly that she didn't know. "But I can't remember anything at all in the memoirs, Ben, that could possibly connect with your mother, ever!"

Mrs. Benson! Bea still couldn't really believe Ben. Mrs. Benson served on every philanthropic board in Valley Ridge, and was a respected elder of the church. Yet, Bea mused, if at one time she had been so out of balance as to indulge in stealing, could her imbalance have returned? Or—and this was more likely—could the judge have got into one of his moods of setting the world right and threatened to expose her? Could Mrs. Benson—Mrs. Benson!—possibly have shot him?

She'd have had to come to the house, get the judge's gun somehow, and dig out the bullet. Suddenly Bea remembered that at one time Mrs. Benson had taken a course for volunteer nursing; but as far as Bea knew she had never practiced. Still, in a return of imbalance and fear of the judge's disclosure, she could have steeled herself to dig out the bullet, and then entered the house in order to find the memoirs. And it would have been simple enough to discover which cabinet contained the memoirs. The judge himself in one of his Jove-like moods, thundering down denunciation, might have told Mrs. Benson or anyone. It was altogether within the realm of possibility.

Ben said, "Are you sure, Bea?"

Sure? Her thoughts had made so swift a journey of conjecture that she had to think back to his question. "Oh, yes, Ben, I'm sure that there was nothing, ever that could suggest your mother's name. Besides—" Besides, the Extracurricular file was gone. She decided not to tell him that.

"There's another thing, Bea. I don't know what to do about it. I don't think my mother would want me to—but right is right," Ben said, again with something like desperation in his voice. "It's about Lorraine; and the murder. One of the police questioned me Sunday. The point is Lorraine was not with me at the time they said the judge was murdered."

"I know that. She told me."

"She told you!"

"She said she didn't really have an alibi."

"But she didn't tell the police that. She told them she was with me. So of course I backed her up. But I got to thinking—well, it's a murder case.

If it comes to the grand jury, as it will, I'll be a witness. But she did disappear at the dance. I thought she'd gone to meet Cecco. So I left too. I knew Cecco was at Valley Inn. I went there, but since Cecco wasn't there at the time, he doesn't have an alibi. Neither does Lorraine."

"Ben—"

"Oh, I know. I ought not to tell you about it. But I *don't* know what to do. I went to Valley Inn, because I knew that Lorraine was thinking of a divorce. I'm a lawyer, and I knew she ought not to be seeing Cecco or—"

"How did you know that he was here? At Valley Inn?"

"Cecco had phoned me that evening just before dinner. Nobody heard him but me. He said he hadn't any money, and then he waited for me to invite him to stay with us; but, of course, I couldn't. Not with Lorraine there and—everything," Ben said miserably.

"Your mother wouldn't have liked it."

Once Ben broke down his own inhibitions he spoke freely. "Mother wouldn't have liked it at all. She never liked Cecco. She doesn't like Lorraine either, but when Lorraine called and talked to her from New York—"

"Go on."

"It doesn't seem possible that— I mean, Lorraine is so darned attractive. I'm not her kind of man. She's used to a different kind of world. More"—he hunted for a word and came out with it—"glamorous. So I just thought I'd tell the police, yes, she had an alibi, me. I could see the police might make things uncomfortable for her. Because of the judge's— Clara's money."

"I know what you mean."

"Naturally. If I could help her— But I never dreamed she was at the club. I looked for her."

"Did you look on the veranda, that end that's just outside the bar?"

"Why, I really don't know. I just got it into my head that she'd gone to meet Cecco."

"The police inquired at the Inn. Cecco was—at least he was supposed to be in his room."

"He wasn't. Nobody saw me at the Inn. I just walked in and no one was in the hall or at the desk so I went up to Cecco's room. He had told me the number. It made me think that perhaps he expected me to call him or get in touch with him."

"But he wasn't there?"

"No. He could have gone down and out the door without being seen, I suppose. But also, you know how the Inn is built, right along the ridge, so some of the second-floor windows are only three or four feet from the ground. Cecco's room was one of those. All he had to do was open the window and step out. He could have returned the same way."

"But where did he go then?"

"I don't know. I told you, I'm a lawyer," Ben said virtuously. "I hope I have the sense to keep quiet about other people's affairs."

Bea sighed. "You didn't keep very quiet about all this tonight. Really, as far as you know, neither Lorraine nor Cecco has an alibi for that night."

"Lorraine wouldn't kill the judge!"

"And you think Cecco would?"

"I think Cecco would do anything he made up his mind to do. As long as it suited his purpose. And by that"—Ben was suddenly quite forceful— "I mean money. The fact is he asked me for a loan. I refused Cecco— Why, it was nothing short of blackmail."

"Blackmail!"

"Well, you see, when we were both young and Mother sent me on a trip to Europe—well," Ben said unhappily, "I wouldn't want my mother to know much of that trip. But all the same I refused to lend Cecco any money." Then he added, "If I tell the police that Cecco was not at the Inn at the time of the murder, then I have to tell them that I was lying when I gave Lorraine an alibi. On the other hand, if Cecco killed the judge—" Again Ben wiped his forehead. "It's a matter of conscience."

"You'll have to make up your mind, Ben. It'll be hard to admit to having lied."

Ben almost groaned. "Yes. But on the other hand if Cecco—"

"Do you think he killed the judge?"

"I don't know what I think. Except," Ben said, suddenly very firm, "I want to keep out of it. The judge is dead. Nobody can bring him back. I see no purpose served in giving the police a reason to dig into Cecco's past."

He meant his own past.

"You must have really kicked up your heels when you and Cecco traveled around Europe."

"Bea! What a dreadful thing to say! All right then. I'll keep quiet about Cecco."

"Perhaps they ought to know," Bea said seriously, thinking it over.

"I'll think about it. Meantime you'll not tell them. I don't want to get involved. And I'm sure my mother wouldn't want to get involved in anything."

"I don't think your mother should have much to object to about Lorraine—considering . . ." Bea said.

"But that was so long ago. My mother wasn't responsible for her own actions—dreadful, of course. But as long as nobody knows about that—unhappy period of her life—"

"Ben," Bea said forcefully, "why don't you marry Lorraine?"

"But my mother—"

"You're a man. Tell your mother to keep out of your affairs. Good Heavens, Ben, don't you see—"

Ben glared at her through the dim light from the dash. "Really, Bea, I confided in you because I thought you were reliable. Now I'm not at all sure I've done the right thing."

Bea interrupted. "You confided in me because you wanted to make sure that there was nothing in the memoirs that could injure your mother. Oh, for Heaven's sake, Ben, grow up!"

She turned away, boiling with a curious kind of wrath. Mrs. Benson had no right to object to Lorraine. No matter how Lorraine had got her jewels and clothes, Bea was sure she hadn't stolen them. Ben's car started up and backed away down the drive.

But then, thinking of Cecco, Bea had a flash of insight. Cecco had hinted, so broadly that there could be little mistake about it, that Lorraine's jewels and clothes had not been paid for by Cecco; it seemed likely that a man had been buying them for her. This could be the reason for her desire to divorce Cecco; but if Clara knew it, Lorraine might feel that it would alter Clara's affection for her and endanger the prospects for a new will. In effect Lorraine might have promised to share with Cecco any money Clara would eventually leave her. In other words, Cecco could be blackmailing his own wife. Although it was in a sense a reasonable hypothesis it was nonetheless based entirely upon Bea's notion that there was some kind of complicity between Lorraine and Cecco.

She went on into the house; the door to the library was open and she saw Clara and Seth there. "Your aunt wants you to hear about her new will. I have notes about it here." He gestured with a yellow, lined tablet in one hand. "I'll have it drawn up properly tomorrow and then Clara can sign it, put it away and forget all about it."

Bea entered the library. Clara was sitting in the armchair near the enormous writing table where she had sat Sunday morning and read the judge's obituary. The lamp on the table had a green shade so everything in the room was slightly tinged with green. Lorraine was leaning against one of the glass-enclosed bookshelves; Bea thought that she was trying to control her emotions even though her eyes were blazing.

Clara said placidly, "Lorraine has already heard it all but if you will, Seth—"

Seth put on horn-rimmed spectacles, which made him look very studious. "There's no use in reading all of it. In a nutshell it's this, Bea. There are a few small bequests, something to the church, something to Velda Mather—if she is still in your aunt's service—" He smiled slightly. "A not unusual provision. Then there's a scholarship fund for the judge's law school. That's a rather large bequest."

"The judge would have liked that," Clara said firmly.

Seth nodded. Lorraine's hands clenched up against her skirt as if she'd like to tear something apart. Seth continued, "The residual estate—and it is a large one—is to be divided equally between you and Lorraine. I think that's all, Clara."

"Yes." Clara rose. "I love both my girls. They have been like children to me. I am grateful to both of them. However," Clara said with decision, "I intend to live for a very long time."

She took up a packet of envelopes, held together by a rubber band. "Here are the cards that came with the flowers. Will you answer them, Bea?"

Bea took the bundle of cards and went to the study where she left it on the judge's desk. When she came back into the hall, Clara had apparently gone upstairs. Bea went to her aunt's room and found her there holding a photograph of the judge in her hands. She turned to Bea. "My new will is right. You should have half. That's fair. You are not to talk to me about it. It's a weight off my mind. When I die you'll be provided for. Lorraine won't have to take what she can get in—any way she can get it."

She must have seen a flicker of question in Bea's face. "Good Heavens, Bea! Don't you think I can see things? Where would Lorraine get such things as—as a sable stole? Jewels. All those clothes. Cecco has no money. Don't look so surprised. I'm not a child!" She smiled unexpectedly. "Goodnight, my dear. We'll not talk of this further."

It was a definite dismissal. Bea went back in her own room when she remembered all the doors and windows to be checked and went back to the hall below. Seth and Lorraine were standing just outside the open door, and Seth held Lorraine in his arms. She was nestling close to him; his head was bent over her. "Don't cry, Lorraine."

"But it's all wrong; *Half* of it to Bea!"

"Never mind now. Your aunt will have time to change her will a dozen times."

"Not," said Lorraine, "if she should die tonight."

TWELVE

Bea went out to the terrace. Seth looked up, embarrassed. Lorraine snuggled closer into his arms. "Lorraine is upset about Clara's will," he said.

"Aunt Clara is not going to die tonight," Bea said.

Lorraine's head moved against his shoulder. The light from the hall streamed out upon them and reflected itself, gleaming, against his car below the steps.

"All right, Lorraine," he said, "even if she shouldn't change her will later you'd have plenty to live on."

"But not what I ought to have." Lorraine's voice came out murmuring sadly but stubbornly. He gave her a little—but gentle—shake. "Now, Lorraine! There's nothing you can do about it tonight."

Lorraine's face jerked around toward Bea. "You did this! You wormed your way in here! All you ever wanted was to get my aunt on your side. She's my aunt, not yours!"

Seth intervened. "I've been wanting to talk to you, Bea. Rufe told me about that thing that happened in the garage—"

"What thing?" Lorraine cried.

"Nothing," Bea said. "The garage doors blew shut. Go on, Seth."

"—and he told me about your room being entered Monday afternoon. I talked to Obrian about it."

"Obrian was here."

"So he told me," Seth said. "He said he searched the house. But then Rufe told me that you thought you saw somebody."

"No, I didn't. I mean yes, I thought there was a movement behind me.

I saw it in the mirror. But then it was gone. Later Cecco found a library window open."

"Didn't you have any idea who it was?"

Lorraine was suddenly as still as a cat at a mousehole.

"No. I went across the road and waited."

"That's what Rufe said. Was anything gone? Money or jewelry or anything?"

"I never carry much money. I had only a little in my handbag and I had taken that with me to New York that day. Aunt Clara keeps what jewels I have with her own. The safe was closed. Nothing was missing. I don't know what anybody could possibly want. Unless to—well, to frighten me and that makes no sense."

Lorraine said suddenly, "It might make sense! If Cecco has anything to do with it! He could have shut the garage doors. I take it you were inside and—yes, he could have done that—"

"He let me out."

"But not till he'd given you a good scare. Am I right? You needn't answer. I know Cecco."

"But why would he do that?" Seth asked.

"There doesn't need to be a reason for Cecco's doing anything he decides to do! Seth, you will get me a divorce at once."

Cecco appeared from the shadow below the terrace. "Not as soon as all that." He smiled, and his white teeth gleamed.

Seth said peaceably, "I ought to do a little more fence-mending tomorrow. I'll send Joe Lathrop around with the will. Goodnight."

"Seth, wait. Could this—this murder injure Rufe? I mean, his career," Bea began.

Seth shook his head. "No. There isn't the slightest real evidence against Rufe. No jury would believe that one or both of you murdered the judge merely because he opposed your marriage. There was nothing in the world to prevent your getting a license and marrying. In my experience the average jury is very clear in its collective mind about reasonable arguments. And remember, Bea, that if someone really was in the house Monday afternoon, it couldn't have been Rufe. He was in Washington that day."

"There was somebody," Bea said stubbornly.

"Then Obrian ought to have seen him. Don't worry, Bea. Get some rest. It's been a very hard day for all of us."

He contrived to move away from Lorraine's clutching arm, and got into his car. Its red rear lights had gone down the drive and turned toward

Stony Road before Lorraine sighed. "He's certainly distinguished-looking."

Cecco laughed. "Get your divorce first, Lorraine. You can't marry anybody until you've divorced me."

"Wait till you hear what Aunt Clara—" Lorraine checked herself. Cecco's smile vanished. His eyes narrowed. Bea said bluntly, "I want to close up the house."

Both Cecco and Lorraine followed her again as she made the tour of doors and windows, and watched again as she set the alarm.

But she had the talk with Ben in her mind. Suddenly she decided to face Cecco with the part of it that affected him. "Cecco, the night the judge was murdered you were not at the Inn as you told the police."

Lorraine grasped it at once, her eyes glittering. "Who told you that?"

Bea ignored the question. "Where did you go, Cecco? Why?"

"I didn't come here and kill the judge." But Cecco, too, was sharply curious. "Who told you that I wasn't at the Inn?"

"It doesn't matter. Where did you go?"

"There is no reason why I should tell you. But I suppose you'll go to the police with this—" Cecco's slender hands made a deprecating gesture. "If you must know, I simply walked out of the Inn and started toward the Benson place to see Ben. But I had forgotten the way. I must have walked miles on these winding roads. Finally I found the way back to the Inn. Nobody saw me leave or return. I did *not* come here. As long as the people at the Inn thought that I was there all the time, why should I tell the police any different?"

Oddly, it sounded true. However, Lorraine's face seemed to tighten with speculation. Cecco saw that. "No, darling, you can't frighten me. I was *not* here. You can't make some neat little plan to suggest to the police that I had anything to do with the judge's murder so—" Cecco smiled but there was cruelty in that smile. "I don't advise you to try it."

Lorraine seemed to think that over. Then she said, "I don't believe he did come here, Bea. He would be afraid of the judge."

Bea, too, believed Cecco. She went into her own room, aware that both of them stood watching her as she closed the door. There was an air of poise in their stillness, as if they were only waiting for a real quarrel—over Clara's will, over Cecco's lack of an alibi. Over anything.

They did quarrel, immediately after entering Lorraine's room. Bea could hear their voices; Lorraine's at first was cool and composed, while Cecco's became angry. This seemed to arouse a like explosion in Lorraine. At last Bea went into the hall, afraid they would wake Clara. She was about to knock on the door when she heard Cecco say, loudly, "—resident! So what do you think of that?"

Lorraine didn't reply for a long moment. Then she said loudly, too, "How do you know?"

"I hear things. It may be only gossip. Your aunt and Bea seem to know nothing of it. But—" Cecco's voice lowered.

Resident, Bea thought. Could some question of Cecco's possible one-time residency in America have arisen? The police might have arrived at a fact about Cecco which none of them had known. If so, they were putting the lives of everybody associated with the judge through a very fine mesh of inquiry. She didn't like Mrs. Benson. She could see now why, although the judge had assisted her, he had never seemed to like her. All the same Bea hoped that the police would not discover the long past shoplifting phase. But if Cecco had in fact lived for some time in America, perhaps in New York, what could that have to do with the judge's murder?

Both Lorraine's and Cecco's voices had fallen into an angry kind of murmur. Just then Clara opened her door, saw Bea and beckoned to her. "What are they quarreling about?"

"I don't know. I was about to tell them not to wake you."

Clara listened. The voices were now very low. She sighed. "Let them quarrel. I suppose it's something about my will. But I really couldn't include Cecco. Not after the way he's treated Lorraine. Oh, I suppose she hasn't treated him very well either. I think they've quieted now." She turned without another word and went back into her own room and closed the door. Bea was still standing in the hall when Cecco flung Lorraine's door wide open.

"I thought I heard someone! Listening at keyholes, Bea?"

"I couldn't help hearing some of it. Please let Aunt Clara have some rest."

Cecco's handsome face with its arched eyebrows and high cheekbones seemed, in the dim light of the hall, more than ever like a portrait of some old-time Spanish grandee—about to give orders to send somebody to torture, Bea thought briefly. "What did you hear?" he demanded.

"Nothing much really. I only knew that you were quarreling."

Lorraine appeared behind him. Cecco's dark eyes gleamed. "You think you've got your aunt's new will all arranged, Lorraine. So now you cast me off. You promised to share her money with me."

"I promised you nothing," she retorted.

"Ah, but you did. And you know what happens to anybody who breaks his word with me. I'm going to tell your aunt all about the man who gave you those jewels, furs, clothes. I couldn't give them to you. But when she hears about him—"

Bea broke in sharply, "Aunt Clara knows."

Cecco's face went stony with surprise. "And yet she is making Lorraine a co-heir to all her money? I don't believe it!"

"It's true. She is nobody's fool. That's one of the reasons she wanted to make sure that Lorraine would have enough money so she wouldn't feel that she had to—take money from anybody."

Lorraine's mouth had opened and stayed open. Cecco seemed to retreat within himself. After a moment Lorraine gave a triumphant giggle. "So what about it, Cecco? What can you do?"

He turned to face her. "I think there may be something I can do. Yes, I think there's something—" He went off toward his room without looking back.

Lorraine watched him now soberly. She looked even a little frightened. "When Cecco acts like that he's got something in mind. I don't like it."

Bea felt that she had had all the emotional storms which she could survive that night. "I'm going to bed."

"Wait a minute." Lorraine followed her into her room and carefully closed the door. "Is it true? Does Aunt Clara know all about Benito?"

Another Ben, Bea thought wearily. "She doesn't know his name. She just knows that there had to be somebody. Are you going to marry him?"

Lorraine's eyes opened wide. "Marry him! Good Heavens! Why should I?"

Bea said in spite of herself, "There must be good and sufficient reasons."

"Reasons? Because we were good friends," Lorraine said smoothly, "for so long? It was a great bore."

Bea stared at Lorraine. Somehow way in the back of Bea's mind an image of a dramatic, all conquering love affair had built itself up.

Lorraine giggled. "Don't look so stunned. Oh, we liked one another after a fashion. He is a brilliant man, too. Knows all sorts of important people. Not that I got to meet many of them. We had to be very discreet. There were two very good reasons why we didn't marry. First, Benito's wife's family is very influential: a divorce is still not looked on with favor in Italy. It might have cost Benito his position; besides, his first interests really were his wife and children. But the other reason is, the whole thing became a great bore. Actually, it was a bit of a bore from the beginning, and in the end we were both so tired of all the nonsense of making excuses and trying to keep—our friendship a secret that both of us were thankful to break it off. He was always very generous. Gave me a nice little sum so I could come back home. It was an easy way out for both of us. Dear old Benito! But marriage. My dear, what an idea!"

"Cecco knew about it."

"Of course. As a matter of fact I expect a number of people knew about it. Benito was important in his way. He was also more than a match for Cecco. I've never known for sure, but I've always suspected that Cecco tried to get money out of Benito—if he did, Benito didn't tell me. It would have been too humiliating to me. Benito was always kind— You needn't look so surprised, Bea. You know only the Valley Ridge world, not the world Cecco introduced me to. Maybe sometimes," Lorraine said with one of her moments of candor, "I wished I hadn't known that world. However, the point is, Cecco agreed to keep quiet about Benito if I would borrow on my expectations and give it to him when Aunt Clara made a new will. But tonight, when I heard the terms of her will—that I was to get only half of her money—I decided I'd have nothing to do with Cecco's scheme. The will is to be signed tomorrow. I don't think Aunt Clara is going to write another one, putting me out of it entirely. At least—well, of course, they way she acts she may write any number of wills. But I—" Lorraine frowned. "It was a poor idea of Cecco's. He had me frightened for a while. But when I thought it over I decided I wouldn't go along with him. So I told Cecco I didn't feel bound by any promise to him. He was very angry. He thought he had quite a firm hold over me. But as you see, he hasn't. Aunt Clara has eyes in her head," Lorraine said with a touch of admiration. "I really thought she was rather an old fool."

"She isn't," Bea said.

But Lorraine went back to Cecco. "When I married Cecco I thought I was getting money, a title, a social position, a fine home, all that. The judge saw through Cecco. He may even have inquired about him somewhere. I don't know. I was a great fool. But honestly, Bea, I don't think Cecco killed the judge. He really is a coward. Oh, he'll do small, mean things, anything for money, but he would never actually face the judge, get his gun away from him, induce him to go down to the wall and shoot him. Not Cecco. So I see no reason to tell the police about the fact that Cecco has no alibi for the time of the judge's murder. Is that all Ben told you?"

"He said you weren't with him for an hour or so."

"Is he going to tell that to the police?"

"I don't know. He was trying to make up his mind."

Lorraine chewed a little on her lower lip. "It'll put Ben in an odd position if he tells the police he was lying for me."

"I don't think he will. He doesn't want to get involved."

Lorraine gave a sudden giggle. "I'd like to see his mother's face if he did that! Goodnight, Bea."

She strolled away.

The house was all at once too quiet. It had been a strange, long day. Somehow, among all the images her memory of the day presented to her, Mrs. Benson—a shoplifter—came first.

She sought in her memory for that portion of the judge's memoirs which he had called Extracurricular Activities. These were rambling dissertations about courts of law, about his quarrels or disagreements—always victorious as the judge told them—with other members of the various boards or trusteeships of which he was a member at one time or another. In some of these memories the judge broke his rule of discretion and named names. There was the library board, the school board, a bank trusteeship, and almost every philanthropic enterprise in Valley Ridge. But even though Bea would leave blanks for the judge to fill in later when his words ran together on the dictaphone, she was sure there had been no mention of shoplifting; she'd have remembered that.

However, amid all the faces of the day, Rufe's became the important one. There was that small, indefinable difference in him. She was dismally afraid that something had been said by his superior concerning her own possible involvement in murder. So it was impossible to marry Rufe until the murderer was convicted. Lorraine would certainly want another husband. She had nestled her head close to Seth, a senator. But Rufe had once been in love with her.

In the morning Rufe and Lorraine disappeared together. Velda saw them, and when Bea came down to breakfast she told her, "They went off together in Rufe's car. I don't know where they were going. I took your aunt's breakfast up to her. She's tired, and no wonder. All that, yesterday. She says young Joe Lathrop is to bring a new will for her to sign some time today. She told me to remind you about those cards that came with the flowers and all those telegrams and letters."

The telegrams were on the judge's desk along with the bundle of cards. Bea spent most of the day writing thank-you notes. Rufe and Lorraine did not return. Sometime after lunch, which Bea had on a tray in the judge's study, Cecco lounged in, watched her for a moment and then settled himself gracefully in a chair. There was nothing about him to remind her of the sense of threat which she had glimpsed in his narrow face the previous night. All the same she wished he would leave; it was as if a slender and elegant spider were sitting at ease but curiously thoughtful and quiet, as if waiting for a chance to strike. She forced herself to keep on steadily writing notes which had by now acquired set phrases.

During the afternoon she heard Clara trotting around overhead in the judge's room. She had promptly seen to her will. Now probably she was working at the next chore, sorting the judge's clothes and belongings, what to be given away, what to keep. Late in the afternoon Lorraine returned, breezing up across the terrace and in the study door. Cecco rose lithely and without a word went out. Lorraine lifted her eyebrows. "What's he doing?"

"Nothing, as far as I know." Bea rubbed her tired hand.

"You can never tell about Cecco." Lorraine flung her hair back in her habitual and this time triumphant gesture. "I've been out with Rufe all day. He's as much in love with me as ever. Of course, being the man he is, he'll expect you to release him from his engagement to you. He wouldn't ask you himself."

THIRTEEN

Bea leaned back in the judge's chair. Lorraine slid down into the chair Cecco had left. "I hope you'll take it sensibly, Bea. Although of course I've got to make up my mind. Rufe—after all he's no great catch. But he adores me."

Like a fresh breeze through the room Bea's common sense operated. To her own surprise she laughed.

Lorraine sat up. "Don't you believe me?"

"Not a word," Bea said cheerfully.

Lorraine thought for a moment, her green eyes bright. "Why not?"

"Because it isn't true, that's all. Why are you lying to me like this?"

Lorraine shifted her position and leaned over so her hair almost hid her lovely face. "I was only thinking that—if you really want him, I'll see to it that you get him. But I want—"

Bea eyed her. "Money?"

"Why not?"

"But I have no money . . . Oh"—a wave of enlightenment came to Bea—"you're thinking of Aunt Clara's will."

Lorraine nodded.

"Aunt Clara is alive and well. She's much sturdier than you seem to think." Bea borrowed from Seth. "She'll have time to make a dozen wills." It was not really hard to find a way through Lorraine's tortuous reasoning. "Are you thinking of a bargain with me?"

"Bargain?" But her voice was entirely too innocent.

Bea didn't even have to grope her way; she spoke, however slowly. "A trade, I suppose. Is that it? You give up Rufe and I try to influence Aunt Clara so she changes her will—"

Lorraine lifted her head boldly. "Of course! Perfectly simple! You talk Aunt Clara into giving me a larger share of her money, and I'll give up Rufe. Of course, I don't mean that you should be cut out of her will entirely but—"

Bea interrupted. "No! For one reason, Aunt Clara is no pushover. She thinks out what she intends to do and then she does it. And another reason is— Oh, Lorraine, how can you be so silly! You can't give up Rufe. He doesn't belong to you to begin with!"

Lorraine thought for a long moment. "But the little money Benito gave me—that is, it was very generous of him of course and all that—but it's not going to last me very long."

"Rufe has no money either. Even when he gets his appointment it will be a minor one. It'll take years—"

"Yes, I thought of that." Lorraine had one of her waves of candor. "He may rise in his career and he may not. I can't exactly see myself waiting around for him to advance and in the meantime doing all the things the wife of a Foreign Service officer is supposed to do."

Bea replied, as she had once said to the judge, "If that kind of thing ever existed it's in the past."

"It's like being the wife of a low-rank officer in the Navy or the Army."

"No. Not any more. The wife of a Foreign Service officer is a private citizen, Lorraine. You don't want Rufe anyway. Why don't you marry Seth?"

"Suppose Seth comes to nothing! Suppose he has to come back here and take up life as a small-town lawyer again."

Bea stared at Lorraine. "You really have thought of everything, haven't you?"

"Not quite," Lorraine said. "Wouldn't you like to know what Rufe and I did today? I'll tell you. We drove and drove in Rufe's old car. We stopped at places where we used to go. On the way home we had a drink at Cobb's Mill. Then we stopped at the Westport Playhouse. It was still closed for the winter, of course, but we looked around. Do you think Rufe would take me on such a drive if he didn't want to?"

"I don't know."

But Rufe wouldn't have taken Lorraine on a long and apparently sentimental journey if he didn't want to, that much was true. Bea bent over her notes again and Lorraine gave a short laugh and went out of the room.

Bea was eying a letter absently when Obrian came. He brought her, wrapped in brown paper, her dressing gown. "They didn't see any need for keeping this," he told her. "It was natural for you to lean over the judge and try to help him."

She took the package. "Does that mean they don't think I—I shot him?"

Obrian's face took on a guarded and unnatural expression; as a rule, he was good-natured and frank. "I don't know what it means or what they they think. Bea—"

He sat down at her gesture, crossed his legs one way, then the other way. It struck her that he was embarrassed, so she braced herself for his next question. It wasn't what she expected. "Bea, that file of the judge's memoirs—"

"Yes—"

"You transcribed them, didn't you?"

"Yes."

"To tell you the truth," he burst out, "I've been kind of worried about them."

"You—"

"He may have said something about me!"

Did *everybody* in Valley Ridge at some time or other ask the judge for help and now expect to find himself in his memoirs! Bea was caught again by an almost hysterical mirth.

"I couldn't do anything about them," Obrian said. "I had to just wait and see if the police or those detectives found anything. I'll not say it was

easy for me. It's been hell, waiting. Now they've apparently finished looking through the memoirs and nobody has said a word to me so— But if I
could be sure there is nothing . . ."

Bea choked back her helpless laughter and said, astounded, "What did
you *do?*"

He stopped looking embarrassed and turned pale. "I took a bribe."

"*You*—I can't believe it!"

"The judge gave me the money. That is, it wasn't his money. It was
from somebody else. I was in a situation that—well, I had just bought a
house. I had a heavy mortgage on it. My wife was ill. I was desperate for
money or I wouldn't have considered a bribe. The judge didn't like offer-
ing it to me either. But he said it would help."

Bea's thoughts made a convincing leap. "Mrs. Benson!"

"So you did find that in the memoirs."

"No, I didn't. Ben told me. He was upset about it. His mother had told
him."

"Oh." Obrian studied her face. "She'd been picked up for shoplifting
and asked the judge to help her. I felt sorry for her. The judge—she gave
him money, she said, to show her appreciation if"—Obrian swallowed
with a gulp—"if I let her off. Quietly. So nobody knew about it. I expect
she paid off the jeweler; she'd picked up some trifle, I don't remember
what. But the judge put it to me so forcefully! He explained her shoplifting to me. She promised to go to a psychiatrist. The judge told me it
would be all right, she wouldn't do anything of the kind again. And she
didn't," he ended with an air of relief.

"There was nothing about that in his memoirs."

"Are you sure?"

"Unless he told it in such general terms that even when I transcribed
it I didn't think of Mrs. Benson. Or you."

He looked around at the cupboard where she kept the used tapes.
"What about those dictated tapes? Could he have said something there?"

"No. I typed every one of them. Then I used them for French practice.
After that, when we'd get to the end of the supply we'd start over again."

"The state police have them, haven't they?"

"They're perfectly worthless." But she went over to the cupboard. "Yes,
the police must have taken them. But I had used each one. I'd do French
verbs or read something and then listen to myself and correct my pronunciation whenever I could."

Obrian said thoughtfully, "They'll get somebody who can understand French to read them, I suppose."

With another quiver of mirth Bea thought of somebody sitting down and intently listening to her fumbles over verbs or her faulty reading of "La Dernière Leçon" or "Le Voyage de M. Perrichon." She wondered if they would get hold of a native Frenchman who was likely to have some hysterics of his own, listening to her. A student from Yale was a possibility; what he would make of them she couldn't guess.

"The memoirs were all arranged in sections. Childhood, school days, university—" She stopped abruptly. There was the Extracurricular file. Obrian had had a chance to enter the house Monday, when no one was at home. But that was wrong. The detectives had looked through the files on Saturday. Almost certainly the Extracurricular file had to be gone before Saturday, that and the Juvenile Court file, for the police had neither returned them nor inquired about them. Further, if Obrian had helped himself to that particular file, he wouldn't now be talking of it. "You must have felt horrible," she said. "Why didn't you just tell the police?"

He heaved an enormous sigh. "You don't know what you're talking about! Even now, after all these years, the taking of a bribe—no, no, I couldn't tell anybody. I just had to wait it out. There was nothing else I could do. I wish Mrs. Benson had taken to shoplifting in some other town."

Bea came back to the judge's desk. "So do I." She hesitated and then decided. "I'd better tell you that there are two missing files. One is what the judge called his Extracurricular Activities."

Obrian stared at her. "Oh, my God."

"I typed them all. I don't remember much that was in that file but there was nothing"—she searched back in her memory—"really *nothing*, Mr. Obrian, that seemed to refer to you."

"Who took the files? You said two are missing."

"Besides the one he called Extracurricular Activities there was one about his term as judge of the juvenile court, and I don't know who took them. Perhaps the state police. I didn't know they were gone until last night."

The experienced police officer abruptly came forth in Obrian. "How did you happen to look in the files last night?"

She thought swiftly: He doesn't know about that suit for malpractice which the judge fixed. "I just happened to. I wondered if they were all there," she added rather lamely.

Obrian seemed to detect her hesitation. "Had the judge fixed things for somebody else?"

"Please, Mr. Obrian."

He rose. "You're not going to tell me who."

"But it—but I—" She took a quick breath. "It's not important."

"The judge was quite a fixer, wasn't he? But the people trusted him. Everybody went to him with troubles. Of course, lately he'd changed. If he got something on his mind that he thought ought to be stopped he'd try to stop it." He brooded for a moment and added, "But he knew I didn't like that bribe from Mrs. Benson. He always trusted me."

She wondered who next would turn up to accuse himself of appearing in the memoirs. Obrian straightened up. "Anything else you haven't told me?"

Anything? Why, yes! He didn't know that after he'd gone Monday, she'd been sure that someone was in the house. She told him quickly.

He listened, all police officer now, and shook his head. "But what could anybody want? I can't make anything of it unless someone else thought he was in the memoirs. By the way, this husband of Lorraine's. Our state police have been in touch with the Italian police, Lieutenant Abbott told me. But there doesn't seem to be anything very revealing so far. Cecco seems to have spent money but didn't have a steady income, not that anybody knows about. There was a hint that he might have been involved in drug rackets but nothing factual enough to make a case of it. He seems to have managed to get fast cars, maybe fast women. Too bad Lorraine didn't take the judge's advice about not marrying him. But Lorraine was always headstrong and somehow everybody in Valley Ridge got the notion that Cecco was rich and had a fine place in Italy." Suddenly Obrian turned a rich red. "They had some things to report about Lorraine, too. Oh, nothing criminal. That is—well, it seems she was the friend—the special friend—of a man there who is very rich. A guy—I can't pronounce his name—"

"His first name is Benito."

"Huh?"

"She told me. That's all over."

"Don't let your aunt hear about it."

"Oh, she knows. That is, she guessed. Lorraine has such good clothes and jewels and—she guessed."

Obrian sighed. "I always said your aunt had more sense than anybody gave her credit for. Furthermore," he said with unexpected perspicuity, "she had the good sense not to let the judge know that she has a good head on her shoulders. He had to be the authority. Of course, lately there was no telling what he might get into his head and worry himself about and— Try to find those missing files, Bea. Especially the— What did he call it?"

"Extracurricular Activities. But it's only a string of anecdotes. Not even very interesting to me as I typed them up. Truly, Mr. Obrian, your name isn't there. As a matter of fact—" Bea was struck rather vividly by that recollection— "I don't think he used many names. He was too cautious of libel or slander. But writing, or rather dictating, kept him entertained and busy."

"Entertained," Obrian said thoughtfully. "I'm not sure I like that idea. The judge was a good man, respected. But lately he could be mean, you know. Headstrong and—mean."

Without another word Obrian went wearily away. Bea listened for his car as it went slowly down the drive. He wouldn't be easy in his mind until the missing file was found; neither would Mrs. Benson if she ever learned of its disappearance.

She pushed back the notes she had written. It was getting late; the afternoon sun sent a rosy glow over the terrace. She heard footsteps on the gravel of the drive. Rufe came along the terrace and looked in the door. "Bea? Can I come in?"

He entered and sat down wearily, then stuck out his long legs and stared at his scuffed loafers. "I didn't accomplish much," he said.

"You took Lorraine for a very long drive." She couldn't help saying it, but Rufe didn't even look up.

"Oh, sure. I was backing out of our drive when she saw me and before I could say anything she hopped in and said she wanted a drive. On the way home we stopped at places she wanted to see again. That was after I had visited Millwood."

"Millwood!" Millwood was a correctional institute for minor offenders.

"I keep thinking that Cecco simply must have been here in America during his childhood. He couldn't possibly pick up such a natural American idiom and pronunciation otherwise. The Juvenile Court file has been taken. I'm sure the police don't have it. If they did have it and kept it for some kind of evidence I think they would have questioned you and Aunt Clara or—oh, somebody.

"And then, you see, Cecco mentioned the time when you had braces on your teeth. How did he know that if he had seen you only when he first knew Lorraine and you were in your teens? You'd stopped wearing braces by then. Perhaps Cecco had lived somewhere near here before, and he could have come up before the judge and been sent to Millwood. It would have been a long time ago. The names of minors are never published. Cecco could have felt himself entirely safe. But that may have been the reason the judge was opposed to Lorraine's marriage."

"I'm sure I never saw Cecco before he started coming to see Lorraine," Bea said after long thought. "Wouldn't Aunt Clara know about it if he'd been sent to Millwood?"

"I doubt it. She's often said that the judge never talked to her about his cases. Of course, there may be nothing to know. It's only Cecco's American way of talking, the braces on your teeth, and the missing file."

"But what could a minor, a boy of sixteen or under, do that would make him an undesirable husband for Lorraine years later?"

Rufe shrugged. "You knew the judge. Anything at all."

"Did you find any records at Millwood referring to Cecco?"

"No. That is, in the first place they were very cagey about giving anybody a look, even at old records. Quite right of course. However, in the end I got hold of an old-timer who knew the judge, told him why I wanted to know if anybody who might have been Cecco had been in the place years ago. He had a very clear memory. He went through records of more than thirty-odd years back. He said it wasn't proper but rules were made to be broken and kind of smiled at me. He conned over everything. There were some boys with foreign-sounding names, but not Cecco di Pallici. Usually the offenses were breaking and entering. He said that he remembered the judge took a great interest in all the boys he had sent to Millwood, tried to get them onto the right course, used his influence about getting them into schools, all that kind of thing. The judge was young then. Only in his mid-thirties. In his day," Rufe said with real respect, "he was a great man."

"But there was nothing about Cecco?"

"Nothing."

"Where was Lorraine while you were at Millwood?"

"Watching a movie." Rufe grinned. "I told her I had to look up something in the Millwood library and it would take a while. She couldn't fancy herself just sitting in the car waiting."

"Sometime you'll really be a diplomat."

"I'll try," Rufe said with a grin.

Just then Lorraine, with her customary flair for entering the room at

the most inconvenient time, came in. She had changed to a thin green
wool dress.

"Rufe! Did you tell Bea what a lovely ride we had today?"

Rufe paid no attention to that. "Lorraine, when did Cecco first come
to America?"

"After you'd gone to Vietnam, Rufe. And then Cecco and I fell in
love and were married. That is, I thought I was in love. I was wrong—"

"How did he happen to come to Valley Ridge?"

"Why, he knew Ben Benson. They had met somewhere, in Paris I
think. Maybe in London. I don't remember. It was during a trip Ben took
while he was still in the university. Anyway they seem to have become
friends. So when he came to America and I met him, the Bensons had
invited him to stay with them. I don't think," Lorraine said in her candid
manner, "Ben's mother liked Cecco much. She didn't really want me to
stay with them for a few days when I came home Wednesday and phoned
them from New York. I could tell. Her precious Ben."

"The Bensons are very rich," Rufe said rather dryly.

"Oh, yes. But Heavens! That Ben! I have never in my life seen anybody
so pompous. The girl who gets him won't have an easy life of it."

"She'll have money."

"Yes." There was now a trace of wistfulness on Lorraine's voice. "But
how would anybody pry money out of Ben? Besides it was all left to his
mother and she'll live to be a hundred. Oh, Ben is no catch."

"So he knew Cecco."

"Oh, yes."

"You're sure that was Cecco's first visit to America?"

Lorraine shot a swift glance at Rufe. "Ask Cecco. I don't know everything about him. It's almost time for dinner. I'll see about cocktails, Bea."

She sauntered out nonchalantly.

Rufe said, "Doesn't know or doesn't want to answer. I've got to get
home for dinner. Miss Dotty will take a knife to me if I don't." He heard
his own words and looked all at once rather white. "I didn't mean that."

"No, I know. We used to laugh and call her—"

"Madame Defarge. But she— I'll see you." He left.

He was not changed at all, Bea told herself, and yet knew that there was
some difference, something too deliberately calm and yet tense about him.
She couldn't analyze the difference but it was there, like an intangible wall
between them. Yet he seemed as frank and open with her as ever.

She took the package Obrian had returned to her, uneasily aware of her stained dressing gown, then thought of Lorraine and Rufe—and suddenly became suspicious of Miss Dotty. But Miss Dotty, devoted though she was to the doctor, would not have shot the judge. The fact of the malpractice suit was buried in the accumulation of years.

But Dr. Thorne couldn't be more than in his middle fifties. He had every reason to look forward to many years of practice unless somebody or something checked his activity. A malpractice suit, even though it had happened years ago and had been covered and kept a secret, would, if it were known, throw mud, and a little mud always sticks. Miss Dotty would have protected the doctor in any way she could. She was quite capable of probing for a bullet.

Bea put the dressing gown in her bathroom laundry hamper, hating to touch it, and changed her dress.

When she went downstairs again, Clara had not yet come down. Lorraine was apparently still in the pantry mixing cocktails. Only Cecco sat in the living room and eyed Bea with a trace of malicious mischief in his dark eyes. He rose gracefully. "Dear Bea, I hoped for a moment alone with you."

"You sat in the study with me most of the afternoon."

"Oh, well, what I have to say didn't occur to me then. The point is, are you going to let Lorraine take your young Rufe away from you?"

"No," Bea said bluntly.

Cecco's slender eyebrows rose. "Dear child! You are so sure of yourself."

"I'm sure of Rufe, if that's what you mean." But in her heart she wondered again—was she really so sure?

Cecco eyed her. "Men have long memories, dear child. Now that Lorraine and Rufe have seen one another again—"

Bea interrupted sharply, "Cecco, when were you first in America?"

"My dear Bea! You know that. It was when I met your cousin Lorraine and fell in love with her."

"That was the first time?"

"In America or the first time I fell in love?"

"You know what I mean."

"I came here to stay with the Bensons, at Ben's invitation. I met Lorraine. She had a notion then that she was in love with this young Rufe Thorne. That didn't last long."

"Lorraine said that you knew Ben Benson in Paris. Or London."

"You asked her? How unimportant. But, of course. We met—let me see—in London. When we were both very young."

"How did you happen to meet?"

Cecco sat forward, his black eyebrows now drawn into a frowning line. "What are you getting at? There's no dark secret about our meeting. Although"—his eyebrows went up again and he smiled—"his mother might not like to hear about it. We met actually over a roulette table."

No, not even the former shoplifter would like that. Cecco went on, his eyes dancing again with a certain malice. "As I say, we were both young. But I had seen something of the world. Ben hadn't. I rather gathered that his mother kept him tied to her apron strings. However, she had released a generous sum of money to permit him to enjoy the culture of Europe, he told me. So we enjoyed European culture, on Ben's money. Horses, gaming clubs—"

"So when you came here to America at that time you intended to see Ben and—"

"Get more money out of him? Why, Bea, what a naughty thought."

"*Did* you get more money out of him?"

Cecco sobered. A reflective look came again into his mobile face. "I thought I did. I was wrong."

"You mean Lorraine."

"Naturally. He introduced us. Here was her rich aunt and Lorraine, I understood, had fine prospects."

"Was Ben glad to see you?"

"I wouldn't say glad. But he invited me to stay with him. Introduced me to his friends. However, Ben had changed. Grown stodgy, adult, had a position in some law firm in the city by then. Possibly," Cecco said delicately, "he really didn't want reminders of his youthful—not excesses but certainly impulses. However, he invited me here."

"And you exercised a neat little blackmail to get him to do that."

"Blackmail! Why, Bea! Truly a naughty thought doesn't become you."

"A naughty thing like blackmail doesn't become anybody," Bea said shortly. "Mrs. Benson must have had some notion that you and Ben had gone about together in Europe."

"I really don't know whether Mrs. Benson knew anything of those tiny blots on her Ben's spotless soul. She wasn't very nice to me. But Ben did take me around and I met Lorraine. And if you want to know why she wishes a divorce, it's because she intends to find another husband."

FOURTEEN

Lorraine, lovely in her pale green wool, carried the cocktail tray into the room. Cecco sprang up to assist her.

Clara came in, and Cecco served cocktails. Lorraine chattered of her long drive with Rufe that afternoon. "And coming home we stopped at Cobb's Mill and had drinks. Nothing had changed much. The same old swans."

"The same old you?" Cecco inquired, smiling.

Clara frowned a little but said nothing. Clara took her place for the first time in the judge's big chair at the head of the table. When she saw that, Velda's eyes popped. Halfway through dinner the telephone rang and Velda, having answered it, relayed a message. "It was Joe Lathrop. He says he's got your new will typed up and ready for signature, Mrs. Bartry."

"Good," Clara said. "Ask him to bring it here now."

Lorraine and Cecco were both very, very still. Clara said, "We'll have coffee, Velda."

Rufe came with Joe Lathrop. "I stopped and asked him to come along," Joe said cheerily. "We need some witnesses to your signature, Mrs. Bartry."

Again both Lorraine and Cecco became extremely quiet.

Clara suggested that they move into the judge's study. "The big desk there," she said and led the way. Joe sat down opposite her and pulled papers from the briefcase he carried.

Clara slowly read every word of the document. There was only the sound of the few pages turning. Finally she reached for the pen, signed her name to the will and to the copy. "Joe?"

Joe leaned over to sign his name as a witness to Clara's signatures. She nodded and said, "Rufe?"

Rufe was eying something on the desk rather closely; he shoved the mass of letters, blotters, writing paper aside and signed the will and the copy.

"All right. Now what do you want me to do with these, Mrs. Bartry?" Joe was being very businesslike.

"I'll put one of them in my safe-deposit box as soon as I can get into it. Do you know when the appraisers will be through with it, Joe?"

Cecco sat up alertly. "Appraisers?"

Joe glanced at him. "It's the law. A safe-deposit box—Mrs. Bartry and the judge used a joint box—is sealed until the appraisers have had a chance to go through it."

"Why?" Cecco said blankly.

Joe allowed himself an unprofessional frown. "For the inheritance taxes of course. Every item in the box must be examined; everything belonging to the judge therefore belongs to his estate and is taxable as such."

Clara eyed her copy of the new will. "The appraisers can take their time. It's not urgent for me. But, Joe, do you know anything about the inquest? When it will take place, and where?"

"No, Mrs. Bartry. But it may be, oh—some time before they get around to it."

"Why so long?" Cecco asked.

Joe was annoyed and frowned. "Several reasons. The medical examiner has made his statement, all that is on record. But one very good reason for not requiring an immediate inquest is that the people concerned are— sometimes, I mean—in an emotional state and their evidence may not be entirely accurate."

Cecco did not look convinced. Clara said, "I wish they'd get it over with. Meeth killed him. No doubt of it." She took the original draft of her will. "Keep the copy in your office safe, will you, Joe?"

"Certainly." Joe had two large envelopes, each with the legend Last Will and Testament in ornate black letters. Clara took her envelope. Joe said, "I think that's all. Feel better about things, Mrs. Bartry?" Young Joe assumed an experience in legal affairs he couldn't possibly have had. "People always do, you know. As if a load had been taken off their minds."

"I expect we ought to have some port on such an occasion," Clara said.

Bea thought rapidly and was about to say, there isn't any, when Joe thanked Clara and said he had to leave. Rufe and Joe said goodnight and left together. There was still in Rufe's pleasant glance something that disturbed Bea, something that seemed to divide them.

Clara had gone calmly away, clasping her copy of the new will. Lorraine had disappeared with her. Cecco sat back in a lounge chair gazing off into space. Bea bent over the desk to rearrange the oddments, which had been shoved out of the way to give space for signing the will. As she picked up some envelopes and a blotter she saw the judge's gold cigar case below them.

She knew it well. She could almost see the judge's gnarled hands turning it over and over. He did not use it much, he complained to Bea privately, saying the cigars dried in it. But Clara had given it to him, so he carried it all the time and pretended to make use of it. The case had not been there during the day. In fact, she could not remember seeing it at all after the judge's murder. So who had had it? Who had placed it on the desk and then neatly covered it with papers, envelopes and blotters?

Joe had shoved aside some of the papers to give a clear space for Clara and again for himself when he signed the will as witness. Rufe had done the same thing, rather swiftly. But Rufe could not have had the gold cigar case.

"What's the matter, Bea?" Cecco said lazily, yet with the sharpness in his eyes which Bea was beginning not only to dislike but to fear.

"Nothing." She put the cigar case in a drawer and rose.

As usual Cecco walked lithely behind her as she made the tour of the house. He laughed softly when she locked the kitchen door. "Velda doesn't seem to think it necessary to lock a door."

"It never was necessary—until lately."

He followed her up the stairs, and watched as she set the alarm.

She was almost asleep when the telephone rang. Clara apparently answered with the extension in her room. A moment later she came to Bea's door, said, "May I come in, Bea?" and entered.

She had wrapped her plumply pretty figure in a pale blue dressing gown. As usual her hair was netted. Yes, Bea thought, remembering Rufe's observation, Clara was a very attractive woman.

"That was Seth on the phone," Clara began. "He's just got back from Bridgeport, and wanted to know if Joe Lathrop had brought the will around. I asked him about Meeth. The police don't seem to be sure of their case against Meeth. I don't see how they can be so stupid. Nobody— nobody else would have killed the judge. He was a good man."

He was also a selfish, domineering and obstinate man, Bea thought, in spite of herself.

"I just thought I'd tell you." Then suddenly she asked, "When are you and Rufe going to get married?"

"I don't know."

Clara's eyes sharpened. "You sound undecided. You can't mean that Rufe is letting himself be taken in by Lorraine!"

"Oh, no!" Bea cried, lying. "No, no. But we—that is he—well, since the murder things have been so hurried. I mean—"

"You mean," Clara said, "that the circumstances and publicity of the murder may reflect upon you or Rufe. You mean you're afraid it would damage his career or even put a stop to it if you marry before the police have found his murderer." She waited a moment, thinking. "Dear Bea, they'll find out that Meeth did it. That will put everything in the clear. Nothing can possibly affect Rufe or you."

"No."

Clara was still not satisfied. "Don't let Lorraine grab him," she said firmly, and then unexpectedly veered from Rufe to his father. "I don't think I've seen Rufus, I mean Dr. Thorne, since Tuesday after the services. It seems strange he doesn't come to see how I—that is, how we are getting on."

"Rufe says he's very busy." Yet it struck Bea, too, that it would have been a normal thing for the doctor to drop in frequently and keep an eye on Clara.

Clara sighed. "Yes, I suppose he is busy. All his patients suddenly getting symptoms so they have to see him—and pump him all they can about the murder."

Her cynicism surprised Bea. She swallowed her shock as Clara waved a hand, said a pleasant goodnight and went away.

Apparently the police were still not sure that Meeth had murdered the judge. She wondered what they were doing.

The next day she found out a part of what they were doing, for Detective Smith came to see her and Clara. He brought with him the boxes of dictated tapes. Clara invited him to sit down. "Those tapes are just what you said they were, Miss Bartry," he said with half a smile. "We got a French teacher from Yale down to translate. He didn't seem very interested himself. I thought that one of those plays, the one about the man who did the favor for Mr. whatever his name was—"

"Perrichon," Bea said.

"Maybe. Anyway, the man who wrote that knew human nature. We always like people we've done a favor for and dislike somebody who does a favor for us. Too bad. But human."

Clara said, "What have the police been doing? I hope not favors for Meeth."

The detective blinked at the sharpness of her voice. "Well, it's still early, you know. A murder case is very serious."

"You needn't tell me that!"

"No, Mrs. Bartry, of course. But we've been busy. The trouble is we have too much work. We can't just drop everything and concentrate on one case although we'd like to. There are other problems, other investigations."

"Not murders, I hope." Clara was still sharp as a little angry bird.

"No," the detective said seriously. "Now, I do want to ask you some questions about the judge. For example, take the day before his murder. Thursday. What did he do that day?"

Clara gave Bea a helpless look. "Well, he was very nervous. I mean— oh, I can't describe it—"

"I thought he was working himself up to a real storm about something," Bea said flatly. "He was not rational, really. I debated calling Dr. Thorne. But then the judge didn't do anything that was uncontrollable."

Clara sighed. "We didn't speak of it, Bea and I, but I could see that he was unusually upset about something."

"Didn't you try to find out why he was acting so peculiar?"

Clara shrugged. "No. We never made a point of questioning him. It would only have made him worse. No, the only thing to do was to wait until he cooled off."

"But you think that this irrational attitude was worse than usual."

Clara bit her lip. Then she said honestly, "We couldn't have sent him to a sanitarium. We couldn't have done that. We always just rode out whatever his moods were."

"But this attack," said the detective kindly, "was worse than usual."

"Yes," Clara said.

Bea nodded.

"And the next day, the day he was shot, he was no better?"

"Worse," Bea said. "But truly we didn't neglect him. We only tried to weather whatever that particular storm might be. We always did that."

"I see. Well, tell me his usual routine."

Bea replied, "In the mornings he would dictate letters or work on his memoirs. Afternoons I would take him for a drive or he'd work in the garden. We lead a very quiet life."

"We looked thoroughly through his files and found nothing that seemed of any special significance. Except, of course, what we took to be his account of Meeth's trial and Meeth's threats. But he did not mention Meeth—or anybody for that matter—by name."

"No. He avoided actual names as a rule," Bea said.

"Afraid of libel? Surely he didn't expect these rambling anecdotes to be read by anybody."

"It gave him something to do." He had not mentioned the two missing files. Bea debated for an instant and then told him, "Mr. Smith, two of the folders are missing."

His gaze brightened. She could feel Clara turn around quickly to look at her. "Do you mean that we didn't see all of the memoirs?" Mr. Smith asked.

"You should know. I looked through the folders. There was one he jokingly called Extracurricular Activities. There was another referring to his term as judge of the juvenile court. Both of them are gone."

The detective waited as if seeking back in his memory. "But those two folders were not in the cabinets when we examined them. I'd remember."

"They're not here now," Bea said flatly. "You can look if you want to."

"Oh, I believe you." The detective got out a pencil and chewed on it thoughtfully. "When did you discover that the folders had been taken?"

"Tuesday night."

"Why did you look at the files?"

Why indeed? To make sure that neither Dr. Thorne nor Mrs. Benson had been mentioned even by implication. "I just happened to," Bea said.

"The two folders were not there on Saturday morning. So someone, presumably the judge's murderer, came into this room after that man Griffin heard the shots. You found this door open. Did you have any impression that whoever had entered the house had gone near the filing cabinets?"

"I don't know. I didn't look at the cabinets or anything, really. I was intent upon finding the judge."

The detective gave a brief nod. "Yes. That would be natural. But if the murderer came into the room and got out those two folders, first he'd have had to know they were there. He'd have had to know that he might have been mentioned in an"--he paused and then brought out the word

—"in an opprobrious way by the judge, a dangerous way. The fact is, the two folders were not in the files the morning we went through them. When did you last see them?"

"I really cannot remember."

"It would help if you could remember."

"I'll try. But just now—no, I can't remember."

"The point is, either they were removed at some unspecified time before the judge's murder, or they were removed the night of his murder while young Thorne and that boy of Obrian's, Tony, were presumably keeping an eye on the files and the house." He paused again. "It seemed to me that Tony and young Thorne are good friends."

"They wouldn't conspire to remove anything from the files."

His face expressed skepticism. She said quickly, "There was a time when they were not in this room at all. They went to the kitchen and had coffee and pie."

"You mean someone could have entered this room and got hold of the folders and gone away without being seen or heard by two ex-soldiers, who were supposedly guarding the room?"

"I think it's possible."

"Well," he said abruptly, "then it wasn't Meeth. We had him that night."

"It was Meeth who killed the judge," Clara said stubbornly.

The detective didn't even look at Clara. "Well, I'll talk to young Thorne and Tony. They'll stick up for each other, but I'll have a try. Meantime, we'll have to search for those folders. They may have been destroyed. Now what about the day *before* he died when you first noted his mood?"

Again Bea scurried through her memory. "That's the day the lawn boys were here. They came to cut the grass and work on the garden. My uncle usually followed them around. It interested him." She thought briefly and sadly of the judge's not always hidden bitterness and regret over his retirement, voluntary though it was.

Clara, sitting now with her hands folded but listening hard, spoke. "Oh yes, he did do something unusual that day. I remember now. He had one of the lawn boys take him out in the car. I don't know where they went. But all that day the judge was very, very upset."

FIFTEEN

"The lawn boys, I have their names. Which one was it who drove for the judge that afternoon?" Detective Smith asked.

Clara didn't remember. "I'm not sure. I only saw the car leaving and I knew that Bea wasn't driving and I thought it unusual."

"Did you know he had taken the car, Miss Bartry?"

"I didn't then. Later, yes, of course. The judge told me that the car was in the drive and asked me to put it away. He said that he didn't trust Bob Forrest—I think it was—to drive into the garage. The entrance is rather narrow."

"I'll talk to Bob. Why do you think the judge would leave like that without telling either of you where he was going?"

Clara shook her head. "The judge did as he pleased. I never questioned him."

"He didn't hint to you that he had something special on his mind?"

Clara shook her head. "He never talked to me of anything that bothered him. Never. He got into the habit while he was judge. He never talked of his cases. He said it wasn't fair, that I just might bias his opinions, something like that. He was always scrupulous."

"But he did seem remarkably disturbed that day?"

Disturbed was not quite the word, but both Clara and Bea nodded.

Bea said, "He had these moods. Especially when he felt he had to do something he really didn't want to do. Like seeing the doctor. That is, he liked Dr. Thorne as a friend. But he hated to go to his office for a checkup."

"My husband was an unusual man," Clara said promptly but rather absently. "Most of that week before his death he was deeply troubled about something. It was as if he had to do something he didn't want to do. It made him"—she paused briefly—"rather difficult. I'm not sure I can make you understand this. But my husband was an extremely conscientious man. Lately though, he—this trait seemed to grow more decisive. I mean—well, once he saw somebody speeding in town and got the number of the car and reported it to the police. He'd do that kind of thing."

The detective looked puzzled. Finally his face cleared. "You mean the kind of person who writes letters to the *Times?*"

"Well, yes," Clara said doubtfully. "But I don't think he ever did just that."

"He didn't," Bea said positively.

Clara went on, "But he did report things that seemed wrong to him. Like the time the Ellison boys made a still in the woods. I understand that poor Mrs. Ellison had a hard time getting the boys off and paying fines."

"Where is she now? I thought that place was closed."

"It's closed. She's in New Mexico. The boys are now in school. They meant no real harm by that still, you know. It was only a boyish kind of—trick," said Clara, running out of words.

The detective seemed to think that over. At last he said, "In other words, the judge still felt himself, in a way, dedicated to upholding the law?"

"Oh yes! He couldn't stand by and see lawbreaking or anything he thought wasn't honest going on. He'd have tried to stop it." Her eyes filled with tears. She leaned forward. "Do you think that could be why he was murdered? I mean, suppose he knew something that somebody wanted to keep him from telling or— Oh, I don't know what I mean!" She flung out her hands and rose. The detective sprang up. "Thank you, Mrs. Bartry. You've been very helpful."

"I don't see how," Clara said in almost a wail. "I don't understand how anybody could hurt such a good man." She went out of the room, her head held high.

The detective shook his head as if he felt sorry for her, and then reached for the telephone book which lay on the desk. Bea heard him dial and ask for Robert Forrest. He talked for a moment, then hung up. "He's not there. He's working over at Dr. Thorne's. I'll talk to him later. I really would like to know where the judge went Thursday afternoon. But now, before I go, you're sure that aside from his mood, there was nothing unusual about Friday. Phone calls, say?"

"There might have been some that I didn't know about. Fridays Velda and I usually do some extra chores in the kitchen. I remember I took the small car early in the morning and did our grocery shopping. Then Rufe got home and came to tell me the good news. He had passed all the tests.

I didn't see much of the judge that day. But that night, after dinner, I decided that I had to tell him about my coming marriage, whether he was in a good mood or not. So I did and—"

"Yes, I know about that. But you think then that he had something else on his mind? That is, something he was determined to make a fuss about?"

"I didn't think of it at the time. It occurred to me only now, when you asked."

The detective picked up his hat. "Think about it. Oh, by the way, Mr. and Mrs. Di Pallici's passports will be given back to them. The dates correspond with the information both Mr. and Mrs. Di Pallici gave us. It was only a question of confirmation."

Bea risked a question. "Do you think there's a suspect besides Meeth?"

The detective evaded that neatly. "We don't know who killed him." He went away, driving a small inconspicuous car, headed toward the Thornes'.

He had barely gone when she found the files. She had sat down on the sofa and found its cushions packed down and needing to be shaken up; she took up one of the cushions to pummel it and discovered the two missing folders beneath it. She riffled through the pages of both folders and found they were all in order, precisely as she had paged them. There was not a sheet missing.

Thinking of Rufe's surmise about Cecco's boyhood, she sat down and went through the notes of the juvenile court file. There were records of a few individual cases but none that seemed to apply to Cecco.

Most of the youthful offenders had been sent to Millwood for such offenses as car stealing, vandalism and breaking and entering; she found nothing involving a more serious charge such as murder or manslaughter. Clearly he was proud when one of these minors showed himself not only repentant but on the way to becoming a worthwhile citizen. He appeared to keep in touch with some of the boys, as if he were in effect a guardian. At last she shoved the unrevealing pages together and put them in the file where they belonged.

Then she addressed herself to the folder labeled Extracurricular Activities. There were occasional, long-winded dissertations about the place of a judge in the law; the power of the judge; the necessity for strict justice. He quoted from Blackstone, Chief Justice John Marshall and Justice Brandeis. He went off into long anecdotes about his quarrels with various board members. But there was nothing even remotely referring to shoplifting or to being the middleman for bribery. That ought to relieve Mrs. Benson and Obrian.

She finally closed the folder and put that away in its proper place, too. Unless the president of the bank had shot the judge for objecting to a change in interest rates, unless the librarian had shot him for insisting that certain books were pornographic and should not have been bought, unless indeed the Reverend Cantwell had shot him because the judge disapproved of a new surface for the parking lot behind the church, then there was absolutely no clue.

She must tell Rufe that the folders had been found and what they contained—or rather what they did not contain. It was, however, an odd place to find them. The only reasonable explanation was that someone had contrived to get at them, but was unable to return them to the cabinet, and so hid them.

She sat at the judge's desk for a long time, thinking of the curious impression which the detective had so gently probed out of her memory. The more she thought of it the more she became convinced that the judge had had a certain air of reluctant but unrelenting decision. He had looked as he did when he reported some infraction of the law.

And then there was always the troublesome fact that the judge's gun was found beside him. He wouldn't have permitted anyone to take it; it would have had to be taken without his knowledge and fired. Then possibly the murderer had used his own gun to kill the judge and had left the judge's gun beside the judge as deliberately as he had extracted the bullet. Perhaps whoever had entered the house and set off the alarm had come into the study in order to secure the judge's gun, to leave it beside the judge as he made his escape!

She thought of that for a moment and saw the flaw; the judge's gun had been fired before the alarm sounded. If after, she and Clara would have heard the gunshot. Probably the police had come to that conclusion long ago.

She was still sitting at the judge's desk when Clara came back. "Has that detective gone?"

"Oh, yes. Long ago."

Clara sat down. "Bea, the police will find that Meeth killed the judge. This dreadful tragedy can't affect Rufe's career. I want you to be married."

"Not now, Aunt Clara."

Clara leaned forward. "Are you thinking of Lorraine?"

"No. But I don't want Rufe unless I'm sure he wants me."

"What makes you think he doesn't want you?"

Bea replied slowly. "I don't know. But there's something—different. I can't explain it."

"I'll talk to Rufe myself."

"No!"

Clara's face was suddenly stern. "Lorraine goes after anything she wants and usually gets it. You've got to tell Rufe that you'll be married as soon as it can be arranged. Of course, we can't have the wedding I had planned for you, a church wedding and a reception and all that. We couldn't do that so soon after the judge— But we can have a quiet little wedding right here in the house. I'd like that." She broke off, listened and said, "There's somebody coming."

There was the familiar sound of gravel in the drive. Bea went to the terrace door; it was a state police car. As she watched, two troopers in smart uniforms got out; between them was another man, a stranger to Bea. The troopers must have seen her in the doorway, for each touched his hat in a formal way as the three approached her. One trooper said, "Miss Bartry, this is James Meeth. He insists that he must talk to your aunt. I hope this is convenient."

"Why—why, I—" She turned toward Clara, who had risen, looking very set and firm. "Let him come in," Clara said. "The troopers, too."

Meeth came in first. He took off his hat, disclosing dark, very short hair; his face was pale with thin lines and a weak chin. He wore a suit which looked new but didn't fit, and new but rather clumsy-looking oxfords. One trooper slid his revolver from its holster and held it closely to his side. The quiet action gave Bea a tremor of fear.

"All right, Meeth," the trooper said. "Say your piece."

Meeth opened his thin lips and then just stood there, turning his hat in his hands. Finally he said to Clara, "Mrs. Bartry?"

"Yes." Clara stood as firm and unyielding as a rock.

"I came to tell you I didn't mean to hurt the judge. I'll never hurt anybody ever again. I did kill my wife but I hadn't intended to. I didn't mean it when I said I'd kill the judge."

"You said you would," Clara said coldly.

He swallowed so hard that Bea could see his throat move. "Yes, I know I did, ma'am. I was furious. I'd only killed my wife because—I was mad. But that's in the past. I threatened to kill the judge, yes, but I was wild and scared and—but then later I knew I never would try to hurt him.

You see—the past years have—they make a mark on anybody and I—"
He had the air of a frightened and desperate child.

"But you came here the night the judge was killed." Clara's eyes were intent.

"Yes, I did. But all I wanted to do was give him a piece of my mind. He wasn't fair to me. The jury wouldn't have given the verdict they gave if he hadn't been against me."

"My husband would never had directed a jury, not in a case like yours."

"No, ma'am. But—" Meeth swallowed nervously again. "That's the way it seemed to me. So I had to get it off my chest. I had to tell him. But there were lights in this room that night and I could see the judge through that door there. It was half open and a young fellow was talking to him. The judge was talking so loud and—so furious that—I guess he scared me. So I left. All at once I decided I'd been wrong to come. It wouldn't change anything to talk to the judge. I'd be just the same, a man on probation. Maybe he'd make it harder for me. It's all the truth, everything I told the police. But I had to see you, ma'am. I had to tell you that I wouldn't have hurt you or the judge, not really. I'm sorry I came that night. I'm sorry I threatened the judge. But I didn't really mean it."

Bea, thinking of her talk with Rufe about the judge's term on the juvenile court, entered the conversation. "Mr. Meeth, did you know the judge? I mean before your case came before him in court?"

He turned faded and rather hopeless gray eyes toward her. "No, miss."

"You never even saw him?"

He shook his head, puzzled. "No, miss. Not that I remember."

"Then," she said directly, "were you, when you were young, ever sent to Millwood?"

Both troopers seemed to stiffen. Meeth merely continued to look puzzled. "Millwood? That's like a reform school for boys, isn't it? No. I was never in any sort of trouble, not even for speeding until—"

He stopped abruptly. There was a short silence. Clara's face was troubled. Then Bea said, directly again, "How did you manage to get the police to bring you here? I thought you were being held as a material witness."

Meeth looked at his hands, still seeming like a frightened child. The trooper with the revolver in his hand said, "He insisted on seeing your aunt. We thought—" He cleared his throat.

Clara looked at him and said, "You thought he might tell something that would add evidence against him?"

The trooper blushed slightly. The other shifted his weight from one foot to the other and said, "We don't know what our superior officer thought."

"I do," Clara said unexpectedly, and turned to Meeth. "What did you do before you went to prison?"

"I drove a truck."

"Do you have a driver's license?"

"Why, I—why, yes, ma'am. That is, I did have."

Clara turned to the troopers. "This man did not kill the judge," she said. "So who did kill him?"

There was a short silence. Meeth's face was childish again in his surprise. The troopers looked bewildered at Clara's abrupt and defiant change of opinion. She said firmly, "It's your duty to find the man who murdered my husband."

SIXTEEN

Clara's abrupt reversal not only bewildered Bea, as it did the troopers, but also frightened her. She had known that Meeth could neither have entered the house on Monday and searched her room, nor have shut her in the garage Sunday night: he had been held as a material witness. But Meeth had always been a kind of buffer between questions she did not want to consider; he had provided a ready-made answer to murder. If he didn't kill the judge, it left too narrow a field of possibility, and, in a dreadful way, too urgent a need for inquiry.

"Thank you both for bringing him here," Clara said suddenly. "I am sure he is telling the truth. Mr. Meeth, when the police let you go, let me know where you are to be found. Thank you, gentlemen. Thank you, Mr. Meeth, for coming to see me."

James Meeth's face brightened, as if a gleam of hope had reached him.

"Come on," a trooper said to Meeth. "We've got to get you back."

Meeth gave a kind of half bow; both troopers said good afternoon.

Clara sat down and said mildly, "I was all wrong. I was sure he had shot the judge. He didn't. Not that man."

"But, Aunt Clara, this could be nothing but a device to help clear himself in the eyes of the police."

"He's not got sense enough for that," Clara said. "And he didn't murder the judge."

"You can't know that. You can't be sure."

"I've lived long enough to know a few things about people."

"You feel sorry for him, Aunt Clara! He managed to get around you."

"You felt sorry for him, too," Clara said shrewdly. "I could tell. Why, that poor man wouldn't intentionally kill a fly!"

"He killed his wife." Now that she had seen James Meeth, though, it was hard to believe.

"They said it was really manslaughter, something not premeditated. Done in a rage or— I don't remember and I don't care, but I've no doubt his wife deserved what she got."

"You are completely—" Bea began, and Clara finished with a gleam of laughter in her eyes, "Unreasonable? Indeed I am sometimes. But I know what I want right now, and that's your marriage."

"But, Aunt Clara, if Meeth didn't kill the judge, then who did?"

"That's the obvious question. Poor Meeth has been a scapegoat, and I helped to make him one."

"But that isn't all—"

"Naturally not. It means that whoever shot the judge must have been somebody he knew. Nobody else could have induced him to stroll down to the wall. Although, of course, if the murderer managed to get hold of the judge's gun—say the judge was threatened and pulled his gun out and the murderer got it away from him and forced him outside the house, far enough away so he hoped nobody would hear the gunshot—oh, yes, I quite see all these possibilities. The murderer might even have known that Meeth was going to be paroled and hoped the blame would fall on Meeth." She thought that over and became less certain of herself. "Of course, that was known by almost everybody. I believe it was in the papers. So that knowledge doesn't narrow the number of people who might have killed him."

Bea said slowly, "The judge would not have gone outside the house if he had felt himself in danger. He'd have done something—fired his gun right here so we'd hear it—even shout for help."

Clara nodded. "Probably. Although you know how stubborn he could be. Remember how violently he objected to having that alarm installed?" Clara's eyes filled with tears. "I wish I hadn't gone upstairs so early. I wish—it's no use wishing now."

There was a light knock on the door. It was the detective again, and when Bea opened the door he came in rather hesitantly. "I met the two troopers with Meeth as they were leaving. I understand that you now think Meeth did not kill the judge, Mrs. Bartry."

"I know he didn't," Clara said simply.

He went on quickly, "Well, I'm sorry to bother you again, Mrs. Bartry. I've been talking to Bob Forrest. He said that he drove the judge into town, and the judge got out at the library steps and told him to meet him there in a half hour. Bob waited, but the judge didn't return for almost an hour and a half. He was positive about that because his working hours for the day were up and he wanted to get the judge home and then go home himself."

"The judge must have been in the library," Clara said. "He was on the library board."

"No. I talked to the librarian and the girls there. No one remembers seeing him in the library at all. Bob says the judge walked up the street but he didn't see where he went. I thought perhaps you might remember something he said which would indicate his errand that afternoon."

Bea shook her head. Clara just looked at the detective, who sighed. "I see you don't. I thought that what Bob told me might jog your memory. But you've been very helpful." Both Bea and Clara looked puzzled; the detective added, "I mean about the judge's behavior. When you said that he was especially disturbed and must have had something on his mind that upset him. Thanks once again." The detective nodded and went away. They heard the closing of a car door and the departure of his car.

"What do you suppose the judge did that afternoon?" Clara said worriedly. "If he didn't go to the library or the bank, where did he go?"

Bea thought it over. The extent of the police inquiry, the fineness of its net, was beginning to impress itself more and more clearly upon her. "If the police have to question everybody in Valley Ridge they'll find out."

"But it seems to me if there was anything important about where he went, then somebody would have come forward by now and told us. Or the police." Clara rose and came over to the desk. "Where did he keep his gun?"

"Here—" Bea opened the drawer; she didn't remember placing the judge's cigar case in the drawer.

Clara saw it and seized it. "Why, Bea! I'm so glad you found that. I haven't seen it since a day or two before the judge was killed. I gave it to him you know. Long ago. Actually he didn't like it much but he pretended he did and constantly used it. But I knew." She took up the gold cigar case and pressed it to her cheek. Tears came to her eyes.

"It was here on the desk. Last night."

"I didn't see it!"

"It was underneath some of the papers that Rufe and Joe had moved to give space for signing your will."

Clara frowned, still smoothing her cheek with the cigar case. "I can't understand—oh, of course Velda found it somewhere and put it here." Clara walked out of the room, holding the cigar case in her hand. Bea sat down again at the desk.

It had been a long morning, yet she was surprised when Velda came in with a luncheon tray, saying, "It's very late. I knew those policemen were here and that man Meeth, so I didn't bother you with lunch then, but you'd better eat. Mrs. Bartry had hers on a tray. Lorraine and Cecco are gone somewhere. I'll not bother with them. When they get back they can fix themselves something."

"Thank you, Velda."

As she was eating, the appraisers arrived along with the other detective, Whipple.

Clara came down to meet them and to escort them to the safe in the judge's room. That was a simple bit of routine; the appraisers kindly overlooked the jewelry belonging to the judge. Shown the Mercedes and looking at the canceled check which Bea had found for them, they also concluded that since Clara had paid for the car, it was not a part of the judge's estate. Clara went with them, then, in the appraisers' car to the bank. When they reutrned Mr. Whipple opened the car door for her with a certain awed respect.

Clara explained it when all of them had gone. "You see, the judge really didn't have much of an estate. He always insisted on paying most of the household expenses. He had a few bonds. They searched through our safe-deposit box but found nothing that could have anything to do with his murder. It held mainly records of my own property and some insurance policies, that's all. I don't think the inheritance taxes will amount to much. I'm going to rest, Bea. It was a tiresome affair, although the bank president couldn't have been more polite. He let us use that little private office of his own."

She went upstairs. Probably the appraisers and the detective had been more or less astonished at the amount of Clara's property, Bea thought. Obviously whatever inheritance taxes there might be would not seem great to Clara.

Bea sat down again at the desk to write some more thank-you notes, vaguely wondering where Lorraine had gone, when Cecco came in whistling a rather merry little tune as if he were pleased with himself. "Still at it?" he said. "It's taking you a long time."

"There were people here."

"Police? Detectives?"

Bea did not want to be led into conversation with him. She nodded and picked up her pen.

"Don't want to talk, is that it?" Cecco's voice was intent and full of interest. "Did they have any news?"

"No," she said flatly.

He sat down and eyed her, but almost as if he didn't see her and was actually intent upon some inner calculation.

Bea suspected that he would not be quite so debonair if he knew of the dossier the police had received from Rome. Still there was apparently nothing in that dossier which proved criminal activities on Cecco's part.

After a while he said, "Do you know where Lorraine is now?"

"No."

"I suppose she is trying to decide where her best chances are. Your Rufe, Ben Benson or Seth. Or perhaps she'll wait and find somebody more promising or more amenable."

"That's her business," Bea said shortly.

"In fact, I saw her coming along the road toward Seth's house on Stoney Road—isn't that what you call it? The same road the Bensons live on."

"Perhaps she went to see Mrs. Benson."

It was more likely that Lorraine had gone to exercise her wiles upon Seth. "When did you see her?"

"Not long ago. Half an hour or so. She was coming from the direction of the Bensons'. Probably making up to Mrs. Benson just in case she decides on Ben. Now I know just where their house is. I can't imagine how I happened to get lost the night the judge was killed." He eyed his glistening oxfords. "My feet hurt. I went for a long walk. These country roads."

Bea addressed an envelope. Cecco said softly, "It's an odd thing about small towns. Gossips, especially the barbers. But in a place like Valley Ridge or Stamford, where I had a haircut Monday, they know all sorts of things. And talk about them."

"They like to entertain their customers." Bea put down her pen. "What are you getting at, Cecco? What particular gossip did you hear when you went to the barber's?"

"Oh, this and that," Cecco replied airily.

On an impulse Bea decided to question him directly. "Cecco, how did you know that I wore braces on my teeth when I was young?"

"You're still young, dear."

"I mean when did you see me wearing braces?"

Cecco's eyes widened merrily. "But I didn't. Lorraine told me. She said once that you were—forgive me, Bea—that you were a beanpole of a child with braces on your teeth. Permit me to say that you look very different now. Not at all like Lorraine's description of you."

"Oh." Bea felt rather flat. It was a reasonable and somehow, she felt, a true explanation.

"Anything else you want to know?" Cecco asked, and as she shook her head he walked out of the room.

So that answered the braces-on-her-teeth question, yet there was about him an aura of mingled calculation and satisfaction. It was nothing tangible, but it struck Bea that he might look like that if he were considering a bet on a horse. Then she called herself fanciful and went back to writing.

Rufe came in half an hour later and flopped wearily down into a chair. "I've been talking to a detective. The police got onto the fact that I'd driven up to Millwood, and then asked about the boys the judge sent there."

"How did they know?"

Rufe shrugged. "How do they know anything? They're extremely efficient. I understand they brought Meeth here this morning."

"Yes. Did they tell you that?"

"The detective named Smith did. He explained that Meeth had something he must say to Aunt Clara, so I suppose they brought him in the hope that whatever he was determined to say would constitute some sort of evidence."

"It did in a dreadful way, Rufe. Now Aunt Clara is sure he didn't kill the judge."

Rufe leaned over, his head in his hands.

"Oh, and Rufe, I asked Cecco when he had seen me wearing braces on my teeth. He said, never. He said Lorraine had told him."

Rufe eyed her thoughtfully. "Did you think he was telling the truth?"

"Well, yes, I did." Lorraine's description of her, as quoted by Cecco, sounded very like Lorraine. She said, "Rufe, I found the two folders that were missing and read them very carefully. There's nothing in them that I can see would be dangerous to anybody."

"Where did you find them?"

"Right here. Under the cushions of the sofa. Anybody might have put them here."

"When?"

"Maybe right after the murder, or it could have been later during the night you and Tony were here. They were not in the files the next morning when the detectives went through them."

Rufe shook his head. "Pull yourself together. I didn't take them. Tony didn't."

"But you were in the kitchen part of the time."

"Meaning a phantom intruder could have got in and taken them. We weren't gone long enough for anybody to read them. Besides we'd have heard anybody in the room."

"He could have come in very quietly, couldn't he?"

Rufe sighed, lifted his head and shoved his hands in his pockets. "I suppose so. I'm beginning to believe almost anything. The wildest sort of ideas—nothing of real evidence. May I see the two folders?"

"Of course." She took them from the cabinet. Rufe settled down to read.

He read rapidly but thoroughly. She had almost come to the end of her letters when he finished, rose and carefully returned the folders to the memoirs file. "Nothing," he said to her inquiring look. "The judge was too cautious about names or even circumstances which would indicate anybody in particular. Except of course his quarrel with Reverend Cantwell. And the banker. And the librarian and— No, there's simply nothing there that could endanger anybody. The page numbers are accurate too, so nothing has been removed."

"No."

"Well— Oh, Lorraine!"

Lorraine, of course. She came in breezily. "I've been driving. That's a beautiful car. Do you think Aunt Clara might give it to me? She can't drive."

"You don't have a driver's license, do you?" Bea asked and thought dismally: Can't I behave just a little more enticingly, more like Lorraine?

Lorraine danced over and sat on the arm of Rufe's chair. "Guess where I went."

"Cecco thought the Bensons'," Bea said.

"Right. I went to call on Mrs. Benson, a duty call. And do you know the strangest thing happened. She actually asked me to stay for lunch. Can you believe it! She talked to me, she asked me about the judge's murder, not that I could tell her anything she didn't know. She even talked about his memoirs. It seems everybody in town knows he was writing his memoirs. She asked if they were interesting."

Bea's hands tightened. "What did you say?"

"Why, I said yes. They were interesting indeed. Especially things about people here in Valley Ridge."

"But, Lorraine—" Rufe began.

Bea said, "Did you read the memoirs?"

"Heavens, no." Lorraine made her habitual gesture of tossing her head gracefully so her black hair fell away from her face. "Do you think I'd be so silly as to plow through all that stuff! But I told her yes, I had read them word for word. What else could I say?" She opened her eyes wide and innocently.

"What did she do then?" Bea said after a moment.

"Oh, what didn't she do! Honestly! Made me stay to lunch. Even gave me a thimbleful of sherry. Talked about Ben all the time; made me look at his baby pictures, school pictures, graduation pictures—all that. I was never so bored. I thought I'd never get away. All the same I thought I'd sort of butter her up—"

Rufe grinned. "You mean Ben?"

"There *is* all that money and to tell you the truth she acted as if she really wanted me for a daughter-in-law. Can you imagine that nice old woman carrying on over me that way?"

I can imagine it, Bea thought; she thinks Lorraine knows about a shoplifting episode. She'd rather have Lorraine for a daughter-in-law, obliged to keep quiet about it, than to have it known all over Valley Ridge.

Lorraine shook back her hair again. "On my way home I passed Seth's place. He was just getting into his car, so of course I stopped and he invited me in and offered me a drink. We chatted, you know. He is so attractive!"

"Seth? Well, of course, he's a senator," Bea said dryly. Then she thought, in pride or something she couldn't account for: Leave her to Rufe. Leave them alone. If Rufe wants her he'll only have to say so.

She gathered up her letters, said something about seeing to dinner and walked out. She could feel Lorraine's green eyes following her. She didn't go to the kitchen. Instead she went to her own room where she paced restlessly up and down, trying to talk herself into some common sense. Suddenly she wanted a cigarette. She had practically stopped smoking after the judge made one of his violent scenes about it a year or so ago. Yet surely there must be some around—dry perhaps but still cigarettes.

She looked in the drawer of the writing table; there was none. There might be some in her handbag, for it was a big utility bag, designed to carry everything from grocery lists to hairbrushes. She glanced through the odd items—change purse, billfold, handkerchiefs, scraps of paper that somehow got in the handbag and were never removed until she had a grand clearing-out day, even a few half-used match packs—but no cigarettes. There were two large pockets with zippers on each side of the handbag. She opened one pocket, feeling a bulge. The bulge was not an ancient package of cigarettes; it was one of the judge's dictated tapes.

It surprised her; yet she must have taken the tape in order to practice French, or perhaps it was one which she had already used for French and had absently put in her handbag and forgotten. She was holding it in her hand when Lorraine strolled in without knocking. "Rufe's gone and— What's that?"

Lorraine's eyes were even greener and more brilliantly set off by the dark-green turtleneck sweater she wore; the clinging black slacks displayed her lovely legs.

"This? It's only an old tape of the judge's. Have you any cigarettes?"

"No, I—no, I don't think so." Lorraine turned and looked out the window for a moment. Then she said, "Oh, I nearly forgot. Aunt Clara wants all those letters put out in the mailbox tonight."

"All right." Bea shoved the used tape back into her handbag. Lorraine went with her into the hall.

Bea went downstairs and into the study, took the letters she'd been writing and brought them down the drive toward the mailbox at the entrance to the road. She drew some letters from the box, mainly notes of condolence, magazines and junk mail, and trudged up the drive again. At the terrace steps she paused. She didn't want to go into the house. She'd been sitting at the desk all day; she needed exercise, and wanted to clear her head of the doubts about Rufe's love for her. She put the assortment of mail on the top step and strolled around the house.

Lights shone from the kitchen windows. She caught a glimpse of Velda adding something to a mixture in a bowl. She went on. The garage doors were closed and bolted on the outside. The evening air was growing chilly, and the tree frogs were starting their musical whistles. The path toward the pond invited her; she thought of old Shadders stalking beside her when he was not diverted by some promising scent. The pines were blue with dusk. She had almost reached the pond when she saw a man's figure. It was Cecco standing at the very edge of the pond, almost concealed by a thicket of laurels. He was simply standing there, gazing down at the pond.

He heard her approach and turned swiftly. In almost the same instant he gave a hoarse gulp and fell backward, half into the pond. She heard the gunshot. It rocked the world. She stumbled and fell herself, heavily, behind the laurels. This saved her life, for there were immediately two more gunshots.

Some birds whirred up, frightened, from the trees.

SEVENTEEN

Somebody was running through the woods. Then there was a heavy splash as though something had been thrown into the water. She could see one of Cecco's shining oxfords at the edge of the pond.

Rufe came plunging along the path out of the sudden evening twilight and found her. He caught her in his arms and then made her crouch down again behind the laurels. He went to look at Cecco. "I think he's dead. Come—"

She was on her feet, Rufe's arms supporting her. "I saw the mail on the steps of the terrace. I guessed that you had come this way, it was always your favorite walk. Hurry, Bea. Shall I carry you?"

She must have said no. When they reached the house it was blazing with lights. Velda met them at the front door, eyes popping. "I heard the gunshots! Is she hurt?"

Rufe shoved her at Velda and ran for the telephone. Clara came from somewhere out of the whirling darkness around Bea. Velda led her firmly to a chair and then stood wringing her floury hands. Lorraine appeared. Bea shook her head dazedly; she was not fainting, yet everything was moving around her. She leaned against somebody who proved to be Lorraine. Lorraine told Velda to get whiskey. Velda went in a flurry out of the room.

"Rufe said it was Cecco. Is that right?" Lorraine asked.

Bea nodded.

Lorraine was sitting on the arm of her chair, one arm around Bea. "Who killed him?"

"I don't know. It happened just as Cecco turned to speak to me. He heard me coming and then he gave a kind of—scream or something and fell over."

Clara came out of the confused dizziness around Bea; she had two glasses. "Drink this," she said. "Here's one for you too, Lorraine."

Lorraine took the glass, downed the whiskey, and half choked as it struck her throat, for neither Velda nor Clara had diluted it with water.

Lorraine said, "He was no good, Cecco—but still—"

"There, there," Clara said in a calm and soothing way. But she had not stood in the evening dusk beside the laurels and seen Cecco topple over into the pond. She had not heard the gunshots so close, so near. She had not dropped down behind the clump of laurels. Bea thought dully: He was shooting at me, too! Then she thought quite clearly: It must have saved my life, stumbling into the laurels. Why would anybody try to kill me?

It was like a nightmare which took on substance. Rufe came back from the study and went to Bea, looked at her, touching her arms, her hands, assuring himself that she was not hurt. Lorraine sank down into an armchair. Clara said, "They're coming. I hear the sirens."

They did come. It was a repetition of the night of the judge's murder.

There was the medical examiner, called from an early dinner, and Obrian, directing Tony and two other policemen. After what seemed a short time the cars carrying the state police arrived. There was Lieutenant Abbott again with some of his men as well as Detective Smith. The police lieutenant showed Clara a search warrant. "Certainly, yes, I understand," she said.

Nobody, however, really understood. Someone repeated what seemed to be a stock formula about willingness to answer questions. Bea was questioned first. How many shots were there? She thought three. Anything else? With a great effort Bea replied, yes, she thought that something had splashed in the pond. What something? She didn't know. Could it have been a gun? She didn't know.

Lorraine sat close beside her all the time they questioned her; Lorraine's dark green turtleneck sweater and her smart slacks looked strangely out of place in a world that had spun off its axis. Dr. Thorne arrived and Bea heard him tell the police that she had had a shock; they must not question her further that night; she had told all she knew.

Seth backed him up. Bea hadn't known that Seth had come, but he was there, telling the police that she couldn't talk to them any more that night. Dr. Thorne took her upstairs.

By then, she realized dimly, it was late. The doctor helped her into bed and put a stethoscope to her chest. Then he tucked an eiderdown around her. Rufe opened the door and came in. "Bea, are you really all right?"

"No," Bea said with truth, "I feel terrible."

"She wasn't hurt though," Dr. Thorne said.

He handed her a glass of water and two capsules, which she swallowed obediently. "I'll go down now and see to Clara. Stay with Bea, Rufe, until she goes to sleep."

Rufe nodded and sat on the edge of Bea's bed, simply holding her hand in his own and asking no questions.

"How about Lorraine?" Bea said presently.

"Okay. Go to sleep."

"Sleep! What are they doing?"

"Same things they did when the judge was shot. Searching all over the place."

Bea opened her eyes to look at Rufe. There was something in his voice that seemed to withhold information. "You're not telling me something. What?"

"I don't know who shot Cecco, if that's what you mean. Not very many people here even knew him."

"Ben Benson knew him."

"Can you imagine Ben lurking behind some shrubbery and shooting somebody?"

"Mrs. Benson might." Bea gave a breathless giggle which she herself recognized as near hysteria.

Rufe eyed her worriedly. "Now, please, Bea, it's been a shock but—" He broke off as Seth knocked and then opened the door. "Rufe, they want to question you again."

"I've told them everything I know! I didn't see who shot Cecco. Do I have to talk to them again?"

Seth replied shortly, "You asked for my advice when you phoned and told me that Cecco had been shot. So here's my advice, take it or leave it. Don't talk too much. Don't say anything that could be—" He checked himself; Rufe finished for him. "Incriminating? I won't."

Bea sat up. "Rufe, do be careful. I mean people can twist words around—"

Seth smiled. "Relax, Bea. Rufe has good sense."

"Don't let them say that Rufe did it."

"I can't tell them what to say, but there's not a chance in the world they'll accuse Rufe. What on earth would be his motive?" Seth's long face sobered; he said suddenly, "Are you thinking of Lorraine? Rufe's getting rid of Cecco because he was Lorraine's husband? Really, Bea—"

"No!"

Rufe at the door whirled around. "For God's sake! Lorraine! Get rid of Cecco because he was Lorraine's husband? A motive for murder? Lorraine doesn't mean anything to me!"

Bea's heart gave a leap; new life seemed to flow all over her.

Rufe looked merely angry and incredulous.

"Of course not. Your girl is right here, Rufe," Seth said good-naturedly. "I was about to scrape up something for dinner when you phoned. Will you ask Velda if she can manage a sandwich or anything to eat?"

"If I can find her. Last time I saw her she was in the kitchen moaning, threatening to leave forever."

Bea sank back on the pillows. "Go with Rufe, Seth. He has a right to have a lawyer present, doesn't he?"

"Well—yes. But I don't think it's come to that. However, I'll go with him. The house is full of people," Seth told her comfortingly. "Nothing for you to be afraid of."

He went out after Rufe and closed the door against a kind of background of sounds, voices from both inside and outside the house. There were cars coming and going.

Dr. Thorne would see to Clara, Bea thought hazily after a while, but how about Lorraine? She must have cared for Cecco once. It seemed to her now that some of the background noises were dying away. Her capsule-induced languor was abating, too. She disentangled herself from the eider-down and went into the hall. There was a steady murmur of voices from below. Lorraine's door was open and she was sitting at the small writing table with a tray set before her. She nodded at Bea, chewing. "Want a sandwich?"

Bea eyed the large plate of sandwiches which was covered neatly with a dinner napkin. "Did Velda fix those?"

Lorraine nodded, still chewing.

"I thought she was having hysterics, threatening to leave."

Lorraine swallowed. "Oh, she did that, all right. Got all the attention she could get. But believe me, she's not going to leave. She's having the time of her life. Here, the chicken ones are best. There's a little salad, too. Coffee? I'll get my bathroom glass."

Bea took a sandwich, discovering with surprise not only that she could eat but that she was very hungry. When Lorraine came back, she stuck a spoon in the glass to prevent it from breaking and then poured hot coffee. Bea said, "What about Aunt Clara?"

"Oh, she's all right. I tried to get her to come upstairs but she wouldn't. Funny," Lorraine said, "it's as if she got a new lease on life since the judge was killed. Different woman altogether. Used to be so mousy."

"I don't think she's changed at all. I think she was always like this. Lorraine, did Cecco tell the truth about where he was the night the judge was killed? I mean when he had gone from the Inn and Ben couldn't find him."

Lorraine took another sandwich, bit into it with vigor and nodded. "I think so. Probably he felt sure that if he actually saw Ben he could"—Lorraine shrugged—"get something out of him. Money or—— Anyway, Cecco always wore tight shoes. His feet began to hurt so he gave up. Yes, I believed him."

"Did the police question you tonight?"

Lorraine's eyes opened wide. "Question me! You were there! Didn't you hear them? Good Heavens, you'd have thought that I got a gun from somewhere, followed Cecco, and took a pot shot at him. Then more shots at you for fear you had recognized me. But I didn't," she said flatly. "Sugar?"

"No, thanks. But, Lorraine, they let you come up here."

"Oh, certainly. I had to do a bit of carrying on—stage weeping, you know. Cecco was my husband. We had our disagreements, but here we were staying in Aunt Clara's house. Sure they let me leave. Bea, didn't you see *anybody* down there at the pond? Besides Cecco, I mean."

Bea shook her head. "I saw him fall. I heard the shots. I scrambled down."

"Yes, I know. I heard you tell them over and over. What does Seth advise?"

"He told Rufe not to talk too much. That's all."

"Bea, do you really think *I* killed Cecco?"

"Do I think—*no!*"

"Well," Lorraine said coolly, "Cecco did try to hold me up for half my share of Aunt Clara's money. I told you all that—his idea of borrowing on what he called my expectations. He really believed that Aunt Clara has a bad heart. But I changed my mind. And after you told me that Aunt Clara knew about Benito there really wasn't anything Cecco could blackmail me about."

Rufe came to the door and saw the plate of sandwiches. He made for it. "Aunt Clara is in her room. I told Velda to take her some soup. The police are still at it. I asked Obrian to let Tony stay around the house tonight. I'll stay too. Any more coffee?"

"I'll rinse out my cup." Lorraine took it to the bathroom. Bea thought suddenly that perhaps Benito was not Cecco's only hold over Lorraine. Perhaps there were other things Cecco could have employed for blackmail. Suppose he knew something which was in fact so damaging to Lorraine's further prospects in life that she had to silence him!

No!

Yet Lorraine *could* have followed him from the house. She could have concealed herself in the clump of pines. Why, she is even wearing colors for concealment, Bea thought, horrified at the swift course of her own reasoning: the dark green sweater, the dark slacks wouldn't have shown in the dusk!

But what about a gun?

Rufe ate voraciously. "I hope I'm not robbing you girls, but I'm starved. They're going to drag the pond tomorrow. I could tell them that the pond has a muddy, swampy bottom. They're not likely to find the gun—if that was what you heard splash in the water, Bea."

"I don't know. I just know there was a splash."

"Bea—" Rufe shot a quick look at the bathroom door; Lorraine was still rinsing the cup. He said in a low voice, "Do you remember that jacket of the judge's? The night he was killed. There in his study."

"Yes. It was on his desk. But then later it was on a chair all folded up."

"When I first came it was just tossed over the desk, as if the judge had thrown it there."

"I suppose the police found it and had gone through the pockets."

Rufe did not look convinced. "Maybe. There's an odd thing. Somebody did pass me as I crossed the road. The lights were full on me. But nobody has come forward and told the police about seeing me. Why?"

"The driver could have been somebody from out of state or—"

"Not on this road. Unless he was lost. Of course he could have been Meeth, not wanting to admit it and place himself on the scene of the murder so close to the time of the murder. It was only later that he talked very fully to the police."

Lorraine came back and Clara appeared in the doorway. She nodded. "It's a good thing to get something to eat. I'm sorry about Cecco, Lorraine. Naturally I know that you were not on good terms but still—"

"Have a sandwich," Lorraine said.

"I've just had about a quart of soup. Velda stood over me." Clara had the judge's gold cigar case in her hands. "I do think it's strange that I didn't find this case sooner. Where has it been all this time?"

Rufe looked steadily at the rest of his sandwich. Seth came to the door. "May I come in? Or is it a family conference?"

"Come in," Clara said. "Sandwiches?" Lorraine asked.

"Velda fed me. I think the police are leaving. Lorraine—" Seth leaned against a chair, his elbows on the back of it. The move brought his face into the shadow of the lamp on the table and again, oddly, there was a teasing, fleeting resemblance to Cecco, although in fact, Bea thought sharply, there was no resemblance at all. He said seriously, "Did Cecco know who killed the judge?"

Lorraine shook her head. "I don't know. If he did he didn't tell me. Cecco—" Lorraine was again overtaken by one of her disarming moments of candor. When she chose to lie, Bea thought, she could lie with the best of them, but when she chose to tell the truth she withheld nothing. "Cecco," Lorraine said, "was by nature a chiseler and a blackmailer. He did it in mean but small ways. He wouldn't have had the courage to blackmail a murderer." She finished calmly and sat down on the bed, looking very lovely. "No," she said decisively, "he wouldn't have had the courage to do anything so dangerous."

Rufe said abruptly, "Why did he go to the pond?"

There was a complete silence. Then Rufe said, "He must have gone to meet somebody."

"And that somebody shot him and shot at Bea?" Seth considered it. "Sounds possible. Unless Cecco just liked to walk and happened to make a target of himself."

"He said he'd been strolling down that way the night I was shut in the garage," Bea said, and then caught Clara's look of inquiry and said quickly, "It wasn't anything, Aunt Clara. An accident. The doors—blew shut and Cecco heard me and let me out."

Rufe bit into another sandwich. "Cecco seems to have been around at odd times. He might have known something."

Seth nodded. "Certainly whoever killed him had to have a reason. People in Valley Ridge don't just go around shooting one another for the fun of it."

"Seth! What a way to talk! I'm going to bed," Clara said firmly. "You girls go to bed, too. It's late."

Seth arranged it so Tony could stay in the house that night. Rufe and Seth stayed, too. Dr. Thorne had gone long ago. Miss Dotty had telephoned for him, saying that there was an urgent call. Gradually the house became quiet. Bea did not set the alarm that night. Tony advised her not to. "You see, we may be out and around the house tonight."

He and Rufe and Seth stood together in the hall. Bea saw Clara to her room and said goodnight.

Bea looked at her watch with incredulity. It was very late. It was also dreadfully like that other night when the judge had been killed. The difference was that she loved the judge; she had never liked, certainly never trusted, Cecco. She tried not to think of Cecco's startled face, his backward plunge, his shining oxford turned at an outrageous angle on the edge of the pond.

She tried not to wonder who had killed him. But it couldn't have been proper stolid Ben Benson and she couldn't imagine why she kept thinking of Ben.

EIGHTEEN

She was still thinking of him the next morning.

Everybody came down late, but this time Velda did not object beyond uttering various threats about leaving a house where murder happened. "Seems as if there's murder right here in the house somewhere," she muttered. Bea felt much the same way.

But she kept on going over in her mind every possible reason for Cecco's murder. She thought about Lorraine, then about Ben. Obviously he had not welcomed Cecco's arrival; if Cecco had been, as Lorraine said, a blackmailer, would correct and proper Ben Benson actually have killed him to prevent Cecco's telling some story of youthful indiscretions? Bea could not seriously accept that as a hypothesis. Yet Ben seemed to be putty in Lorraine's hands. Could he have thought that in killing Cecco he was removing an obstacle to his marriage to her? That didn't seem reasonable either. The troublesome point was, again, that so few people knew Cecco. One must know someone very well or fear him very much to bring one's self to murder.

She didn't see Clara until noon. Lorraine came down as Bea was sitting at the table eying a cup of cold coffee. Police, Velda told them, were dragging the pond. Lorraine shook her head. "They'll never find anything in that pond. Are you going anywhere this morning, Bea?"

Bea replied, "No, I expect the police will be here sometime—"

"The drive is already full of photographers and reporters." Lorraine snapped off a grape and swallowed it whole apparently. "It's like the time when the judge was killed. Only worse. I suppose I'll have to give some sort of interview."

Rufe came in as she spoke. "Don't do that, Lorraine. You're the widow, remember. Doesn't do you or anybody any good to go posing in front of cameras." He sat down wearily.

Velda came bustling in. "You haven't had any breakfast and it's almost time for lunch!"

"I wanted to see how my father is doing. He's getting too old to work so hard. Needs a younger man to help him."

"Huh—" Velda said scornfully. "He'd never consent to that. I'll get you something to eat." She bustled off again. No, Velda wouldn't leave in spite of her mumbled threats; her eyes were agleam and excited.

Rufe fiddled with a spoon. "There are some policemen down at the pond now. Cecco—" He glanced swiftly and rather apologetically at Lorraine, who said, "Of course, they'll do an autopsy. I agreed to that last night. They'd have done it anyway. They'll find the bullet that killed him. But if it was a gun that splashed into the pond I doubt if anybody can ever find it."

Rufe frowned. "Things have been hurried. I didn't ask you, Lorraine, if there were relatives in Italy who ought to be notified. I mean, any cables you want to send. Or you could phone."

Lorraine shook her head, brooded for a moment and suddenly chose to explain Cecco's American accent. "There's nobody now. His mother was a New Yorker. She was separated from his father ages ago when Cecco was a boy. I didn't learn this until after I had married Cecco. She died."

Rufe said quickly, "Then he lived there as Cecco di Pallici?"

"Oh, no," Lorraine replied airily. "His mother gave him another name."

"What?" Rufe asked sharply.

Lorraine seemed to think back. "I really don't remember. Something that sounded American. Her maiden name probably. I think it was something like Brown or White or Johnson. When she died Cecco went back to Italy. I don't know what happened to his father, probably he came to no good end. I didn't tell you that Cecco was brought up in New York because I—oh, I was afraid you'd connect him and me with the judge's murder. Cecco couldn't have been a very nice boy. I didn't know, I was afraid that some time he had been in this vicinity and had come up before the judge and that was why the judge didn't want me to marry him. Well, to tell you the truth I was afraid somebody would take a notion that Cecco and I were working together to get rid of the judge and to get Aunt Clara's— Never mind that." Lorraine's typical burst of candor seemed to relieve her. "But now, you see, Cecco couldn't have killed the judge. No, there's really nobody to notify. He's to be sent to Italy to the family mausoleum. It's hard to tell the difference between his so-called *palazzo* and a mausoleum, but the mausoleum exists and they can make room for Cecco. I arranged all that with the police last night. They searched Cecco's room and all his luggage. Did you know that?"

Rufe was looking very thoughtful; probably, Bea thought, he was searching his memory of the records at Millwood and trying to discover any connection between a White, a Brown, a Johnson—or even a quite different name—and Cecco. If it existed, it would be necessary to trace Cecco's mother's residence in New York, his own residence there and countless details.

Rufe did not seem to hear Lorraine's question for a moment; then he nodded. "Apparently they found nothing of any special interest. Except a few bills, not paid."

"They'll never be paid as far as I am concerned," Lorraine said coolly. "No letters from any of his dear little friends?"

"I don't think so. In any event I don't think one of them would follow Cecco here and kill him. Do you?"

Lorraine's green eyes widened. "I never thought of that."

"I don't think it likely," Rufe said and Velda returned with bacon, eggs and toast. "Enough for a regiment," Rufe said. "Thank you."

He absently ate his meal in brooding silence, finished, said thank you and left, his shabby loafers flopping along the hall and out.

The day went on. Bea occupied herself by replying to the letters she had found in the mailbox and left on the terrace steps. She wondered, coldly, what would have happened if she had not left the stack of mail on the steps, and Rufe had not come along.

She had read all the letters and made a list which required replies when Clara came down. Clara was fresh and neat, her hair done carefully, her eyes as blue as her favorite blue suit. She said mildly, "It's odd but there have been no phone call. bout Cecco. I wonder why."

As she spoke, Lorraine came in. "Darling, nobody here knew Cecco."

"But the idea of the tragedy! I should think somebody would phone me."

Nobody had. Ben was the only person to whom Cecco's death might have a personal significance. Unless, of course, Seth had actually fallen in love with Lorraine at once . . . But that was absurd. Bea was appalled at the extent of her own speculations; the next thing she knew she would be mentally accusing Velda, Miss Dotty and again Dr. Thorne.

Clara peered up suddenly over her glasses. "I don't think a single one of us had an alibi for the time of Cecco's murder. I don't have an alibi. I was in the judge's room, just sitting there thinking of him."

Lorraine came to the desk and perched on the edge of it. That day she wore almost flagrantly bright colors as if she defied the role of widow, as by law she certainly was. Her dress was a tangerine-colored wool. A jade-green sweater was slung over her shoulders. The tangerine dress was so well cut and simple that it must have cost a great deal. Bea thought of Benito, who had supplied Lorraine with money and from whom she had parted with apparently no regret on either side.

"I was taking a shower," Lorraine giggled. "Nobody saw me there naturally. When I heard Velda yelling her head off I just dashed into the sweater and slacks I had taken off and ran down to see what was going on."

"We have answered everything the police asked us. It does seem really too dreadful." Clara sighed. "Lorraine, are you going back to Italy with Cecco?"

Lorraine stared at Clara. "No!"

"But there must be— Things have to be done."

"There is nothing at all for me to do there and I don't intend to go back."

Clara sighed again. "Well, as you wish. I do think it would be more becoming, but then we can always make some excuse."

"There's a very good excuse," Lorraine said flatly. "I loathed Cecco."

"Lorraine, don't speak like that! Or—" Clara said prudently, "don't let anyone else hear you speak like that."

Lorraine recovered her sweet and loving manner. "Darling, don't you think I have any sense. I'll be the grief-stricken widow if you insist but it'll be hard."

"Bea," Clara said, looking rather shocked. "What about meals? Do you think Velda—"

"I'll talk to her."

In the kitchen Velda was muttering gloomily again. "A funny thing! Nobody has come. Nobody has phoned."

"Nobody knew him," Bea said placatingly.

"Somebody," Velda said darkly and truthfully, "knew him well enough to kill him. Well, we'll just have to hang in. Can't cop out on Mrs. Bartry. I'll see to meals, don't worry. We'll skip lunch; breakfast was too late. Will Rufe and Tony or the senator be here tonight? If so, I'd better make something for them to eat." Velda's bark was always worse than her bite, although, if put to it, she could bite, too.

"I don't know. I hope so." Bea did indeed hope so. Three women alone in the big house with murder in the woods, murder down by the stone wall, murder!

Velda said, "You're scared. I don't blame you. Honestly, now didn't you see whoever killed that Cecco?"

"No! I didn't see anybody. I just heard the shots."

Velda stared at her for a moment. "Well, I was only going to say if you *do* have some idea about the murderer, you'd better tell the police right away."

"But I tell you I *don't* know." Bea went back to the study and Clara's letters.

The day went along with what seemed remarkable quiet. The telephone did not ring and nobody came to call. Rufe did not return. Nobody questioned them. Once Bea thought she caught sight of Detective Smith walking slowly past the garage and down toward the pond.

If the men dragging the pond found a gun or anything else of any significance, Bea knew nothing of it. As dinner time approached the one remaining police car departed. The rosy spring twilight fell softly as though there were no such things as murder and fear in the world.

Seth came in after dinner. "Have you heard?" he asked. He looked angry. When Clara cried, "Heard what?" he told them. "Joe Lathrop! In my office! Knocked out, gagged and bound up with tape."

There was a silence. Lorraine recovered first. "Did they get Aunt Clara's will?"

"Oh, no. No reason for that! Besides the safe was closed. Only Joe knows the combination—Joe and I. So far I haven't discovered anything missing."

"But doesn't Joe know who—" Clara began.

Joe had said that he didn't know; Seth had found Joe about five o'clock. He had stripped off the tape and got out the gag—a hand towel from the office washroom. Joe said he'd been bending over a bookshelf near the door but with his back to the door. It had opened quietly and as he began to turn he felt a smashing blow. When he became conscious again, he said that he could neither move nor yell for help. He didn't know how long he had remained unconscious. Seth had called Obrian. "He and a couple of his men are going through the office now for fingerprints. I took Joe home. He said he had a headache but that was all."

He wouldn't have coffee; he was tired, but he'd come back and spend the night in the house if they wanted him. Clara summoned the courage to refuse. "Get some rest, Seth. We won't need you tonight."

Seth offered a vague protest, but then went on home.

Rufe still did not come or telephone. Velda left after warning them, unnecessarily, to lock the house. A moment later Obrian pulled up to the front door and came in for a moment. "If you're afraid, I'll try to get somebody to stay here. I don't know who but somebody. We're so short of men."

Clara refused. "It's all right, Mr. Obrian. We'll set the alarm and nothing will happen to us. I have the phone right beside my bed."

Seeming somewhat relieved, Obrian left.

After Clara had set the alarm and said goodnight as calmly as if it were any night, and the key in the door of Lorraine's room had clicked, the house seemed very quiet.

Too quiet, Bea thought after a long time; she wished for some normal and customary sound. She also wished she could stop going over and over again all the known facts of the judge's murder—and Cecco's murder. It struck her suddenly that she—all of them—appeared to have taken it for granted that whoever had murdered the judge had also murdered Cecco. Perhaps this was simply because murder is unusual; it did not seem likely that there were two murderers, one intent upon killing the judge and the second on killing Cecco. It did seem likely that Cecco's murder was somehow linked to or even a result of the judge's murder. She hadn't heard the police say that; it was only a reasonable hypothesis.

According to Lorraine, Cecco had never hesitated if he happened upon an opportunity to indulge in a little blackmailing. Yet if he knew anything of the judge's murderer it would have been a very dangerous kind of blackmailing.

It *had* been dangerous; Bea remembered Cecco's startled face and the way he had plunged backward. Yet he couldn't have been such a fool as to place himself, like a target, down by the pond.

Nobody could get into the house that night without rousing the three women and giving Clara time to use the telephone. There was no reason for anybody to attack Lorraine or Clara or Bea herself. Yet reason couldn't conquer instinct. Bea did eventually drop into a troubled sleep, struggled out of its uneasy darkness and knew that someone was in the room. It was Clara, whispering. "Bea, wake up. The judge is talking. I can hear his voice."

NINETEEN

The judge *was* talking. His rasping, rather harsh voice came clearly, yet distantly up the stairwell. It was eerie, unnatural, not quite lifelike; yet it was the judge's voice. Clara held Bea's wrist tightly; Bea could feel her hand tremble. The voice went steadily on, but there were no distinguishable words. Then all at once there was merely the cadence of a word or two and Bea's common sense came back. "It's the dictating machine," she whispered. "Somebody is running through one of the judge's dictated tapes."

"Are you sure?"

"Oh, yes. I heard him say, 'Paragraph here, Bea.' I'll turn off the alarm and go and see."

The alarm was already turned off. Clara said, "You'll not go down there! Use the phone in my room. Call Rufe. Seth. Anybody. Be quiet though."

She trotted into Bea's room and came back with a dressing gown, which she draped over Bea's shoulders, as Bea dialed the Thorne number; there was a repeated buzz, then a woman's voice said sleepily, "Dr. Thorne's wire."

It was his answering service. Bea said, "Did he go out or did he tell you not to call him except in an emergency?"

The woman apparently debated; finally she said, "Who is this?"

Bea told her. "I don't want the doctor. I want to talk to his son."

"Is it serious?"

"Yes. Hurry, *please.*"

She rang and rang; finally a voice said drowsily, "Dr. Thorne."

"Oh, Doctor, it's Bea. I want to talk to Rufe."

The doctor seemed to pull himself together and awaken. "Rufe, why, yes! Certainly. Hold on. I'll call him."

As she waited she could still hear the judge's voice from below, so lifelike and yet subtly unlifelike, droning on and on. After what seemed a long time the doctor came back on the telephone. "Rufe's gone. He's not in his room. His car is gone, too. I looked. Do you want me to come?"

Bea debated for a second and said, "No, thanks. But if you hear Rufe come back will you tell him I phoned?"

"Yes, certainly. But why? Is Clara all right?"

"Yes. I'm sorry I wakened you."

His voice was dull with drowsiness. She put down the telephone and as she did so the faraway drone of the judge's voice from the study simply stopped.

Just then Lorraine came swiftly up the stairs. "Bea! Aunt Clara!" She reached the hall and paused for a moment; there was the swish of silk, then she came to the door. "Oh, there you are!"

Clara said, "You were downstairs. Why?"

"I thought I heard someone talking in the study. It was like the judge's voice. I had to go down and see who—but I remembered to turn off the alarm. When I got there whoever it was had gone."

This time Bea couldn't tell whether she was lying or telling the truth. Obviously she had no reel of tape in her hand. Besides, the used tapes which the police had heard had none of the judge's dictation, not a word of the judge's voice, only her own— But those weren't all the tapes!

That memory was like a dash of cold water in her face. She herself had a reel in her handbag. She still couldn't remember putting it there, pushed neatly down into the zippered compartment, yet she must have done so, absently, intending to use it again. But that reel just might be a recording that the judge had made and she had not transcribed. Suppose that was the reel somebody had been listening to, on the machine in the study. Suppose there was something on it which could give information about the judge's murder.

Lorraine had seen her, surprised, with the reel in her hand.

She ran back into her own room. Her big black handbag stood on the table. She opened it swiftly. The reel was gone.

Clara and Lorraine had followed her. "What is it?" Clara asked. "Bea, what—"

Lorraine didn't ask. Lorraine knew. Bea was now sure that the reel was the reason for the search of her room Monday when she was in New York —her handbag with her. Lorraine couldn't have searched her room. She had been away that afternoon, shopping for a black dress. Cecco—yes, Cecco could have returned by taxi from Stamford, searched Bea's room, then left to return again later, with the excuse that he had had to wait for a haircut. But Cecco himself had been murdered. He couldn't have found the reel, for she had it with her. So he couldn't have used it for blackmail.

All that shot through her mind like a series of pictures in fast motion.

However, someone had taken the reel and was curious enough about it to run it through the machine. Since Lorraine had admitted she turned off the alarm, Bea had to ask, "Lorraine, did you take that reel of tape from my handbag?"

Lorraine blinked. "That thing you had in your handbag! Heavens no! Why should I?"

"Bea—" Rufe shouted from the hall below. "Anything wrong?"

Everything was wrong, Bea thought dismally. Clara turned back into the hall. "Rufe, we were phoning to you. Your father said you weren't at home."

"I wasn't." Rufe ran up the stairs. "I was out in the drive. Parked my car and intended to stay there all night. I didn't like the idea of you three women left alone. Why did you phone me?"

Bea told him briefly. "Someone was in the study, running a tape through the dictating machine. There was one reel of the judge's dictation in my handbag. I didn't know it. I don't remember putting it there. Now it's gone. I don't know what he said on the tape. Lorraine saw the reel when I found it."

Lorraine interrupted. "She's going to tell you that I took that tape and tried to hear what the judge had said. She's going to accuse me of Heaven knows what!"

Clara said, "Why did you come in, Rufe?"

"I saw the light in the study. Then it was turned off. I didn't see anyone and the light made me wonder what was going on. I tried the front door but it was locked. The terrace door was open so I came in that way. Bea, where did you last see the tape?"

"Yesterday afternoon, late. I told you Lorraine saw it."

There was a flash of mischief in Lorraine's green eyes. She put out her arms toward Rufe. She was wearing a flesh-colored silk dressing gown, her blue-black hair tumbled over her shoulders and she looked stunningly beautiful. "Don't you want to search me, Rufe?" she said, smiling.

"I don't see how you could have a reel of tape concealed anywhere about you." Rufe's voice had a slight edge to it but he looked amused, too. Then he sobered. "I suppose there just could be something on the tape which would supply evidence about the judge's murder, even a motive. Did you hear anything important, Lorraine?"

"Why, I told you I didn't touch that reel! I don't think you believe me!"

"I don't think I do," Rufe said bluntly. "Lorraine, if you have that tape it might be very dangerous to you."

She smiled. "Darling, I told you. I don't have it!"

Rufe said abruptly, "I'm going down to the study."

Without a word, moved by a shared impulse, the three women followed him. There were lights in the study. Miss Dotty sat on the sofa; she wore her white uniform under a gray coat; her nurse's comfortable shoes were planted firmly on the floor. Madame Defarge, Bea thought irresistibly, although Miss Dotty had no knitting. Miss Dotty looked at Rufe and it seemed to Bea that there was a flash of some intelligence between them. If so, it was so fully understood by both that neither of them spoke. Clara cried, "Why, Miss Dotty!"

Miss Dotty simply sat and said nothing. Lorraine came nearer, looking puzzled. "But you weren't here when I came down."

"No," said Miss Dotty.

"Well, why did you come?" Lorraine said in a burst.

Rufe walked behind Miss Dotty and the sofa to the judge's desk. He put his hand on the dictating machine and nodded. "It's still warm. Well, Lorraine, where's the tape?"

"*Stop asking me that!*" All at once Lorraine turned sharp and angry.

Rufe looked at Miss Dotty. "When did you get here?" he asked in a casual way, which seemed to Bea a little too casual.

"Just now. Door was open. Thought I'd wait." Miss Dotty vouchsafed that much and stopped, looking stolid and completely immovable.

The telephone rang. Rufe was nearest it, but his proximity didn't quite account for the dash he made for it. "Yes, it's Rufe. I see. Right. Well, hold it. Right."

Miss Dotty looked at the floor in a remarkably knowing way. Lorraine, Clara and Bea stared at Rufe, who had suddenly grown rather pale. He sank down into the judge's chair. After a long moment he seemed to become aware of the unspoken questions hurtling around him, for he said, "Wait—I've got to think—I've got to—"

"Who was that on the phone?" Clara demanded in a tone that brooked no evasion.

"Joe."

"Joe Lathrop! But how did he know where to find you?"

"He thought I might be here."

"You mean you told him you'd be here! Why?"

Miss Dotty said, "I'm going," and rose.

Clara turned a distracted face to Miss Dotty. "Where—why—" Miss Dotty started on a plodding but determined way toward the open terrace door.

Lorraine watched her, then looked at Rufe and snapped, "I don't know what Joe had to say at this time of night but he must be out of his head to call here."

"I think I'm out of my head." But Rufe seemed to make a decision, that or Miss Dotty somehow had made up his mind for him. He rose. "I'll take you in my car." He addressed Miss Dotty's solid back.

"My bike," Miss Dotty said over her shoulder.

"I'll put it in the back of my car." Without another word, without even a look at the three women, he followed Miss Dotty. She reached back to hold the door open for him. They disappeared into the dark spring night. There was the barest sound of their footsteps outside. Bea went up to the terrace door and closed it.

"What are they up to?" Lorraine demanded. "That Miss Dotty and Rufe are in cahoots! Anybody can see that. But what has Joe Lathrop to do with it?"

"I'm going back to bed," Clara said. "It was a shock, you know, hearing the judge's voice and— I'm going to bed."

She went slowly but with resolution. It had been a shock to Bea, too. She turned to Lorraine. "You *did* take that reel of dictation! You did run it through the machine. What was on it? What had the judge said?"

"I told you I didn't take it."

Bea thought for a moment. Clara wouldn't like it, but she went to the telephone.

Lorraine came up beside her. "What are you doing?"

"Calling Obrian. I'm going to tell him about the tape and somebody running it on the machine."

"Aunt Clara will be very upset. Call Seth. That's better. He'll know what to do. I'll call him. What's his number?"

"I don't see what he can do. But—all right." Bea told her the number and Lorraine dialed quickly. There was, however, a repeated buzz at the other end of the telephone. Lorraine put down the receiver with a bang. "Line's busy. Wouldn't you know it! Well, we can wait."

"No. Aunt Clara looks too tired. Let's go upstairs. I'll set the alarm. Tomorrow we can talk to Obrian and Seth and Rufe."

"Do you think you can make Rufe tell you what's on his mind? I don't." Lorraine waited while Bea turned off the lights. They went up the stairs together, and then Bea made sure that the alarm was set again. Lorraine suddenly seemed to listen. "I don't know why," she said in a whisper. "But somehow it's as if—oh, I don't know. The house feels wrong."

"Wrong!" Bea's heart gave a disconcerting jump.

"As if somebody is in the house."

Someone had been in the house Monday afternoon and had slid out of sight, a mere flicker in the mirror. Lorraine said quickly, "But there can't be anybody here!" She went to her room and locked the door emphatically. Clara's door too was firmly secured.

Nobody could get into the house or come upstairs without rousing the whole place. Bea hoped though that Rufe had deposited Miss Dotty at her small apartment and driven back home across the road. The house was so still she could have heard the faintest motion anywhere. She sat for a long time, staring at nothing until at last she dropped over onto the pillow.

After a while it seemed she must have begun dreaming, for the pillow suddenly reversed itself. It pressed so hard she couldn't breathe. Then she knew that somebody's hand held the pillow over her face, smothering her. She kicked; she struggled; she clutched into the darkness with both hands, yet someone evaded her and pressed even more relentlessly. Darts and flashes of light seemed to shoot across her eyes. The eiderdown seemed to hold her as if it too had hands.

But suddenly the pressure was gone. There was a flurried scramble and hard thud on the floor near her. She pushed the pillow aside, took a great breath of air and reached automatically to turn on the bedside light. Seth lay, sprawled on the wrinkled rug, rubbing his head.

"Seth!"

"He got away." He struggled awkwardly to his feet and rubbed his head. "He knocked me down. Half killed me—"

"But you—I didn't know you were here."

"Oh, sure. I couldn't let you three women stay in the house alone. Didn't want to alarm you either by insisting on staying with you. The terrace door was open so I came up the back stairs and just sat in that little bedroom. Must have fallen asleep. But then all at once I thought I heard someone here. I grabbed for him."

"Who?"

"I couldn't see. He knocked me down and—he's got to be somewhere in the house or near—" He rubbed his elbow this time. "Damn near broken. I'll call Obrian."

"We tried to call you. Your line was busy."

"Call me? Why?"

"I'll explain later. Call Obrian."

"Right."

"Oh, Seth." Her senses were returning. "Rufe may be outside in his car. Get him first."

"Rufe! Why, all right—all right." Seth went out, half running.

So Lorraine had been right, Bea thought. Someone had been in the house, hidden himself, but had not reckoned with Seth.

There was a sudden sound which ought to be familiar. It was familiar. The alarm was shrieking.

TWENTY

Somebody turned it off. The silence was like a blow. Then she could hear voices in the house. She didn't know who and didn't care. But the door swung open, light streamed in from the hall and Rufe ran to her and caught her in his arms.

She clung to him; she would never let him go. He pushed back her hair, he turned her face toward him and said, "Bea, Bea—" over and over again.

"Somebody was here—the pillow—Seth took it away. He went to call you—"

"We were watching and broke in. That started the alarm. I turned it off."

"We—?"

"Joe and Tony and Miss Dotty."

"You mean all three of you were out there watching the house?"

"Sure."

"But—but Joe—"

"Oh, he's all right. I knocked him out this afternoon, you know. He insisted. I made it gentle and then wound him up in office tape. Tony has put in a police call. He had his radio car down there in the entrance of the Ellison place. The police will be here. They'll find the tape. I think that may explain it."

"Who—"

Lorraine said from the doorway, "Here's the tape, Rufe. I hid it in the linen closet after taking it from Bea's handbag. I ran it through and heard enough to—" She gave the tape to Rufe. "Perhaps I picked up some hints about blackmailing from Cecco. So I decided to keep it in the event of— Oh, never mind. Here come the police."

The police siren was wailing. Cars thudded up the drive. Lorraine, her head held high, led the day down to the judge's study. Seth leaned on the judge's desk, a red blotch showing up now on his temple. Clara sat like a pretty little statue, her hands folded around the judge's gold cigar case. She looked up as Bea, Rufe and Lorraine came in. "Is that the tape?" she asked.

Rufe nodded. "Put it on the machine, will you, Bea?"

Bea adjusted the tape in the machine and turned it on. Clara flinched a little as the judge's voice came out, but then she leaned forward, listening intently. Obrian came in as they listened. Unexpectedly Ben Benson stuck his head in the door and came in. He looked weird in a raincoat over pajamas. He mumbled something about hearing the police car and then he, too, listened.

The judge said from the machine, "Now take this down, Bea, exactly as I say it. But you must never never tell anybody at all what I'm saying. This is a solemn order. You must never tell even your aunt. I think it will work out all right. Not many people here in Valley Ridge know of it. We so seldom get out and see people. I only happened to hear a rumor of it a few days ago when I was in the bank and was asked my opinion. I was deeply shocked. Seth cannot run for President. He cannot become President."

Clara cried, "President! Seth! Is that true, Seth?"

Seth smiled, shook his head and rubbed his elbow again.

Rufe stopped the machine. "I heard a rumor of it, too, when I was in Washington, Seth. Old Upson told me when I had dinner with him."

Lorraine said coolly, "Cecco heard it, too. That afternoon he went to the barber shop in Stamford for a haircut. He told me. That's why I— Never mind," she said again and might as well have said that she had thought of just possibly becoming a President's wife—with the help of the tape.

Suddenly Bea remembered when Cecco had told Lorraine; Bea herself had heard it. Rather she thought she had heard Cecco say only "resident" and had taken it to refer to something of his own or Lorraine's affairs. He had actually said "President." She was sure of it.

Seth didn't even look at Lorraine. "Go on with the tape, Rufe."

Rufe started the machine again; the judge's voice went on inexorably. He was working up to one of his irrational moods of what he would have considered justifiable anger. "I must consider my duty as a lawyer and former judge.

"I'll begin at the beginning. Seth was brought before me on a breaking and entering charge while I was judge of the juvenile court. I had to send him to Millwood but I was interested in him. He did very well; he always learned rapidly. His name was kept out of the papers because he was a minor. When he came out of Millwood his father and I determined to keep his presence there a secret. That is, the man we thought of as Seth's father was his stepfather. He gave Seth his name. Seth was born in Spain of Spanish parents; his mother married old Seth Hobson when Seth was a child. Seth's real name was Juan Perez. But some time or other Seth trumped up a false birth certificate. He admitted that yesterday. I went to see him in his office. He showed it to me but I know that it is a forgery. He had sent Joe Lathrop out on an errand so I was there alone with Seth. I told him I couldn't stand by knowing that a law might be broken.

"Paragraph here, Bea."

Paragraph here, Bea. It was the familiar cadence of the words which Bea had recognized. At the same time a fleeting recollection nudged her; she had felt once or twice that there was a resemblance between Cecco and Seth; now she knew what that was. Cecco, though Italian, had reminded her of portraits of Spanish grandees. Seth had almost the same kind of long, slender face; she had thought it a New England face; but it was Spanish.

Clara was sitting very straight and implacable. "Is all this true, Seth?"

Seth shrugged. "Some of it. My foreign birth. Sure. There was no point in advertising the fact, either that I had served some time at Millwood when I was a youngster or that my stepfather had adopted me and given me his name. No point at all. The judge agreed."

Clara insisted. "But are you going to try to run for the Presidency?"

"Certainly not!"

"But the rumor the judge heard—"

Seth sighed. "I can't help it if some of my friends start up such talk. I've made a good record in my years in the Senate. They need a candidate. I suppose it's natural that they should think of me. But I had no intention of ever becoming a candidate. The judge—well, we know how he was recently. Go on with the tape, Rufe."

The judge coughed and went on. "I am giving Seth till tonight to make up his mind. I realize that this is too lenient, but I have followed Seth's career with pride. He became a senator because he was brilliant. He has made a fine record. There is nothing in the Constitution to prevent his acting well as a senator. No one knew anything about his background. No one questioned it. But he can't be President. He was not born in the United States. His forged birth certificate shows premeditation. He'll be here tonight and promise to withdraw from the candidacy which he hoped to get. I'm sure of this. However, it's a very—" There was a long pause as though the judge were trying to think of a suitable word; finally it came out, "a tremendous temptation to any man, especially an ambitious man and Seth is ambitious. He is also ruthless. I may be obliged to use strong measures to persuade him. Of course, a gun— No, that can't be necessary—yet Seth will not give up easily. If I show him that I mean what I say—"

The judge's voice was harsh, which Bea recognized as the prelude to a fit of anger. He went on in disconnected phrases. "I know—I'll get out my gun and show him that if he gets mean." His voice began to take on a rasping, frenzied note. "I must defend the Constitution. I'm the only person who knows the fact about Seth. He knows that only I can accuse him." He seemed to pause here and consider. He mumbled into the microphone; then his voice became louder, almost incoherent. "Yes, he is a ruthless man. He'll try to stop me the only way I can be stopped. But I'll defend myself, I've got to defend the Constitution. I'm the only one who can do that—Bea, think of it—I'm the only person in the United States to defend—to save the law of the land. I'm the only one." There was another pause, filled only with heavy breathing. The now hoarse and jerky voice of the judge came out again. "He's been my friend. But my oath of office long ago—I've always tried to see that the law is upheld— it's very hard. But I'll do it. I'm an old man, I'm a sick old man. They try to hide it from me, but I'm past my useful years. But not now! *I'll be useful!* I'll kill him if I have to— Bea, don't write down all this." His voice seemed to take on a more normal tone for an instant. "No, no, I don't mean to kill him." But then his voice rose again in a grasping kind of scream. "But I'll do it! My forefathers fought for the Constitution. I can fight for it too. How can a man die better than facing fearful odds, for the ashes of his fathers and the temples of his gods?" Another pause; then he went on rather sadly. "I was so proud of him. But now I have to kill him or he'll kill me. I could see it in his eyes when I accused him of forging the certificate. Seth will try to talk me around. He's a smooth politician. But I have given my life for the law— I'll give my life for the law, Seth." The judge's voice became low. There was another short return to the normal. "Bea, I'll put this record in that big black purse of yours, on the hall table. I'll tell Seth that you have it and— Now, Bea, if there is any trouble with Seth—now, Bea, you have this tape so take care of it. If Seth gives up his plan I'll tell you and you're to forget that you know this at all. Never mention it to a soul."

The tape clicked. After a moment Rufe turned off the machine. "Too bad he didn't go on. Did you come here the night he was killed, Seth?"

Seth eyed him. "No. I knew the judge. I decided to give him time to settle down. He did come to see me at my office here. He did accuse me. I couldn't make him understand that I had no intention of becoming a candidate. Then I never saw him alive again. He was one of the best friends I had in my life. He was right. I couldn't have taken on candidacy for President even if—" Seth smiled. "Even if it was eventually offered to me."

Bea said, "Seth saved me tonight. There was someone in my room."

"Seth, you said that you didn't know the medical examiner." Rufe said slowly.

Seth lifted his arched eyebrows. "I don't. Except as a name. I've been away from Valley Ridge so much in recent years."

Rufe looked down at the desk. "And you didn't know that he spent four years as a Navy surgeon in the South Pacific."

"But what does that have to do with anything?"

"Whoever dug that bullet out of the judge couldn't have known that the medical examiner had had all that experience with bullet wounds. Of course, any good doctor could have found evidence of cutting out the bullet. But ordinarily a doctor wouldn't have looked for it. Seth couldn't have known that the medical examiner would instantly tell the difference between a normal exit wound of a bullet and an extraction with a knife. Most people would have assumed that it was only the wound a bullet would make. But the medical examiner knew at once that a knife had been used."

Clara rose, still holding the judge's gold cigar case; she walked slowly and with dignity to the judge's desk. Seth moved aside; she sat down at the desk and looked as grave and judicial as the judge himself. "This is a very serious accusation, Rufe," she said. "What it comes down to, however, is Seth's word against the judge's word. The judge told the truth. Seth admits that. But we all know that the judge sometimes was not clear in his mind." She looked at Rufe. "How long have you believed Seth shot the judge?"

Seth half smiled. Rufe said steadily, "I wasn't really sure. But at first I wondered why the person who saw me come here the night the judge was killed didn't come forward and tell the police he had seen me in his car lights. It had to be someone from out of state who either did not read of the murder or didn't want to get involved—or the murderer. The car came from the direction of Seth's house not a mile away. Then when I went to Washington old Upson told me that there was already a strong organization building up to run Seth for the presidential nomination. I knew that the judge's term on the juvenile court had been omitted from his obituary; that portion of his memoirs was missing and later found. Seth had given the obituary to Joe to phone in and omitted the judge's term in the juvenile court. Seth could have tried to get hold of that part of the memoirs and later take a look at it."

Bea broke in. "It's true. Seth did have a chance to open the filing cabinet and take out that portion of the memoirs. He was alone here in the study the next morning, Saturday, after Rufe and Tony left. But then somebody was in my room. Seth did come in time to save my life."

Seth nodded at her and said quietly, "I'll reserve my defense. Go on, Rufe."

Rufe continued, "Things just added up. There had to be a really important reason for the judge's murder. Then I had an idea. I read the Constitution again to make sure of my memory. If Seth had been guilty of a felony or a misdemeanor when he was young and had been sent to Millwood, it wouldn't help his candidacy if it were known, but it wouldn't prevent it legally. However, if he were born in a foreign country he couldn't be elected. I told Joe what I was afraid of. We took a quick look through Seth's office this afternoon. But it was getting late. We weren't sure we had put everything back just right so Joe made me slug him and tie him up. Then tonight Joe went back and got into the safe and there was the birth certificate. He phoned here to tell me."

"You were a little rough on poor Joe," Seth said good-naturedly. "No need for all that nonsense. If you had asked for my birth certificate, I'd have shown it to you."

"Would you?" Rufe said. There was a curious expression in his face. "A forged certificate—that does show premeditation, you know. The judge was right. What about his coat, Seth? How did you get him to remove his coat?"

"Coat? I don't know anything about a coat. Oh, yes—I remember now. That old jacket was thrown over his desk. It was a very warm night. Of course," Seth said slowly, "if your father had come over to take his blood pressure the judge would have had to remove his coat."

"No," Rufe said. "The police found it on the desk. They had examined it and folded it over a chair before you got here, Seth. So when did you see it over the desk?"

Seth's long face was still good-natured. "I grant you, Rufe, that you have a motive which some people might consider a real motive for killing the judge. But a jury wants proof. You have made out a case against me. There is no solid proof whatever. Try to convince a jury and you'll see how theoretical it is. Surely you don't think that a jury would accept as sensible evidence that tape—obviously the ravings of a sick old man! I didn't kill the judge. You say I did. Prove it."

Obrian stepped forward. "I've known you a long time, Seth. You've made a fine record. But I'm going to have to bring all this to the inquest, and the case against you is sure then to go to the grand jury. The publicity will completely finish your career. I'm sorry, really sorry. But I think you shot the judge."

"No, no!" Bea cried. "I tell you he saved my life tonight. Someone had a pillow over my face and I fought and fought and then Seth came and whoever it was knocked him down and—and—" Her voice dwindled away as a small, domestic memory struck her. "Oh," she said. "It was the rug."

"Rug?" Obrian stared at her.

"There's a little rug by my bed. The floor is polished. Sometimes the rug slips and—and I suppose it slipped and he fell and then he said— Oh—" Bea turned to Clara, who held out her hand.

Lorraine said coolly, "We tried to phone Seth tonight. The line was busy. Nothing easier than to leave it off the hook so as to give the impression that he was at home and talking if anybody happened to phone." She had turned instantly from Seth to Ben, that was clear.

Obrian said, "You see, Seth, you have too many things to explain. Even if you could convince a jury you didn't kill the judge, it would end your career. But I don't think you can convince a jury. The minute that birth certificate of yours gets into the hands of experts . . ."

Seth had been leaning against a chair near Ben Benson. His lanky figure seemed scarcely to move, but suddenly Ben went sprawling on the floor, screaming as he went down. Everybody yelled. Rufe shot for the door and tripped over Ben, who struck wildly at Rufe. It was a nightmarish scene for a second or two. Then Seth, Rufe and Obrian were gone, Ben Benson surging out the door after them. With shocking loudness there were several gunshots echoing through the night, shouts, the thud of a car racing and then nothing.

Lorraine sat down. Clara clasped the judge's cigar case more tightly. Rufe and Obrian and Ben came back into the house. "Never mind," Obrian said. "Can't be helped." He mopped his face. "Seth was a hunter, liked nothing better than a hunting trip. He'd have been able to extract the bullet." Obrian thought for a moment. "Seth had to get out a bullet which could be identified as coming from his own gun. He must have promised the judge to give up his plans. The judge felt safe."

Rufe said, "He also, in a friendly and agreeable way, must have induced the judge to remove his coat. It really was an unseasonably warm night. But Seth would have known that a thirty-two wouldn't penetrate the coat and that he couldn't get it out. He got hold of the judge's gun, too—easy enough I'd say, the way the judge was when he was upset. Probably the judge had put his gun on his desk or in his belt or even carried it in his hand. Perhaps he wasn't entirely sure of Seth, yet Seth must have promised him to forget all about his ambition to become a candidate. It must have been that way, for apparently the judge went out willingly with Seth for a stroll. Seth shot him with his own gun, then he had to dig out the bullet. He fired the judge's gun and left it beside him to suggest suicide."

Clara nodded soberly. Rufe went on, "But in the meantime Aunt Clara had set the alarm. Seth didn't know that. He came in to find the tape the judge had told him he had dictated. When the alarm went Seth got out as fast as he could. But later—"

Bea said, "Someone had searched my room twice, not thoroughly the first time when I was shut in the garage, but very thoroughly the second time when nobody was in the house."

Lorraine said, "Cecco must have seen him close the garage doors the night Bea was shut in there. Cecco waited a while before he let Bea out.

That would have amused Cecco. But Cecco would not have made an appointment with him if he'd thought Seth was a murderer. He'd have been afraid to tackle him. He only meant to embarrass Seth. It would have been hard for Seth to explain."

Rufe said, "And Cecco thought that Seth might have paid him to keep quiet. But Seth believed Cecco knew more than he knew."

"Cecco had been at Seth's house this afternoon," Lorraine said. "I saw him walking down the road. He must have told Seth then whatever it was that he could use as a threat for blackmail."

"Why shoot at Bea?" Ben said.

"Probably because the judge told him that he had dictated the whole thing to Bea. Seth must have been on pins and needles for fear Bea would run the tape and know all about his motive for killing the judge." Lorraine spoke with such sharp impatience that a twinge of alarm went over Ben's face. Lorraine put her hand quickly on Ben's arm and held on.

"What happened tonight then, Rufe?" Obrian asked.

"Miss Dotty told me yesterday. It almost proved the notion I had and didn't want to have. She said that when she went home Friday night she had seen Seth's car parked in the Carter drive. Joe phoned tonight to tell me about the birth certificate. He thought it didn't look just right. Tony was already waiting with me in the drive behind that big clump of cedars. Joe came too. Miss Dotty had taken her bike to Seth's place as soon as it was dark and watched there. When he drove out she followed him and he parked again at the Carter place. We were sure that Seth would make another attempt to get the tape and he had to be caught in the act. I thought we could stop him before he got into the house. But then—" He looked at Lorraine.

"I took the tape. I wanted to know what the judge had said." Lorraine shrugged but held Ben's arm.

Rufe said, "Did you open the terrace door?"

"Oh, yes. I had turned off the alarm before I came downstairs. It seemed stuffy here and I wanted some fresh air. But I didn't see Seth."

"He heard the voice on the tape. He must have got very close to the house, in the shrubbery. But he must have thought it was Bea running the tape and listening. He had to stop her. He got into the house while Aunt Clara and Lorraine and you, Bea, were in the upper hall talking and the alarm was off. He went up the back stairs. We didn't search the house. Like a fool I didn't think of that until it was almost too late. Then we broke in."

He didn't look at Bea; he only looked very white and frightened and Bea loved him. Clara said, "The judge's cigar case—"

"Oh, that was another thing, small, but Joe found it in Seth's office, recognized it as belonging to the judge, knew that the judge must have gone to see Seth the day before the judge was murdered. Seth had sent Joe out of the office to close a real estate deal. Joe forgot about the case. He intended to return it to you, Aunt Clara. After I saw that on the desk where Joe left it, I was sure Seth had killed him—but I had no real proof."

Ben said stolidly, "I'm not sure you have real jury proof yet. There's motive, yes. There's Miss Dotty's story of seeing his car the night the judge was murdered. There's his presence in the house tonight, but nobody saw him kill the judge or Cecco or shoot at Bea or—"

Obrian gave him an exasperated glance. "People don't as a rule invite other people to watch them kill somebody."

Just then the door opened and Dr. Thorne came in. "I saw the police cars," he said. "Heard about . . . It can't be Seth."

Rufe replied. "It was. And when I began to wonder about Seth I remembered what the judge said just as he died. He asked for you, Father. He said 'doctor'—then he muttered something about 'will'—but then he said 'Seth' and died. He didn't want to see Seth about his will. He was trying to tell Bea that Seth had shot him."

Bea could see the rosy light from the alarm flashing. She could hear the sudden burst of the judge's voice and then the silence. But she had given the judge's words what seemed a clear interpretation then.

Obrian said soberly, "The Juvenile Court record was—before Cecco tried to do a little blackmailing—the only danger that Seth knew about. He was the judge's friend, he was the family lawyer. Nobody would have suspected him." The telephone rang, interrupting him.

Obrian was nearest and he picked it up, listened, and his face seemed to clear. He put down the receiver almost solemnly. "Well, that ends it. We don't need jury proof. Seth tried to get a gun from one of my men and somehow in the fracas Seth was shot. There'll not be a trial." He looked at Clara. "It's better that way."

It was better. Miss Dotty marched in from the terrace, took the doctor's arm and without a word marched him sternly out again.

Obrian said vageuly, "Tomorrow—the police and—" He walked out, too.

Lorraine said flatly, "I was a great fool. I'm sorry, Bea. I almost got you killed." She came to Bea and put out her hand. Bea took it. They walked hand in hand like two little girls toward the terrace, where Ben waited for Lorraine. Bea turned back to Rufe, who sat down at the judge's desk and put his head in his hands. "I was a great fool, too, Bea. I nearly got you killed for trying to get a hard and fast case."

Clara stopped him. "I expect Ben and Lorraine will want to live here rather than with his mother. So you and Bea can get married as soon as you like. I'll not be alone."

Bea's mouth opened and shut. Clara, the realist, smiled. "Lorraine would rather have been the President's wife. That is, if Seth had made it. But it didn't take her long to change her course. I expect she'll be very good for Ben really. Now let's get the date set for you two."

Bea said slowly, "Rufe, it wasn't the Foreign Office. It wasn't Lorraine. It was when you began to suspect Seth that you—oh, it seemed to me you had changed. About me, I mean."

Rufe looked up. "About you! Why, I didn't change! It was a hard thing for me to accept, hard to try either to prove or disprove it. I didn't want to tell even you but—"

"Oh, never mind." Bea went to him and stood close, so he could put his arm around her. Clara said, "Make up your minds about the date," and walked out, holding the judge's cigar case against her cheek.

THE END